Praise for
RED SPARROW

"A great and dangerous spy-game is being played today between Russian intelligence and the CIA. . . . Jason Matthews's **thrilling** *Red Sparrow* takes us deep inside this treacherous world. He's an insider's insider. He knows the secrets. And he is also **a masterful storyteller.**"
—*New York Times* bestselling author Vince Flynn

"**Sublime and sophisticated**. . . . The stakes here are high, with agents on both sides desperately following streams of sensitive information, but . . . **veteran CIA operative turned novelist** Matthews . . . focuses on the people and the intelligence community's day-to-day routine. . . . More than a primer in tradecraft, *Red Sparrow* offers an advanced study . . . and **the prose rivals the plotline for energy and urgency**."
—*The Washington Post*

"There hasn't been a **first-rate** American spy novelist who claims to have worked as an intelligence officer before turning his hand to fiction. Until now, that is. . . . Lord knows how [Matthews] got the manuscript of *Red Sparrow* past the redacting committee at Langley, but he has turned his considerable knowledge of espionage into **a startling debut**. . . . I have rarely encountered a nonfiction title, much less a novel, so **rich in what would have once been regarded as classified information**. . . . From dead drops to honey traps, trunk escapes to burst transmissions, Matthews offers the reader **a primer in 21st-century spying**. His former foes in Moscow will be choking on their blinis when they read how much has been revealed about their tradecraft . . . **terrifically good**."
—*The New York Times Book Review*

“The pages of this flinty tale are **laced with mole hunts, double traps, triple crosses** and enough spy tradecraft to fill a manual. . . . This is a global story, packed with foot pursuits, car chases, and safe houses.”

—*USA Today*

“Intense. . . . Readers will welcome this debut from **a writer who supersizes his spies. . . . Realistic tradecraft, horrific villainy, and stunning plot twists** as the opponents vie for control. . . .”

—*Library Journal* (starred review)

“Move over, George Smiley. The great fictional spy has new, intriguing company. . . . [*Red Sparrow* is] **fresh and gripping**. The reader has a front seat to the painstaking art of mole detection and agent development, spy craft, and political interference in the mysterious world of espionage. **Excitement and tension build until a pulse-pounding finale**.”

—*The Columbus Dispatch*

“I have not read a more **exciting, gripping** novel in a long time. . . . I read until eleven and woke up at five a.m. to finish this book. If it doesn’t supplant *The Girl with the Dragon Tattoo* as **the next mammoth read**, and if it doesn’t take its place alongside le Carré’s *The Spy Who Came In from the Cold*, the love of literature and **jaw-dropping thrills** really is dead. I learned more about the former Soviets and the new Russians, and about our US of A, than I ever gleaned from the hardest-working journalists writing today. Halfway through, I was afraid Putin would find out I was reading *Red Sparrow* and have me arrested.”

—Doug Stanton, author of *Horse Soldiers*

"Exceptional. . . . The author's career in the CIA allows him to showcase **all the tradecraft and authenticity that readers in this genre demand**. . . . [A] complex, high-stakes plot."

—*Publishers Weekly* (starred review)

"Jason Matthews's thirty-three years as a CIA field operative enriches his first novel with **startling verisimilitude**. . . . That sense of authenticity, along with vividly drawn characters, much detail about tradecraft, and an appropriately convoluted plot . . . make this **a compelling and propulsive tale of spy-versus-spy**. . . . Espionage aficionados will love this one."

—*Booklist* (starred review)

"All the **tradecraft and cat-and-mouse tension** of a classic spy thriller—a terrific read."

—Joseph Kanon, author of *Istanbul Passage*

"Not since the good old days of the Cold War has **a classic spy thriller** like *Red Sparrow* come along."

—*New York Times* bestselling author Nelson DeMille

"Matthews's first novel, a globe-trotting spy thriller, **features enough action to satisfy even the most demanding of adrenaline junkies**. . . . The author's CIA background and the smart dialogue make this an entertaining tale for spy-novel enthusiasts."

—*Kirkus Reviews*

RED SPARROW

JASON MATTHEWS

POCKET BOOKS

NEW YORK LONDON TORONTO SYDNEY NEW DELHI

Pocket Books
A Division of Simon & Schuster, Inc.
1230 Avenue of the Americas
New York, NY 10020

First Pocket Books paperback edition May 2014

Manufactured in the United States of America

10 9 8 7 6 5 4 3 2 1

ISBN 978-1-4767-6417-7
ISBN 978-1-4767-0614-6 (ebook)

To Suzanne, Alexandra, and Sophia

1

Twelve hours into his SDR Nathaniel Nash was numb from the waist down. His feet and legs were wooden on the cobblestones of the Moscow side street. It had long since gotten dark as Nate ran the surveillance detection route designed to tickle the belly hairs of surveillance, to stretch them, to get them excited enough to show themselves. There was nothing, not a hint of units swirling, leapfrogging, banging around corners on the streets behind him, no reaction to his moves. Was he black? Or was he being had by a massive team? In the nature of the Game, not seeing coverage felt worse than confirming you were covered in ticks.

Early September, but it had snowed between the first and third hours of his SDR, which had helped cover his car escape. Late that morning, Nate bailed out of a moving Lada Combi driven by Leavitt from the Station, who, as he calculated the gap, wordlessly held up three fingers as they turned a corner onto an industrial side street, then tapped Nate's arm. FSB trailing surveillance, the Federal Security Service, didn't catch the escape in the three-second interval and blew past Nate hiding behind a snowbank, Leavitt leading them away. Nate left his active cover cell phone from the Embassy Economic Section with Leavitt in the car—the FSB were welcome to track the phone between Moscow's cell towers for the next three hours. Nate had banged his knee on the pavement when he rolled, and it had stiffened up in the first hours, but now it was as numb as the rest of him. As night fell, he had walked, slid, climbed, and scrambled over half of Moscow without detecting surveillance. It felt like he was in the clear.

Nate was one of a small group of CIA "internal ops" officers trained to operate under surveillance on the opposition's home ground. When he was on the street working against them, there was no doubt, no introspection. The familiar fear of failing, of not excelling, disappeared. Tonight he was running hot and cool, working well. *Ignore the cold that wraps around your chest, pushing tight. Stay in the sensory bubble, let it expand under the stress.* His vision was acute. *Focus on the middle distance, look for repeat pedestrians and vehicles. Mark colors and shapes. Hats, coats, vehicles.* Without thinking much about it, he registered the sounds of the darkening city around him. The zing of the electric buses running on the overhead wires, the hiss of car tires on wet pavement, the crackling of coal dust underfoot. He smelled the bitterness of diesel fumes and burning coal in the air and, from some unseen exhaust vent, the loamy aroma of beet soup cooking. He was a tuning fork resonating in the frosty air, keyed and primed, but strangely calm. After twelve hours he was as sure as he could be: He was black.

Time check: 2217. Twenty-seven-year-old Nate Nash was two minutes away from meeting the legend, the jewel in the tiara, the most valuable asset in CIA's stable. Only three hundred meters from the quiet street where he would meet MARBLE: sophisticated, urbane, in his sixties, major general in the SVR, which was the successor to the KGB's First Chief Directorate, the Russian Foreign Intelligence Service, the Kremlin's overseas spies. MARBLE had been in harness for fourteen years, a remarkable run considering that Cold War Russian sources survived an average of eighteen months. The grainy photos of history's lost agents clicked behind Nate's eyes as he scanned the street: Penkovsky, Motorin, Tolkachev, Polyakov, all the others, all gone. *Not this one, not on my watch.* He would not fail.

MARBLE was now chief of the Americas Department in the SVR, a position of colossal access, but he was old-school KGB, had earned his spurs (and general's star) during an overseas career spectacular not only for its operational triumphs, but also because MARBLE had survived the purges and reforms and internal power struggles. He did not delude himself as to the nature of the system he was serving, and he had grown to loathe the charade, but he was a professional and loyal. When he was forty, already a colonel and serving in New York, the Center refused permission to take his wife to an American oncologist, a mindless display of Soviet intransigence, and she died instead on a gurney in a Moscow hospital corridor. It took MARBLE another eight years to decide, to prepare a secure approach to the Americans, to volunteer.

As he became a foreign spy—an agent, in intelligence lexicon—MARBLE quietly and with courtly grace had spoken softly to his CIA case officers—his handlers—apologizing self-deprecatingly for the meager information he reported. Langley was stunned. Here was incalculably valuable intelligence on KGB and SVR operations, penetrations of foreign governments, and, occasionally, when he could, the crown jewels: the names of Americans spying for Russia. He was an uncommon, inestimable asset.

2218. Nate rounded the corner and started down the narrow street, apartment buildings on either side, the uneven sidewalk lined with trees now bare and blown with snow. At the far end of the street, silhouetted in the light from the intersection beyond, a familiar shape turned the corner and began walking toward him. The old man was a pro: He had nailed the four-minute window.

Nate's fatigue fell away and he could feel himself rev up. As MARBLE approached, Nate automatically scanned the empty street for anomalies. *No cars. Look up. No windows open, apartments dark. Look back. Cross streets quiet. Scan the shadows. No street sweeper, no lolling bum.* A mistake, despite all the hours of his SDR, of provocative maneuvers, of waiting and watching in the snow and cold, a single mistake would have one inescapable result—the death of MARBLE. Not, to Nate, so much the loss of a source of intelligence or the beginning of a diplomatic flap, but the death of this man. Nate would not fail.

MARBLE walked unhurriedly forward. They had met twice before. MARBLE had been assigned a succession of CIA handlers—had educated every one. Some of them had been accomplished. In a few MARBLE had suspected galloping stupidity. And one or two had displayed a terrifying *langueur,* a potentially fatal disinterest in being professional. Nate was different, interesting. There was something, an edge, a focus, an aggression in pursuit of doing the thing correctly. A little raw—a little compulsive, MARBLE thought—but not many had the fire, and MARBLE approved.

MARBLE's eyes narrowed with pleasure at seeing the young American. Nate was average height and thin-framed, with straight black hair over a straight nose and brown eyes that kept moving, glancing over the older man's shoulder as he approached, watchful rather than jittery.

"Good evening, Nathaniel," said MARBLE. Slight British accent from the assignment in London, leavened by his time in New York. A whim to use English, to be closer to his case officer, despite Nate's nearly fluent Russian. MARBLE was short and stocky, with deep brown eyes separated by a fleshy nose. He had bushy white eyebrows, which matched his full head of wavy white hair, giving him the appearance of an elegant boulevardier.

They were supposed to use aliases, but that was ridiculous. MARBLE had access to the SVR foreign diplomatic mug book and knew Nate's name perfectly well. "It's good to see you. Are you well?" MARBLE looked carefully at Nate's face. "Are you tired? How many hours did you spend tonight?" MARBLE's questions were perfectly polite, but he still wanted to know. He never took anything for granted.

"*Dobryj vecher, dyadya,*" said Nate. He had begun using the familiar "uncle," part tradecraft to show respect, part a display of real affection. He checked his watch. "It's been twelve hours. The street feels loose." A patois they both understood, and Nate knew MARBLE was checking to hear how thorough his SDR had been.

MARBLE did not comment. The two began walking together in the shadows cast by the trees along the sidewalk. The air was frosty, still, there was no wind. They had approximately seven minutes for the meeting.

Nate let MARBLE do most of the talking, and he listened carefully. The older man spoke quickly but without haste, a mix of gossip and politics in MARBLE's service, who was up, who was down. A summary of a new operation, a successful SVR recruitment in a foreign country. Details would be on the discs. This was as much a conversation between two human beings as a debriefing. The sounds of their voices, the eye contact, MARBLE's low chuckle. That was the point.

As they walked they both resisted a natural impulse to link arms, like father and son. They both knew there could be no contact, a bitter necessity, for fear of contamination with *metka,* spy dust. MARBLE himself had reported on the secret program to pollinate suspect CIA officers in the US Embassy in Moscow. Yellow, yeasty, powdery, the chemical compound nitrophenylpentadienal, NPPD. Pockmarked Russian techs squeezed the rubber bulbs and it was spritzed on clothing, floor mats, steering wheels. NPPD was designed to spread like sticky pollen from a daffodil, from a handshake to a sheet of paper to a coat lapel. It would invisibly mark anything an American CIA officer touched. Therefore, if you were a Russian official under suspicion and your hands or clothes or desk blotter fluoresced with NPPD, you were cooked. MARBLE had traumatized Langley by subsequently reporting that different batches of *metka* were tagged with distinct marking compounds that could identify the specific American host.

As they walked and spoke, Nate reached into his pocket, pulled out a sealed plastic bag. Replacement batteries for MARBLE's covert communications equipment: three steel-gray cigarette packs, inordinately heavy. They used covcom to transmit fast-breaking news and to keep contact warm during the gaps between personal meetings. But these brief encounters, mortally risky, were infinitely more productive. It was during these that MARBLE passed volumes of intelligence on discs or drives, and equipment and rubles were replenished. And there was the human contact, the opportunity to exchange a few words, time to renew the almost religious partnership.

Nate carefully opened the plastic bag and held it out to MARBLE, who reached in and extracted the prewrapped brick of batteries, which had been packed in a sterile lab in Virginia. MARBLE then dropped two discs into the bag. "I estimate there are about five linear meters of files on those discs," he said. "With my compliments."

Nate noted that the old spook still thought in terms of linear feet of file folders even as he was stealing digital secrets. "Thank you. Did you include the summary?" The intel hacks had begged Nate to remind MARBLE to include a summary of the take, to prioritize translation and processing of his raw reports.

"Yes, this time I remembered. I have also included a new office directory in the second disc. A few changes of personnel, nothing too startling. And a schedule of my foreign travel plans for the next year. I am looking for operational reasons to travel, I included the details," he said, nodding at the disc in the bag.

"I look forward to seeing you outside Moscow," said Nate, "at your leisure." Time was ticking and the two had already reached the end of the street, had turned and were walking slowly back to the other end.

MARBLE grew pensive. "You know, I have been thinking about my career, about my relationship with my American friends, about life ahead of me," he said. "I probably have several more years before retiring. Politics, old age, the unthinkable mistake. Perhaps three or four, perhaps two years. I sometimes think it would be pleasant to retire in New York City. What do you think of that, Nathaniel?" Nate paused and half turned toward him. What was this? His street hum faded. Was his agent in trouble? MARBLE raised his hand as if to squeeze Nate's arm, but stopped it in midair. "No alarm, please, I'm just thinking out loud." Nate looked sideways at MARBLE: The old man was confident, calm. It was natural for an agent to think about retiring, to dream about the end to the danger and the double life, to stop listening for the knock on the door. The Life eventually causes great fatigue, and that leads to mistakes. Was there fatigue in MARBLE's voice? Nate would have to report the nuances of this conversation carefully in his ops cable tomorrow. Inexorably, problems in a case always rebounded to the handling officer, problems he didn't need.

"Is there anything wrong, a security problem?" said Nate. "You know your bank account is waiting for you. You can retire anywhere you want. We support you in every way."

"No, I'm fine. We have more work to do. Then we can rest," said MARBLE.

"It is an honor working with you," said Nate, and he meant it. "Your contribution is impossible to measure." The older man looked down at the sidewalk as they walked along the darkened street. Their meeting was stretching now to six minutes. It was time to go.

"Is there anything you need?" asked Nate. He closed his eyes and concentrated. Batteries passed, discs received, summary included, foreign travel schedule. The only thing remaining was to schedule the next personal meeting three months from now. "Shall we meet again in three months?" asked Nate. "It will be dead winter by then, December. The new site, EAGLE, near the river?"

"Yes, of course," said MARBLE. "*Orel.* I will confirm in a message the week before." They were approaching the end of the street again, moving slowly toward the brighter lights of the intersection. A neon sign marked a Metro station entrance across the street. Nate suddenly felt a wash of alarm running up his back.

A battered Lada sedan cruised slowly through the intersection, two men in the front seat. Nate and MARBLE flattened themselves against the wall of a building, completely in shadow. MARBLE had seen the car too, the old man was every bit the street pro as his young handler. Another car, a newer Opel, crossed in the opposite direction. Two men inside were looking the other way. Glancing behind him,

Nate saw a third car slowly turning into the street. It was running only with its parking lights.

"It's a sweep search," hissed MARBLE. "You didn't park a vehicle nearby, did you?"

Nate shook his head no. No, no, fuck no. His heart was pounding. This was going to be a close thing. He looked at MARBLE for a beat, then the two of them moved as one. Forgetting spy dust, forgetting everything else, Nate helped MARBLE take off his dark overcoat, turning it inside out as he pulled it off his arms, transformed into a light-colored coat of a different cut, stained and frayed at the sleeves and hem. Nate helped MARBLE shrug it on. Reaching into an inside coat pocket, Nate unfolded a moth-eaten fur hat—a part of his own disguise—and jammed it on MARBLE's bare head. MARBLE took heavy-rimmed eyeglasses, one stem wrapped with white tape, out of his front pocket and put them on. Nate reached into another pocket and removed a short staff that he shook lightly downward. An elastic cord inside the staff snapped the three lengths together to create a cane that he thrust into MARBLE's hand.

The middle-aged Muscovite was gone, replaced in eight seconds by a creaky old pensioner wearing a cheap cloth coat and hobbling along with a cane. Nate pushed him gently in the direction of the intersection and the Metro station. This action defied the catechism, it was dangerous to use the Metro, to trap oneself underground, but if MARBLE could get away from the area, the risk was worth it. His disguise would have to be enough against the multiple surveillance cameras on the platforms.

"I'll get them away from here," said Nate, as MARBLE bent over and began shuffling to cross the intersection. The old spook looked at him once, grave but cool, and winked. *This guy is a legend,* thought Nate. But now his only priority was to distract the surveillance cars and get them to start vectoring on him, away from MARBLE. He must not be detained, however. MARBLE's discs in his pocket would kill the old man as surely as if surveillance arrested him.

Not on his watch. The icy burn started in his head and throat. The collar of his coat was up, and his guts were set, and he quickly crossed in front of the surveillance car slowly cruising up the street toward him half a block away. This would be the FSB, the thugs working internal espionage inside the Russian Federation. Their turf.

The 1200cc Lada engine screamed and they caught him in the reflected light of the high beams off the glistening street, and he ran to the next block, ducked into a basement stairwell that reeked of urine and vodka, and behind him came the sound of wailing tires, so, *Wait, wait, now move again,* sprinting through alleyways, ghosting across pedestrian overpasses, pounding down stairs to the river. *Use barriers, cross railroad tracks, change vector and direction once out of physical sight, make them guess wrong, squeeze past their picket line.* Time check: nearly two hours.

He was shaking with fatigue and he ran, then walked, then crouched behind parked cars, hearing engine noises all around him as they converged, then spread out, then converged again, trying to get close enough to see his face, close enough to tackle him facedown in the street, to jam their hands into his pockets. He could hear the squelch breaks, hear them yelling into their radios, they were getting desperate.

His first surveillance instructor had told him, *You will feel the street, Mr. Nash, it doesn't matter whether it's Wisconsin Avenue or Tverskaya, you will feel it,* and Nate was fucking feeling it, but there were a lot of them, even if they did not know exactly where he was. Car tires squealed on the wet cobblestones as they sped back and forth, and the good news was that they didn't have enough of him yet to deploy feet, and the bad news was that time was on their side. Thank God they were beating up on him, which meant they had not focused on MARBLE. Nate said a prayer, that the old man had been missed as he limped into the Metro, and that this surveillance had not been on him from the beginning, because that would mean that a second team was now following MARBLE. They weren't getting his agent, *his agent,* and they weren't getting the package of MARBLE's discs, volatile as nitro in his pocket. The squealing tires died away and the streets were quiet.

Time check: Two-plus hours, leg- and spine-weary, with vision gray around the edges, and he went down a narrow alleyway, hugging the wall in the shadows, hoping they were gone, imagining the dented cars all back in the garage, ticking hot metal and dripping mud, while the team leader screamed at them in the ready room. Nate hadn't seen a car in several minutes, and he thought he had slipped outside their search perimeter. It had started snowing again.

Up ahead a vehicle screeched to a stop, then reversed and turned into the alley, its headlights catching the snow. Nate turned toward the wall, trying to reduce his outline and the contrasts, but he knew they must have seen him, and as the lights swept over Nate the car accelerated toward him, edging over to his side of the alley. Nate watched in fascinated disbelief as the car kept coming, its passenger-side door inches away from the wall and the two intent faces straining forward, wipers going full tilt. These FSB animals, didn't they see him? Then he realized they saw him perfectly well, they were trying for a wall smear. *It is an unwritten rule that surveillance teams following a foreign diplomat never, ever offer violence to a target,* the instructors had said, and really, seriously, what the fuck were these guys doing? He looked back and saw the entrance to the alley was too far away.

Feel the street, Mr. Nash, and the second-best option was feeling the cast-iron drainpipe running down the building a foot away from him with the rusty metal straps bolted to the brickwork, and as the car bore down, he leapt up and grabbed the drainpipe, using the metal fasteners to clamber higher, and the car slammed into the wall, splintering the drainpipe, the car's roof just below Nate's lifted-up legs. With a heavy grinding sound, the car scraped along the wall and came to a stop. They had stalled the engine, and his grip was gone, and Nate fell onto the roof of the car and then to the pavement. The driver's door was opening, a big man in a fur hat was getting out, but they never, ever offer violence to a target and Nate shouldered the door back onto the head and neck of the thug, heard a scream, saw a face contorted with pain. Nate slammed the door on his head two more times, very quickly, and the man fell back into the car. The passenger door was pinned shut by the wall and Nate could see the other goon trying to climb over the front seat to get at the rear door, so it was time to run again and Nate sprinted down the alley into the shadows and around the corner.

Three doors down was a grimy soup kitchen, open at this late hour, its lights spilling onto the snowy sidewalk. Nate could hear the car in the alley-way backing up, engine whining. He ducked into the tiny, empty restaurant and closed the door. A single room, nothing more than a service counter at one end with several well-worn wooden tables and benches, stained wallpaper, and grimy lace curtains over the window. An old woman with two can-opener teeth sat behind the counter listening to a scratchy radio and reading a paper. Two battered aluminum pots of soup simmered on electric rings behind her. The aroma of cooked onions filled the room.

Fighting to keep his hands from shaking, Nate walked up to the counter, and in Russian ordered a bowl of beet soup to the woman's blank stare. He sat with his back to the curtained window and listened. A car roared by, then another, then nothing. On the radio a comedian was telling a joke:

Khrushchev visited a pig farm and was photographed there. In the village newspaper office there was a heated discussion about the photo caption. "Comrade Khrushchev among Pigs"? "Comrade Khrushchev and Pigs"? "Pigs around Comrade Khrushchev"? None will do. The editor finally makes a decision: "Third from left—Comrade Khrushchev." The old lady behind the counter cackled.

He had not eaten or drunk anything in more than twelve hours, and he began wolfing down the thick soup with a shaking spoon. The old woman stared at him, got up, and walked around the counter to the front door. Nate watched her out of the corner of his eye. She opened the door and he felt the blast of cold outside air. The old woman looked out at the street, up and down the block, then slammed the door shut. She returned to her stool behind the counter and picked up her paper. When Nate finished his soup and bread, he walked up to the counter and counted out a few kopeks. The crone gathered the coins and swept them into a drawer. She slammed the drawer and looked at Nate. "All clear," she said. "Go with God." Nate avoided looking at her and left.

In another hour, drenched with sweat and trembling with fatigue, Nate stumbled past the militiaman's booth at the front entrance to the Embassy housing compound. MARBLE's discs were finally safe. It was not the approved way to end an operational night, but he had missed by hours the pickup in the Station car. His entry was noted, and within a half hour the FSB, and instantly after that the SVR, knew that it was young Mr. Nash of the Embassy Economic Section who had been out of pocket for most of the evening. And they thought they knew why.

OLD LADY'S BEET SOUP

Melt butter in a large pot; add a chopped onion and sauté until translucent; stir in three grated beets and one chopped tomato. Pour in beef stock, vinegar, sugar, salt, and pepper. Broth should be tart and sweet. Bring to a boil, then simmer for an hour. Serve hot with a dollop of sour cream and chopped dill.

2

The next morning, at opposite ends of Moscow, in two separate offices, there was unpleasantness. At SVR headquarters in Yasenevo, First Deputy Director Ivan (Vanya) Dimitrevich Egorov was reading the FSB surveillance logs from the previous night. Watery sunlight filtered through massive plate-glass windows overlooking the dark pine forest that surrounded the building. Alexei Zyuganov, Egorov's diminutive Line KR counterintelligence chief, stood in front of his desk, not having been invited to sit down. Zyuganov's close friends, or perhaps just his mother, called the poisonous dwarf "Lyosha," but not this morning.

Vanya Egorov was sixty-five years old, a major general with seniority. He had a large head with tufts of graying hair over the ears, but otherwise he was bald. His wide-set brown eyes, fleshy lips, broad shoulders, ample belly, and large muscular hands gave him the look of a circus strongman. He wore a beautifully cut dark winter-weight suit, an Augusto Caraceni from Milan, with a somber dark blue necktie. His shoes, glossy black, were Edward Green of London, out of the dip pouch.

Egorov had been an average KGB field officer in the early years of his career. Several tepid tours in Asia convinced him that life in the field was not his preference. Once back in Moscow, he excelled in the internecine politics of the organization. He mastered a succession of high-profile internal jobs, first in planning positions, then in administration, and finally in the newly created Inspector General's position. He was active and prominent in the change-over from KGB to SVR in 1991, chose the right side during Kryuchkov's abortive 1992 KGB coup against Gorbachev, and in 1999 was noticed by the phlegmatic First Deputy Prime Minister Vladimir Vladimirovich Putin, a blond scorpion with languid blue eyes. The next year Yeltsin was out and Putin was, remarkably, implausibly, in the Kremlin, and Vanya Egorov waited for the call he knew must come.

"I want you to look after things," Putin had then told him in a heady five-minute interview in the elegant Kremlin office, the rich wood of the walls eerily reflected in the new president's eyes. They both knew what he meant, and Vanya went back to Yasenevo first as Third Deputy Director, then Second, until last year, when he moved into the First Deputy Director's office, across the carpeted hallway from the Director's suite.

There had been some anxiety leading up to the elections last March, the goddamn journalists and opposition parties unfettered as never before. The SVR had looked after some dissidents, had discreetly operated at polling places, and had reported on select opposition parliamentarians. A cooperative oligarch had been directed to form a splinter party to siphon off votes and fracture the field.

Then Vanya himself had risked everything, had really taken a chance, when he personally suggested that Putin blame Western—specifically US—interference for the demonstrations leading up to the elections. The candidate loved the suggestion, eyes unblinking, as he contemplated Russia's comeback on the world stage. He had clapped Vanya on the back. Perhaps it was because their careers so resembled each other, perhaps because they both had accomplished little as intel officers during brief overseas assignments, or perhaps one informant recognized a fellow *nashnik*. Whatever it was, Putin liked him, and

Vanya Egorov knew he would be rewarded. He was close to the top. He had the time, and the power, to continue to advance. It was what he wanted.

But the handler at a snake farm inevitably is bitten unless he exercises great care. Today's Kremlin was suits and ties, press secretaries, smiling summit meetings, but anyone who had been around for any length of time knew that nothing had changed since Stalin, really. Friendship? Loyalty? Patronage? A misstep, an operational or diplomatic failure, or, worst of all, embarrassing the president, would bring the *burya,* the tempest, from which there would be no shelter. Vanya shook his head. *Chert vozmi*. Shit. This Nash episode was exactly what he didn't need.

"Could surveillance have been more poorly managed?" Egorov raged. He was generally given to mild theatrics in front of his subordinates. "It's obvious this little prick Nash met with a source last night. How could he have been out of pocket for more than twelve hours? What was surveillance doing in that district in the first place?"

"It appears they were looking for Chechens doing drug deals. God knows what the FSB is doing these days," said Zyuganov. "That district, it's a shithole down there."

"And what about the crash in the alley? What was that?"

"It's not clear. They claim the team thought they had cornered a Chechen and believed he was armed. I doubt it. They may have gotten excited in the chase."

"*Kolkhozniki*. Peasants could do it better. I'll have the director mention it to the president next Monday. We cannot have foreign diplomats harmed on the streets, even if they are meeting with Russian traitors," said Egorov with a snort. "The FBI will start mugging our officers in Georgetown if this happens again."

"I will pass the word too, at my level, General. The surveillance teams will get the message, especially, if I may suggest, if some time at *katorga* could be arranged."

Egorov looked at his CI chief blankly, noting that he used the czarist name for gulag with wet-lipped relish. Jesus. Alexei Zyuganov was short and dark, with a fry-pan-flat face and prominent ears. Tent-peg teeth and a perpetual smirk completed the Lubyanka look. Still, Zyuganov was thorough, a malevolent minion who had his uses.

"We can criticize the FSB, but I tell you this, this American is meeting someone important. And those idiots just missed him, I'm sure of it." Egorov threw the report on his desk. "So, can you guess what your job is going to be from this point onward?" He paused. "Find. Out. Who. It. Is." Each word was punctuated with a tap on Egorov's desk with a thick index finger. "I want that traitor's head in a wicker basket."

"I'll make it a priority," said Zyuganov, knowing that without more to go on, or without a specific lead from a mole inside the CIA, or without a break on the street, they would have to wait. In the meantime he could begin a few investigations, conduct an interrogation, just for art's sake.

Egorov looked again at the surveillance report, a futile piece of work. The only confirmed fact was the identification of Nathaniel Nash at the embassy gate. No sighting or description of anyone else. The driver of one of the surveillance cars (a photo of him with a sticking plaster over his left eye was included in the report, as if to justify the incident in the alley) positively identified Nash, as did the militiaman at the US Embassy compound entrance.

This could turn sweet or sour, thought Egorov. A splashy spy case solved to his credit while mortifying the Americans, or an embarrassing debacle displeasing the Kremlin and Egorov's testosterone-fueled patron, resulting in the sudden end of his career. Depending on the president's ire, this could include a bunk next to that ruined oligarch Khodorkovsky in Segezha Prison Colony Number Nine.

Morbidly contemplating the potential opportunities while recognizing the political consequences, Egorov that morning had called for and read Nate's *liternoye delo,* the operational file: *Young, active, disciplined, good Russian. Behaves himself regarding women and alcohol. No drugs. Diligent in cover position in the Embassy Economic Section. Effective while on the street, does not telegraph his operational intent.* Egorov grunted. *Molokosos.* Whippersnapper. He looked up at his KR chief.

The hairs growing out of Zyuganov's brain tingled and he sensed that he had to show more enthusiasm. First Deputy Director Egorov might not be a street operator, but he was a well-known species in the SVR zoo, a politically ambitious bureaucrat.

"Mr. Deputy Director, the key to finding the bastard who is selling our secrets is to focus on this young Yankee *geroy,* this hero. Put three teams on him. Wrap him in onionskins. Twenty-four hours a day. Order—better yet, ask—FSB to increase coverage, let them rattle around behind him, then put our own teams out at the margins. Give him a look, then take it away. See if he's re-casing meeting sites. There will be another meeting in three to six months, that's certain."

Egorov liked the bit about onionskins, he would repeat it to the Director later today.

"All right, get started, let me know what your plans are so I can brief the director on our strategy," said Egorov, dismissing the chief with a wave.

Brief the director on our *strategy,* thought Zyuganov as he left the office.

The US Embassy compound in Moscow is located northwest of Yasenevo, in the Presnensky District near the Kremlin and a sweeping bend in the Moskva River. Late that afternoon, another unpleasant conversation transpired in the office of the CIA Chief of Station, Gordon Gondorf. Much like the Line KR chief who had not been invited to sit down, Nate stood in front of Gondorf's desk. His knee throbbed from the day before.

If Egorov's imposing bulk made him look like a circus strongman, Gondorf's small frame and pinched features made him look like a whippet in a circus dog act. Only about five feet six, Gondorf had thinning hair, pig's eyes set too close together, and tiny feet. What he lacked in stature he amply made up for in venom. He trusted no one, and was unaware of the irony that he himself instilled trust in no one. Gondorf ("Gondork" behind his back) lived in a secret hell known only to a certain type of senior intelligence officer: He was in over his head.

"I read your ops report about the run last night," said Gondorf. "Based on your write-up, I suppose you think the outcome was satisfactory?" Gondorf's voice was flat and he spoke slowly, waveringly. Nate's gut flipped in anticipation of the impending confrontation. *Stand your ground.*

"If you mean do I think the agent is safe, yes," said Nate. He knew where Gondorf was going with this but left him to get there on his own.

"You almost got the Agency's most prolific and important asset arrested last night. Your meeting was busted by surveillance, for Christ's sake."

Nate tamped down building anger. "I ran a twelve-hour SDR yesterday. The very SDR you approved. I confirmed my status. I was black when I got to the site, and so was MARBLE," said Nate.

"How do you explain the surveillance, then?" said

Gondorf. "You can't possibly think it was random surveillance in the area. Tell me you don't think that." Gondorf's voice dripped with sarcasm.

"That's exactly what it was. There is no way they were searching for me, that bullshit in the alley, they weren't following me from the start, no way. It was random and they reacted, no attempt to be discreet. MARBLE got away clean." Nate registered that Gondorf wasn't even concerned about the attempted wall smear. A different chief would have been in the ambassador's office, raising hell, demanding the Embassy file a protest.

Switching barrels, Gondorf said, "Nonsense. The whole thing was a disaster. How could you have directed him to go down into the Metro? That's a mousetrap. You ignored procedure when you pawed him to change his overcoat. He is supposed to do that himself. You know that! What if he's fluorescing under a light wand right now?"

"I made the determination and the decision. I thought changing his profile and getting him out of the area was the priority. MARBLE's a pro, he'll know to get rid of the coat and cane. We can send him a message, I'll verify with him at our next meeting," said Nate. It was agony to argue this way, especially with a chief who didn't know the street.

"There's not going to be a next meeting. At least not with you. You're too hot now. They ID'd you a dozen times last night, your Econ cover is gone, you'll have half the surveillance directorate in Moscow on your ass from now on," said Gondorf. He was visibly relishing the moment.

"They always knew this cover position. I always had coverage, you know that. I still can meet assets," said Nate, leaning against a chair. Gondorf had a dummy hand grenade mounted on a wooden base on his desk. The plaque on it read COMPLAINT DEPARTMENT. PULL PIN FOR FASTER SERVICE.

"No, I don't believe you can meet agents. You're now a shit magnet," said Gondorf.

"If they put that many resources on me we can bankrupt them," argued Nate. "I can drain their manpower by driving all over town for the next six months. And the more coverage I get, the better we'll be able to manipulate them." *Stand your ground.*

Gondorf was unimpressed and unconvinced. This young case officer stud represented too much of a risk to him personally. Gondorf had his sights set on one of the big component jobs in Headquarters next year when he returned to Washington. It wasn't worth the risk. "Nash, I'm recommending that your tour in Moscow be curtailed. You're too hot and the opposition will be looking for a way to pick you off, catch your agents." He looked up. "Don't worry, I'll make sure you get a good follow-on assignment."

Nate was shocked. Even a first-tour officer knew a short-of-tour expulsion submitted by a COS—whatever the reason—could derail a career. He also was sure that Gondorf would use back channels to hint that Nate had fucked up. Nate's unofficial reputation, his "hall file," would take a hit, it would affect his promotions and future assignments. The old feeling of standing in black quicksand started coming back.

Nate knew the truth: He had saved MARBLE last night with quick and correct action. He looked down at Gondorf's impassive face. They both knew what was happening and why. So to Nate there didn't seem to be any point not to finish the conversation with a flourish. "Gondorf, you're a gutless pussy who's terrified of the street. You're fucking me to avoid your responsibility. It's been an education serving in your Station."

As he left the office, Nate noted that the absence of a screaming tirade from his chief was indeed the measure of the man.

Kicked out of Station short of tour. Not as bad as getting an agent killed, stealing official funds, or fabricating reports, but still a disaster. How it would affect future assignments, promotions, Nate couldn't tell, but the news would get around the minute the cable from Gondorf hit Headquarters. Some of his classmates from training were already on their second tours, making their bones. Rumor had it that one of them already had been offered a chief's job in a small Station. The additional months of training for Moscow had put Nate behind the curve, and now this.

Even as he told himself not to fixate, Nate fretted. He had always been told to keep up, of the necessity of not falling behind, of the absolute requirement to win. He grew up in the genteel southern equivalent of a cage match where generations of Nashes had been raised in the Palladian family mansion on the bluffs along the south shore of the James. Nate's grandfather and his father after him, respectively founder and reigning partner of Nash, Waryng, and Royall in Richmond, had sat in green-shaded studies, and sucked their teeth, and shot their cuffs. They had nodded approval as Nate's brothers, one implausible with Julius Caesar curls, the other sweating and outrageous in a gamine comb-over, wrestled in their suits on the carpet, and learned just enough of the law, and married chesty belles who stopped talking when the men came into the room, blue eyes searching for approval.

But what y'all suppose we do about young Nate? they had asked one another. Graduated from Johns Hopkins with a degree in Russian literature, Nate sought refuge in the spiritual, ascetic world of Gogol, Chekhov, Turgenev, a world that brick-paved Richmond could not invade. His brothers howled and his father thought it a waste. It was expected that he would attend a law school—he was preapproved for acceptance at Richmond—and eventually fill a junior partner's chair at the firm. The graduate degree in Russian from faraway Middlebury was therefore a problem, and the subsequent application to the CIA a family crisis.

"I believe you'll find the life of a civil servant less than fulfilling," his father had said. "I frankly cannot see you happy in that bureaucracy." Nate's father had known past directors. His brothers were less circumspect in their criticism. During a particularly riotous holiday meal, they started a family pool to predict how long Nate would last in the CIA. The high field was three or fewer years.

His application to the Central Intelligence Agency had nothing to do with escaping the suspenders and cuff links, with the crushing absoluteness of Richmond, or with the inevitability of the colonnaded mansion overlooking the river. It had nothing to do with patriotism either, really, though Nate was as patriotic as the next person. It had everything to do with the hammer in his chest when he at ten years of age *made himself* walk along the ledge of the mansion three floors up, level with the hawks over the river, to beat down the dread, to confront the raptors of fear and failure. It was about the strain between him and his father and grandfather and omnivore brothers, raucously demanding compliance from him while practicing none themselves.

It was the same hammer in his chest during interviews as he applied to the CIA, the heartbeat he had to still as he dissembled and jauntily affirmed how much he liked talking to people and meeting challenges and confronting ambiguity. But as the heartbeat slowed and his voice steadied, he had the quite remarkable epiphany that he actually could be coolheaded, and he could confront things he didn't control. Working in the CIA was something he needed.

But real alarm slammed through him when a CIA

recruiter informed Nate that it was unlikely his application would be accepted, mainly because he had no postgraduate "life experience." Another interviewer, more optimistic than the other, confidentially told him his excellent Russian test scores made him a very attractive candidate. It took the CIA three months to decide, during which time his brothers noisily revised the family pool predicting the date *of his return* from the CIA. They were no less noisy when the envelope arrived. He was in.

Report for duty, sign the endless forms, file into a dozen classrooms, the months in Headquarters, cubicles, and conference rooms with the uninterested briefers and the eternity of projected presentations. Then finally the Farm, with the macadam roads running straight through the sandy pine forests and the linoleum dorm rooms, and the stale homerooms and the classrooms carpeted in gray, and the numbered students' seats which belonged previously to last year's heroes, to heroes forty years ago, faceless recruits, great spies or not, some gone wrong, the traitors, some long dead and remembered only by those who knew them.

They planned clandestine meetings and attended mock diplomatic receptions, mingling with loud, red-faced instructors wearing Soviet Army uniforms and Mao suits. They walked wet-to-the-knee through the piney woods, peering through a night scope and counting paces until they came to the hollow stump and the burlap-wrapped brick, the owls in the branches congratulating them for finding the cache. They were laid over the hot ticking hoods of their vehicles at pretend roadblocks, as instructor "border guards" shook sheaves of papers in their faces and demanded explanations. They sat in swaybacked American Gothic farmhouses along lonely country roads and drank vodka and convinced gibbering role players to commit treason. Through the pines, the slate-black river was furrowed by the talons of dusk-feeding ospreys.

What instinct enabled Nate to excel in practical exercises? He didn't know, but he left the drag of family and Richmond behind and ran effortlessly on the street, under surveillance, coolly meeting instructor-agents bundled in coats and wearing implausible hats. They said he had the eye. He started to believe it, but the jackdaw challenges of his brothers hung over his head like a blunt instrument. Nate's nightmare was failing, getting kicked out, showing back up in Richmond. They dropped people from training without warning.

"We look for integrity from you students," said a tradecraft instructor to the class. "We send people home for trying to G-2 the scenarios for upcoming problems. Just to max the exercises," he said loudly. "You get caught with an instructor notebook, or any other restricted course material, it's an immediate drop from the program, people." Which, to be perfectly honest, thought Nate, meant, *Try it.*

They were a class, but of individuals, all dreaming of first assignments, first tours to Caracas, Delhi, Athens, or Tokyo. The ache for class standing and first choice of assignments was acute, and culminated in excruciating receptions in the student center hosted by various Headquarters divisions, a bizarre sorority rush week for fledgling spies.

At one of these end-of-training cocktail parties, a man and a woman from Russia House took him aside and told him he was preapproved and accepted in the Russia Division, so he didn't have to request assignments elsewhere. Nate mildly asked if he couldn't use his Russian language to chase Russians in, say, the Mideast or Africa Divisions, but they smiled at him and said they looked forward to seeing him in Headquarters at the end of the month.

He was through, and provisionally accepted. He was part of the elite.

Now came lectures about modern Russia. They discussed Moscow's Damoclean politics of natural gas, hanging plumb over Europe, and the Kremlin's chronic inclination to sponsor rogue states in the name of fairness, but really to make mischief and, well, to prove Russia was still in the Game. Furry men lectured about the promise of post-Soviet Russia, and elections and health reforms and demographic crises, and about the heartbreak of the curtain being drawn closed again, and behind it the icy blue eyes that missed nothing. The *Rodina,* sacred Motherland of black earth and endless sky, would have to endure a while longer, as the chain-wrapped corpse of the Soviet was exhumed, hauled dripping out of the swamp, and its heart was started again, and the old prisons were filled anew with men who did not see it their way.

And a flinty woman lectured about a new Cold War, about the sly disarmament negotiations and the new supersonic fighters that can fly sideways but still show Red Star roundels on the wings, and Moscow's rage over a Western missile defense shield in Central Europe—oh, how they resented the loss of their elegant slave states!—and the sabers scraping in the rusty scabbards, familiar music from the days of Brezhnev and Chernenko. And the point of it all, they said, the point of Russia House, was the unceasing requirement to know the plans and intentions behind the blue-eyed stare and the smooth blond brow, different secrets nowadays, but the same as ever, secrets that needed stealing.

Then a retired ops officer—he looked like a Silk Road peddler, but with green eyes and a lopsided mouth—came to Russia House for an informal presentation.

"Energy, population decline, natural resources,

client states. Forget all that. Russia is still the only country that can put an ICBM into Lafayette Square across from the White House. The only one, and they have thousands of nukes." He paused and rubbed his nose, his voice deep and throaty.

"Russians. They hate foreigners only a little less than they hate themselves, and they're born conspirators. Oh, they know very well they're superior, but your Russki is insecure, wants to be respected, to be feared like the old Soviet Union. They need recognition, and they hate their second-tier status in the superpower stakes. That's why Putin's putting together USSR 2.0, and no one is going to stand in his way.

"The kid who pulls the tablecloth and smashes the crockery to get attention—that's Moscow. They don't want to be ignored and they'll break the dishes to make sure it doesn't happen. Sell chemical weapons to Syria, give fuel rods to Iran, teach Indonesia centrifuge design, build a light water reactor in Burma, oh, yeah, people, nothing's out of bounds.

"But the real danger is the instability all this creates, the juice it gives the next generation of world-stopping crazies. People, the second Cold War is all about the resurgent Russian Empire, and don't kid yourselves Moscow is gonna sit back and see how the Chinese navy handles itself when—not if—the shooting starts in the Taiwan Strait." He shrugged on a shiny suit coat.

"It's not as easy this time around; you men and women will have to figure it out. I envy you." He lifted his hand. "Good hunting," he said, and walked out. The room was quiet and they all stayed in their seats.

Nate was now in the vaunted Moscow pipeline, dipped in specialized training, compartmented internal ops training, and as the Moscow tour loomed, he studied operational vocabulary in Russian, and he was allowed to review the "books," the agent files, read the names and examine the flat-faced passport photos of the Russian sources he would meet on the street, under the nose of surveillance. Life and death in the snow, the tip of the spear, as big as it comes. His Farm class was dispersed and largely forgotten. Now there were other lives at stake. He could not—would not—fail.

Three days after his talk with Gondorf, Nate was sitting in a small restaurant in Moscow's Sheremetyevo Airport, waiting for his flight to be called. He ordered a "sanwitz Cubano" and a beer off the greasy menu.

The Embassy had offered to send an admin facilitator with him to help with tickets and passport control, but he had politely refused. The night before, Leavitt had brought out some beers at the end of the workday, and they sat around talking quietly, avoiding the obvious subjects, certainly not mentioning what all the other officers thought, that Nate's career in general and reputation in particular were going to take a hit. Good-byes were strained.

The only bright spot was that two days before, in response to Gondorf's short-of-tour notification, Headquarters cabled that a case-officer position in neighboring Helsinki had suddenly come open. Given Nate's nearly fluent Russian, the abundance of Russians in Finland, his instant mobility as an unmarried officer, and his unexpected availability, Headquarters inquired whether Nate would consider a lateral assignment to Helsinki, effective immediately. Nate accepted, as Gondork bridled at the reprieve, but concurred. Helsinki Station's formal assignment cable arrived, followed by an informal note from Tom Forsyth, his soon-to-be new Chief of Station in Helsinki, simply saying he was glad to welcome Nate to the Station.

Nate's Finnair flight was called and he walked out

onto the tarmac with the other passengers toward the plane. High above him, from a glassed-in observation room in the control tower of the airport, a two-man team cranked frames with a long lens. FSB surveillance had followed Nate to the airport to say good-bye. The FSB, the SVR, and especially Vanya Egorov were certain that Nate's sudden departure was significant. As Nate mounted the aircraft stairs and the cameras clicked, Egorov sat in his office immersed in thought. A shame. His best chance to find the spy the CIA was running was fading away. It would take months, perhaps years, to develop a better lead in this case, if at all.

Nash was still the key, thought Egorov. He presumably would still handle his source from outside Russia. Egorov decided not to let up on Nash, and the lateral assignment to Finland was an opening. *Let's work him a little in Helsinki,* he thought. The SVR could operate virtually at will in Finland, and better yet, they had primacy in the foreign field. No more FSB bum-boys to coordinate with. *We'll see,* thought Vanya. The world was too small a place to hide.

MOSCOW AIRPORT CUBAN SANDWICH

Slice a twelve-inch loaf of Cuban bread partway through lengthwise and fold flat. Drizzle olive oil on outside and slather yellow mustard inside. Layer glazed ham, roast pork, Swiss cheese, and thinly sliced pickles. Close and press for ten minutes in a plancha or between two hot foil-wrapped bricks (heat bricks for an hour in a 500-degree oven). Cut in thirds on the diagonal.

3

Dominika Egorova was sitting at a private corner banquette in the crystal-and-marble opulence of Baccara, the most elegant of the new restaurants in Moscow, located a few steps from Lubyanka Square. The forest of crystal and silver on a dazzling white tablecloth was unlike anything she had experienced before. She was enjoying herself and, despite the operational nature of the evening, was determined to enjoy the sinfully expensive dinner.

Dimitri Ustinov sat across from her, humming with horny. Tall, heavily built, with a shock of black hair and a lantern jaw, Ustinov was a leading member of the fraternity of gangster Russian oil and mining oligarchs who had amassed billion-dollar empires in the boom years after the Cold War. He had started as a local enforcer in organized crime, but he had come up in the world.

Ustinov was dressed in a flawless shawl-collar tuxedo over a ribbed white dress shirt with blue diamond studs and cuff links. He wore a Tourbillon watch by Corum, one of only ten produced each year. His bear-paw hands rested easily over a blue-enameled Fabergé cigarette case, made in 1908 for the czar. He took a cigarette out of the case and lit it with a solid-gold Ligne Deux, snapping it shut with the distinctive musical note of all Dupont lighters.

Ustinov was the third-wealthiest man in Russia, but for all his wealth he was not the smartest. He had feuded publicly with the government, most notably with Prime Minister Vladimir Putin, and had refused to acknowledge or accept government regulation of his enterprises. Three months ago, at the height of the feud, Ustinov airily made obscenely disparaging remarks about Putin on a Moscow TV interview show. People in the know were amazed that Ustinov was still alive.

Ustinov wasn't thinking about anything that evening except Dominika. He had seen her at the television station a month after his interview. Her beauty and elemental sexuality took his breath away. He had been prepared to buy the television station on the spot just to meet her again, but it wasn't necessary. She immediately and delightedly had accepted his invitation for dinner. As he looked at her across the table, Ustinov wanted his thumbprints all over her.

Dominika was twenty-five years old, with dark chestnut hair worn up and tied with a black ribbon. Her cobalt-blue eyes matched his cigarette case and he said so, then compulsively slid the priceless bauble across the table to her. "This is for you." She had full lips and slim, elegant arms that tonight were bare. She wore a simple black dress with a plunging neckline that revealed a spectacular cleavage. The diffused candlelight barely illuminated one fine blue vein on her breast beneath flawless skin. She reached out and fingered the magnificent case with long, elegant hands. Her nails were short and square-cut, without any polish. She looked at him with wide eyes and he felt a string being plucked somewhere between his gut and groin.

She knew enough to follow her instincts, to swallow the bile in her throat. She smiled at this elemental lizard. "Dimitri, this is magnificent, I cannot possibly accept such a gift," she said. "It's too generous."

"Of course you can," Ustinov said, struggling to be charming. "You are the most beautiful woman I have ever met, and you being here is the most wonderful gift I could ever receive." He took a sip of champagne and imagined that little black dress in a discarded heap in the corner of his bedroom. "I am very fond of you already," said Ustinov.

Dominika willed herself not to laugh at him, even as she felt a delicious iciness run up her back and down her arms. This *derevenshchina,* this rube, had as much sophistication as a provincial bully-boy enforcer, which was exactly what he had been years before. But Lord, he was wealthy now. During the week of preparation, Dominika had been told a few facts about Ustinov: Yachts. Villas. Penthouse apartments. Oil and mineral holdings around the world. A private security army made up of well-paid mercenaries. Three private jets.

Dominika was the only child of Nina and Vassily Egorov. Nina had been concertmaster in the Moscow State Symphony, a rising virtuoso who had studied with Klimov and had such massive potential that she was allocated Guarneri's magnificent 1741 Kochanski del Gesù by the Glinka State Central Museum of Music and Culture. Fifteen years ago her anticipated promotion to the Russian National Symphony Orchestra was denied her when Prokhor Belenko, a toad-eating violinist of inferior talent—but married to the daughter of a Politburo member—demanded that he be promoted, and was given the position. Everyone knew what had happened, but no one said a thing.

Along with her brilliance in playing the red-varnished *skripka,* Nina Egorova was known for her fiery disposition, including a simmering temper that exploded whenever she had seen enough. Before the amused eyes of eighty fellow orchestra members, Nina had walloped Belenko above the right ear with his own music stand during his last rehearsal with the State Symphony. Nina was unrepentant. She was also a woman in the then–Soviet Union. They took away the Guarneri. She refused to play a lesser instrument. They moved her from the first to the third seat in strings. She sent them to hell. Administrative leave morphed into dismissal when the Ministry of Culture called the symphony director and her career was over. Now, years later, the elegant neck had bent, the strong hands had curled, the dark hair was gray and in a bun.

Dominika's father was the famous academician Professor Vassily Egorov, Senior Professor of History at Moscow University. He was one of the most respected and influential figures in Russian letters, with the rank of Meritorious Professor. His gold-and-blue Order of St. Andrew hung framed on the wall; the claret bowknot he wore every day on his lapel was the Medal Pushkina, the Pushkin Medal for achievement in literature and education. Ironically, Vasya Egorov didn't look distinguished or influential. He was short and slight, with thinning hair combed carefully across his head.

Unlike his wife, Vassily Egorov had survived the Soviet years by avoiding politics, allegiances, and controversy. Cocooned in the university, he succeeded chiefly by carefully cultivating a persona of studious fair-mindedness, discretion, and loyalty. What no one knew was that Meritorious Comrade Professor Vassily Egorov maintained a secret, separate soul, the conscience of a totally different being, in which he harbored a moral thinker's revulsion for the Soviet. Like all Russians, he had lost family in the 1930s and 1940s to Stalin, resisting the Germans, the purges, the *katorga*. But more than that. He rejected the imbalance and illogic of the Soviet system, he despised the top-heavy favoritism of the *cheloveki,* the insiders' sloth and self-indulgence that crushed the human spirit and had robbed Russians of their lives, their country, their patrimony. It was an apostasy shared only with Nina.

All Russians harbor secret thoughts, they are accustomed to it. So it was with Vassily and Nina, who hid their revulsion at how modern Russia had not changed. Even as Dominika grew older and could begin to understand, Vassily dared not speak to her of their feelings. Both parents yearned to give her a clear vision of the world, to let her see the truth for herself. If they could not expose Russia's hellish evolution—from Bolshevik rage to Soviet rot and now, even after glasnost, into the Federation's parasitic greed—Vassily at least resolved to instill in Dominika the real majesty of Russia.

The spacious three-room apartment (after Nina's dismissal they were permitted to keep it, thanks only to the continued position and prestige of Vassily) was filled with books, music, art, and conversation in three different languages. Her parents noticed, when Dominika turned five, that the little girl had a prodigious memory. She could recite lines from Pushkin, identify the concertos of Tchaikovsky. And when music was played, Dominika would dance barefoot around the Oriental carpet in the living room, perfectly in time with the notes, twirling and jumping, perfectly in balance, her eyes gleaming, her hands flashing. Vassily and Nina looked at each other, and her mother asked Dominika how she had learned all this. "I follow the colors," said the little girl.

"What do you mean, 'the colors'?" asked her mother. Dominika gravely explained that when the music played, or when her father read aloud to her, colors would fill the room. Different colors, some bright, some dark, sometimes they "jumped in the air" and all Dominika had to do was follow them. It was how she could remember so much. When she danced, she leapt over bars of bright blue, followed shimmering spots of red on the floor. The parents looked at each other again.

"I like red and blue and purple," said Dominika. "When Batushka reads, or when Mamulya plays, they are beautiful."

"And when Mama is cross with you?" asked Vassily.

"Yellow, I don't like the yellow," said the little girl, turning the pages of a book. "And the black cloud. I do not like that."

Vassily asked a colleague from the Faculty of Psychology about the colors. "I have read about a similar condition," said the colleague. "Sensing letters as colors. It's quite interesting. Why don't you bring her by one afternoon?"

Vassily waited in his office while his professor friend sat with Dominika in a nearby classroom. One hour stretched to three. They came back, little Dominika happy and distracted, the professor pensive. "What?" asked Vassily, looking sideways at his daughter.

"I could sit with her for days," said the professor, packing his pipe. "Your little girl shows the attributes of a synesthete. Someone who perceives sounds, or letters, or numbers as colors. Fascinating." Vassily looked at Dominika again. She was now happily coloring at her father's desk.

"My God," said Vassily. "Is it an illness, is it insanity?"

"Illness, burden, curse, who can say?" He stuffed his pipe. "On the other hand, Vasya, perhaps she is *odarennyi*, gifted." Vassily, the brilliant man of letters, was at a loss. "There's something else," said the professor, looking over at Dominika, her head bent over her drawing. "Her synesthesia appears to extend to human reactions. Not only words or sounds, she also sees emotional content as colors. She spoke to me about what sounds like halos of color around people's heads and shoulders." Vassily stared at his friend. "Perhaps she will develop into something of a savant in matters of human intentions.

"Of course, there is the prodigious memory. She flawlessly repeated twenty-five digits back to me several times. It is not uncommon in these cases," continued the professor. "But you already have seen that." Vassily nodded. "And another thing, not so common. Your little girl is prone to *buistvo,* define it as you like, temper, mischief, a short fuse. She swept my papers to the floor when she could not solve a puzzle. Something she will have to control later in life, I would imagine."

"*Bozhe,*" said Vassily, and hurried home to tell his wife.

"This comes from your family," said Vassily dryly to Nina, as red-faced Dominika would glower when the music was turned off, gravely displeased, eyes ablaze. If she was this way at age five, what would she be like later on?

When at the age of ten Dominika auditioned at the Moscow State Academy of Choreography at second Frunzenskaya 5 she impressed the admissions panel. She had no technique, no formal discipline, but even at that young age they saw in her the intensity, the natural skill, the instincts of a great dancer. They had asked her why she wanted to dance, and had laughed at her answer, "Because I can see the music," and the room grew still as her already strikingly beautiful face darkened and she regarded the panel through narrowed eyes as if contemplating doing them all physical harm.

Dominika made her saucy, triumphant way through the academy, the great feeder school for the Bolshoi. She flourished despite the rigors of the classical Vaganova method. She had by then become accustomed to living with the colors. Her ability to see them, whether while listening to music, or dancing, or simply talking to people, now felt more refined, somehow more under her control. And she began deciphering the colors, associating them with moods and emotions. It was not a burden. To her it was simply something she lived with.

Dominika continued to excel, but not only in dancing. She achieved highest marks in the academy's middle and upper schools, where her ability to remember everything she had been taught served her well. This was something new, something different. Dominika listened to the political lectures, the ideological lessons, the history of communism, the rise and fall of the socialist state, the history of Soviet ballet. Of course, there had been excesses, and there had been corrections. And now modern Russia would continue to grow, a sum greater than its parts. Her young mind made the leap, accepted the cant.

By age eighteen, Dominika was promoted to the first student troupe at school and led her study class in political achievement. Each night she would return home to tell her secretly horrified father what she had learned. He tried to counterbalance her growing enthusiasms with the lessons of literature and history. But Dominika was in the full flight of her adolescence, in the grip of her young career. If she sensed the nature of his desperate message, if she read the colors above his head, she gave no sign. Vassily could not be more clear. He dared not speak out openly against the system.

Of course, Nina was pleased that her daughter was progressing so rapidly in the junior ballet company. It was fine, a secure future was assured. But she too watched in dismay as her little girl became a model Modern Russian Woman, an ultranationalist, a tall, chestnut-haired beauty who walked with the elegance of a ballerina, and who behaved like the *apparatchiki* of the old days.

Dominika lay on the carpet in the living room, her mother combing her dark hair softly, rhythmically, with the long-handled brush that belonged to her great-grandmother. The tortoiseshell brush with gently curved handle that, along with a framed photograph and a silver samovar, was the only family belonging rescued from the elegant house in pre-Bolshevik Petersburg. The hog's-hair bristles made a quiet stirring sound, crimson in the air. Her hair was radiant. Dominika, stretching after a long day of ballet, interrupted her father's soft-spoken narrative by relating what she had heard at school. "Father, do you realize that *outside influences* are threatening the country? Are you aware of the growing number of dissidents *advocating chaos*? Have you read V. V. Putin's article concerning *Zionists* working against the state?"

With a dull ache, the parents looked down at their daughter. *Gospodi pomiluj!* God forbid! *The state. V. V. Putin. Dissidents.* On the floor, Dominika stretched deeply, her long legs and lithe figure already Their instrument, her good mind slowly being brought into Their service. Nina looked at Vassily. She wanted to tell her daughter the truth, to warn her about the pitfalls of the system that had killed her career, of a system that had forced Vassily to blank his exceptional mind and stay silent for his entire life. Vassily shook his head. "Not now, not ever," he said.

At twenty, Dominika was selected prima ballerina of the First Troupe. Her evaluations uniformly were outstanding and her athletic ability prompted her ballet master to compare her to "a young Galina Ulanova" the *prima ballerina assoluta* of the Bolshoi after the war. Now, when she danced, the colors she saw no longer were elemental shapes and hues, but sophisticated waves of variegated lights, rolling and pulsing and carrying her aloft. The sepia tones surrounding her dancing partners let her more perfectly combine with them. She was hot to the touch, precise, strong in back and leg, exquisite and tall on her toes. The ballet master insisted it was time she began preparing for the yearly audition to join the Bolshoi troupe.

As she grew stronger and more supple, there was something else coming alive within Dominika's body, an extension of the rigors of dance, an awareness of her own body. It was not lasciviousness, for she carried her sexuality within her. It was a private awakening, and she tested her corporeal boundaries without a thought of shame. As far as she could determine, neither of her parents was this way, so perhaps a long-forgotten relative had been a libertine.

In her darkened bedroom, when her body called her, she explored her sensations, explored them as intently as she practiced at the barre, her breathing deep red behind her eyelids, and she shuddered as she discovered how she was wired. It was not a fetish, nor an addiction, but rather a secret self that grew more aware as she grew older. She enjoyed her secret self. It was not all nature-child innocence, however. She occasionally felt the need for something edgy, forbidden, and she closed her eyes tight, on a night of a colossal thunderstorm outside her window, amazed at herself, as she held the swan-necked handle of *Prababushka*'s brush in her long fingers, timing the lightning flashes to match her own rhythms. Wanting more and more, amazed still, she trailed the humid point lower and held her breath and felt the even sweeter surge of the handle suddenly pinning her like a beetle in a display case. Thank God she had now taken to combing her own hair in the evenings after ballet school.

Though she had casual friends, Dominika was not friendly with her classmates. For all that, she was class leader, concerned and consumed with nothing but the troupe's progress, its record of excellence, the triumphs in competitions with other schools, especially those from Saint Petersburg, the spiritual center of Russian ballet of the imperial style. Dominika lectured her weary fellow dancers about the Moscow School's purity, its essential Russian nature. They all called her *klikusha,* the demoniac, behind her back, the New Russian Woman, the gladiator, the star, the devoted, the true believer. *Oh, shut up,* they thought.

At twenty-two, Sonya Moroyeva probably had one final year to move up from the academy to the Bolshoi, but with Egorova in the running that year, her chances were not good. She had been dancing all her life, was the daughter of a full member of the Duma, and was at the core a spoiled and vain young woman. She was, frankly, desperate. She had been recklessly sleeping with a boy in the troupe, blond, lynx-eyed Konstantin, an incredibly risky activity that if discovered by the instructors would have guaranteed their instant dismissal from the school. But after fifteen years in the academy she knew the quiet times, and when the sauna room was deserted, and how long they had for their sweaty sessions, with her supple legs bent over her head, and she whispered in Konstantin's ear for a week, and told him she loved him, and ground her hips up at him, licking the sweat from his face, and begged him to save her career, her life.

Experienced ballet students know as much about anatomy and joints and injuries as a doctor. Konstantin, rabbit-mad in his gluttony for Sonya's *pizda,* waited until he was paired with Dominika. Practicing a pas de deux on a crowded floor, he stepped hard on her heel when she was *en pointe,* forcing her foot forward, and the colors bled and her world went swirling black, and she buckled to searing pain and total collapse. They carried her to the infirmary, her classmates frozen and pale along the barre, Sonya palest of all. Dominika had looked at her then, had seen her guilty expression, the gray miasma swirling unseen around her head, and knew. On the infirmary table her foot was turning black and eggplant-purple, the worst, and the pain radiated up her leg. The doctor muttered, "Lisfranc fracture of the midfoot," and after a series of orthopedic examinations and surgery, and a cast on her foot to the ankle, Dominika was dropped from the academy; her dancing career, her life for ten years, was over. It was that fast, that final. All the honeyed phrases about her being the next Ulanova evaporated. The masters, the coaches, the trainers wouldn't look at her.

In young adulthood she had learned to cope with the *buistvo,* the mounting rage, but now she let it grow, tasted it in her throat. She hysterically considered denouncing Konstantin and Sonya for having sabotaged her. They too would be expelled if their assignation was revealed, but in the end she knew she could not. She was still numbly contemplating her future when the call came from her mother.

Her father had suffered a massive stroke and had died on the way to Kremlyovka Clinic in Kuntsevo, reserved for citizens of privilege and wealth. He had been the most important person in her life, her guide, her protector, and now he was gone. She would have held his hand to her cheek, told him of her release from the ballet academy, of the treachery of her classmates. She would have asked him for advice, for him to tell her what she should do. She could not know it, but Vassily would have whispered to his idealistic daughter that one may fall in love with the State, but the State does not reciprocate, ever.

Two days later, Dominika sat in the formal parlor of their apartment, her right foot extended in the cast, her eyes dry, her elegant neck and head held high. Her mother sat beside her, in black, quiet and calm. The house was full of guests, scores of people who came to pay their respects, academics, artists, government officials, and politicians. The sound of their voices filled the air with elemental shades of green, the color she associated with sorrow and grief, and which seemed to push the air out of the room. Dominika struggled to breathe. There was food from the kitchen, traditional blini with red caviar, smoked sturgeon and trout. On the sideboard, carafes of mineral water, a steaming silver samovar, fruit juice, whiskey, and iced vodka.

Then, looming in front of the couch was Uncle Vanya, leaning over her mother, mouthing words of condolence. The brothers had never been close, their personalities and temperaments nearly polar opposites. Dominika was not sure what he did, but one hardly uttered the letters KGB or SVR. Then he came close, sitting beside her, his beefy features inches from her face, intruding on her grief. She saw him appraise her, dressed in black, hair back, in mourning. Her throat constricted in the familiar way, and her mother reached over to squeeze her hand. *Control yourself.*

"Dominika, my deepest condolences," said Vanya. "I know how close you were to your father."

He reached out and gave her a paternal embrace, brushing his cheek against hers. His cologne (Houbigant from Paris) was lavender-scented and strong. "Let me also say that I regret your injury, how it affects your career." He nodded at her cast. "I know what a good student you had become, both with the dancing and in school as well. Your father was always very proud of you." He sat back in the couch as another family friend passed by, shaking hands.

Up till now, Dominika had only looked at Vanya, she had not spoken. "What are your plans now?" he asked. "Perhaps the university?"

Dominika shrugged. "I am not sure what comes next. Dancing was my life, I have to find something else." She felt him staring at her.

He smoothed his tie and stood, looking down at her. "Dominushka, I have a favor to ask. I need your assistance." Dominika looked up at him, startled. Uncle Vanya shrugged. "It's not so mysterious. I need you to do something for me, quite unofficial, a small little thing, but important."

"For the Secret Service?" Dominika asked, astonished.

Vanya put a finger to his lips. He led her limping to the side of the living room. The day of her father's funeral. He had chosen this time purposely, hadn't he? They always did.

"I need your talent, *dorogaya moya,* my dear, and your beauty," Uncle Vanya had said. "Someone I can trust, someone with your well-known discretion." He moved closer, and Dominika felt the flattery wrapped in his body heat.

"It is a simple task, almost a game, to meet a man, to get to know him. I can provide the details later." *Zmeya,* serpent.

"Will you agree to help your old uncle?" Vanya asked, his hands on her shoulders. A serpent, flicking its tongue, tasting the air. For him to ask her now was monstrous, typical, beastly. Dominika could feel her heartbeat in her throbbing foot.

A halo of yellow bloomed behind Vanya's head as if he were a Byzantine saint. Then her breath came back, and with it a hollow calm. Precisely because he expected her to refuse, Dominika accepted. She looked back evenly, seeing the narrowing of his eyes, seeing him calculate. She saw him searching her face, but she gave him nothing, and his face had reacted to that.

"Excellent," said Vanya. "You know that your father would be extremely proud. There was no bigger patriot than your father. And he raised his daughter to be a patriot too. A Russian patriot."

Continue speaking of my father and I shall lean forward and bite your lower lip off, she thought. Instead, Dominika gave him a smile that only recently she had come to recognize had an effect on people. "Now that my ballet career is over," she said, "I may as well do *secret chores* for you." Vanya's face moved, then he recovered. He took his hands from her shoulders.

"Come to see me next week," he said, looking down at her cast. "If you are able. I will send a car for you." Vanya buttoned his light woolen suit. He took her hand in his big paw, his face inches from hers. "Come give your uncle a proper good-bye." Dominika put her hands on his shoulders and pecked him lightly on either cheek, looking for a moment at his wet liver lips. Lavender scent and a yellow halo.

He whispered in her ear. "I do not ask you to help me for nothing in return," he said. "I believe I can intervene in the matter of this apartment." Dominika pulled back. "Your mother would not lose it, even after your father's death. It would be a great comfort to her." Vanya let go of her hand, straightened, and walked out of the room. Astonished, she watched him close the door behind him. *A first taste of the yoke,* thought Dominika.

On the street, Vanya motioned his driver to get going and settled into the backseat of his Mercedes. *There,* he thought with a sigh, *I've paid my respects. Brother Vassily was a fuzzy-headed academic, living in the past. And that sister-in-law. She's already lost her mind, a* sumashedshij, *a lunatic. But that niece—she's a real Greek statue—is perfect for this matter, I'm glad I thought of her. Now that she's ruined her foot she has no options. She can learn other things. That apartment would sell for millions,* Vanya thought. *Yes, after all, this is family and it's the least I can do.*

That evening after the guests had left she sat with her mother in the darkened living room. Bach was playing softly, accompanied by the nearly empty samovar that sighed occasionally with the last of its steam. Dominika didn't need lights in the room. Great waves of deep red pulsed past her from the music. Holding both her hands in her lap, Nina looked at her daughter and knew she was "looking at the colors." She squeezed Dominika's hands to get her to concentrate, and began talking in a low, slow voice. She whispered to her, leaning close to her daughter, and spoke about her father and his life. She spoke about ballet school and Russia and what had happened to her. And then Nina spoke of darker things, of promise and betrayal and revenge. Two figures in a darkened room filled with vermilion Bach, two *klikushy* in a forest glen, planning mayhem.

Two days later, Dominika returned to the academy, ostensibly to talk with the doctors and to collect her belongings. She was already an outsider, it was as if they were waiting for her to leave. She lingered unobtrusively, sitting in a chair near the exit, watching Sonya Moroyeva and Konstantin dancing, Sonya's right leg impossibly high, impossibly straight *en penché,* Konstantin turning her in a slow promenade. His eyes were on the slash of black leotard stretched across her crotch. At the evening break, with shadows lengthening in the nearly empty practice hall, Dominika watched Sonya and Konstantin slip down the hall toward the sauna room. There had been rumors about the two, of course, but now Dominika knew. She waited and watched the light on the practice hall's parquet floor fade, feeling the familiar tightening, controlling it, bringing the ice.

The building had grown silent, the various offices dark. The ballet master and two matrons were still in their offices farther down; dim lights shone at the far end of the otherwise darkened hallway. Dominika hobbled silently to the door of the anteroom of the large wood-paneled sauna used by students and pushed through it, silently walked to the door of the steam chamber and peered through the smoked-glass port in the cedar door. They were both naked on the wooden slats of the top bench, barely illuminated by the single bulb in the ceiling. Konstantin had just raised his face from between Sonya's wide-spread legs and was poised over her like a great beast. Sonya clasped her hands behind Konstantin's neck and swung her legs over his shoulders. Through the glass, Dominika saw the calluses on the pads of Sonya's feet and the splay of battered ballerina toes.

Her mouth was open and her head was back on the bench, but the heavy door of the sauna muffled Sonya's moans. Dominika stepped back and willed the ice to take over the rage. A twist of the steam dial and a broomstick through the outer door handles would poach them both in twenty minutes. No. Something elegant, undetectable, poisonous, final. The two had ended Dominika's career, now it was time to end theirs, but without a trace, without a hint of revenge.

Dominika propped open the hallway door to the anteroom and turned on the overhead light, which shone into the darkened corridor. In the long hallway she swung one of the exterior windows open. The cool night air rushed in and Dominika followed the cold air, pinpricks of ice-blue light like fireflies swirling down the hallway toward the matrons' offices. She slipped into a darkened office two doors down and leaned against the wall and listened.

In three minutes the matron—which one was it? Dominika wondered—felt the cold air and went down the hallway to investigate. The light in the sauna anteroom and the open door opposite the window had her muttering to herself. It sounded like Madame Butyrskaya, the most strict, the most ferocious of the academy watchdogs. Dominika waited in the silence, counting the seconds, then heard the hiss of the sauna door and then Madame's bellows and what sounded like a strangled sob. Sounds of feet on the linoleum and continued bellowing and now mewling, whimpering, receded down the hallway. Not even her daddy in the Duma could save her, she thought.

Dominika put her hand up in front of her face in the nearly dark office. It was steady and luminous and she felt air coursing back into her lungs, as if someone had opened the valve to an oxygen bottle, and she realized, with a little huff of surprise, that she felt no emotion over having destroyed those two, and she reveled in the elegance and simplicity of what she had done, and then thought about her father and was a little ashamed.

The cast came off her foot. SVR planners intended to dangle Dominika in front of Ustinov at the television station. They wanted him to invite her to spend time with him. They didn't tell her to sleep with him, it wasn't necessary, they had said, but she knew it was implied. Their deceit lay on the table. She surprised herself by not caring about that. The briefers looked at her cautiously, unsettled by her level gaze and slight smile, not sure what they had on their hands.

All right, all right, they said, they needed to know

more about his business, his international travel schedule, his contacts. They said he was being investigated for fraud and misappropriation of State funds. The colors of their words were pale, washed out, as if they were not fully formed. Yes, what they needed was clear, she said, she could do it. The men in the room looked at one another and back to her, and she read them like a hymnal. This was an exceedingly interesting discovery, this SVR, this Russian Secret Service, she thought. *Gusi,* a gaggle of geese.

As she read the reports, themselves a riot of color, she resolved to silence the smug counterintelligence planners who sat looking at her through smoke-filled eyes, to wipe the smile off the face of her dear Uncle Vanya. She remembered the lavender smell of him. His poor little niece, the broken ballerina, his dead brother's beautiful daughter. Care to help me in a delicate matter? Perhaps we can keep your mother in the apartment after all. *Ochen horosho*. Very good.

Now the candlelight flickered and the crystal clinked, and as Ustinov shoveled food into his mouth, Dominika felt an even, slow contempt for him that infused her with an icy detachment. She was prepared to do whatever was necessary to complete the assignment, and she knew precisely what to do and how to do it.

So she did. Dominika was captivating at dinner. Educated, attentive, distracting. She trailed a fingertip across the hollow of her throat, watching the parabolas of orange around his shoulders. Interesting, thought Dominika, the yellow of deceit mixed with the red of passion. *Zhivotnoe*. Animal.

He could barely sit still through dinner—she saw him gulping his champagne with the thirst that comes from building lust. His shirt studs vibrated. At the end of dinner, he told her he had a bottle of three-hundred-year-old cognac in his apartment, better than anything the restaurant could offer. Would she come home with him? Dominika looked at him and conspiratorially leaned forward. Her breasts swelled together in the candlelight. "I've never tried cognac," she said. Ustinov could feel his heartbeat in his mouth.

BLINIS SERVED AT VASSILY EGOROV'S WAKE

Season one cup flour with baking powder and kosher salt. Add milk, egg, and clarified butter, and blend into a smooth batter. Cook a tablespoon of the batter at a time over medium low heat until blini are golden on both sides. Serve topped with red caviar, salmon, crème fraîche, sour cream, and fresh dill.

4

They left the restaurant in Ustinov's sleek BMW, the windows of which were heavily armored. Ustinov's apartment sprawled on the top floor of a massive neoclassical building in the "Golden Mile" section of the Arbat. It was a superb penthouse made up of two contiguous apartments with marble floors, massive white leather furniture, and gilt fixtures on the walls. City rooftops and the lights of Moscow were visible through the floor-to-ceiling windows that ran the length of the apartment.

The air was scented with incense. Enormous Chinese lamps cast warm light in pools throughout the room, and in one corner hung an abstract reclining nude, fingers and eyes and toes pointing in all directions, a Picasso, Dominika guessed. *That will be me in fifteen minutes,* she thought wryly.

Ustinov dismissed his security detail with a wave, and the door clicked closed. On an ebony sideboard, among a forest of bottles, Dominika saw a squat bottle of cognac, presumably the three-hundred-year stuff. Ustinov poured into seventeenth-century Bohemian crystal and made her sip. From another tray, she sampled an earthy pâté with a sublime hint of lemon on a delicate toast point.

Ustinov took Dominika's hand and led her down a broad hall hung with lighted paintings and up three wide steps to the darkened bedroom. He did not notice the hint of a limp from her mended foot, more a hitch in her stride than anything. He was too busy looking at her hair, her neck, the softness of her bosom.

Their motion into the room triggered recessed lighting and Dominika stared in amazement from the doorway. The bedroom was a cavernous space, the size of a throne room, decorated in white and black contrasts. An enormous circular bed on a platform in the middle of the room was covered with plush fur throws. The walls were lined with scores of full-length mirrors. Ustinov picked up a remote and pressed a button. Fabric shades on the ceiling mechanically drew back to reveal a star-filled black sky through a cantilevered glass roof. "I can follow the moon and stars as they move across the sky," he said. "Will you watch the sunrise with me tomorrow?"

Dominika forced herself to smile. The *svin'ya* in his sty. But how could such a man amass such wealth while others still stood in lines for bread? The atmosphere in the bedroom was heavy, with a fragrance of sandalwood. The ivory carpet beneath her feet was soft and thick. A collection of silver dishes on a white ash sideboard winked in the revolving lights. A separate spot illuminated a framed Ebru panel with spidery calligraphy. Ustinov saw her look at it. "Sixteenth century," he said, as if he were prepared to take it off the wall and give it to her.

Now that they were standing in his bedroom, the game was a little more serious, the sexuality she had thrown around during dinner suddenly not so clever. The physical act was easy enough, she was not a prude. But she wondered what she would lose if she seduced this man. Nothing, she told herself. Ustinov couldn't take anything away from her, neither could the leering briefers from the Service, nor lavender-scented Uncle Vanya with his mouthed condolences. "Serious work for the Service," Vanya had said. *Nonsense,* Dominika thought. *It was a political game to unseat a rival, but anyway this* blyad, *this gilded bas-*

tard, deserved to lose what he had, to go to prison. She would gut him, and Uncle Vanya would wonder what sort of person he had recruited for this task.

Dominika turned to Ustinov and let her wrap fall from her shoulders. She kissed him once lightly on the mouth and ran her hand across his cheek. He pulled her close and kissed her back roughly. Their two figures were reflected in a hundred mirror images.

Ustinov pulled away and looked at Dominika through tunnel-visioned eyes. His body was an exposed nerve; his brain was detaching itself from the anchor points inside his skull. He shrugged his dinner jacket to the floor and pawed at his silk bow tie. The oligarch who had made a fortune by outplaying other dangerous men, by cheating and hammering and, even, by eliminating his competition, saw only the blue eyes, the tendril of brown hair falling to the slender white throat, the lips still wet from their kiss. Dominika put her hands on his chest and whispered, "*Dushka,* wait for me on the bed. I will be two minutes."

In the gilt-bedecked bathroom, Dominika looked at herself in the mirror. *You said yes,* she thought, *first to Vanya and now to this* medved, *this drooling bear, so important to prove yourself, now get on with it.* She reached behind her, unzipped, and stepped out of her dress. *You use this,* she thought, looking at her body in the mirror, *and you get the thing done, captivate him, find out what they want to know.* They had told her Ustinov was dangerous, he was a brute who had killed men. Fine. Tomorrow morning she would be spooning iced consommé into his upturned mouth like a baby bird, and he would be chirping his secrets to her, and then the brute would be looking at the world through bars. Then she remembered something from the briefing and quickly reached into her clutch and popped a Benzedrine tablet they had given her, for the physical lift, they had told her.

Ustinov was lying on the bed on his back, propped up on his elbows, naked except for a pair of black silk shorts. Dominika walked slowly up to the foot of the bed, wondering how to start. She remembered how good it felt when trainers had rubbed their inflamed feet at the ballet academy, so she knelt and rubbed her thumbs hard across the arch of his foot. Ustinov looked at her blankly. *Idiotka,* she thought, *some courtesan you are,* and with desperate intuition put her mouth over the big toe of Ustinov's right foot and swirled her tongue around the length of it. He groaned and fell back on the bed. Better. His trembling hand reached into a recess on the frame of the bed and instantly the room was bathed in deep red light, coloring the bed, their faces, their skin. It was augmented by smaller dots of pink, swirling around the room, off the mirrors and over Dominika's crimson body. With a low hum, the bed began revolving. *God preserve us from gangsters,* thought Dominika.

Ustinov grunted something at her and reached out his hand. The revolving pink lights against the all-red background of the room turned into double pink dots, then triple dots, revolving around one another in their respective paths across the room. Dominika was overloading on the lights and the colors, and Ustinov continued beckoning for her. His guttural obscenities came out as slashes of dark orange, elemental, brutal; they somehow slid beneath, not over, the pink dots.

Dominika looked at him from under half-closed lids and wondered whether she should lick her lips for effect. As he revolved like a Bundt cake in a microwave, Ustinov's eyes never left her. Dominika knew she had to simultaneously obliterate his body as well as his head, he had to want her to stay with him. A week, two weeks, two months. Any amount of time would satisfy the requirements, the longer the better, they said. They had told her the sidewalk outside Ustinov's apartment was stained with the tears of his one-night stands.

Ustinov was slowly revolving toward her. When he came even with where Dominika was kneeling, he put his arms around her waist, threw her on her back—she registered the tug of tearing panties—hunched over her like a gargoyle and began making passionate, if feral, love to her.

In the red light, Ustinov's clenched teeth—normally white and even—appeared blue and black-rimmed. Dominika threw her head back and closed her eyes. She felt Ustinov's hot breath on her breasts. The pink sparks of light flowed over her quivering legs, their bodies, and the mirrors. She lifted her buttocks and rocked her pelvis to meet each of his lupine thrusts, clapped her hands around his arms and concentrated on making him lose his sanity. Ustinov pulled his head back in a paroxysm of impending meltdown. Dominika involuntarily huffed as he began moving harder and faster. Apart from the red light, and his blue teeth, and his grunting, Dominika was surprised to feel her own body—her secret self—responding; the bitter-tongue lift from the Benzedrine had arrived. She looked past his chin at the glass ceiling but she could not see any celestial bodies. Where were the stars?

What she did see was an Angel of Death. First she saw a reflected blur on the glass ceiling panels. The blur became a shadow gliding toward the bed, across each mirrored panel like poured black mercury, reflected a hundred times. Dominika felt a pulse of air as the apparition floated above Ustinov's head. The gangster's eyes were sightless with passion. He sensed nothing. A sprung steel wire flashed across Ustinov's throat, drawing tight with a musical zing, cutting into his flesh. Ustinov's eyes snapped open, and his hands scrabbled at the wire garrote now cutting into his windpipe. With his fingers digging at the wire, Ustinov's face hung suspended inches from Dominika's. Her mouth was frozen in a silent scream. He looked at her uncomprehendingly with red-rimmed eyes, a vein on his forehead bulging, his fingers trying for purchase on the wire. His mouth sagged open, a black thread of his saliva falling on her cheek. Ustinov's body began convulsing. He shook side to side like a fish trying to throw a hook. Dominika registered that he was still inside her; she pushed at his chest, turned her head to avoid his spittle and blood, and tried to slip out from underneath him. But he was a big man, suddenly very heavy, and she couldn't move. Dominika could only close her eyes, cross her arms across her face, and feel Dimitri Ustinov's life ebb out of his body. She could feel blood, from the wire cutting his throat, dripping onto her neck and breasts. Ustinov was making a gurgling sound and started going limp, his breath bubbling through the blood, blue-black in this light, of his severed windpipe. Dominika felt a tremor pass through his body, his feet drummed on the bed quickly two or three times, and then he was still. The bed revolved in the pinky silence.

Nothing happened for another terrifying minute. Dominika opened one eye to see Ustinov's face hanging above hers, eyes open, tongue visible in an open mouth. The indistinct black figure loomed over them both, unmoving, speckled by the pink dots. Were those black wings behind his shoulders, or just the reflection of the mirrors? The tableau of three motionless bodies revolved endlessly around the room. As if in a coordinated action, Ustinov slipped out of her and the black figure with a single movement dragged the body off her. It rolled off the bed onto the floor. The killer ignored the corpse, reaching over to the controls to stop the bed. Dominika made to get up, but the figure in black put his hand on her shoulder and pushed her gently back onto the bed. She was trembling, naked, and covered in blood. Her breasts were wetly black with it. The bedclothes were a tangle, but she gathered them up and tried wiping the gore off her body.

She would not look at the man, yet somehow knew he was not going to harm her. He stood at the foot of the bed, motionless, and Dominika stopped trying to sop up the blood and held the blood-black sheet in her hands. Her breath was ragged with fear and shock. The man was studying her foot, visible from beneath the sheet. He reached for her and she began to withdraw it, then out of some primal instinct kept it still. The man stroked the top of her foot lightly. Most people shake hands, but with Matorin, it was a little different.

Formally, Sergey Matorin was an SVR staff officer with the rank of major assigned to the Executive Action Department (Department V). Informally, he was a *chistilshchik,* a "mechanic," an executioner of the Russian Secret Service. In the KGB years, this department was known variously as the Thirteenth Department or Line F, or simply as *mokroye delo,* "wet work." During the height of the Cold War, Line F had managed kidnappings, interrogations, and assassinations, but in the new SVR such things were said not to be even remotely contemplated or condoned. Granted, fractious Russian journalists were found shot in Moscow elevators, or regime critics succumbed to high concentrations of radionuclide polonium in their livers, but that had nothing to do with the modern Russian Foreign Intelligence Service. The age of the "umbrella pokers" had passed.

During the Soviet invasion of Afghanistan, Matorin served as a team commander in the elite Alpha Group of Spetsnaz, at that time under the command of the KGB. A screw came loose during Matorin's five years in the valleys of Afghanistan, and the threads were permanently stripped. His eight-man team had followed orders, but Matorin didn't much care about command. He was essentially a loner who liked to kill people.

He was hit during combat by a metal splinter that blinded his right eye, leaving it an opaque milky white. Tall, whip-thin, his face pocked and scarred, Matorin wore his gray hair plastered over a cadaverous skull. This and a sharp hook nose gave him the appearance of an undertaker. After the withdrawal from Afghanistan, on rare occasions he was seen in SVR headquarters ghosting through the offices of Department V. Younger officers stared in fascination at this throwback Polyphemus. Older employees turned away and crossed themselves.

Even though he was now deployed on occasional "special tasks," Matorin missed the action of Afghanistan. He thought about it often. He had the ability to go back there in his mind, to see the sights, to hear the sounds, to smell the smells. Certain moments would spontaneously trigger his memories. These unexpected trips were the best, the most vivid, including the music. He could hear perfectly the staccato notes from the *rubab* and the crescendo beat from the tablas.

Matorin stroked Dominika's foot just as he had stroked the foot of the pegged-out Afghan bint that one afternoon in the Panjshir Valley. His team had rigged a canopy over the blades of the Mi-24 helicopter and tied down the corners so there was a large shaded area for the men to sit. Earlier they had gunned a group of muj on the road, landed to collect booty, and found the girl hiding among the rocks by the roaring river.

She was about fifteen years old, dark hair, almond eyes, her clothes worn and dusty, the usual filthy camp follower. Every Soviet military man serving in Afghanistan had heard stories about what Afghan women did to Russians taken prisoner, so there was no love lost for the girl. She was straining with the cords around her wrists, but the double loop around her neck threatened to strangle her if she struggled too much. She swore and screamed and spat at the eight Alpha Group commandos who stood in a circle around her. Matorin squatted between her wide-spread legs, secured at the ankles, and watched her struggle. He reached out and held her sandy foot and caressed it. At the touch of the infidel the girl screamed and bellowed and called out to the hills, to her fellow fighters, to come to rescue her.

She needn't have objected to someone simply touching her foot. There was more to come. In the next fifteen minutes Matorin had carefully sliced off her clothes with a short sheath knife and had unwrapped her hijab. She lay supine in the dust, under the canopy that billowed gently in the wind. A soldier poured water over her face, washing it clean, but she spat back at him, thrashing her body against the cords. Matorin reached behind his back and unsheathed a Khyber knife, two feet long, the edge of the elegantly curved, T-shaped blade bright silver from constant honing.

Lying flat behind a boulder a hundred meters up the rocky slope, an Afghan teenager put down his AK-47 and peeked around the rock. He could see the big mottled-green helicopter—he knew it only as "Shaitan Arba"—on the ground, its stationary rotors drooping with their own weight. He saw a circle of figures beneath the billowing canopy. Over the faint roar of the river and the wind in the rocks, the boy heard another sound from the valley floor: a shrill keening, a young woman's screams, which went on and on. The boy uttered a prayer and slipped away. He knew there was something down there that was more terrifying than just infidel Russians.

Matorin got his nickname that day from his men, at least the ones who could continue watching him use his knife. "Khyber" looked down at Dominika with his poached-egg eye, took his hand off her foot, and said, "Get dressed." She had an appointment with Uncle Vanya.

USTINOV'S RUSTIC PÂTÉ

Caramelize chicken livers, pancetta, and garlic, then deglaze pan with brandy. Hand-chop mixture with parsley, capers, shallots, lemon zest, lemon juice, and olive oil into a coarse texture. Add additional olive oil. Serve on toast with lemon.

5

After the murder of Ustinov, Uncle Vanya had summoned Dominika to Yasenevo. She was escorted to the executive elevator bank of SVR headquarters. The SVR shield of Star and Globe hung inside the elevator. Dominika still had a copper taste in her mouth, still felt the slippery sensation of Ustinov's blood on her body. For a week she fought down the recurring horror, tried vainly to sleep, resisted the crawly impulse to physically slough the skin off her breasts and belly. The nightmares had faded, but now she was sick, and depressed, and livid at the way she had been manipulated. Then Uncle Vanya had sent for her.

She had never been to Yasenevo, inside SVR headquarters, much less on the executive fourth floor. It was deathly still; no sound came from any of the closed doors visible down the corridors. She was walked past airbrushed official portraits—each one discretely spotlighted—of former KGB directors lining one side of the long, red-carpeted hallway that led from the elevator to the executive suite: Andropov, Fedorchuk, Chebrikov, Kryuchkov. Berlin, Hungary, Czechoslovakia, Afghanistan. On the opposite wall hung the portraits of the new leadership of SVR: Primakov, Trubnikov, Lebedev, Fradkov. Chechnya, Georgia, Ukraine. Were they all in heaven or hell? The old boys' eyes followed her as she walked down the hall.

To the right were the imposing doors of the Director's office. To the left, identical doors led to the First Deputy Director's office. Dominika was shown in. Uncle Vanya sat behind a large desk of polished, light-colored wood. A heavy piece of glass covered the top of the desk. Apart from a red leather blotter in front of him, the desk was clean. A bank of white telephones squatted on a credenza behind the desk. The large office, carpeted in a deep blue, had a comfortable couch and chairs at the opposite end, next to three picture windows that had a magnificent view of the pine forest. It was a brilliant winter day and sunlight streamed into the office.

Vanya motioned Dominika to take a seat. He looked at her closely. She was wearing a dark blue skirt and crisp white shirt nipped at the waist by a narrow black belt. She looked as beautiful as ever, but she had dark circles under her eyes and was noticeably pale. Using her on the Ustinov thing had been an inspired move. Too bad the experience for her had been so . . . extreme. It was her bad luck that the urgent order from the Kremlin to settle Ustinov's hash had coincided with her departure from ballet school and her father's death.

Neither of them spoke. According to the report, she had performed creditably, had charmed the pants off Ustinov, so much so that he had dismissed his security detail and thus given Matorin the opening to get to the target. Even though she had not had hysterics, he gathered it had been a little rough for her. Matorin was a bit much for the uninitiated. She would get over all that.

"Dominika, I commend you on your excellent performance in the recent operation," said Vanya. He looked evenly at his niece from across the desk. "I know it must have been difficult, a shock." He leaned forward. "It's over now, you can forget the unpleasantness. Of course, I don't have to tell you about your duty, *your responsibility,* never to mention this to anyone, ever."

Her mother had told her to always be careful

around him, but she was wound up. Throat tightening, Dominika looked at the yellow haze around him. Her voice quavered. "You say 'unpleasantness.' I watched a man murdered a foot from my face. We were naked, he was on top of me, as you well know. I was covered in his blood, my hair was matted with it. I can still smell it." She saw her uncle's eyes and felt his unease. *Be careful,* she thought, there was an undercurrent of anger there too. Her voice soft again: "Just a little favor, a simple matter, you said, I'd be helping you out." She smiled. "He must have really done something, that you had to kill him."

Damned impertinence. Vanya was not about to discuss politics, nor Putin's toxic narcissism, nor the necessity of making an example of Ustinov for the benefit of the other kulaks. No, he had summoned his niece for two reasons. He wanted to assess her state of mind, to judge whether she could keep her mouth shut, whether she could put the incident behind her, recover from her trauma. And depending on the answer to the first question, he would have to consider two further options.

If Dominika rose from her chair, unhinged and refusing to listen, she could not leave the headquarters building alive. Matorin would solve the problem. Dominika might not realize it, but she was an eyewitness to a political assassination that Putin's enemies would love to document for the world. If that happened, he, Egorov, would be forfeit. Right now certain State organs were covering Ustinov's death as a grisly murder at the hands of a business rival. Everyone knew the truth; this had been expected. But if his twenty-five-year-old niece with Fabergé-blue eyes and a 95C bosom subsequently stood up and told what she had seen, and from what vantage point, the opposition press would never stop.

If, however, she seemed under control, he would

take steps to ensure her continued discretion. His political well-being hinged on her future good behavior. He had already decided that he would accomplish this by bringing her inside, into the Service, under the permanent discipline and supervision of the Center. There would be no difficulty doing so. A job in records, in the archives. She would be accounted for, engaged in training, learning procedures and regulations. They could keep an eye on her. Depending on her performance—he did not expect much—she could be given a clerical job in one of the departments, an ornament in the outer office of some general. Later, perhaps, she could be assigned abroad, buried in a *rezidentura* in Africa or Latin America. After five years—by that time the directorship would be his—she could even be cashiered for cause and kicked out.

Vanya spoke softly. "Niece, it is your duty to be always loyal, to do your utmost, to serve your country. There is no question of your discretion. It is absolutely required of you. Is this going to be a problem between us?" Vanya looked at Dominika steadily as he knocked the ash off the end of his cigarette.

It was the exact moment where the next part of her life would be decided. The usual yellow halo around Vanya's head had grown darker, as if suffused with blood, and the timbre of his voice had changed, taken on an edge. In a telepathic flash Dominika realized it, remembered her mother's whispers. *Zaledenet,* she thought, summoning control. *Become ice.* She looked up at her uncle, whom she was beginning to detest, and also beginning to fear. Their eyes met.

"You can depend on my discretion," she said woodenly.

"I knew I could," said Vanya. She was a smart girl, he could see her instincts at play, she had sense. Now to put a cube of sugar on the teaspoon. "And because you have performed so well, I have a proposal." He leaned back in his chair and lit another cigarette. "I am offering you a starting position as a staff member of the Service. I want you to join me in our work here."

Dominika willed herself to remain expressionless, and was satisfied watching Vanya's eyes searching her face for a reaction. "In the Service?" she said. "I have never considered it."

"This would be a fine opportunity for you right now. Steady employment, start accumulating a pension. If you belong to the Service, I can continue to guarantee your mother can keep her apartment. Besides, what else would you do, look for a job as, what, a dance instructor?" He crossed his hands on his desk.

Dominika mentally marked the spot on Uncle Vanya's shirt where she would plunge the pencil lying on his desk. She lowered her eyes and kept her voice calm. "Helping Mother would be important," she said. Vanya made an *Of course* gesture with his hand. "It would be strange to work here," she added.

"Not so strange," said Vanya. "And we could work together." The words floated above his head, changing color with the sunlight outside. *Of course,* thought Dominika, *a staff recruit would work closely every day with the Deputy Director.*

"What sorts of duties would I be assigned?" said Dominika. She knew enough already to guess the answer.

"You would have to begin at the entry level, of course," said Vanya. "But all the functions of the Service satisfy a critical need. Records, research, archives. An intelligence organization survives or perishes on how it manages information." Of course, they wanted her buried in the third subbasement.

"I'm not sure I know about such duties, Uncle,"

said Dominika. "I don't think I would do well." Vanya hid his irritation. He really had only two choices with this Venus de Milo. Matorin could dispose of her before lunch, or he could get her into the Service, under control. The middle ground was unacceptable. She couldn't be left walking around Moscow, resentment growing, perhaps thinking of getting even. *Sookin syn.*

"I'm sure you would learn quickly. It's quite important work," Vanya said. Now he was reduced to trying to convince this silly twit.

"I do think I would have an interest in another part of the Service," said Dominika. Vanya peered over the desk at her, hands clasped and motionless. She was still sitting with a straight back, head erect, stricken. Vanya said nothing, waited. "I would like to be admitted to the Foreign Intelligence Academy as a candidate trainee."

"The Academy, the AVR," said Vanya slowly. "You want to be an intelligence officer. In the Service?"

"Yes, I think I would do well," said Dominika. "You yourself said I performed satisfactorily with Ustinov in gaining his trust." Raising Ustinov made the point. Vanya lit his third cigarette in as many minutes. Not counting the women in support functions, there had been two, perhaps three, women in the First Chief Directorate in the old KGB, and one of them was an old battleax in the Presidium. None had ever been admitted to the old KGB Higher School or to the Andropov Institute or to the current AVR. The only women involved in field operations were the coopted wives of *rezidenturi* officers, and the *vorobey,* the trained "Sparrows" who seduced recruitment targets.

But in thirty seconds Vanya Egorov made a lightning calculation. As a candidate in AVR, his niece would be under even more stringent control. Her performance, attitude, and physical whereabouts for the foreseeable future would be constantly monitored. She would be physically out of Moscow for long periods of time. If she strayed and was tempted to open her mouth, she would fall under the disciplinary jurisdiction of the Service. Her dismissal, even imprisonment, would be a matter of a stroke of the pen.

More broadly, he could generate some political profit from putting her name forward as a candidate for the Academy. He would be the high-minded deputy director who for the first time selected a woman—athletic, educated, fluent in languages—for formal training in the modern SVR. Bosses in the Kremlin would see the public-relations benefits.

From across the desk, Dominika saw his face, followed his calculations. Now would come the reluctant agreement, the inevitable stern warnings.

"You're asking a lot," Vanya said. "There's an entrance examination, a high refusal rate, then long training, quite rigorous." He swiveled in his chair to look out the picture window, considering. He had made up his mind. "Are you prepared to commit yourself to this path?" he asked.

Dominika nodded. She wasn't absolutely sure, of course. But it would be a challenge, and that appealed to her. She was also loyal, she loved her country, she knew she wanted to try to join one of the premier organizations in Russia, perhaps, she thought, even to contribute. The Ustinov killing had repulsed her, but it also had shown her, in the space of an evening, that she could handle secret work, that she had the brains, and the courage, and the fortitude.

There was something else, she knew, something ill-defined, something accumulating in her breast. They had used her. Now she wanted to intrude into their world, these *domovladel'tsy,* these landlords who abused the system and its people. She wondered what her father would think.

"I will consider it," said Vanya, swiveling back to look at her. "If I decide to submit your name, and if you are selected, your performance in the AVR will be a reflection on me, on the whole family. You realize that, do you not?" Charming. His concern for her and the family had not kept him from throwing her at Ustinov.

She almost said, *I'll be sure to preserve your reputation,* but pushed the anger back down and instead nodded again, more sure now about wanting the Academy. Vanya stood up. "Why don't you go downstairs and have lunch? I will tell you my decision this afternoon." He would have to clear it with the Director (gentle persuasion) and the director of training would have to be browbeaten (a pleasure). But Dominika's place would be reserved, and the thing would be done, and his problem with her would be solved. When she left, Vanya picked up the phone and spoke briefly into it.

Dominika was escorted back down the hallway to the elevator. The former directors all looked as if they had faint smiles on their faces. In the sprawling cafeteria, Dominika ordered the *kotleta po-kievski,* a hard roll, and a bottle of mineral water. The cafeteria was moderately crowded and Dominika had to search for an empty seat. She found a table where two middle-aged women were sitting at the other end. They looked at the beautiful young girl with the tired eyes and the visitor's badge, but said nothing. Dominika began eating. The chicken was lightly breaded, golden brown, and delicious. A trickle of butter came from the rolled-up cutlet; there was the rich taste of garlic and tarragon. The cutlet morphed into Ustinov's throat and the butter sauce turned vermilion. She put down her knife and fork with trembling hands.

Dominika closed her eyes and fought the nausea. The two women at her table were looking at her. This was not something you see every day. They didn't know how right they were.

Dominika looked up and saw swirling black. Sergey Matorin was sitting at the table across from hers, leaning over a bowl, spooning soup into his mouth. He was staring at her as he ate, his dead eye unblinking, just as a wolf watches even while drinking at a brook.

SVR CAFETERIA CHICKEN KIEV

Mix and chill compound butter with garlic, tarragon, lemon juice, and parsley. Pound chicken breasts into wafer-thin cutlets. Roll tightly around thumb-sized pieces of compound butter, tie with twine. Dust with seasoned flour, dip in egg wash, coat with bread crumbs. Fry until golden brown.

6

Dominika entered the SVR's Academy of Foreign Intelligence (AVR) soon after her father's funeral. The school had been renamed several times during the Cold War, from the Higher Intelligence School to the Red Banner Institute to the AVR, but veterans simply called it School No. 101. The main campus for decades had been located north of Moscow, near the village of Chelobityevo. By the time it became the AVR, the school had been modernized, the curriculum streamlined, admission criteria liberalized. The campus had moved to a clearing in the dense forests east of the city at kilometer twenty-five on the Gorky Highway. It was therefore now referred to as "Kilometer 25" or simply "the Forest."

In the early weeks, wary and excited, Dominika, the only woman, and a dozen new classmates were driven in rattling PAZ buses with darkly tinted windows to various locations around Moscow and the surrounding suburbs. They rolled through sliding metal gates into anonymous walled compounds registered as laboratories, research centers, or Pioneer Youth camps. The days were filled with lectures about the history of the Services, of Russia, of the Cold War, and the Soviet Union.

Whereas the chief attribute previously required for acceptance into former KGB schools was fealty to the Communist Party, the modern SVR required of its trainees an overarching devotion to the Russian Federation and a commitment to protect it from enemies within and without.

For the first period of indoctrination, trainees

were evaluated not only for aptitude but also for what in the old KGB would have been called "political reliability." Dominika excelled in class discussions and written assignments. There was a hint of the independent streak in her, of impatience with time-tested formulations and dicta. An instructor had written that Cadet Egorova would hesitate for just a second before answering a question, *as if she were considering whether she chose to answer,* then invariably respond with excellence.

Dominika knew what they wanted to hear. The slogans in the books and on the chalkboards were kaleidoscopes of color, they were easy to categorize and memorize. Tenets of duty, loyalty, and defense of the country. She was a candidate to become a part of Russia's elite, the Sword and Shield of yesterday, the Globe and Star of today. Her youthful ideology had once horrified her freethinking father—she knew that now—and she no longer *totally* accepted the ideology. Still, she wanted to do well.

The start of the second training block. The class had moved permanently to the Kilometer 25 campus, a cluster of long, low buildings with pitched-tile roofs, surrounded by pines and stands of birch. Sweeping lawns separated the buildings, gravel paths led to the sports fields behind the buildings. The campus was a kilometer off the four-lane Gorkovskoye shosse, screened first by a tall wooden palisade, painted green to blend in with the trees. Past this "forest fence," three kilometers farther into the woods, ran two additional wire fence lines, between which black Belgian Malinois hounds ran free. The dog run could be seen from the windows of the small classrooms, and from their rooms in the two-story barracks the students could hear the dogs panting at night.

She was the only woman in the dormitory and they gave her a single room at the end of the corridor, but she still had to share the bathroom and shower room with twelve men, which meant she had to find quiet times in the mornings and evenings. Most of her classmates were harmless enough, the privileged sons of important families, young men with connections to the Duma or to the armed forces or to the Kremlin. Some were bright, very bright, some were not. A few brave ones, used to getting what they wanted and seeing that silhouette behind the shower curtain, were ready to risk it all for a tumble.

She had reached for her towel on the hook outside the shower stall in the gang bathroom late one night. It was gone. Then a knuckly classmate with sandy hair, the burly one from Novosibirsk, stepped into the stall with her, crowding behind her, his arms around her waist. She could feel he was naked as he pushed her face against the wall of the shower and nuzzled her wet hair from behind. He was whispering something she couldn't understand; she couldn't see the colors. He pressed up against her harder and one hand drifted from around her waist to her breasts. As he squeezed her, she wondered if he could feel her heartbeat, if he could feel her breathing. Her cheek was pressed against the white tiles of the stall, she could feel them changing like prisms hung in sunlight, they were turning dark red.

The tapered, three-inch faucet handle for the cold water had always been loose, and Dominika wiggled it back and forth until it came off in her hand. She turned slippery and breathy to face him, breasts now crushed against his chest, and said, "*Stojat,*" wait, wait a second, through a constricted throat. He was smiling as Dominika drove the pointed end of the faucet handle into his left eye up to her knuckle and his vomit-green scream of pain and terror washed over her as he slid down the wall clutching his face, his knees pulled up tight. "*Sto-*

jat," she said again, looking down at him, "I asked you to wait a second."

"Attempted rape and justifiable self-defense" was the secret AVR review board's judgment, and Novosibirsk gained a one-eyed bus conductor and the board recommended that Dominika be separated from Academy training. She told them she had done nothing to cause the incident, and the panel—a woman and two men—looked her up and down and kept straight faces. They were going to do it to her again. Ballet school, Ustinov, now the AVR, and Dominika told the panel she would lodge a formal complaint. To whom would she complain? But word of the incident got back to Yasenevo and Deputy Director Egorov cursed so foully over the phone that Dominika would have seen brown treacle flowing out of the earpiece, and they told her the decision had been made to give her another chance, under probationary status. From then on the rest of her class ignored her, avoided her, a *klikusha* walking between the buildings in the Forest, an impossibly straight back and long elegant steps with the faintest hitch in her stride.

The start of the third block of AVR. They filed into classrooms with plastic chairs, and pebbled acoustic tiles on the walls, and clunky projectors hanging from the ceiling. Dead flies lay in piles between the double windowpanes. Now came instruction in world economies, energy, politics, the Third World, international affairs, and "global problems." And America. No longer referred to as the Main Enemy, the United States nevertheless was her country's main competitor. It was all Russia could do to maintain superpower parity. Lectures on the subject took on an edge.

The Americans took them for granted, they ignored Russia, they *tried to* manipulate Russia. Washington had interfered in recent elections, thankfully to no avail. America supported Russian dissidents and encouraged disruptive behavior in this delicate period of Russian reconstruction. American military forces challenged Russian sovereignty, from the Baltic to the Sea of Japan. The recent "reset" policy was an insult, nothing needed to be reset. It was simply that Russia deserved respect, the *Rodina* deserved respect. Well, if, as an SVR officer, Dominika ever met an American, she would show him that Russia deserved respect.

The irony was that America was in decline, said the lecturers, no longer the high-and-mighty US. Overextended in wars, struggling economically, the supposed birthplace of equality was now divided by class warfare and the poisonous politics of conflicting ideologies. And the foolish Americans didn't yet realize they would soon need Russia to hem in a galloping China, they would need Russia as an ally in a future war.

But if Americans chose to pit themselves against Russia, thinking she was feeble and weak, they would be surprised. A student in the class disagreed. He suggested that yesterday's notions of "East and West" were antiquated. Besides, Russia had lost the Cold War, get over it. There was a hush in the classroom. Another classmate stood, eyes flashing. "Russia most certainly *did not* lose the Cold War," he said. "*It never ended.*" Dominika watched the scarlet letters ascend to the ceiling. Good words, strong words. Interesting. The Cold War never ended.

Not long after, Dominika was separated from the rest of her class. She had no need for language instruction, for she could have been an instructor herself in spoken English or French. Nor was she hustled off to the administrative track. Her instructors had seen her potential, had passed it on to AVR administrators, who in turn had called Yasenevo and requested the Center's permission to admit Dominika Egorova—niece of the First Deputy Director—into the practical, or operational, phase of training. She would be the rare female candidate trained by the SVR as an *operupolnomochenny,* an operations officer. There were no delays. Approvals from the Center had already been granted.

She had been admitted to operations training, the Real Steel, the Game; she had entered a special phase, the last chrysalis stage before she would emerge to serve the Motherland. The time passed without her knowing it. Seasons seemed to change without her being aware of them. Classes, lectures, laboratories, interviews all came in a dizzying rush.

It started with ridiculous subjects. Sabotage, explosives, infiltration, first taught when Stalin raved and the Wehrmacht encircled Moscow. Then came the more practical lessons, and they worked her hard. She developed legends, *zashifrovat',* her cover for movement, ran routes to detect opposition surveillance on the street, found safe houses, transmitted secure messages, found meeting sites, *yavki,* ran *vstrechi,* agent meetings, plotted recruitment approaches. She practiced with disguises and digital communications, signals and caches. Her memory for detail, for lessons learned, astounded them.

Instructors in unarmed-combat class were impressed by her strength and balance. They grew a little alarmed at her intensity and the way she wouldn't stay down on the mat after having been thrown. Everyone had heard the story from the Forest, and the wide-eyed men in the class watched her hands and knees and protected their *mudya* when sparring with her. She saw their faces, saw the green breath of their disapproval and fear as they huffed and grunted in the gymnasium. No one came near her voluntarily.

The practical instruction continued. They brought her to downtown Moscow, to the streets that were used as a living classroom to practice tradecraft principles taught in the dingy classrooms around Yasenevo. The streetcraft instructors were *pensionerki,* old spooks, some of them seventy years old, retired decades ago. They had some difficulty keeping up with Dominika as the exercises accelerated. They watched her bunched dancer's calves striding long on the shimmering Moscow sidewalks. The slight telltale limp from her shattered foot, now mended, was endearing. She was driven, determined to excel. Her face shone with perspiration, the sweat darkened her shirt between her breasts and across her ribs.

The colors helped her on the street; the blues and greens from the teams in the radio cars and the watcher vans made it possible to pick out coverage among the crowds on broad boulevards. She twisted surveillance teams around themselves, meticulously timed brush passes on crowded Metro platforms, met practice agents in dirty stairwells at midnight, controlled the meetings, read their minds. The old men would mop their faces and mutter, "*Fanatichka,*" and she would laugh at them, her hair pulled back tight on her head, her shoulders straight, secretly reading the colors of their breathless approval. *Come on,* dinozavry, *come on, you old dinosaurs.* The gruff old men secretly loved her, and she knew it.

These ancient instructors were supposed to coach her on what conditions would be like abroad, on what she could expect on the street, on how to operate in foreign capitals. *Glupost,* thought Dominika, what stupidity, that these old men who had last been overseas when Brezhnev ordered troops into Afghanistan were telling her what to expect on the streets of modern-day London, New York, or Beijing. She had the temerity to mention the incongruity to a course coordinator, who told her to shut her mouth and reported her comments up the line. Her face flushed at being spoken to that way, but she turned away, cursing herself. She was learning.

As she was being evaluated, Dominika began courses on the psychology of intelligence collection, the psyche of sources, on understanding human motivations and identifying vulnerabilities. An instructor named Mikhail called it "opening the human envelope." He was a forty-five-year-old SVR psychologist from the Center; Dominika was his only student. He walked her around Moscow, both observing people, watching interactions. Dominika did not tell him about seeing colors, for her mother long ago had made her swear never to mention it. "And how in God's name do you know that about him?" Mikhail would ask when Dominika whispered that the man sitting on the next park bench was waiting for a woman.

"It just seems that way," she would reply, never explaining that the bloom of passion-purple around the man flared when the woman came around the corner. Mikhail laughed and looked at her in amazement when it turned out to be right.

As Dominika focused on these practice sessions, her refined intuition told her she was having an effect on Mikhail. Even though he initially featured himself as a stern instructor from Directorate T, she would catch him looking at her hair or stealing darting glimpses at her body. She mentally counted the times he contrived to bump into her, or touch her on the shoulder, or put his hand on the small of her back when going through a door. He radiated desire, a dark crimson fog lingered around his head and shoulders.

She knew how he liked his tea, when he needed his glasses to read a menu, the rate of his heartbeat when pushed close against her in the Metro. She could see Mikhail stealing looks at her unpolished nails, or watching her dangle a shoe off her foot at the café table.

It was a monstrous risk to sleep with him. He was an instructor, and a psychologist to boot, charged with evaluating her personality and suitability for operations. Yet she knew he would say nothing, she knew she had an indefinable hold over him, and making love, a grave dereliction during training, was an edgy thrill, more than physical pleasure.

Of which there was a considerable amount. An afternoon after a street exercise, they found themselves in the apartment Mikhail shared with his parents and brother, all at work or away from the house. The coverlet from his bed was on the floor and her thighs trembled and her shoulders shook and her hair framed her face as she straddled him, pulses running up her spine and down to her toes, especially those of her once-broken foot. She knew what she wanted, her secret self had been neglected of late, what with school and training and barracks. She trapped him—who was impaled upon whom?—and rocked strongly downward, giving herself what she needed, while she was still fresh. There would be time for softness and cooing and sighing later. Right now her eyes were half-closed, and she concentrated on coaxing the building pressure, stronger, stronger—*povorachivaisya! come on!*—into the sudden teetering flush that made her double over, too sensitive to continue, too sweet to stop. Her vision cleared and she brushed the hair off her face, aftershocks cramping her thighs and toes. Mikhail lay wide-eyed and silent beneath her, a bystander unsure of what he had just witnessed.

Afterward, he kept taking sidelong glances at her

while he made a pot of tea. Wrapped in a sweater and sitting at the kitchen table, Dominika guilelessly looked at him, and the psychologist in Mikhail simultaneously knew the sex had had nothing to do with him. He likewise knew he would say nothing about it, ever. And that they would never do it again. In a way, Mikhail was relieved.

The operations course was coming to an end, the last leg of the tripod of training nearly complete. The exhausted pensioners who trained Dominika had long ago nicknamed her *mushka,* beauty spot, also the colloquialism for the front sight of a gun, the sight that picks up the target first. Completing their evaluations, they positively assessed her industrious spirit, they remarked on her intellect and wit and on her sometimes inexplicable intuitions on the street. Her loyalty and dedication to the *Rodina* were unquestioned. One or two pensioners noted that she was impatient. She could be argumentative, she needed to develop more flexibility in recruitment approaches. One old-timer alone wrote that despite her superior performance he believed she lacked true patriotic zeal. Her natural independence eventually would unseat her devotion. It was a feeling, an impression; he could not cite any examples. The comment was discarded as the addled thought of an old fool. In any case, Dominika was never shown any of the evaluations.

All that remained was a final practical exam on the street, using techniques, honing her tradecraft. A final exercise, a written examination, an exit interview. She was almost through. Before any of that happened, however, and to the consternation of her instructors, Dominika disappeared from the course: summoned immediately to the Center, “required for special duty,” was all they said.

Dominika was told to report to a room at the other end of the fourth floor of Yasenevo, near the portraits of the directors. She knocked at a plain mahogany door and went inside. It was an executive dining room, small, wood-paneled, carpeted in deep wine-red, windowless. Polished wood and antique sideboards gleamed in the recessed lighting. Uncle Vanya was seated at the far end of a dining table covered by a snowy white tablecloth and set with Vinogradov porcelain. Crystal glasses twinkled in the light. He got up from his chair when he saw Dominika enter and walked down the length of the table to greet her with a vigorous hug around the shoulders. "The graduate has come home." He beamed, holding her at arm's length. "Top of your class, top marks on the street, I knew it!" He put her arm in his and walked her down the room.

There was another man sitting at the other side of the table, quietly smoking a cigarette. He looked to be fifty years old, with a red-veined tetrahedron for a nose. His eyes were dull and watery, his teeth corrugated and stained, and he slouched with the familiar casual authority honed on the razor strop of decades of Soviet officialdom. His tie was askew, his suit was a washed-out brown that recalled low tide at the beach. It matched the gaseous brown bubble that surrounded him as he sat. It was not the color—blacks and grays and browns assuredly were trouble—it was the paleness of the color and how it enveloped him in soft focus. *He is* bluzhdayushchiy, *devious,* thought Dominika, *not to be trusted.*

Dominika sat across from him, meeting his appraising stare with unblinking eyes. Vanya sat at his place at the head of the table, his paws folded demurely in front of him. Unlike the former Soviet apparatchik across from her, Vanya as usual wore an elegant pearl-gray suit, blue shirt with starched collar, and a navy tie with minute white dots. On his lapel he wore a small red ribbon with a sky-blue star—for Merit to the Fatherland, *Za Zaslugi Pered Otechestvom*—for significant contributions to the defense of the Fatherland. Vanya lit a cigarette with a well-used silver lighter, which he snapped closed.

"This is Colonel Simyonov," said Vanya, nodding in the direction of the slouching man. "He is the chief of the Fifth Department." Simyonov said nothing, but leaned forward and flicked ash into a copper ashtray beside his plate. "We have identified a singular operational opportunity," continued Vanya. "The Fifth has been given the responsibility to carry it out." Dominika looked from Vanya to Simyonov dully. "I have recommended to the colonel that you would be uniquely suited to assist in the operation, especially since you have completed your training at the Academy with an excellent record. I wanted the two of you to meet."

What is this nonsense? thought Dominika. "Thank you, General," she said. She took care not to call him "Uncle" in the presence of a senior officer. "I still have two weeks to complete. There is a final exercise and the closing evaluations. I—"

"Your final evaluation is complete," interrupted Vanya. "There is no need to return to the AVR. In fact, I want you to begin additional training in preparation for this operational assignment with Simyonov." Vanya stubbed out his cigarette in an identical ashtray at his side.

"May I ask the nature of the assignment, General?" said Dominika. She looked at the two impassive faces. They both were too smart to give anything away with a look, but they didn't know what else Dominika could see. Their respective bubbles swelled around their heads.

"For now it is sufficient to tell you that this is a potentially important case, a *konspiratsia* of some delicacy and sensitivity," said Vanya.

"And the nature of the additional training?" asked Dominika. She kept her voice level, respectful. A door at the end of the room opened and an orderly entered carrying a silver salver on a tray.

"Lunch has arrived," said Vanya, sitting up. "Let us talk about the project after we eat." The waiter lifted the lid and began serving steaming *golubtsy,* large square cabbage rolls, fried brown and swimming in a thick sauce of tomato purée and sour cream. "The best of Russian cooking," said Vanya, pouring red wine into Dominika's glass from a silver decanter. This was a charade: Dominika's newly trained operational antennae were buzzing. She had no appetite for the heavy food.

Lunch lasted a dreary half hour. Simyonov uttered three words the entire time, though he continued to stare at Dominika from across the table. His expression was one of distinct boredom, with an air of not wanting to be in the room. Finished eating, he scrubbed his mouth with his napkin and pushed away from the table. "By your leave, General," he said. He gave Dominika another appraising look, nodded in her general direction, and left the room.

"Let's have tea in my office," said Vanya pushing back his chair. "We'll be more comfortable there."

Dominika sat warily upright on the couch in Vanya's office, the view of the Yasenevo forest in front of them. Dominika was dressed in a white shirt and black skirt, her hair pinned up, the informal uniform at the Academy. Two glasses of steaming tea in magnificent antique Kolchugino *podstakanniki* tea-glass holders sat on the table in front of them.

"Your father would be proud," said Vanya, sipping carefully.

"Thank you," said Dominika, waiting.

"I congratulate you on your achievement and on your entrance to the Service."

"The training was challenging, but everything I could have hoped for," said Dominika. "I am ready to start work." It was true. She soon would be on the front lines.

"It is always an honor to serve your country," he said, fingering the rosette on his lapel. "There is no greater honor." He looked at his niece carefully. "This operation with the Fifth, it's not something that comes along every day, especially not for a recent graduate." He sipped at his tea.

"I am eager to learn more," said Dominika.

"Suffice it to say that the operation is a recruitment approach to a foreign diplomat. It is of utmost importance that there be no *razoblachenie,* no exposure, no unmasking of the hand of the Service. The diplomat must be compromised, thoroughly and without a misstep." His voice had grown thin, serious. Dominika said nothing, waiting for him to continue. She couldn't exactly see his words, they were indistinct and pale.

"Naturally, Colonel Simyonov expressed concern that your overall inexperience in operations, despite your excellent training record, could be a disadvantage. I assured him my *niece*"—he hung on the word to indicate that he had exerted his influence—"was the perfect choice. He of course soon recognized the logic of using you, especially in light of the additional training I proposed." Dominika waited. What office would they send her to? Technical measures? Language? Subject matter tutorial? Vanya lit a cigarette and blew smoke at the ceiling. "You have been enrolled in the specialized course at the Kon Institute."

Dominika willed herself to remain still, expressionless, coldly feeling the physical blow that started in her stomach and radiated up her back. People had whispered about the institute during training: formerly State School Four, more commonly referred to as Sparrow School, where men and women were trained in the art of espionage seduction. *You're sending me to whore school,* she thought.

"This is what they call Sparrow School?" she asked, controlling the quaver in her voice. "Uncle, I thought I would be entering the Service as an officer, to be assigned to a department, to begin practicing intelligence work. This is training for *prostitutki,* not staff officers." She felt she could hardly breathe.

Vanya looked at her evenly. "You must look at this interval positively—this training will reveal to you other options when you begin managing operations on your own in the future." He sat farther back on the couch.

"And the operation against the diplomat, do you intend that it should be a *polovaya zapadnya,* a honey trap?" She had read about the grimy sex operations while in the Academy.

"The target is *zastenchivyj,* timid, shy. We have assessed his vulnerabilities over many months. Colonel Simyonov agrees that he is susceptible."

Dominika stiffened. "The colonel knows about what you want me to do, about *Sparrow School*?" She shook her head. "He was staring at me across the table. He might as well have opened my mouth and checked my teeth."

Vanya interrupted, his voice now a little edgy. "I'm sure he was very impressed, he is a veteran officer. And all operations are unique in their own ways. There has been no final decision made as yet on how to proceed. Nevertheless, this is an immense opportunity for you, Dominika."

"I cannot do this," Dominika said. "After the previous operation, how it ended, it took me months to forget Ustinov's—"

"You're bringing that up? Didn't you remember my instructions to you to forget that episode, never to refer to it?" Vanya said. "I require absolute compliance in that regard."

"I have never uttered a word," Dominika snapped back. "It's just that if this is another of those operations, I'd rather—"

"You'd rather? You are a graduate of the Academy and a junior officer in the Service now. You will obey orders, accept assignments given to you, and do your duty. You will defend the *Rodina*."

"I am committed to serving Russia," said Dominika. "It's just that I object to being used in these sorts of operations . . . There are people who do this work regularly, I have heard about them. Why not use one of them?"

Vanya frowned. "Stop talking. Not another word. You don't have the sense to see what I'm offering you. You're thinking about yourself, about your childish preoccupations. As an SVR officer you have no preferences, no choices. You accomplish what you are told to do with excellence. If you choose not to accept, to allow your frantic prejudices to derail your career before it begins, tell me now. We will release you from the Service, close your file, cancel your pension, and withdraw your privileges—*all of them*."

How many times will my mother's neck be put into the noose? thought Dominika. What else would they make her do to let her serve with honor? Vanya saw her shoulders slump. "Very well," she said, rising. "With your permission, may I go?"

Dominika got up and walked in front of the picture window toward the door, the sun highlighting her hair, framing her classic profile. Vanya watched her walk across the carpet—did she limp a little?—and stop briefly at the door to turn and look back at him. A shiver ran over his scalp as he saw the blue eyes, intense and unblinking, ripsaws and scalpels, fix on his face for three alarming seconds. Glowing like wolves' eyes just beyond the lights of the *blizhnyaya*, the dacha. He had never seen a look like that in his life. Before he could say anything else, she was gone, like a *klikusha* in the Krasny Bor Forest.

SVR GOLUBTSY

Blanche cabbage leaves, cook rice. Sauté chopped onions, carrots, and peeled and seeded tomatoes until soft, incorporate with the rice and ground beef. Fold cabbage leaves around two spoons of mixture to form large square envelopes. Fry in butter until brown, then simmer for one hour in stock, tomato sauce, and bay leaves. Serve with reduced sauce and sour cream.

7

Nate Nash arrived at Helsinki-Vantaa Airport after a two-hour flight. The modern airport was sparkling and well-lit. Like at Sheremetyevo, there were flashy advertisements for cologne, watches, and vacation trips. Airport shops stocked with lingerie, gourmet food items, and magazines stretched down the airy terminal. But the lingering smell of cooked cabbage, rosewater cologne, and wet wool was missing. Instead, cinnamon buns were baking somewhere. As Nate collected his single suitcase, cleared customs, and headed to the taxi stand outside, he did not see a short man in a plain dark suit watching him from across the arrival hall. This man spoke briefly into a cell phone and turned away. In thirty minutes, nine hundred kilometers to the east, Vanya Egorov knew that Nash had arrived in Finland. The Game would begin.

The next morning, Nate walked into the office of Tom Forsyth, Chief of Station in Helsinki. Forsyth's office was small but comfortable, with a single nautical painting hanging above his desk and a small couch against the opposite wall. A framed photo of a sailboat on a glassy ocean stood on a table beside the couch, with another framed photo of what appeared to be a youthful Forsyth at the wheel beside it. Shades in the office were drawn over a single window.

Forsyth was tall and lean, in his late forties, with receding gray hair and a strong chin. Intense brown eyes looked up at Nate over the top of half-moon glasses. Forsyth smiled, threw a sheaf of papers into an in-box, and got up to shake hands from across the desk. His handshake was firm and dry. "Nate Nash," he said with a smooth voice. "Welcome to Station." He gestured for Nate to sit in a leather chair in front of his desk.

"Thanks, Chief," said Nate.

"You in an apartment? Where did the Embassy put you?" asked Forsyth. The Embassy housing office had that morning deposited him in a comfortable two-bedroom flat in Kruununhaka. Nate had been delighted when opening the double doors to a small balcony with a view of the marina, the ferry terminal, and the sea beyond, and he told Forsyth so.

"It's a nice area, an easy walk to work," said Forsyth. "I'd like you to huddle with me and Marty Gable to get an idea of what we've got going." Gable was the Deputy Chief of Station, whom Nate had not met yet. "We've got a couple of good cases, but there's more we can do.

"Forget about the internal target, the Finns are allies and we've got them covered. Marty and I work liaison, so you don't have to worry about the internal service. We'll pass along any unilateral possibilities that we develop.

"All the usual Arabs—Hezbollah, Hamas, Palestinians—they've all got reps in town. Might be tricky getting close to them, so think about access agents. Iranians, Syrians, Chinese. Small embassies, and they feel safe here in neutral Scandinavia. The Persians might be looking for embargoed equipment. Check them out on the dip circuit," Forsyth said, tilting back in his office chair.

"I want to go after something bigger," said Nate. "I have to score big after what happened to me in Moscow." *Indeed,* thought Forsyth. He saw worry behind the eyes, determination in the set of the jaw. Nate sat upright in his chair.

"That's fine, Nate," said Forsyth, "but any recruitment, as long as it's productive, is a good recruitment. And you land the big fish by being patient, by working the circuit, by generating a dozen developmental contacts."

"I know that, Chief," said Nate quickly. "But I don't have the luxury of time. That Gondorf is gunning for me. If it weren't for you, I'd be back in Russian Ops in front of a computer, pushing a mouse. I never told you how much I appreciate your asking for me."

Forsyth had read Nate's personnel file, sent out to Station when Nate's lateral assignment had been approved. Not many young case officers with near-fluent Russian. Top marks throughout training at the Farm, and subsequently in "denied area" training for Moscow, the art of operating under constant hostile surveillance. The file also positively noted Nate's performance in Russia, especially his handling of a sensitive restricted case—no details.

But Forsyth now saw a distracted young case officer squirming in front of him. With something to prove. *Not good, makes you accident-prone, always swinging for the fences with your eyes closed.*

"I don't want you worrying about Moscow. I talked to some people in Headquarters and you're fine." He saw Nate's face working at the thought of his hall file. "And I want you to listen to me," said Forsyth. He stopped until he had Nate's attention. "I want you to work smart, good tradecraft, no shortcuts. We all want the big cases—hell, you're handling one now—but I won't accept half-assed operations. Clear?" Forsyth looked hard at Nate. "Clear?" he repeated.

"Yessir," said Nate. He got the message, but told himself he was going to find agents, he wasn't going to flame out as a case officer. He was not going home. He flashed to crazy-quilt images of him in a Richmond country club sitting across from Sue Ann or Mindy, bee-stung lips and frosted hair piled high, as his brothers putted golf balls across the tartan plaid rug into one of Missy's pink Lilly Pulitzer flats lying on the rug across the club room. Fuck no.

"Okay," said Forsyth. "Find your desk. It'll be the first office down the hallway. Get out of here and go find Gable," he said, reaching for his in-box.

DCOS Marty Gable was sitting at his terminal in another small office one door down from Forsyth's, trying to figure out how to write a cable to Headquarters without using the word "cocksucker." Older than Forsyth, Gable was in his late fifties, big and broad shouldered, with white brush-cut hair, blue eyes, and a steel girder for a nose. His forehead was tanned and ruddy, the weather-beaten face of an outdoorsman. Knuckly brown hands dwarfed his keyboard, immobile. He hated drafting cables, hated typing with two fingers, hated the bureaucracy. He was a street guy. Nate stood in the doorway of his office. It was totally bare, unadorned save for a government-issue picture of the Washington Monument on the wall. His desktop was empty. Before Nate could knock courteously on the doorframe, Gable swiveled in his chair and looked at Nate with a scowl.

"You the new guy? Cash?" bawled Gable. The accent was somewhere from the Rust Belt.

"Nash. Nate Nash," said Nate, as he walked to the desk. Gable remained sitting but extended his frying-pan hand. Nate tensed for the inevitable bone-crushing grip.

"You took your time getting here. You recruit anyone on the way in from the airport?" Gable laughed. "No? Well, there's time after lunch," he said. "Let's go." On the way out of the Station, Gable stuck his big Rottweiler head into several offices along the hallway, checking to see what the other Station case officers were doing. They were empty. "Good," said Gable, "everyone's ass out on the street. The fucking world as it should be."

Gable took Nate to lunch in a grubby little Turkish restaurant in a small snow-filled alley near the train station. The steamy single dining room had half a dozen tables, a pass-through window from the kitchen, and a framed portrait of Atatürk on the wall. People were yelling in the kitchen, but when Gable went to the window and clapped his hands the noise stopped. A thin dark man with a black mustache and an apron parted the bead curtain and came out of the kitchen. He embraced Gable briefly and was introduced as Tarik, the owner. The Turk shook hands loosely without looking into Nate's eyes. They took a corner table and Gable pulled out the chair he wanted Nate to sit in, against the wall with a view of the door. Gable sat with his back to the other wall. Speaking Turkish, Gable ordered two Adana kebabs, two beers, bread, and salad.

"I hope you like spicy," said Gable. "This little shithole has the best Turkish food in the city. There are a lot of immigrants from Turkey around here." Gable looked at the kitchen. He leaned forward. "I popped Tarik about a year ago, support asset, you know, pick up mail, pay rent on a safe house, keep his ear to the ground. A couple hundred a month and he's happy. If we need to, we can tap into the expat community in Helsinki." Gable straightened as the food came, two long flat kebabs speckled with red pepper, grilled a dark brown. A large broiled flatbread, splashed with melted butter, was underneath. Raw onion salad sprinkled with dark red sumac and lemon was piled on the side of the plate. Two sweating bottles of beer were plunked on the table as Tarik muttered, "*Afiyet olsun,* may it be good for you," and withdrew.

Gable began eating before Nate picked up his fork. He wolfed food, talking and moving his big mitts in the air. "Not bad, eh?" he asked of the kebabs, his mouth full. He upended his beer and drank half the bottle. His jaws snatched at the food, gazelle going down the gullet of a crocodile. Without preamble or embarrassment, he asked Nate what the fuck had happened in Moscow between him and that asshole Gondorf.

Mortified, his worries rekindled, Nate explained briefly, a few sentences. Gable pointed at him with his fork. "Listen up: Remember two things about this fucking business. You can never mature as an operator unless you've failed, large, at least once. And you're judged by your accomplishments, the results you bring, and how you protect your agents. Nothing else matters." The other half of the bottle disappeared and Gable called for another. "Oh, and there's another thing," he said. "Gondorf's a douche bag. Don't worry about him."

Gable was finished with his entire plate before Nate even had gotten through half of his. "Did you ever fail in your career?" he asked Gable.

"Are you kidding?" said Gable, tilting back his chair. "I was in the shit so often I rented the top floor of the latrine. That's how I got here. After the most recent train wreck, Forsyth saved my ass."

Gable's career had been spent primarily on the Shithole Tour—Third World countries in Africa and Asia. Some case officers make their bones in the restaurants and hotel rooms and sidewalk cafés of Paris. Gable's world was one of midnight meetings on deserted dirt roads in red-dust-covered Land Rovers. Other officers tape-recorded their meetings with government ministers. Gable wrote secrets into a sweat-damp notebook while sitting with agents sour with fear, making them concentrate, making them stay fucking on topic. They would sit in the heat, engine block ticking, with the windows up, watching the heads of the mambas part the tops of the tall grass on either side of the vehicle. Nate had heard that Gable was a legend. He was loyal to his assets, then to his friends, then to the CIA, in that order. There was nothing he hadn't seen, and he knew what was important.

Gable sat back and sipped his beer, started talking. Last assignment was in Istanbul, big fucking town, good ops, Dodge City. Spoke pretty good Turkish, knew where to go, who to see. Pretty fast he'd recruited a member of the PKK, the benighted Kurdish separatist terror group from eastern Turkey. They'd been leaving bombs in briefcases in government buildings, or shoeshine kits in the bazaar, or paper sacks in trash cans in Taksim Square.

One day Gable got into a taxi driven by a Kurd kid, twenty, twenty-one years old. Sounded sharp, drove okay. Listen up, you got to keep your eyes open, all the time. He had a hunch, an instinct, so he told the kid to stop at a restaurant, invited him to eat with him, this Kurd kid. He had to stare down the fat Turk motherfucker behind the counter, they all hated Kurds, called them "mountain Turks."

Kid ate like he was hungry. Talked about his family. Gable smelled PKK, so he hired the taxi for a week of driving around. Hunch paid off. Kid was a member of a local cell but didn't buy the terrorism bullshit. A little respect, five hundred euros a month, a nice little recruitment. All because Gable kept his eyes fucking open in a taxi. Don't forget that.

The kid started with useless shit, but Gable straightened him out—called *agent handling* for a fucking reason—and they focused on cell leaders, how they got their orders, how the couriers traveled. Not bad, but Gable pushed the kid, and they started getting the locations of PKK warehouses where they stored the Semtex or whatever they were using, Nitrolit from Poland. Then he started passing the names of the bomb-makers.

It was getting good and we had to keep a cold compress on the Turkish National Police because they wanted to wrap them up, "capture them dead," they used to say. COS in Ankara was happy and the suits in Headquarters were bobbing their heads. Then Gable got cocky, lost the bubble; lesson for Nate, you always have to keep the bubble.

Young Kurd lived in Tepebaşi, fundo neighborhood down the hill from Pera, the old European quarter. Gable normally met the kid in his taxi, driving around town, never stopping, nighttime always, on the fly. Broke the rules and visited the kid's house to meet the family. At his house. The kid had invited him, it would have been an insult to refuse, got to be culturally sensitive, goddamn it. Besides, Gable wanted to see where his agent lived. Listen up, you always know where your agents live, you never know whether you're going to have to dig them out of the woodwork some night.

The street was steep, lined with peeling wooden row houses, faded splendor, narrow front steps, double front doors, etched-glass sidelights, all broken and boarded. Former European neighborhood, now littered with garbage and smelling of drains. In Istanbul you get used to smelling sewage, actually smells sort of sweet. Anyway, it was getting dark and lights in the houses were starting to come on. Evening call to prayer had just ended.

Gable had come down the hill dreading it. This was going to be an awkward hour full of shy, downcast eyes and endless glasses of tea. Fuck it, part of the job. As he approached the house he heard screams. His agent's front door was open. Something breaking. Fuck, not good, neighbors would be gathering soon. Gable thought it would be a circus in approximately two minutes. He started drifting away from the house. Pretty dark by now, no one would notice him.

Trouble was, at the front door two guys were marching Gable's agent out of the house by the armpits. The kid's wife was slight and dark with almond eyes from the south slopes of the Taurus Mountains, torn T-shirt, barefoot. She was right behind them, screaming, beating at the men. A baby about two years old stood in the doorway buck-naked, crying. These two dickheads were as skinny as Gable's agent, but there was no resistance, maybe because one of the dickheads held a pistol.

Jesus Christ, the kid's in trouble with the PKK. Maybe spent the extra money, maybe bragged about his new foreign friend. Listen up, it goes south that fast. You got to protect them, sometimes you got to do it for them. The PKK took a medieval view when dealing with countrymen they thought were traitors.

Gable could have walked away. Saw the baby girl in the door—cute little thing, bubble butt and slobbering nose—and he thought, *Naw, fuck it.* Stepped up to the first step of the house and smiled at the dickheads. They stopped and let go of the kid, who fell on his ass on the top step. Little wife stopped screaming and looked at Gable, big fucking *yabanci,* foreigner with big knuckles. A dozen neighbors edging around, all Kurds. Fucking neighborhood was dead quiet, not a sound, water running down the center of the street. The dickhead with the pistol yelled something in Kurdish, sounded like sash weights in a washtub.

Big Mouth began waving the pistol, pointing it at the kid, at the wife, shaking it like a finger. Kid was one hundred percent dead if Gable didn't do something. Fuck it, anyway, because this was the absofuckinglutely end of the case, the kid would have to skip Turkey if he wanted to stay alive. PKK guy came down a step and continued yelling at Gable. Ignored the beady eyes, focused on the pistol. Little fuck's knuckles whiten on the grip, you know you got about three seconds. Barrel started coming up.

Gable was carrying a Hi-Power in a Bianchi belt loop behind his hip. He cleared the Browning and shot the Kurd, pop-pop-pop. Call it the Mozambique, double-tap center mass, third round forehead, suppose it was invented over there or something. Dickhead's eyes opened, fell straight down in a heap. Slid skull-first down the stairs. Pistol bounced after him, Gable picked it up, threw it clattering down a sewer grate, got to be a million guns in Istanbul's sewers. Gable's spent brass hadn't hit the pavement before the neighbors bolted like fucking squirrels, going in all directions, shutters slamming up and down the hill.

The Kurd kid held his wife. Wondered if the kid realized their new life started right then, maybe, the wife probably did, looked smart, nipples showing through that T-shirt. Gable looked at the other PKK guy, who's seen Jesus, or Muhammad, whatever, and the guy held his hands in front of him, palms out, walked down the steps, and ran down the street into the dark.

Gable gave the kid five grand to clear out, couldn't get any more out of Headquarters. Don't know where they went, maybe they're in Germany or France. Five Kurdish kids learning German. When *they* turn twenty, Nate's *son* can find and recruit *them*. Fucking crazy. Okay, now the point of this long fucking story.

Aftermath was a veritable shitstorm, I kid you not, Gable said. First it was the Consulate and the hysterical Consul General, tinny voice like a music box, then the Embassy in Ankara, then the knife-and-fork set at the State Department. Diplomat involved in fatal shooting, they were very upset, a lot of weeping. Grave repercussions. Had to leave Istanbul. The Turkish National Police gave me a plaque and a farewell dinner; they were delighted. Turkish cops love a good shoot-out. But everyone else was seriously pissed, and official CIA investigation hadn't even started.

Gable waltzed around with Office of Security at Headquarters for a month. After forty hours of conversation they settled on "deficient tradecraft." COS Ankara didn't back Gable up, too much political heat, sounds like Gondorf, doesn't it? Plenty of assholes to go in your career. Gable's prospects for foreign operations were over for the indefinite future, it seemed, and he was stuck in a four-by-four cubicle on the Turkish desk in Headquarters, listening to a twenty-three-year-old new hire on the other side of the partition talking on the outside line to her girlfriend about getting up the nerve to fellate her boyfriend that weekend. None of the young officers even wore wristwatches, goddamn it: they told time with their fucking phones, or tablets, or whatever they're called.

Gable didn't feel sorry for himself, it was operations. All this happened to him, but for the right reason. Listen up, the most important thing is your agent, his security, saving his life. It's the only thing.

At about the same time, Forsyth had just concluded his own personal shitstorm, but had bounced back and landed in Helsinki. He heard Gable was fucked—that was nothing new—and sent for him as his number two, like the old days, only there aren't any good old days, it's a myth. The ecstatics at Headquarters were happy to let Gable go to Finland as DCOS, no one else wanted the job and they wanted him off the desk, bad influence.

"So here we are, three fuckups, in the field, operating near the fricking Arctic Circle. And you and me drinking beer in a Turkish hash house." Gable finished his beer and yelled, "*Hesap*." When Tarik came out of the kitchen, Gable motioned to Nate. "He's paying." Nate laughed.

"Wait a minute," said Nate. "What do you mean,

Forsyth went through his own shitstorm? What happened to him?" Nate dug out a few euros and handed them to Tarik. "Keep the change." Tarik smiled thinly, nodded to Gable, and retreated to the kitchen. "You overtipped, rookie," said Gable. "Don't let them get used to you paying out. Got to keep them hungry." Gable got up and shrugged on his coat.

"Bullshit," said Nate. "You paid that young Kurd five grand to get him out of Dodge, but even you admitted he was burned, useless. You didn't have to pay him squat." Nate looked at Gable as they turned out of the alley and walked in front of the train station. Gable avoided looking back at him, and Nate knew that Gable was more than just a tough guy. But he wasn't going to test the limits anytime soon.

The air was cold and Nate flipped up the collar of his overcoat. "You didn't answer me about Forsyth," said Nate. "What's the story?"

Gable ignored the question and continued walking down the sidewalk. "Do you know where the Russian Embassy is?" asked Gable. "China, Iran, Syria? You should be able to get in a car and drive directly to any one of them. You might have to exfil some poor bastard someday. I'll give you a week to find 'em all."

"Yeah, okay, no problem. But what about Forsyth? What happened?" Nate had to keep dodging around pedestrians on the snowy sidewalk as Gable bulled his way through the afternoon crowds. They got to a corner and waited to cross. Nate saw a coffee shop on the opposite side of the street. "Quick cup of coffee? Come on, I'll buy." Gable looked at Nate sideways and nodded.

Over coffee and a short brandy, Gable told the story. Forsyth was considered one of the shit-hot Chiefs of Station in the Service. Throughout his twenty-five-year career, Forsyth came up the ranks with a brilliant record. As a young officer he recruited the first-ever North Korean reporting asset. Before the Wall came down, he directed a Polish colonel who brought Forsyth the complete war plans for Warsaw Pact Southern Command. A few years later, he recruited the Georgian defense minister, who, in exchange for a Swiss bank account, arranged for a T-80 tank with the new reactive armor to be driven at 0300 across the shale beach at Batumi and up the ramp of a heavy landing craft leased by the CIA from the Romanians.

As he moved up, Forsyth was one of the senior managers who had done the work and knew what the Game was about. Case officers loved him. Ambassadors came to him for advice. Seventh-Floor suits at Headquarters trusted him, and at age forty-seven he was rewarded with the plum COS Rome job. Forsyth's first year in Rome was, as expected, a solid success.

What no one expected was that politically savvy Tom Forsyth would tell the supercilious staff aide of a senator visiting Rome on a congressional delegation to shut up and listen instead of talking during a Station briefing. She had questioned the "condign wisdom" of a controversial and compartmented Rome Station operation. The twenty-three-year-old political science major from Yale with twenty months of experience on the Hill had moreover personally criticized Forsyth's management of the case by saying she thought the "tradecraft employed was, in a word, subpar." This elicited from the usually phlegmatic Forsyth a cryptic "Go fuck yourself," which days later resulted in the Headquarters notification that the senator had complained, that Forsyth's Rome assignment was curtailed, that he was being relieved for cause.

After the usual righteous letter of reprimand in Forsyth's file, the Seventh Floor quietly offered Forsyth the COS Helsinki job. The offer was made to demonstrate to Congress that Headquarters sympathized with Forsyth's reaction to fatuous oversight inflicted on hardworking field operators during Codel shopping junkets camouflaged as fact-finding trips. Offering Forsyth Helsinki was, in addition, an insincere and calculated offer because no one thought Forsyth would accept. The Station was one-sixth the size of Rome's, in arguably the least important of four somewhat sleepy Scandinavian countries, a post for a junior COS. They expected Forsyth to decline, find a place to park himself, and leave in two years when he became eligible to retire.

"By accepting the assignment he basically told the Seventh Floor to go fuck themselves," said Gable. "A half year later he got me as his deputy, and yesterday you arrive. Not that you're a fuckup." Gable laughed. "You're just known as one."

Gable saw Nate's face, the faraway stare. *Okay,* he told himself, *this kid has a worm in his guts.* He'd seen it before, the talented case officer too fucking afeared for his rep and future to be able to relax and let it flow. That whey-faced Gondorf had rattled the kid, should be ashamed of himself, and now he and Forsyth had to get Nash thinking straight. He made a mental note to talk to the COS. The last thing Station needed was a c/o who didn't know the right time to pull the recruitment trigger.

TARIK'S ADANA KEBAB

Purée red bell and hot peppers with salt and olive oil. Add purée to ground lamb, chopped onion, garlic and parsley, finely cubed butter, coriander, cumin, paprika, olive oil, salt, and pepper. Knead and shape into flat kebabs; grill until almost charred. Serve with grilled pide bread and thinly sliced purple onions sprinkled with lemon and sumac.

8

The white-and-blue Voskhod hydrofoil settled into the water and approached the dock in a trailing cloud of blue diesel smoke. Carrying a small suitcase, Dominika stepped onto the steep pontoon ramp on the edge of the tarry mudflats and walked up to a bus waiting on the gravel road above the river. Eleven young people—seven women and four men—trudged up the pier behind her. They were all silent and tired and put their bags down in front of the open baggage compartment of the bus. No one spoke, they didn't glance at one another. Dominika turned and looked out over the wide Volga River, pine trees lining both sides down to the shoreline. The air was humid and the river smelled of diesel fuel. Three kilometers north, around a bend in the river, the steeples and minarets around the Kazan Kremlin could just be seen in the morning haze.

Dominika knew it was Kazan because they had driven through the city from the airfield, past all the highway signs. That meant they were in Tatarstan, still in European Russia. At midnight, they had flown seven hundred kilometers from Moscow to a darkened military airfield. Unlit signs had read BORISOGLEBSKOYE AERODROME and KAZAN STATE AIRCRAFT PLANT. They had silently boarded a bus, the star-cracked windows covered by stained gray curtains. They drove through quiet predawn streets to a waterfront pier, where they boarded the wallowing hydrofoil as the sun was coming up over the city.

They waited wordlessly for an hour in the aircraft-style seats of the hydrofoil in stifling air. The arrhythmic rocking of the hull, the slopping water against the pier, and the creaking of the frayed nylon lines straining against the bollards made her queasy, then sleepy. Apart from the driver of the bus and a man on the bridge of the vessel, they had seen no one. Dominika watched the sunlight spread on the water and counted the seabirds.

Eventually a gray Lada pulled up to the gangplank and a man and woman got out, carrying two flat cardboard boxes. They boarded the boat, placed the boxes on the counter at the front of the cabin, and opened the flaps. "Come and help yourselves," said the woman, and sat down in a front-row seat with her back to the passengers. They rose slowly and made their way to the front. They had not eaten since breakfast the day before. One box was full of fresh-baked *bulochki,* sweet buns with raisins, the other filled with waxed containers of warm orangeade. The man watched the passengers return to their seats, then went out and spoke to the man on the bridge. The vessel's engines started with a rumble, and a shudder went through the seats. The aluminum gangway banged onto the pier and the lines were cast off.

The hydrofoil was on plane, up on its foils, and the whole ship trembled as it sped downriver. The seat in front of her vibrated, the cabin headliner grommets buzzed, the metal ashtray inserts chattered in the armrests. Fighting down nausea, Dominika focused on the fabric of the grimy headrest in front of her. Courtesan College. She was flying down the Volga toward a colossal indignity.

Now they were on the bus, the nameless woman sitting in the front seat. They swayed through a sun-dappled pine forest, finally stopping at a concrete slab wall. The sun caught the broken glass mortared along the top. The bus sounded its horn, then squeezed through the gate and up a sweeping drive and stopped in front of a two-story neoclassical mansion with a mansard roof of spalling slate. It was absolutely quiet in the woods, without a breath of a breeze, and there was no movement from within the mansion.

Deep breath. *Come on, snap out of it.* This disgusting school was another obstacle, more sacrifice, another test of her loyalty. She stood in the piney woods in front of the mustard-colored mansion and waited. She had arrived at Sparrow School.

After talking with her uncle, Dominika had thought hard about telling them all to go to hell. She contemplated taking her mother back to Strelna on the shores of the Nevskaya Guba, near Petersburg. She could find work as a teacher or a gym coach. With luck and time she might find employment at the Vaganova Academy, back into ballet. But no, she decided she was not going to run away. She would do this, whatever it took. They were not going to shoot her. This was about physical love, it would not matter what they made her do, they could not defeat her spirit.

And even as she revolted against the thought, Dominika's secret self, the humming servo of her body, wondered whether the grimy catechisms resident in the ocher building before her would in any small way fulfill her. She hated the thought of Sparrow School and was abashed at having been sent here, but she privately was expectant, watchful.

"Leave your bags in the hallway and follow me," said the woman, who had preceded them up the front steps and through the towering front doors of weathered wood. They gathered in an auditorium. Judging by the bookshelves, it had formerly been a library that had been converted to a lecture hall with a raised wooden platform and dais and several rows of creaking wooden seats at one end of the room. The woman, dressed in a shapeless black suit, walked among them and passed out envelopes by hand. "Inside you will find your room assignments," she said, "and the names you will use during your training. Use only these names. You will not relate any personal information about yourselves to other students. Any infraction will result in immediate dismissal." In her early fifties, the administrator had upswept gray hair, a square face, and a straight nose. She looked like the woman on the stamps, Tereshkova, the first woman in space. Her words came out in gouts of yellow.

"You have been chosen for specialized training," said the matron. "It is a great honor. The nature of the training may seem alien and strange to some of you. Concentrate on the lessons and the exercises. Nothing else is important." Her voice echoed in the high-ceilinged hall. "Now go upstairs and find your rooms. Dinner is at six in the dining room across the hall. Instruction will begin here this evening at seven o'clock. Go now. Dismiss."

In the upper hallway Dominika counted twelve rooms, six either side, numbers in cracked-enamel lozenges screwed into the wood. Between the bedroom doors along the hallway were other plain doors without knobs or handles. These could be opened only by use of a key. Her room was painted light green and was spare but comfortable, with a single bed, standing closet, table, and chair. There was a faint but constant odor of disinfectant, on the bedspread, in the closet, in the stack of sheets on the shelf. The room had a curtained-off toilet (above which hung a hand shower) and a rust-stained sink. Above the writing table was a large mirror, too large, incongruous in the barracks-style room. Dominika put her cheek flat against the mirror and looked at the surface in glancing light, like in training. The silver smokiness of a two-way mirror. Welcome to Sparrow School.

Dusk, and the night sky not visible through the

pine tops. The house was dimly lit; there were no clocks in the mansion, anywhere. No telephone rang. The hallways and staircases and ground-floor rooms were silent; the night invaded the house. The walls were bare, held none of the daguerreotype official portraits of Lenin or Marx, though moldy outlines where portraits once hung were still visible on the panels. What Tatar noble family had lived here before the Revolution? Did resplendent parties ride and hunt in these pines? Did they hear the whistle of the Moscow steam packet from the river? What Soviet instinct had put the school this far away from Moscow?

She looked around the dining table at the eleven other "students" silently spooning *tokmach,* a thick noodle soup that had been ladled into their bowls from a colossal blue-and-white porcelain tureen by a wordless waiter. A plate of boiled meat followed. The women and three of the men were all in their twenties; the fourth man seemed even younger, in his teens, thin and pale. Were any of them also SVR-trained? Dominika turned to the woman on her left and smiled. "My name is Katia," she said, using her training alias.

The woman smiled back. "I am Anya." She was slight and blond, with a wide mouth and high cheekbones lightly dusted by freckles. She looked like an elegant milkmaid with pale blue eyes. Her halting words were cornflower-blue, innocence and artlessness. Others shyly recited their aliases. After dinner they filed quietly into the library.

It was absolutely quiet in the room, then the lights dimmed. Welcome to Sparrow School instruction. A film started, stark black-and-white images, brutal, feral, sawtoothed, it burst onto a screen at the front of the room with straining faces, clasping bodies, organs shafting endlessly, everywhere, now in such close focus to become gynecological, unrecognizable, unworldly. The sound started at full volume and Dominika saw the heads of her classmates jerk back at the sudden assault of sound and sight. The air was filled with spinning color for her; she knew the signs of overload when the bleeding sequence red-violet-blue-green-yellow began. She had no control and closed her eyes to escape the onslaught. Then a speaker popped and the sound suddenly went down to barely audible, so that the woman on the screen seemed as if she were whispering, even as her hair stuck to the side of her face and her body was jolted endlessly by an offscreen partner.

The light flickered on the ceiling beams twenty feet above her head. Could she last here for the duration? What would they expect her to do? What would they do if she got up and walked out of the room? Would she be dismissed from the Service? The hell with them. They wanted a Sparrow, they would get a Sparrow. No one knew she could see the colors. Mikhail had said she was the best student he ever had in seeing people. She would stay. She would learn.

She told herself this wasn't love. This school, this mansion secluded behind walls topped with broken glass, was an engine of the State that institutionalized and dehumanized love. It didn't count, it was physical sex, it was training, like ballet school. In the flickering light in the musty library Dominika told herself she was going to go through with this, to spite these *vnebrachnye deti,* these bastards.

The lights came on and the students sat red-faced and embarrassed. Anya sniffled and wiped her eyes with the back of her fist. The matron addressed the students in a flat, hard voice. "You have had a long journey. Return to your rooms and get some rest. Instruction resumes tomorrow morning at oh-seven-hundred. Dismiss." Nothing in her manner would have even remotely indicated that they had been watching a film of people engaged in coitus for the last ninety minutes. They filed out and up the grand staircase with the massive wooden banisters. Anya nodded good night before closing her door. Dominika wondered whether Anya or the others knew that tonight the as-yet-unseen staff of the Kon Institute, stuffed into the *cabinets de voyeur* between rooms, would be watching them undressing, bathing, and sleeping.

Dominika stood in front of the mirror, ran the long-handled brush through her hair, the only familiar token she had brought from home, and she looked at it in her hand, as if it could mock her. She stood and unbuttoned her blouse. She slipped the blouse on a bent wire hanger and nonchalantly hooked it on the frame of the mirror, covering one end of it. She set her little suitcase on the table and opened the lid against the mirror, blocking a further third. She stepped out of her skirt and pirouetted unconsciously to look at the curve of her back and the swell of her bottom in the nylon panties before casually flipping the skirt over the frame of the mirror, covering the last third. They would clear the mirror in the morning, perhaps speak sharply to her about it, but it was worth it tonight. Then she brushed her teeth, got under sheets in a disinfectant bloom of camphor and rose oil, and flipped off the light. She left the hairbrush on the dresser.

The men were separated from the women and the days spilled into one another and they lost a sense of time. Soporific mornings were devoted to endless lectures on anatomy, physiology, the psychology of the human sexual response. A few new staff appeared. A female doctor droned endlessly about sexual practices in different cultures. Then came the classes on male anatomy, knowing how a man's body works, how to excite a male. The techniques, positions, movements numbered in the hundreds. They were studied, repeated, memorized, an Upper Volga Kama Sutra. Dominika marveled at this monstrous encyclopedia, at the sticky epiphanies that ruined normality, that forever would rob Dominika of her innocence. Could she ever make love again?

Afternoons were reserved for "practical subjects," as if they were training to be ice-skaters. They practiced walking, they practiced conversation, they practiced pulling the cork out of a champagne bottle. There were rooms of used clothes, scuffed shoes, sweat-stained lingerie. They dressed up and practiced talking to one another, learned to listen, to show interest, to make compliments and to flatter and, most important, to elicit information during conversation.

A rare afternoon of camaraderie, five of them sitting on the floor of the library in a circle, knees almost touching, laughing, chattering, practicing what they called "sex talk" from what they had heard in the nightly films.

"It's like this," said a dark-haired girl with the heavy accent of the Black Sea, and she closed her eyes and murmured in cast-iron English, "Yah, lovers, you are making me to come." Gales of laughter, and Dominika looked at the blushing faces and wondered how soon some of them would find themselves in their underwear in the Intourist Hotel in Volgograd watching skinny Vietnamese trade reps shuck off their shoes.

"Katia, you try," said the girl to Dominika. From the first night they had all sensed she was somehow different, somehow special. Beside her, Anya looked at her expectantly.

Without knowing why, perhaps to show them, perhaps to show herself, Dominika half closed her eyes and whispered, "Yes, honey . . . just like that . . . Oh, God," and pushing the sound up from her belly: "UNNGGGHHH." Shocked silence, and then the circle of girls roared their approval and applauded. Anya stared, flaxen-haired and wide-eyed and wordless, mindless of the general hilarity of the moment.

Anya of the meadow-flower-blue halo. She was struggling, aghast at the most salacious aspects of training, and clung to Dominika for courage and support. "You have to get used to it," Dominika told her, but Anya cringed during the nightly films, holding Dominika's hand tightly as the fuck circus raged on the screen in front of them. *The little farm girl isn't going to make it,* Dominika thought. *Her color is getting weaker, not stronger.*

Then one night, after an impossibly depraved film that had her silently weeping, Anya came to Dominika's room, eyes red and lips trembling, her cornflower syllables barely visible. She had come to her friend for solace, she was losing her mind. She had told them she was quitting, but they had said something to her—God only knew what—and she could not leave. Dominika pulled her by the hand behind the bathroom curtain. "You have to get through this," she whispered, shaking Anya gently by the shoulders.

Anya sobbed and threw her arms around Dominika's neck. She pressed her lips against Dominika's mouth. The little idiot was trembling and Dominika did not pull away, did not reject her. They were on the floor of the little bathroom. Dominika cradled Anya in her arms, felt her shake. Anya turned her head up for another kiss, and Dominika almost refused, but then relented and kissed her again.

The kiss had an effect on Anya and she reached for Dominika's hand, pulled it to her body, and slid it beneath her bathrobe onto her breast. *Oh, for God's sake,* thought Dominika. She herself felt no passion, but rather sadness for the girl in her arms. Was this the bisexuality they had lectured to them about downstairs? Could they be observed behind the curtain? Was there audio in the room? Was this a serious offense?

Anya held her hand by the wrist and trailed it over her nipple, which swelled under Dominika's fingertips. The bathrobe fell open and Anya pulled the captured hand lower, between her legs. Perversion? An act of kindness? Something else? Dominika's unknown ancestral libertine—whoever she was—kept her going, an inexplicable out-of-body state where stopping now was only slightly less possible than going ahead. Dominika's feather-light fingertips traced minute, perfect circles and Anya melted, her head turned in to Dominika, the line of her neck soft and vulnerable.

Sitting up against the bathroom tiles, Dominika felt Anya's breath between her own legs and there was no reason now to stop. Her secret self told her to feel her body, and the sensation of Anya's breathy exhalations radiated up her stomach. Dominika's head dropped back against the tile and her arm gripped the side of the sink for support. She felt *Prababushka*'s tortoiseshell brush in her hand and pulled it down. Her great-grandmother's hairbrush, her mother had brushed her own hair with it, it was her secret companion during the thunderstorms of her girlhood.

Dominika trailed the handle down Anya's stomach, making the soft amber curve infinitely light, infinitely insistent. Anya held her breath and her eyes fluttered behind tight-shut eyes. Looking at Anya's face, Dominika positioned the handle and flexed her wrist. Anya's mouth opened partway, and her eyes showed a sliver of white, like the slack face of a corpse on a slab.

Anya stiffened and began shaking against the slow

plunge and drag of tortoiseshell. She turned chin-wet to look up at Dominika and whispered, "Yes baby, just so, you're cumming me," and Dominika smiled and watched the little milkmaid thrash about while she put her own secret self back in the hurricane room inside her and closed the door.

After a few minutes, Anya sighed and turned her face up to be kissed again. *Enough.* "You have to go, quickly, now," Dominika said. Red-faced, Anya gathered her bathrobe around her, looked at Dominika, and went silently out. Would there be bellowed accusations tomorrow morning? Was there anyone behind the mirror right now? Too tired to care, Dominika got into bed in the darkened room. The brush lay forgotten on the floor under the sink.

The next morning, in a large downstairs salon, wood-paneled and carpeted with a huge blue-and-ivory Kazakh carpet, the women were ordered to sit in chairs set in a circle in the center of the room. The first student, a slight young brunette with the lilting western accent of Novgorod, was ordered to stand up, undress, and walk around the circle to be critiqued by the others. There was shocked silence. She hesitated but then disrobed. The female doctor and her assistant, both in lab coats, acted as moderators, noting strengths and weaknesses. Finished, the student was ordered to sit in her chair, but to remain naked. The next student was called and the process was repeated. Flushed faces, goose bumps, and bitten lips, the room slowly was filled with incongruous, shivering naked bodies, a pitiful pile of clothes and shoes beneath each chair.

Thank God there were no men present! Anya twisted her hands nervously as her turn inexorably came, and she looked over to Dominika in a panic. Dominika looked away. The doctor snapped at Anya to hurry up when she hesitated to peel off her panties. Now it was her turn, and Dominika ignored her nervousness and stood up when she was called. It was monstrous to be ordered to strip off in the presence of half a dozen strangers, but she forced herself. Anya looked at her intently. Dominika was embarrassed as much by her nudity as by the awed silence in the room when she walked around the circle of chairs. "Best in breed," whispered the assistant. "Best in show," corrected the doctor.

The following day a man stood in the circle of chairs and took off a short bathrobe. He was naked underneath and needed to bathe and clean his toenails. The doctor evaluated the pale body for the students, and close-up assessment followed. The next day the man in the bathrobe was back, this time with a short, stocky woman with iodine-red hair and chapped cheeks and elbows. They disrobed and unconcernedly made love on a mattress in the center of the students' circle of chairs. The doctor pointed out different lovemaking positions; she would order the couple to stop in mid-act to illustrate a relevant point or to demonstrate a physical refinement. The models showed no emotion, neither for themselves nor for their partners, their colors so washed out as to be invisible. It was soulless.

"I cannot look at them," Anya confessed to Dominika. They had grown into the habit of walking together around the shabby garden of the mansion in the few free minutes after breakfast. "I cannot do this, I simply cannot."

"Listen, you can become used to anything," said Dominika. How was this girl ever selected? From what provincial capital had she been picked? Then she wondered to herself, *What about you, can* you *become accustomed to anything after enough time?*

The next week was, as Dominika anticipated, a

multiplication of indignity. Again the salon and the familiar circle of chairs, but this time men, brusque men in tight suits and bad haircuts, sat in the circle. The female students were told to undress in front of these men, who then proceeded to critique each of the students, pointing out flaws in her figure or complexion or face. They were never identified; their yeasty yellow bubbles combined to tarnish the atmosphere of the entire room.

Anya covered her tear-streaked face with her hands until the doctor told her to stop being a silly cow and to take her hands away this instant. Feeling as if she were in a dream, Dominika left her body, closed her mind, and endured the stares of a man with a terribly pocked face. The color coming from inside him made his eyes yellow, like a civet in an alley. She stared back at him without blinking as his eyes wandered over her. "Not enough meat on her," he said aloud to nobody in particular. "And her nipples are too small." Two other men nodded in agreement. Dominika stared them all down until they looked away or got busy lighting their cigarettes.

Dominika was surprised to note that she was beginning to go numb. Numb to nakedness, numb to lewd commentary, numb to strangers' eyes looking at her breasts or her sex or her buttocks. *They can do what they like,* she told herself, *but I won't let them look me in the eyes.* Other students reacted in their own ways. One silly little idiot from Smolensk with the lilt of southern Russian dialect vamped and hip-shot her way through the sessions. Anya never seemed to get over her shame. The defining smell of disinfectant in the mansion now was overlaid with the pungency of their bodies, musk and sweat and rosewater and brown soap. And after lights out, the sweating staff sat in the *cabinets* and took notes and made sure the cameras were not blocked.

Anya knocked softly at her door late one night, and Dominika opened it a crack and told her to go away. "I can't help you anymore," she said, and Anya turned and disappeared down the darkened hallway. *It isn't my problem,* thought Dominika. *It's enough that I'm fighting for my own sanity.*

Then the bus came with the military cadets, the ones who had scored at the top of their class. The women waited for them in their rooms, and sat on the beds and watched the skinny, bruised bodies as the boys ripped off their tunic shirts and boots and trousers, and held on tight as they rutted like stoats until time was up. The cadets left without looking back at the women, and the bus swayed as it went out through the gate into the pine forest.

The next morning in the curtained, darkened library the projector began, but instead of the usual film, they saw their classmate in room number five on the single bed with a skinny, shaved-headed cadet from the day before. The women could barely look at the screen. This was shame, this was indignity, seeing yourself with legs hooked around a pimply back, hands formed into claws on bony shoulders. The doctor would freeze-frame the films to add commentary, suggest improvements. Worse, they all now guessed that the films would come in order—rooms five, six, seven, and so on. Anya's head was down, her face in her hands. She was in room eleven and would have to endure not only the films, but also the wait. She ran from the room weeping as her segment ended. The doctor let her flee. She prattled on about what had been done wrong, how it could be improved.

Dominika was in room number twelve, at the end of the hall. The filmed segment of the interlude with her cadet therefore was the last. Disembodied, she watched herself, surprised at her slack face, how mechanically she had grasped the young man and guided him, how she had pulled his ear to get him off when he collapsed on top of her. Her head was spinning, yet she felt no shame, no embarrassment. She looked at the images on the screen without feeling and kept telling herself that she was a member of the *Sluzhba Vneshney Razvedki,* the Foreign Intelligence Service of the Russian Federation.

The next morning Anya did not come down to breakfast, and two girls found her in her room. They had to push the door open with their shoulders. She had knotted panty hose around her neck, wrapped the end around a coat hook on the back of the door, and simply had drawn her legs up and strangled herself. She had had the strength to keep her feet off the floor until she blacked out. The weight of her lolling body had kept the noose tight. In the garden, Dominika heard the screams. She raced upstairs, pushed the others aside, and lifted Anya off the hook and laid her on the floor. She felt guilt and anger. What did the little twit expect from her anyway? How could she have had the courage to choke to death, she thought, but not to lie with a man for thirty minutes?

There barely was a reaction. The bear sniffed at the body, then turned its back. Anya was carried out of the mansion on a canvas stretcher, covered by a blanket, her blond hair sticking out from under. Nothing was mentioned, by anybody. The day's instruction continued as before.

The course was coming to an end. The six Sparrows watched as the four young men filed back into the dining room. They were fledgling "Ravens" now, trained in a smaller villa down the road, three of them expert in the art of seducing the vulnerable and lonely women targeted by the SVR—the minister's spinster secretary, the ambassador's frustrated wife, the underappreciated female aide of a general. The fourth young man had learned another specialty: befriending the sensitive, fearful men—cipher clerks, military attachés, sometimes senior diplomats—who secretly yearned for male friendship, companionship, love, but who were heart-piercingly vulnerable to the threat of exposure. The Ravens loftily declared that they had suffered during their training. Training partners were not readily available, whispered Dmitri; they practiced on unwashed girls from nearby villages, made love to sallow slatterns bused from factories in Kazan. Dominika did not ask about the fourth boy, how and with whom he had practiced. "But now we're trained to excel in love," said Dmitri. "We are experts." He opened his arms and stared at them through his eyelashes.

The women looked back at him wordlessly. Dominika saw the women's faces were closed down, saw the skepticism and fatalism and mistrust. These were like the vacant faces of the hookers on Tverskaya Ulitsa in Moscow. *The fruits of Sparrow School,* thought Dominika. Anya's empty place at the table was not the only cost.

They departed for the airport at midnight, carrying their cheap cardboard suitcases, leaving the blacked-out mansion without a look back. Whore School was closed until the next group arrived. The pinewoods were black, silent. The plane circled the smokestacks of Kazan and flew west over the invisible landscape. In another hour they were over the lights of Nizhniy Novgorod, bisected by the black ribbon of the Volga. Then came the gradual descent toward the glow of sleepless Moscow. She would never see any of the other trainees again.

She was to report to the Center the next morning, to the Fifth Department, to start her career as a junior intelligence officer. She thought about Simyonov, chief of the Fifth, and about the other officers she would meet, how they would look at her, what they would say. *Well,* she thought, *the trained courtesan is back from the steppes,* and she intended to inhabit their world.

The living room was dark when she tiptoed into the apartment in the hours before dawn, but her mother appeared in the hallway, dressed in a bathrobe. "I heard your steps," she said, and Dominika knew she meant her uneven tread in the stairwell. Dominika hugged her, then took her mother's hand and kissed it—with lips that had been trained to ruin a man—an act of expiation.

SPARROW SCHOOL TOKMACH SOUP

Boil coarsely chopped potato, thinly sliced onions, and carrots in beef broth until soft. Add thin noodles and cook until done. Put boiled beef in bottom of bowl and pour broth and vegetables over.

9

Dominika reported to the Fifth the next morning, still exhausted by the flight from Kazan. Walking down the long headquarters corridor with light green walls, she went to Simyonov's office to report for duty but was told the colonel was out and to come back later. Instead they sent her to Personnel, then to Registry, then to Records.

She walked around a corner in the hallway and came upon Simyonov himself, talking to a white-haired man in a dark gray suit. She noticed the man's bushy white eyebrows and kindly smile. His liquid brown eyes narrowed as Simyonov made a brief introduction: General Korchnoi, chief of the Americas Department, Corporal Egorova. She vaguely knew the name, was aware of his seniority. Compared to the pale aura around Simyonov's head, Korchnoi was bathed in a flaming mantle of color, as bright as Dominika had seen in anyone. Purple velvet, deep and rich.

"The corporal just returned from the course at Kazan," said Simyonov with a smirk. Everyone in the Service knew what that meant. Dominika felt the blood rush to her cheeks. "And she is *assisting* in the approach to the diplomat, the case I was telling you about, General."

"More than just assist," said Dominika, looking at Simyonov, then at Korchnoi. "I graduated from the Forest in the last class." She ignored Sparrow School, cursing Simyonov under her breath. She knew what Simyonov was doing, but she sensed nothing from the older man. Hard to read.

"I heard about your record at the Academy, Corporal," said the general enigmatically. "I am glad to meet you." Korchnoi shook her hand with a dry, firm grasp. Simyonov looked on, smiling, thinking this would be the first of many senior officers who would try to dive down the front of her blouse. She'd be working in the front office of some general (and on his leather couch) within six months. Surprised and flattered, Dominika shook his hand, thanked the general, and continued down the corridor. The men's eyes followed her.

"More steam than a *banya* in Yakutsk," whispered Simyonov when Dominika had walked around the corner. "You know she's the niece of the deputy?"

Korchnoi nodded.

"Niece or not, she's going to be a pain in the ass," muttered Simyonov. Korchnoi said nothing. "She wants to be an operator. But look at her, she's built to be a *vorobey*. That's why Egorov sent her to Kazan."

"And the Frenchman?" asked Korchnoi.

Another snort. "*Polovaya zapadnya*. A straight honey trap. A matter of weeks. He's a commercial type, we squeeze him dry, and it's done." He nodded his head down the hallway. "She wants to read the file, to get involved. The only thing she's going to get involved in is what's between the Frenchman's legs."

Korchnoi smiled. "Good luck, Colonel," he said, shaking hands.

"Thank you, General," said Simyonov.

They had pointed her to a corner of the French Section of the Fifth Department. She had stared at the windowless angle of the walls as they met at the corner of the chipped desk, which was bare save for a cracked wooden in-tray. Two fat file folders were thrown rudely on her desk. Simyonov had finally released them to her to get her off his back. The dull blue covers with black diagonal stripes were dog-eared, spines fuzzy from sweaty hands. *Osobaya papka.* Her first operational file. She opened the cover and drank in the words, the colors.

The target was Simon Delon, forty-eight, first secretary in the Commercial Section of the Embassy of France in Moscow. Delon was married but his wife remained in Paris. He traveled infrequently to France for conjugal visits. As a geographical bachelor in Moscow, Delon had been noticed by the FSB almost immediately. They assigned a single watcher at first, but as time passed and interest in him peaked, he was covered in FSB ticks. They spent a lot of time with their *krolik,* their rabbit. A twelve-man team took him to work and put him to bed. Photos spilled out of an envelope stuck between the pages of the file. Delon walking alone along the river, alone watching the skaters at the Dynamo rink, alone eating at a restaurant table.

Dominika smoothed the creased blue surveillance flimsies. They had used the mirror to watch a long-legged hooker slide her hand up Delon's leg in a little escort bar off Krymskiy Val Ulitsa. *Subject uncomfortable, nervous, refused (unable?) to pick up hooker,* read the entry. Poor devil, he didn't belong there, thought Dominika.

Technical annex: An audio implant in a living-room electrical outlet produced hours of tape: *2036:29, Sounds of dish in the sink. 2212:34, music softly played. 2301:47, retired for night.*

They had spiked his phone from the central exchange to cover the weekly call to his wife in Paris. Dominika read the transcripts in French. Madame Delon was imperious and dismissive on one end, Delon small and silent on the other. *A sexless, joyless marriage with an impatient woman,* an unknown transcriber had written in the margin.

Sometime during the assessment process, the

SVR had elbowed its way in and declared primacy over the FSB—it was a foreign case, not domestic. The second volume of the file began with an operational assessment, written in the abbreviated style of the semiliterate Soviet, the kind of writing they had mocked at the Academy. *Subject potential for operational exploitation excellent. No identifiable vices. Sexually unfulfilled. Access to restricted information good. Assessed to be retiring and unaggressive. Susceptible to blackmail given lucrative marriage.* And so on.

Dominika sat back and looked at the pages and thought about her Academy training. It was clear that this was a small case, with a small target, and with a small payout. Delon might be a lonely little man, vulnerable perhaps, but his access in his embassy was low-level. The Fifth didn't have anything better than this, this *navoz,* this manure? Simyonov was building this up, inflating the case, it was clear. She had gone through the Academy, had endured whore school, only to find herself now among a different kind of prostitute? Was the entire Service like this?

She took the elevator to the cafeteria, took an apple, and went out onto the terrace in the sunshine. She sat away from the bench seats, on a low wall along a hedge, flicked off her shoes, closed her eyes, and felt the warmth of the bricks on her feet.

"May I join you?" said a voice, startling her. She opened her eyes and saw the tidy figure of General Korchnoi of the Americas Department standing before her. His suit coat was buttoned and he stood with his feet together, as if he were a maître d'. The sunlight made his purple halo deeper in color, almost with a discernible texture. Dominika jerked upright, fumbling with her flats, trying to get them back on. "Leave your shoes off, Corporal," Korchnoi said with a laugh. "I wish I could take mine off and find a fish pond in which to dangle them."

Dominika laughed. "Why don't you? It feels wonderful." Korchnoi looked at the blue eyes and the chestnut hair and the guileless face. What sort of provisional officer would make that outrageous suggestion to a general-grade officer? What kind of junior graduate would have the nerve? Then the head of the SVR Directorate responsible for all offensive intelligence operations in the Northern Hemisphere leaned down and pulled off his shoes and socks. They sat in the sun together.

"How is your work, Corporal?" asked Korchnoi, looking at the trees around the terrace.

"It is my first week. I have a desk and an in-box, and I'm reading the file."

"Your first case file. How do you like it?"

"It's interesting," Dominika said, thinking about the general shabbiness of the file, the dubious conclusions, the spurious recommendations.

"You don't sound entirely enthusiastic," said Korchnoi.

"Oh, no, I am," said Dominika.

"But . . . ?" said Korchnoi, turning toward her slightly. The sunlight cast a spidery shadow on his bushy eyebrows.

"I think I need time to become familiar with operational files," said Dominika.

"Meaning what?" said Korchnoi. His manner was gentle, reassuring. Dominika felt comfortable speaking to him.

"After I read the file, I did not agree with the conclusion. I don't see how they arrived at it."

"What part don't you agree with?"

"They are looking at a low-level target," she said, consciously not giving too many details, mindful of security. "He is lonely, vulnerable, but I don't think he is worth the effort. At the Forest they spoke often about squandering operational resources, about not chasing unprofitable targets."

"There was a time," said Korchnoi, testing her, "when women were excluded from the Academy. There was a time when it would have been unthinkable for a junior officer to read into an ongoing operation, much less comment on it." He looked up at the midday sun and squinted. Royal purple.

"I'm sorry, General," Dominika said mildly. She knew, was certain, that he was not angry. "It was not my intention to criticize, or to speak inappropriately." She looked at him squinting up at the sun, quiet, waiting. She had an instinct to speak her mind to this man. "Forgive me, General, I meant only to comment that I think the case is weak. I cannot see how they arrived at the operational conclusions. I know I have scant experience, but anyone could see this."

Korchnoi turned to look at Dominika—she was serene and confident. He chuckled. "You are supposed to read with a critical eye. And those idiots at the Academy are right. We have to be more efficient. The old days are over. We have difficulty forgetting that."

"I did not mean to be disrespectful," said Dominika. "I want to do a good job."

"And you are right." Korchnoi smiled. "Marshal your facts, order your arguments, and speak up. There will be disapproval, but keep on. I wish you luck." He rose from the wall, holding his shoes and socks. "By the way, Corporal, what is the name of the target?" He saw her hesitate. "Just curious." Dominika in a flash knew this was not the time to be a novice. If he didn't already know the name, he could find out in ten seconds.

"Delon," she said. "French Embassy."

"Thank you." And he turned, still holding his shoes and socks, and walked away down the path.

She expected nothing less, but the difficulties began during the daily planning sessions. Holding the two-volume file in her arms, Dominika entered the conference room and sat at the end of a faded table with three officers, all draped in browns and grays, from the Fifth Department (responsible for France, Benelux, Southern Europe, and Romania). She sensed the lack of energy in the room. There was no emotional output from these men, no imagination, no passion.

An enormous map of Eurasia covered an entire wall, several telephones were on a dusty credenza at the end of the room. The men stopped talking when she entered. Rumors were already circulating about the beautiful Sparrow School graduate. Dominika returned their stares, barely registering the hard faces, the question-mark smirks. Browns, grays, dingy colors from dingy minds. Cigarette butts filled the cheap aluminum ashtrays in the center of the table.

"Are there any preliminary comments?" asked Simyonov at the far end of the table. He was as expressionless and uninterested as he had been when Dominika first met him. He looked at the three faces around the table. No one spoke. He turned toward Dominika, daring her to speak. She took a breath.

"With the colonel's permission, I would like to discuss the target's access," Dominika said. She could hear her heartbeat.

"We have assessed his access," said Simyonov. His tone implied that Dominika was not to concern herself with the intricacies of the operation. "He is a worthwhile target. What is left now is to determine an approach," he said, looking at the officer seated beside him.

"I'm afraid that's not entirely correct," said Dominika. Heads came up to look at her. What was this? An attitude? From an Academy graduate? From a Sparrow? Eyes swiveled toward Simyonov for his reaction. This was going to be good.

Simyonov slouched over the table, hands in front of him. Today he radiated a faint yellow glow. This man was not going to stand for any contradictions. His eyes were red and watery, his gray hair lay slack on his head.

"You are here, comrade," he said, "to assist in the *approach* to the Frenchman. Matters of access, handling, and production will be the responsibility of the officers of this department." He leaned a little farther forward and stared at Dominika. Heads swiveled back in her direction. Surely that would be the end of the discussion.

Dominika kept her hands clasped firmly on the file folders in front of her to keep them from trembling. "I'm sorry to contradict you, *comrade,*" said Dominika, echoing his word, an anachronism. "But I was assigned to participate in this operation as an operations officer. I look forward to being included in all phases of the case."

"An operations officer, you say?" said Simyonov. "A graduate of the Forest?"

"Yes," said Dominika.

"When did you graduate?" he asked.

"The most recent class," said Dominika.

"And since then?" Simyonov looked around the table expectantly.

"Specialized training."

"What sort of specialized training?" asked Simyonov quietly.

She had prepared for this. Simyonov knew very well where she had been. He was trying to humiliate her. "I audited the basic course at the Kon Institute," said Dominika, her lips tight against her teeth. She was not going to back down to these *lichinki,* these maggots. She cursed Uncle Vanya in the same breath.

"Ah, yes, Sparrow School," said Simyonov. "And that, precisely, is why you are here. To *participate* in the entrapment of the target, Delon." One of the men at the table nearly, but not quite, stifled a smirk.

"I'm sorry, Colonel," said Dominika, "I was assigned to this department as a full member of the team."

"I see," he said. "Have you read Delon's *delo*?"

"Both volumes," said Dominika.

"Admirable," he said. "What preliminary observations do you have about the case and its merits?" Smoke drifted to the ceiling as the room fell silent. Dominika looked at the faces appraising her.

She swallowed. "The issue of his access is critical. The target, Delon, in his capacity as a midlevel commercial officer, does not have access to classified material sufficient to justify a politically delicate *chernota*."

"And what do you know of blackmail?" Simyonov said evenly, slightly amused. "Just out of the Academy and all?"

"Delon himself is not worth the effort," repeated Dominika.

"There are a number of analysts in Line R who would disagree with you," said Simyonov, his tone hardening. "Delon has access to French and EU commercial data. Budget figures. Programs. Investment strategies, energy policies. You would throw this information away?"

Dominika shook her head. "Delon knows nothing that one of our low-grade assets in any of a half dozen French commercial or trade ministries in Paris could not provide directly. Surely that avenue would be a more efficient way to service general requirements?"

Simyonov, face hardening, sat back in his chair. "You apparently learned quite a lot at the Academy.

So, you would propose that the department not validate the operation? That we disengage and do nothing against the target, Delon?"

"I say only that the potential risk of compromising a Western diplomat in Moscow is not justified by his low potential as a source."

"Go back and read the file again, Corporal," said Simyonov. "And come back when you have something constructive to add." They all stared at Dominika as she rose from the table, collected the file, and walked the long length of the room to the door. She kept her back straight and focused on the door handle. She closed the door to muffled murmurs and chuckles.

The next morning Dominika arrived at her empty desk to find a plain white envelope in her spavined in-box. She carefully slit it open with a thumbnail and unfolded the single sheet of paper. Written in purple ink in a classic script was a single line:

Delon has a daughter. Follow your instincts. K.

The next day they were back around the table piled high with photographs and surveillance reports. The ashtrays were overflowing. Dominika walked to her place at the end of the conference table. The men ignored her. They were reviewing Delon's profile, a smoke-polluted exercise conducted with disinterest and one eye on the wall clock. There were no primary colors from any of them. They walked through his habits and patterns, as described by the teams, arguing about places where they could engineer contact. Bored as usual, Simyonov looked up at Dominika. "Well, Corporal, do you have any ideas about contact points? Assuming you have reconsidered your earlier objections to the operation."

Dominika kept her voice steady. "I have reread the file, Colonel," she said, "and I still believe this man is not a valid target." Heads around the table did not come up this time; the men kept their eyes on the papers in front of them. This *vorobey* was not long for the Fifth, they thought, possibly not long for the Service.

"Still you take this line? How interesting," said Simyonov. "So we drop him, is that your recommendation?"

"I said no such thing," said Dominika. "I believe we should indeed pursue him as a target, exploiting his lonely solitude." She flipped open the cover of the file in front of her. "But the ultimate target, the end goal of the operation, should not be Delon himself."

"What nonsense are you talking?" said Simyonov.

"It's already in the file. I completed a bit of extra research," said Dominika.

Simyonov looked around the table, then back at Dominika. "The case has been thoroughly researched already—"

"And discovered that Monsieur Delon has a daughter," interrupted Dominika.

"And a wife in Paris, yes, we know all that!"

"And the daughter works in the French Ministry of Defense."

"Unlikely," fumed Simyonov. "The entire family was traced. The Paris *rezidentura* checked all local records."

"Then it appears they missed something. She is twenty-five years old, unmarried, lives with her mother. Her name is Cécile," said Dominika.

"This is preposterous," said Simyonov.

"She was mentioned only once in the transcripts. I checked the foreign directories in Line R's library," said Dominika, flipping more pages in the file. "Cécile Denise Delon is listed in the Rue Saint-Dominique registry. That means the central registry at the Defense Ministry." Dominika looked around the table at the faces staring at her. "That suggests, as far as I could determine, that she has access to classified defense bulletins distributed daily to the government. She is one of the custodians of planning documents for the French military. She likely handles the dissemination and storage of a wide variety of French military budget, readiness, and manpower reports."

"Conjecture, at this point," said Simyonov.

"We don't know where the French store their nuclear secrets, but I wouldn't be surprised—"

"There's no need for idle speculation," said Simyonov. The yellow fog around his head was growing, and getting darker too. Dominika knew that he was frustrated, angry, calculating, and she knew that her defiance and insubordination were already more than enough to have her cashiered from the Service.

The room was deathly still. Simyonov's antediluvian Soviet instincts were alerted; the bureaucrat in him calculated. His thoughts in an instant proceeded in the nature of the traditional KGB functionary: *This little* tsarevna *with the big last name is making me look lacking and stupid. How can I profit in the end from her work? If this* maneken *is correct, the rewards could be huge, but so are the risks. An operation targeting the French Ministry of Defense would need to be approved all the way to the top.*

"If this is true," he said stingily, "there *could* be an added benefit." He spoke as if he had known all along. He flicked ash into the ashtray.

She could read his oily, humid mind. "I agree with you, Colonel. It's Delon's real potential, it's what makes him worth pursuing, what makes it worth the risk to recruit him."

Simyonov shook his head. "The daughter is in Paris, twenty-five hundred kilometers away."

"Not so far, I think," said Dominika, smiling. "We will see." Simyonov was unsettled by that smile. "Of course, we'll have to develop a more detailed profile about the relationship between father and daughter."

"Of course, thank you, Corporal," Simyonov said. A few more minutes of this and she would be taking over the Fifth Department. All right, he thought, she could do the preparatory work, as much as she liked. As the operation proceeded he'd ensure she'd be on her back with her legs in the air with the cameras rolling, and that would take care of that.

"Very well, Corporal, since you uncovered this interesting detail, I want you to draw up your own thoughts about contact with the target Delon," he said to Dominika.

"With your permission, Colonel, I have already drawn up a plan to engineer first contact," said Dominika.

"I see . . ."

The Fifth Department officers pushed back in their chairs and crushed their unfinished cigarettes in the ashtrays. Jesus, the gossip about this Sparrow had been limited to blue eyes, how she filled out her regulation skirt, the size of her chest. No one had mentioned anything about her *yaitsa,* her set of balls. They filed out of the room, leaving Dominika to gather the paper scattered around the table, the new girl left behind to clean up the room. She didn't mind. She stacked the papers, piled them on top of the dog-eared folders of Delon's file, and walked out of the conference room, closing the door behind her.

In the Arbat, at number 12 Nikitsky Bulvar, there is a small restaurant called Jean Jacques. It is something like a French brasserie, noisy, smoky, filled with the winey aroma of cassoulets and stews. Tables covered with white tablecloths are jammed nearly edge to edge on a black-and-white tile floor, bentwood chairs tucked in tight. The walls are covered in wine bottles on shelves to the ceiling, the curving bar is lined with stools. Jean Jacques is always crowded with Muscovites. At lunchtime, if one is alone one shares a table with a stranger.

Midday on a rainy Tuesday, Jean Jacques was even more busy than usual. Customers stood inside the front door or under the canopy outside, waiting for single seats to come free. The din was overwhelming, cigarette smoke hung heavy. Waiters scurried between tables, opening bottles and carrying trays. After a fifteen-minute wait, Simon Delon of the French Embassy in Moscow was shown to a two-cover in the corner of the room. A young man sat in the other seat, finishing a deep bowl of Dijonnaise stew thick with vegetables and chunks of meat. He dipped black bread into the gravy. As Delon sat at the table, the young man barely looked up in acknowledgment.

Despite the crowds and the noise, Delon liked the restaurant, it reminded him of Paris. Better still, the Russian lunchtime practice of seating strangers together occasionally provided an opportunity to be seated beside a cute university student or an attractive shopgirl. Sometimes they even smiled at him, as if they were together. At least it would look that way from across the room.

Delon ordered a glass of wine while he looked at the menu. The young man sitting across from him paid his check, wiped his mouth, and reached for his jacket on the back of his chair. Delon looked up to see a stunning dark-haired woman with ice-blue eyes walk toward his table. He held his breath. The woman actually sat down in the seat just vacated by the young man. She wore her hair up, there was a single strand of pearls beneath her collar. Under a light raincoat she was wearing a beige satin shirt over a darker chocolate-colored skirt, with a brown alligator belt. Delon took a ragged pull of his wine as he peeked and saw how the shirt moved over the woman's body.

She took a small pair of square reading glasses out of an alligator clutch; they perched on the end of her nose as she looked at her menu. She sensed him looking at her and she raised her eyes. He dove back behind his menu in a panic. Another peek, he took in the elegant fingers holding the menu, the curve of her neck, the eyelashes over those X-ray eyes. She looked at him again.

"*Izvinite,* excuse me, is there something wrong?" said Dominika in Russian. Delon shook himself and gulped self-consciously. He looked to be in his fifties, with strawlike brown hair combed across a big head balanced on a skinny neck perched on narrow, rounded shoulders. Small black eyes, a pointy nose, and pursed mouth topped with a little mustache completed the whiskered-mouse effect. One point of his collar slightly stuck out of his blue-black suit, and the knot of his tie was small and uneven. Dominika resisted the impulse to tuck in his collar and straighten his tie. She knew his birth date, what kind of aspirin was in the cabinet above his bathroom sink, the color of the bedspread on his lonely bed. Well, she thought, he certainly looked like a commercial attaché.

Delon could barely look her in the eye. Dominika sensed the effort he made to speak to her. When he finally did, the words were the palest of blue, not unlike the cornflower blue that had defined Anya at Sparrow School. He took a breath and Dominika waited. She already knew her assessment of him was correct, that her plans for him were beginning.

"I beg your pardon," said Delon. "I'm sorry, I do not speak Russian. Do you speak English?"

"Yes, of course," said Dominika in English.

"*Et français?*" asked Delon.

"*Oui,*" said Dominika.

"How wonderful. I did not mean to stare," he stammered in French. "I was just thinking how fortunate you were to be seated. Have you been waiting long?"

"Not too long," said Dominika, looking around the restaurant and at the front door. "In any case, it looks like the crowd is less."

"Well, I'm glad you got a seat," said Delon, running out of things to say.

Dominika nodded and looked back down at the menu. Fortune had nothing to do with Dominika getting that particular seat in the corner of the room. Every customer that day in Jean Jacques was an SVR officer.

A second chance encounter at Jean Jacques provided the excuse to introduce herself in alias "Nadia" to the owlish little diplomat. Another bump on the sidewalk outside the brasserie days later somehow gave him nerve enough to suggest that they lunch together. After that they tried another restaurant for lunch. Delon was excruciatingly shy, with courtly good manners. He drank in moderation, spoke haltingly about himself, and furtively mopped at his glistening forehead as he watched Dominika absentmindedly brush a strand of hair behind her ear. Over the space of these contacts, Delon's reticence began fading, while his azure aura was strengthening. It was what she was looking for.

Delon had accepted without suspicion the legend that Nadia was a language teacher at Liden & Denz in Gruzinsky Street. He studiously did not react when she spoke of an estranged husband, a geologist, working out east in another time zone, and he feigned polite disinterest when Dominika vaguely mentioned her small apartment whose only redeeming feature was that she did not share it with anyone. Privately, Delon's thoughts raced.

Simyonov wanted to move fast, he wanted

Dominika to lure the little man into bed and drop the house on him. Dominika resisted, stalled, pushed back to the limits of insubordination. She knew Simyonov intended to use her as a Sparrow, that his vision in the recruitment attempt stopped at a sex-entrapment operation, that he had no appreciation of the promise in the case. She argued forcefully for a period of careful development of Delon, doubly important because of his daughter's potential as a stupendous source. He would need to be brought along gently. Simyonov controlled his temper as this curvy Academy graduate lectured him, reported progress, and proposed next steps.

It was a classic *razrabotka,* developmental, over the following weeks. Dominika took Delon through the stages of casual acquaintance to comfortable friendship, watching how he relaxed with her, grew cautiously more familiar, how he hid his growing longing for her. She anticipated his desires, prompted him, hinted how she was becoming fond of him. He could scarcely believe it. The Frenchman was besotted with her, but Dominika knew he was too timid, too fearful to ever push himself at her. There could be no recruitment of him if he felt deceived or compromised, she decided. The recruitment would come based only on friendship, on Delon's growing infatuation, on his eventual inability to refuse her anything.

They met once a week, then twice a week, then began meeting on the weekends for walks around town, visits to museums. By mutual inclination they were discreet. They both were married, after all. They talked about his family, a carefree childhood in Brittany, his parents. Dominika had to be soft. Delon was a turtle who would jerk his head back under his shell if startled.

In time, Delon spoke haltingly about a loveless marriage. His wife was several years older than he, tall and patrician, she ran things her way. Her family had money, lots of it, and they had married after a brief courtship. Delon told Dominika that his wife had resolved to make something out of him, grand ideas of position and title, abetted by her family's influence. When his reticence and mildness revealed themselves, his wife had turned her back on the marriage. She preserved appearances, of course, but she did not mind the separation required by his diplomatic assignment. His standing in the Foreign Service depended on her.

Delon adored Cécile, their only child. A photo of her revealed a slight, dark-haired young woman with a willowy smile. She was a lot like Delon, shy and tentative and reserved. With growing familiarity and trust, he finally revealed to Dominika that his daughter worked at the Defense Ministry. He of course was immensely proud of her young career, which had been arranged by his wife and influential father-in-law. Delon spoke with good humor about his hopes for his daughter. A good marriage, a strong career, a comfortable life. That he was willing to talk about Cécile was an important milestone in the development.

Over the rim of a demitasse at a café, Dominika one afternoon asked Delon whether he worried about the future, worried that his wife would leave him, worried that his daughter would meet the wrong man and be trapped in a melancholy life like his own. Delon looked at Dominika—the object of his growing affection—and for the first time should have felt the silken touch of the SVR glove brush against his cheek. A danger signal. But he ignored the frisson, distracted by her blue eyes and tumbled hair and, he was scandalized to admit to himself, the horizontal stripes of the jersey that traced the curve of her breasts. Still they continued their chaste friendship.

Outings ended with awkward good-byes, red-faced handshakes, and, once, a hurried, perfumed kiss on the cheek that made his head swim.

"What are you waiting for?" raved Simyonov. "We're here to trap this *robkij francuz*, this timorous Frenchie, not to write his biography."

"This is no time to be stupid," Dominika said to Simyonov, knowing she was committing a grave offense of discipline. "Let me run this and I will have the Frenchman *and his daughter* recruited," she pleaded.

Simyonov seethed, the pulsing yellow fog around him paled, then strengthened, then paled again. He was dissembling, planning treachery, she was sure. She continued crowding him, with her argument but physically as well, standing right up to him. The ensnarement of Delon was nearly complete. He was ready for the hook, she was sure of it. He wanted to start spying for her, he just didn't know it yet. She remembered a phrase from her old pensioner instructors during the ops course.

"Don't worry, comrade," Dominika said. "This *svekla*, this beet, is almost cooked." She felt like a veteran repeating it.

"Look," said Simyonov, pointing his finger at her, "forget the old bullshit jokes and wrap this target up. Stop wasting time." But even as he scolded, he could sense the nuances Dominika was building into this operation, refinements that he knew were beyond him and were in consequence not at all to his liking.

Dominika finally invited Delon to her ostensible apartment in northern Moscow, near the Belarus train terminal and not far from the language school where she claimed to work. It was a small two-room flat with a sitting room, an attached kitchen with curtained lavatory, and a tiny bedroom. The carpet was threadbare, the wallpaper faded and bubbled with age. A battered teapot on a single-element propane stove was too old to whistle. It was small and dingy, but a Moscow apartment not shared with relatives or work colleagues was still an inexpressible luxury.

Another unappreciated—for Delon—aspect was that the walls, ceilings, and fixtures were peppered with lenses and microphones. The apartments on both sides, above, and below were likewise SVR-controlled units. The energy draw from this apartment block alone could have air-started a Tupolev Tu-95. Sometimes, late at night, you could hear the transformers humming in the basement.

"Simon, I need your help," Dominika said, opening the door to her apartment. A clutch of blue flowers in his hand and a bottle of wine under his arm, Delon immediately looked concerned. This was the third visit to Nadia's apartment, and previous visits had been limited to chastely listening to tapes, drinking wine, and conversation. Dominika put a little panic into her voice and shook her head. "I accepted a temporary job as an interpreter, French to Russian, for the ITFM trade fair next month. To make a little extra money. What was I thinking? I don't know any of the vocabulary for industry, energy, commerce—in either language, for that matter."

Delon smiled. Dominika noted that his blue aura glowed with confidence and affection. They sat down on the little divan in the tiny living room. He knew all about the fair, it was his job. At least six SVR technicians beyond the walls watched and recorded the scene. "Is that all?" said Delon. "In a month I can teach you all the French words you'll need." He patted her hand. "Don't worry." Dominika leaned toward him, took his face in her hands, and planted a big vaudeville kiss on his lips. She had calculated the time and the nature of the kiss carefully. Showy and girlish as the smooch may have been, it nevertheless was the first time Delon had felt Dominika's lips. "Don't worry," he repeated shakily. He could taste her lipstick. The blue words now were uniformly colored and darker. He had decided.

Dominika had always displayed an interest in his job, his duties as a diplomat, and Delon had grown accustomed to describing his work, pleased to have someone show an interest. Now he could do something for her, and the next evening Delon came to Nadia's apartment straight from the embassy carrying his briefcase, and produced a twenty-page report from the embassy's Commercial Section on investment challenges and opportunities in Russia. He read through it with her. The word *Confidentiel* was printed on the top and bottom of each page.

More sessions, more documents. When Delon could not bring out originals, or copy them, he would take adequate pictures of documents with his cell phone. They worked with his technical dictionaries in French and with hers in Russian. As befitting a language teacher, Dominika was mastering the vocabulary, and he could see with the pride of a tutor that she likewise was mastering the issues regarding international trade and energy. Delon set his jaw with conviction. He would teach her, train her, make her an expert. He loved her, he told himself.

To solve the problem of leaving embassy documents overnight so Dominika could study, Delon himself began making copies for her, a step not so important for the SVR in terms of document copy—the overhead cameras in the ceiling above the table could focus on a single comma—but as an act of commission, an irreversible step beyond the regulations of embassy security. Dominika knew he was hers now. For Delon, the fiction of "vocabulary study" faded into the fiction of "educating Nadia," which was morphing now into an overwhelming devotion to her, to do whatever she asked. This motivation was stronger than any agent salary she could have offered, stronger than any blackmail threats from a bedroom sting. If he realized he was dealing with Russian intelligence, he never acknowledged it.

Simyonov watched the progress and called another meeting, making a show and raving about moving forward, about bedding the diminutive Frenchman. "Go ahead, *you* take him to bed," said Dominika to Simyonov and the men around the table. "Which one of you wants to fuck him?" The room fell silent.

Dominika tried to be a little softer. "Look," she said. "The next step is supremely delicate." She had to move Delon first to agree to contact his daughter, then gently to ask her to provide defense secrets. It was like pulling strings to control one puppet that in turn was attached to another puppet. Once his daughter had crossed the line, Delon had to ensure her continued participation. "Once the French defense documents start flowing, the case will be made," said Dominika.

Simyonov listened sourly and was not convinced. The plan was too complicated. This *diletantka* was insubordinate. But he resolved to wait a while longer. He was confirmed in his plans after another hallway conversation with General Korchnoi. The veteran senior spy said he absolutely agreed with the need to move forward with the recruitment pitch, and commiserated with Simyonov when he heard about Dominika's headstrong attitudes. "These young officers," said Korchnoi. "Tell me more about her."

Ironically, it was the timorous Delon who forced the timeline. Sitting next to Dominika on the couch one evening, reviewing another midlevel commercial document, Delon had impulsively reached out and taken her hands in his. He then had leaned toward her and kissed her tenderly. Perhaps the intimacy of working together finally overcame him, perhaps an instinct about being dragged slowly into the funnel web of espionage made him fatalistic. Whatever had awakened him, Dominika kissed him back tenderly while frantically calculating. They were at a critical juncture of the operation. Sleeping with him now, before she could bring the daughter into the plan, could jeopardize the transition. Conversely, it could cement her control over him. Dominika thought about the glistening jowls, the overhanging bellies of the men in the hot little room on the other side of the wall.

As if he had sensed her indecision, Delon's lips faltered, his eyes popped open. At the least likely moment he was going to stop. The halo around his head was blazing, incandescent. In that instant Dominika knew she must go forward, they would have to become lovers. She would carry him along, help him seduce her.

She registered a little regret at reaching this stage. He was so trusting and sweet—how unlike her romp with Ustinov. And now she had Sparrow training, prompts from which began popping uncontrollably into her brain.

Dominika put her hand behind his head and pressed their lips together more tightly (*No. 13, "Unambiguously signal sexual willingness"*) and took a trembling breath (*No. 4, "Build passionate response by evincing passion"*). He pulled away and looked at her with wide eyes. She caressed his cheek and then, staring into his eyes, placed his hand on her breast. He could feel her heart beating and she pressed his hand more hotly against her (*No. 55, "Display carnal abandon to authenticate physical arousal"*). She shuddered. Delon was still staring, his hand motionless. "Nadia," he whispered.

Eyes now closed, Dominika brushed her cheek against his and brought her mouth close to his ear (*No. 23, "Provide aural prompts to spur desire"*). "Simon, *baise-moi,*" she whispered, and they were up and staggering into the dim little bedroom (which was in truth illuminated brighter than Moscow's Dynamo soccer stadium but with invisible infrared light), and Dominika stepped out of her skirt, shrugged off her blouse, but kept her low-cut brassiere in place (*No. 27, "Employ incongruity of nudity and vestments to whiplash the senses"*), and watched Delon hopping ridiculously out of his trousers while she trailed her hands down her thighs (*No. 51, "Autostimulate to generate pheromones"*).

He was like a mating turtledove in bed, fluttering, feathery, weightless as he lay on her body. He nuzzled gently between her breasts; she hardly felt him, but she arched her back, threw out her legs (*No. 49, "Generate dynamic tension in the extremities to hasten nerve response"*) and focused for an instant on the aperture in the light fixture on the ceiling, but his head was lifting from between her breasts to look at her again, and she met his eyes and he sighed and fluttered more energetically on top of her. Dominika closed her eyes (*No. 46, "Block distractions which derail responsiveness"*) and called his name again and again and felt a building tremor run through his body, and she helped him (*No. 9, "Develop the pubococcygeus muscle"*), and he whimpered, "*Nadia, je t'aime.*"

She ran her fingers along his neck and whispered, "*Lyubov' moja,*" my love, and knew what was happening when the door to the bedroom exploded inward and the orange-tinted bulb (better contrast for the digital cameras) in the overhead fixture flooded the room with light and three men in suits crowded into the room. Their shirt collars were wet and their eyes shone like pig eyes in a truffle forest. They had been watching from next door, and the smells of their sweat and day-old shirts and week-old socks filled the room.

The minute the door opened, Dominika sat up in bed and clasped the terrified, shrinking Delon to her like a favorite doll and started screaming in Russian for them to get out. She knew Simyonov was blowing her careful recruitment to smithereens. He could not wait, he had to proceed according to his artless script. It was a blow against her. She was paying for her glib performances around the conference table, her disrespectful interruptions. She remembered trying to talk like one of the old boys: "This beet is almost cooked," she had said. Well, the old boys were showing her who ran things.

They tore Delon from her, dragged him off the bed, and marched him naked to the living room. They pushed him on the couch and threw him his crumpled trousers. He looked up at the hulking men without comprehension. Dominika continued swearing at them from the bed as she gathered up a sheet to cover herself and get to her feet. She was nearly blind with rage and her body, throat, head felt tight, and her ears were filled with a rushing sound.

She was determined to drive them out of the room and retrieve the situation. Before she could stand, the third man grabbed her by the wrist and pulled her off the bed and into the living room. When Delon saw her being manhandled he made to rise, but the other two men pushed him back down. The man spun Dominika to face him and slapped her across the cheek. "*Shalava, suka!*" he spat, and threw her to the floor. Staged scenario or not, Dominika looked up at the bastard who had called her a slut and a whore, and measured the distance to his eyes.

Dominika got to her feet and let the sheet fall to the floor. Every eye in the room was transfixed by her body, chest heaving, legs braced. Her foot flashed out in a feint, and the SVR man bent forward to protect himself. Dominika quickly reached out and dug the nails of her thumb and forefinger into the septum between his nostrils, pinched hard, and pulled him toward her, a torture-cell NKVD come-along from the 1930s. Dominika pulled the howling and unresisting thug's head sharply downward against the little table in the room—littered with French Embassy commercial documents—the corner of which caught him on the cheek, knocking the table and the papers over and dropping the man into a heap on the floor. He didn't move. From the couch Delon looked at her in disbelief.

The entire sequence had taken less than ten seconds. One of the other SVR men grabbed Dominika and hustled her out of the apartment, frog-marched her down the hall, and shoved her into another room. "Take your hands off me," she said as the door slammed shut in her face. The man was gone. A voice came from the back of the room.

"An effective performance, Corporal, a strong finish to a discreet intelligence operation." Dominika turned to see Simyonov sitting on a couch in front of two monitors. One screen showed the apartment, a man bending over the insensate lump on the floor, while the other man stood over Delon, who was still holding his trousers in his hands, his face looking up at him, upturned as if in prayer. The other screen replayed Dominika and Delon in bed. With the sound muted, their lovemaking looked clinical, staged. She ignored it.

Dominika clutched the sheet around her with one hand while fingering her throbbing cheek with the other. "*Zhopa!* Asshole! We would have gotten it all," she screamed. Simyonov did not respond. His eyes darted from one monitor to the other. "He would have recruited his own daughter for me," she raved. Simyonov did not turn to look at her but muttered, "He will do so at any rate." He pointed a remote and the sound came from the live monitor. The two SVR men were now screaming at Delon, who sat motionless on the couch. Dominika took another barefoot step into the room toward Simyonov, seriously contemplating driving a thumbnail into his eye. "Don't you know he will not succumb to blackmail? He is not brave enough. Do you really think . . . ?"

Simyonov turned to her as he lit a cigarette. His eyes blazed yellow. "If it doesn't work, we can log it into your copy book as a failure, then," he said. "It's not your decision and it never was," he said, smiling at her. "And this Service is not your private preserve." He turned to the silent monitor. Dominika dully watched herself wrap her legs around Delon's waist.

"What is the purpose of replaying the bedroom film, comrade?" she said to Simyonov. He did not reply but blew cigarette smoke at the ceiling.

"Given the fact that Serov struck you, I will not initiate charges against you for what you did to him." He pointed at the other monitor and at Serov, still unconscious on the floor. "You have quite a temper, don't you, *Vorobey*? It should be an asset to you in your budding career." He smiled again and nodded at the door to an adjoining room.

"There is a change of clothing in there if you want to get dressed, Corporal. That is, unless you choose to remain naked all night." Dominika went into the little room and quickly threw on a formless smock and plastic belt, a pair of black tied shoes. The approved look for the last fifty years for the Modern Soviet Woman.

Dominika never saw Delon again. The story came out in segments. An SVR informant working in the clerical pool of the French Embassy reported that Delon requested an appointment with the ambassador the next morning. Delon confessed to an "unreported, intimate relationship with a Russian woman." The little man had shown quite a lot of courage as he described the number and nature of the commercial documents that he had shared, copied, or otherwise compromised. The DGSE chief in Moscow cabled his headquarters in Paris, as well as the Counterintelligence Division of the DST. There had been knowing shakes of the head. A beautiful woman, *que faire?* What could you do?

The Germans would have found him *shuldhaft*, culpable, and given him three years. The Americans would have pegged the poor sap a victim of sexpionage and sentenced him to eight years. In Russia the *predatel'*, the traitor, would have been liquidated. French investigators handed down a stern finding of *négligent*. Delon was transferred home quickly—out of reach—and consigned to duties without access to classified information for eighteen months. He was near his daughter and back in Paris. His ultimate penance was living again in his wife's elegant, lofty house in the Sixteenth with only the memories—in the sleepless early mornings—of a dingy little Moscow apartment and a pair of cobalt-blue eyes.

JEAN JACQUES BEEF STEW DIJONNAISE

Season and dust with flour small cubes of beef and brown aggressively. Remove meat. Sauté chopped bacon, diced onion, tomatoes, carrots, potatoes, and thyme until soft. Return meat to pan, cover with beef broth, and simmer until meat is tender. Blend in Dijon mustard, splash of heavy cream; reheat and serve.

10

Vanya Egorov was chain-smoking Gitanes sent to him via SVR couriers by the *rezident* in Paris. His eyes were tired and it felt as if there were a steel band around his chest. On his red leather blotter lay another FSB surveillance report, the third in as many months. An American diplomat—suspect CIA—had been followed during a twelve-hour SDR two nights ago. There had been multiple teams on the young American, and the number of surveillants deployed had grown through the late afternoon and into the night when it seemed increasingly likely that the Yankee was operational and was headed for a meeting with an asset. The teams had grown excited when it appeared that the young American fool had not detected coverage. That was very rare.

The final number of surveillants topped out at one hundred twenty, the FSB report baldly boasted. Driving snow flurries during the day had grounded spotter aircraft, but ground units followed in multiple layers, switching the eye frequently. Foot assets were salted ahead of the American along likely routes, teams paralleled on the flanks. There had been at least one FSB static surveillant in sixty of Moscow Metro's one hundred eighty stations, in case the American changed course suddenly. Egorov flipped the last pages of the report impatiently. FSB *dolboyoby,* those fuckheads.

The American entered Sokolniki Park in northeast Moscow at dusk, walked through the decrepit amusement park, dark and frozen, past the rusted Ferris wheel, and entered the labyrinth of lanes and alleys lined with black, bare trees. He stopped at an empty ornamental fountain and sat on the cement rim in the cold, stupidly contemplating the barren flower beds. Encrypted radio traffic spiked. This was it. A meeting. Keep the night-vision goggles on the Yank, but fan out and lock on to anyone in the vicinity, anyone. A solitary pedestrian, furtive, nervous, moving in the direction of the fountain.

Reading the report, Egorov could imagine FSB men darting from tree to tree, NVGs strapped to their heads, a forest full of green, bug-eyed aliens. A tracking dog was brought up to look for buried drops. The keyed-up Alsatian was used to follow Americans, trained to focus specifically on the scent generated by Dial soap and Sure deodorant—the scent of America.

And they waited. And the American waited. Well beyond the traditional four-minute window. Ten, twenty, thirty minutes. Nothing. The rest of the park was empty. The dog was run back along the American's foot route but did not alert on anything. No caches, ground spikes, devices, nothing. Radio cars on the outer edges of the park cruised slowly, recording one hundred license plates in the area that would be checked and cross-referenced. Nothing. The American then left the park and, again nontraditionally, proceeded directly home, with no effort to test for coverage. FSB radios went silent.

Egorov flipped the report into his out-box disgustedly. The FSB were congratulating themselves on a "perfect surveillance evolution," in that the rabbit had no idea he had been stoppered in the bottle. Big deal, thought Egorov, what had they accomplished?

Vanya Egorov did not know it, but the thrashing about of FSB coverage on the American case officer created enough of a stir that MARBLE, headed into Sokolniki Park to attempt a meeting with the American, instead decided to wait and watch from a covered bus stop on Malenkovskaya Ulitsa, several blocks from the entrance to the park. His exceptional street instincts were confirmed when he saw three surveillance radio cars pull abreast of each other a hundred meters from him. The surveillance team leaned against the fenders of their cars, smoked cigarettes, and not-so-furtively passed around a bottle. This was the classic surveillance error on the street, bunching and scuttling together like *tarakany.* Cockroaches.

Very well, another reprieve in the life I have chosen, thought MARBLE as he walked away from the neighborhood. How many more did he have left? He thought about what he would write in his burst transmission tonight, and how he had to urgently find a reason to travel abroad. He had to meet Nathaniel again.

The next morning Line KR Chief Zyuganov sent a classified *sluzhebnaya zapiska* to General Egorov, a memo designed to demonstrate Zyuganov's prescience and command of the situation.

> There could be a limited number of explanations for the American officer's activities. 1. This could have been an exercise to draw, then quantify, FSB surveillance capabilities, including collecting signals intelligence on FSB encrypted frequencies; 2. The American did detect coverage and aborted his meeting plans, leading surveillance into the park to misdirect; 3. The American was oblivious but his agent aborted the meeting for unknown reasons.
>
> This activity by the Americans seems poorly planned and clumsily executed and reflects our continued assessment of the CIA Station Chief Gondorf as a senior officer unsuited for dealing with the intricacies of his grade, the unhappy product of long-time patronage.

Who cares about that polyp? thought Egorov. *We have enough dim-witted, vain, pampered bunglers in our own Service.*

Vanya knew, was *certain,* that they had missed again, that the mole was still out there, sweating in his bed at night, betraying Russia, jeopardizing his—Vanya's—own political and personal future.

Then the day had been shattered by a midafternoon telephone call from the Kremlin, the smooth voice of the president hollow over the encrypted line. President Putin knew about the last night's surveillance in Sokolniki Park, recited back the various interpretations of what had happened. Vanya mentally filed away the fact that Zyuganov's *zapiska* had found its way to that office.

"A counterespionage success against the Americans would not be unwelcome now," the president had purred into the phone. "In a time of crisis for the Motherland, there is less time for *hozjajki,* these housewives, to bang pots and pans in protest." The line went silent but Vanya did not interrupt. He was familiar with the cadences of the president's speech. "We do not have the luxury of time," said Putin finally, and the line was disconnected.

Vanya stared into the phone receiver and replaced it on the instrument. *Sookin syn.* Son of a bitch. He pushed the key on his intercom. "Zyuganov, immediately." The mole was still out there, but if clandestine meetings in Moscow were not working, third-country meetings outside Russia were the key. And Nash was right next door in Finland. Nash. He pushed his intercom again. "Egorova. My niece. This instant."

In twenty minutes, Dominika was sitting in front of his desk. CI Chief Zyuganov, his feet not touching the floor, sat on the other side of her. All three buttons of the dwarf's shapeless black suit were buttoned and he gripped both arms of the chair. His perpetual bland little smile aggravated Vanya. His poisonous dwarf.

As usual, Dominika was a vision, dressed in a navy-blue wool skirt and jacket, her hair up in the regulation bun. She looked quickly at Alexei Zyuganov, and the black triangles behind his head. She was not so new in the Service as not to have heard about his handiwork in the torture cells of the Lubyanka during the waning years of the Soviet Union.

They were whispered stories, unbelievable, repeated only between close friends inside the Service. Zyuganov had been one of two chief Lubyanka executioners in the old days, young for the job but suited to it simply because he was immune to its horrors. It was said the dwarf had a fascination for his executed prisoners as they hung from the overhead beams, or lay on the tables or splayed on the sloping floor, heads down toward the drains. He would handle them, move them around—"ragdolling," they called it—would lean them up against the wall so he could talk to them while fussily arranging and rearranging their limbs. Dominika imagined the dirty smocks, the purple necks, the—

"It seems like we are always sitting here, you and I," said Vanya brightly. Dominika cleared her head of the cellars. She saw Vanya's yellow halo, bright and broad. This would be an interesting meeting. "It's good to see you again."

"Thank you," she said quietly. She braced herself.

"I am pleased to hear that General Korchnoi offered you a seat in the Americas Department."

Oh, get on with it, she thought. "When Colonel Simyonov released me from the Fifth, I had no office. I am grateful to the general for the opportunity," Dominika said.

"Korchnoi told me he was impressed with your work against the Frenchman," said Vanya.

"Despite the fact that the operation was unsuccessful," said Dominika.

"We all have our successes and failures," said Vanya, bathed in yellow, acting sweet.

Dominika's voice rose a little. "The operation against Delon would still be progressing if the Fifth Department had not acted prematurely. We could have developed a penetration of the French Defense Ministry."

"I read the file. There was promise. Why did we not?" interrupted Zyuganov mildly. Dominika willed her eyes not to grow large as she saw the parabolas of black unfold from behind Zyuganov's shoulders like bat wings. *Shaitan,* thought Dominika, *pure evil.*

"You'll have to ask the chief of the Fifth Department," said Dominika, not looking into Zyuganov's eyes, not wanting to see what lived behind them.

"Perhaps I shall," said Zyuganov.

"Enough. There's no value in recriminations. Corporal Egorova, it is not your place to question the decisions made by senior officers," said Vanya mildly.

Dominika kept her voice level as her eyes never left her uncle's. "This is why the Service is struggling to exist. This is why Russia cannot compete. Attitudes like this. Officers like Simyonov. They are *krovopiytsy,* attached to the belly, sucking blood, impossible to remove." There was silence in the room as they stared at each other. Zyuganov watched her face; his hands did not move on the arms of his chair.

"What am I to do with you, niece?" said Vanya finally, getting up from his desk and walking to stand in front of the picture window. "Your record is strong, you should not jeopardize the career ahead of you. The manner in which you have spoken to me already is enough for your separation from the Service. Do you wish to continue your complaints?" *And think about your mother,* thought Dominika.

"And think about your mother," said Vanya. "She needs your support."

"I am taking advantage of our relationship, I know," said Dominika. "But our work is too important to let it be done *starinnyj,* in the manner it has always been done." She turned to watch her uncle at the window and knew two things. Vanya did not care about any of this, he had another agenda that involved her, and she had some latitude in her comments. She also knew Zyuganov was drinking her words in, she could feel him radiating like a furnace. He was a creature that was not content unless he had prey. She did not look at him.

Looking out the window, Vanya shook his head. *Welcome to the modern SVR,* he thought—*improvements, reforms, public relations, and women in the Service.* Junior officers could criticize the old ways. "So you do not like the old ways?" said Vanya.

"I do not like to fail at an operation that could have succeeded, whatever the reason," said Dominika.

"And you believe you are ready to manage your own operation?" said Vanya softly.

"With guidance and advice from officers like you and General Korchnoi . . . and Colonel Zyuganov, of course," said Dominika. She forced herself to include the little cadaver-lover sitting beside her. He turned his head toward her, jug-handle ears extended, and nodded.

"Most would say you are too young, too inexperienced, but we shall see." Dominika noted the tone of Vanya's voice, the honeyed phrase before the knout. "The nature of the assignment I have in mind unfortunately will take you out of the Americas Department."

"What is the assignment?" she asked. She would scream if he told her she would have to seduce someone.

"It is a foreign assignment, to a *rezidentura,* to do real operational work. A recruitment operation." Vanya's own recollection of foreign operations was dim, but he spoke as if he relished it himself.

"A foreign assignment?" Dominika did not know what to say. She had never been out of Russia.

"To Scandinavia. I need someone new, fresh, with those instincts you have displayed," he said. *You mean with a man,* she thought bitterly. He saw her eyes and put up his hand. "I don't mean what you're thinking. I need you as an *operupolnomochenny,* an operations officer."

"That's what I want to be," said Dominika. "To be a member of the Service, to work for Russia."

Zyuganov spoke, his voice mild and oily, the words coal-black. "And so you shall. This is a delicate task which will require great skill. One of the most difficult tasks. You must destroy an American CIA officer."

From his office, Maxim Volontov, SVR *rezident* in the Russian Embassy in Helsinki, watched Dominika walk across the hall to return the dun-colored file to the file room for the evening. Since she had arrived in the *rezidentura* from Moscow, Dominika would check out the file each morning and take it to a work area to read, usually writing in a notebook, taking notes. At the end of each day she would return it to the file clerk per established *rezidentura* practice. Besides Volontov, Dominika was the only officer allowed to check out this particular file. It was a copy of the SVR *delo* on the American CIA officer Nathaniel Nash, transmitted from Yasenevo.

Volontov noted the dancer's legs, the body beneath the tailored shirt. Volontov was fifty-five years old, warty and stout, with a silver-gray 1950s Soviet pompadour. He had one steel tooth in the back of his mouth, visible only when he smiled, which was never. His suit was dark, baggy, and shiny in places. If modern spies today are made of space-age composites, Volontov was still steel plates and rivets.

Dominika observed with interest the orange haze of deceit and careerism around his bullet head. Orange, different from the yellow-tinted walruses back home. But he had been around for many years, during the really difficult times in the KGB, and was a protean survivor. Those specific instincts told him to handle the niece of SVR First Deputy Director Egorov carefully, even though it rankled. Plus this young bombshell was here on a special assignment. A sensitive one. After a week of preparation, Dominika tonight was to attend her first diplomatic reception—National Day at the elegant Spanish Embassy—to see if she could spot the American Nash. Volontov would also be there, watching from across the room. It would be interesting to see how she would work the reception. Volontov's diesel-fueled thoughts turned to the excellent hors d'oeuvres the Spaniards always served.

Dominika had been put in a temporary apartment in the old quarter of Helsinki hurriedly rented by the *rezidentura* per directions from Moscow, separated by design from the Russian Embassy community typically jammed into tiny apartments on the compound. Helsinki was a wonder. She had looked in amazement at the tidy streets, buildings with scalloped cornices, painted yellow and red and orange, and lacy curtains in the windows, even the shops.

In the comfortable little flat, Dominika got ready for Spanish National Day. She put on her makeup, slipped into her clothes. She brushed her hair; the brush handle felt hot in her hand. For that matter, *she* felt hot, ready for battle. Her little flat was awash in undulating bars of color: red, crimson, lavender;

passion, excitement, challenge. She reviewed what she had been instructed by Volontov to accomplish with the American. This first night, establish contact; in the coming weeks, arrange a follow-up, then regularize encounters, develop bonds of friendship, build trust, uncover his patterns and movements. Get him talking.

She had been briefed in the Center. Before she left Moscow, Zyuganov had spoken to her briefly. "Corporal, have you any questions?" he asked. Without waiting for her reply, he continued. "You realize that this is not a recruitment operation, at least not in the classic sense. The primary goal is not foreign intelligence." He licked his lips. Dominika kept quiet and kept still. "No," said Zyuganov, "this is more a trap, a snare. All we require is an indication—active or passive, it doesn't matter—when and how this American meets his agent. I will do the rest." He looked at Dominika with his head tilted slightly. "Do you understand?" His voice grew silkier. "*Obdirat,* I want you to *flense* the flesh from his bones. I leave it to you how to do it." He locked on her eyes. Dominika was sure he knew she could see colors. His own eyes said, *Read me, if you can.* Dominika had thanked him for the instruction and had hurried away.

This Nash was a trained CIA officer. Even a single contact with him was going to require great care. But the difference was that this operation against the American was hers to manage now. It was *hers*. She put down the brush and gripped the edge of the vanity as she looked into the mirror.

She stared back at herself. What would he be like? Could she sustain contact with him? What if he did not like her? Could she insert herself into his activities? She would have to determine the right approach to him quickly. *Remember your techniques: elicit, assess, manipulate his vulnerabilities.*

She leaned closer to the mirror. *Rezident* Volontov would be watching, and the *buivoli* in the Center would also be observing the outcome, the buffalo eyes of the herd all turned her way. All right, she would show them what she could do.

Americans were materialistic, vain, *nekulturny*. The lectures at the Academy insisted that the CIA accomplished everything with money and technology, that they had no soul. She would show him soul. *Amerikantsy* were also soft, avoiding conflict, avoiding risk. She would reassure him. The KGB had dominated the Americans in the sixties during Khrushchev's Cold War. It was her turn now. Her hands ached from gripping the vanity. Dominika shrugged on her winter coat and turned for the door. This CIA boy had no idea what was going to happen to him.

The palatial ground-floor public room of the Spanish Embassy was brightly lit by three massive glittering crystal chandeliers. Rows of French doors lined one side of the room leading to the ornamental garden, but were closed against the late fall frost. The room was jammed full, and a hundred images scrolled past Dominika as she stood on the low landing looking down at the guests. Business suits, tuxedos, evening gowns, bare throats, upswept hair, whispered asides, guffaws with heads held back. Cigarette ash on lapels, a dozen languages going at the same time, glasses wrapped with wet paper napkins. The partygoers circulated in a constantly changing pattern, the din of their voices a steady roar. Groaning boards were arranged along the outer margins of the room with food and drink. People were lined up three deep. Dominika forced herself to tamp down the kaleidoscope of colors, to manage the overload.

She wondered how she was going to catch sight of Nathaniel Nash in this herd. He might not even be here tonight. Minutes after she had entered the reception room, she had already been cornered by several older men, diplomats by the look of them, who leaned in too closely, spoke too loudly, looked too obviously at her chest. Dominika wore a muted gray suit with a single string of pearls; the jacket was buttoned, with occasionally a hint of black lace underneath. *Nothing slutty,* Dominika thought, *but sophisticated-sexy.* Certainly Scandinavian women could dress tarty. For instance, that statuesque blonde standing beside double French doors swelled out of her cashmere top, every terrain feature visible. Her hair was so blond it was almost white, and she played with it as she laughed at something a young man said to her. The young man. It was Nash. She knew his face from a hundred surveillance photos in his file.

Dominika slowly made her way toward the French doors, but it was like pushing through evening crowds in the Moscow Metro. When she got to the French doors, Miss Scandinavia and Nash were gone. Dominika tried looking for the woman's blond head—the Amazon was half a head taller than everyone else in the room—but could not see her. As taught at the Academy, Dominika walked clockwise around the outer edges of the reception room, scouting for Nash. She approached one of the buffet tables where Rezident Volontov was standing, his plate and his shovel mouth both brimming with tapas. He was making no attempt to talk to anyone. He popped a piece of tortilla española into his mouth, oblivious to the crowd around him.

Dominika continued circling the outer edges of the room. She could see the broad shoulders of the big blonde, surrounded by the delighted, sweaty faces of at least four other men. But no Nash. Finally, Dominika saw him in the corner of the room, near one of the service bars.

Dark hair, trim figure, he was dressed in a dark blue suit with a pale blue shirt and simple black tie. His face was open, his expression active. *He has a dazzling smile,* Dominika thought; it radiated sincerity. She stood close beside a column in the ballroom, casually enough, but unobserved by the American. What was most remarkable, what surprised Dominika the most, was that Nash was suffused with a deep purple, a good color, warm and honest and safe. She had seen it around only two other people before: her father and General Korchnoi.

Nash was speaking to a short, balding man in his fifties with a bulbous nose who she recognized as one of the translators in the Russian Embassy, what was his name? Trentov? Titov? No, Tishkov. The ambassador's translator. Spoke English, French, German, Finnish. She edged closer, using the crowd at the bar as cover, reached for a glass of champagne. She heard Nash speaking excellent, unaccented Russian to the sweaty Tishkov, who was holding a water glass half-full of scotch. He was listening to Nash nervously, giving him fitful upward glances, nodding his head occasionally. Nash even talked like a Russian: His hands opened and closed, pushed the words around in the air. Remarkable.

Dominika sipped from her champagne glass and moved closer. She watched Nash over the rim of her glass. He stood easily, not crowding Tishkov, but leaning forward to be heard over the din in the room. He was telling the little potato the story of a Soviet citizen who parked in front of the Kremlin. "*A policeman rushed over to him and yelled, 'Are you crazy? This is where the whole government is.' 'No problem,' said the man. 'I have good locks on my car.'*" Tishkov was trying not to laugh.

From the other end of the buffet, Dominika watched Nash fetch another scotch for Tishkov.

Tishkov was now telling his own story, holding on to Nash's arm as he spoke. Nash laughed, and Dominika could actually see him applying the force of his charm on the man. Attentive, charming, discreet, Nash was putting Tishkov at ease. *He's a spy,* thought Dominika.

Dominika looked beyond Nash and Tishkov at Volontov halfway down the room. The warthog *rezident* was oblivious to a textbook encounter between an American intelligence officer and a potential target. Nash looked up for a second and quickly scanned the room. Their eyes met and caught for a beat, Dominika looked away, and Nash quickly turned his attention back to Tishkov. He didn't register seeing her. But in that split second, Dominika felt a jolt, the first-time electric zing of seeing your target up close. Her quarry. They used to call them the Main Enemy.

Dominika eased back behind the column and watched the American. Fascinating, that easy-standing attitude. The younger man was keeping the older Tishkov interested. Confident but not *nevospitannyi,* not boorish or swaggering, nothing like her former colleagues in the Fifth. *Sympatichnyi.* Her earlier nerves about making contact, about engaging with the American, evaporated. She itched to approach him right then, get into his space, into his head, as she had practiced with Mikhail in Moscow, using her face and figure to get his attention. A simple matter of edging closer, a quick introduction . . .

No. Calm yourself. With Tishkov around, Dominika would not approach him. Instructions from the Center regarding Nash were specific. Contact must be private, unofficial, and no one in the embassy was to know, save Volontov. She would stay professional, exacting, calculating. It was what the operation required, and she was not going to deviate. To meet him, Dominika needed a better strategy than simply planning to attend all the diplomatic functions in Helsinki for the next calendar year.

Several days later, fate supplied Dominika the opportunity she needed, at a venue she could not have predicted. Despite a modest street entrance under an unassuming neon sign, the Yrjönkatu Swimming Hall in downtown Helsinki was a neoclassical gem, built in the 1920s, located several blocks from the train terminal. Copper Art Deco lamps along a balustraded mezzanine above the elegant pool cast movie-set shadows on the gray marble pilasters and glimmering tile floors.

Thanks to constant swimming-therapy sessions at ballet school, Dominika was a strong and devoted swimmer. She began going to the pool, a few blocks from her apartment, as an outlet. She favored the noon hour. Going in the evenings was too dark, too cold, the walk home alone too depressing. Besides, she was becoming increasingly lonely and fitful. Volontov, reflecting Moscow's impatience, was pressing her for progress on meeting Nash; he didn't care that engineering a plausible, random "bump" on a target, even considering the smallish size of Helsinki, was not automatic.

Dominika's breakthrough came when she was asked by Volontov to complete an urgent update report to Yasenevo. She missed her noonday swim. So she went after work, despite the dark and cold. And saw Nate come out of the men's locker room and walk around the edge of the pool, a towel draped around his neck. Dominika was sitting at the far end of the pool, legs trailing in the water, when she saw him. Without haste she got up and moved closer to one of the marble pillars and watched him. He swam smoothly and powerfully. Dominika watched his shoulders bunch and flex as he plowed through the water.

Dominika fought down her nervousness. Should she take the plunge, literally and figuratively? She could wait and report to Volontov that she had discovered one of Nash's patterns and that she was moving ahead with plans to establish contact. But that would be viewed only as a delay. She should move now, this instant: *Privodit' v dejstvie,* they had said at the Academy, throw the operation into action. This was a perfect chance for a first contact that would seem random and uncontrived. *Move.*

Dominika was wearing a modest one-piece racing suit and a plain white swimming cap. She slipped into the water and slowly made her way across several lanes to the one beside Nate's. She began swimming slowly down the lane, letting Nash pass her, then pass her again on the next length. She timed his third overtaking pass to occur at the end of the pool as Nate made a relaxed open turn and started another lap.

Dominika began swimming to stay even with Nash, which she found she could do with ease. Neither was swimming very hard. Through her goggles, Dominika could see his body underwater, rolling rhythmically in a smooth freestyle. At the far wall, Dominika and Nate both touched at the same time and started the return lap to the deep end. By this time, Nate noticed another swimmer keeping pace with him. Looking underwater, he saw it was a woman, sleek in a racing suit, stroking smoothly and strongly.

Nate dug a little harder to see if a dozen deeper pulls would draw him slightly ahead of the mystery swimmer. She stayed even, without apparent effort. Nate pulled harder, flexing his lats. She kept up. Nate increased his kick rate slightly and checked. She was still there. The wall was coming up and Nate decided to go at it hard, nail a flip turn, and crank up his stroke rate to the opposite wall. *Let's see if she can hit a turn and finish with a sprint.* He took a breath as he came up to the wall. Nate's legs came over his shoulders, his feet slapped explosively on the tiles, and he came off the wall clean and hard, ready to motor. He cycled his arms, elbows high, driving, pulling, the metronome *chop chop chop* of them entering the water filling his ears. He cranked up his kick and felt the lift of the bow wave around his head and shoulders. Smooth and fast, he limited breaths to one side, away from the girl. There would be plenty of time when he touched to wait for her to come churning up to the wall. For the last five yards, Nate stretched and glided, turning on his side to face in the girl's direction. But she was already there, her wake hitting the wall as he touched. She had touched him out. She looked over at him as she stood up in the shallow end, peeled the cap off her head, and shook her slightly damp hair.

"You swim beautifully," Nate said in English. "Are you on a team?"

"No, not really," said Dominika. Nate took in her strong shoulders, elegant hands holding the wall, plain short nails, and those blue eyes, electric, wide. Nate had pegged her accented English as Baltic or Russian. There were a lot of Finns who spoke English with a Russian accent.

"Are you from Helsinki?" asked Nate.

"No, I'm Russian," said Dominika, watching his face for a reaction, for contempt, dismissal. Instead, there was the brilliant smile. *Go ahead, Mr. CIA,* she thought. *What will you say now?*

"I saw the Dynamo Swim Team compete in Philadelphia once," said Nate. "They were very good, especially in the butterfly." The water of the pool sloshed over his shoulders, reflecting his purple haze.

"Of course," said Dominika. "Russian swimmers are the best in the world." She was going to say, *As in all sport,* but kept quiet. *Too much,* she thought, *settle down. All right, contact made, nationality established, now set the hook.* Tradecraft from the Forest. She moved to the ladder to climb out of the pool.

"Do you come here in the evenings?" Nate asked when Dominika said she had to go. The muscles in her back flexed as she climbed up the ladder.

"No, my schedule is irregular," said Dominika, trying not to sound like Garbo, "very irregular." She searched his face; he looked disappointed. Good. "I don't know when I will be back, but perhaps we'll meet again." She felt his eyes on her as she climbed out of the pool and walked into the women's locker room.

As it turned out, Dominika and Nate met again at the pool two days later. She nodded noncommittally to his wave. They swam more laps, swimming side by side. Dominika played it slow, indifferent. She was correct, reserved, a conscious counterbalance to his shambling American informality. She constantly told herself not to be so nervous. When he looked at her she knew from his expression that he was unsuspecting. *He doesn't know what this is,* she thought with a thrill. The CIA officer doesn't know who he's up against. When it was time to go, she again got out of the pool without delay. This time she looked back at him. An unsmiling wave. That was enough for now.

Over the course of several weeks they met five or six times, and not one of them was by chance. Dominika had cased the Torni Hotel, diagonally across the street from the pool entrance. Most evenings Dominika would be in the sitting room at the window observing his arrival. As far as she could tell, he never was accompanied by anyone. He was surveillance-free.

Dominika tried to build momentum in minute

and undetectable stages. As they continued meeting at the pool it was natural that they introduced themselves. Nate said he was a diplomat in the American Embassy working in the Economic Section, Dominika said she was an administrative assistant in the Russian Embassy. She heard him recite his cover legend, and gave her own. *He's very natural,* thought Dominika. *What sort of training do they get?* Typical, trusting American, incapable of a true *konspiratsiya.* He looked at her without guile, his purple halo never changed.

God, she's serious, thought Nate. *Typical Russian, afraid of putting a foot wrong.* But he liked her reserve, her underlying sensuality, the way she looked at him with her blue eyes. He especially liked the way she pronounced his name, "Neyt." But he gloomily told himself she could not have access to secrets. *Come off it, she's just a beautiful Russian Embassy clerk. Twenty-four, twenty-five, Muscovite, Foreign Service, junior admin, remember to get the patronymic and family name off the registration card at the pool. To have gotten out of Moscow this young, she probably has a sugar daddy.* Not hard to believe, looking at that face, the body underneath the spandex. Unattainable. Nate decided to send in traces, just for form's sake, but knew he'd be moving on.

This was not a honey trap against a hapless European on her home turf, Dominika told herself. This was an operation in the foreign field against a foreign intelligence officer. She was Center-trained, she knew she would have to reel him in carefully. She had filed an initial contact report to Yasenevo, detailing the first few contacts. Volontov was pressing for forward movement.

A couple of weeks, no response from Langley on the trace cable. *Typical, but who cares?* thought Nate. It was enough to meet her occasionally and drink in that face. He had gotten her to smile twice, her English was good enough to get a joke. He wasn't going to spout off in Russian and scare her.

One evening, as they finished swimming, they turned to climb the ladder to get out of the pool. They bumped into each other. Her suit clung to her curves. Nate could see her heartbeat beneath the drum skin of spandex. He offered Dominika his hand climbing up the ladder. Her hand was strong, hot to the touch. He held it for a beat and let go. Face impassive, no reaction. He held her eyes for another beat. She took off her swim cap and shook her hair.

Dominika knew he was looking at her, kept calm, distant. What would he say if he knew she had been trained as a Sparrow, if he knew what she had done with Delon and Ustinov? She would not, absolutely not, seduce him. She would hear the cackles all the way from Moscow. No, she was going to accomplish this with discipline, with cleverness. *Move it forward,* she thought. *Time to start opening the human envelope, to shake up that frustratingly consistent purple mantle.*

Dominika said yes to Nate's suggestion that evening that they stop for a glass of wine in a neighborhood bar. His face had lit up with surprise, then pleasure. Seeing each other in street clothes on the sidewalk seemed strange. Dominika sat firmly on the other side of the little table, nursing a glass of wine.

Now elicitation: Where are you from in the United States? Do you have brothers and sisters? What does your family do? She was going down the list, filling in the blanks in his *papka.*

If Nate didn't know better, this would have sounded like a debriefing. *Maybe she's just nervous, deflecting questions about herself. When Russians aren't being intense,* he thought, *they're being obtuse.* Well, let her relax. He was not going to spook her by going in too hard. Spook her from what? he asked himself. She wasn't a target and he wasn't going to bed her.

He ordered black bread and cheese. *Very clever,* she thought, *he thinks that's all we Russians eat.* A second glass of wine? No, thank you. It was Dominika who finally said she had to go home. Nate asked if he could walk her home. At the front door to her small, modern apartment block, she saw him wrestle with the enormousness of leaning in for a peck on the cheek, she watched him trying to decide—men are all alike—then gave him her hand, shook his once firmly, and went inside. Through the glass door she saw him turn away, hands in his pockets.

The trained SVR intelligence officer, graduate of Sparrow School and the AVR, congratulated herself on a good evening, good progress, especially how she had cut him off from that kiss. Then she laughed. *Some courtesan you are,* she thought, the slayer of gangsters, the seducer of diplomats, and now *otkazatsya,* denying a good-night kiss.

"Hey, Romeo," said Forsyth, leaning into Nate's small office in the Station, "did you see the incoming from Headquarters this morning on Esther Williams?" Forsyth was referring to the results of the name-trace request Nate had cabled in on Dominika Egorova; DPOB: 1989, Moscow; Occ: Administrative assistant, Russian Embassy. He had drafted the cable more than a month ago. Nate expected that there would be "No Hqs traces" on the woman, she wasn't even on the local dip list. She had told Nate she held a junior admin rank, the absolute bottom. The rest of Nate's cable vaguely outlined the contact based on aperiodic meetings at the swimming pool. Totally useless, no access, no potential.

"No, I haven't seen the cable," said Nate. "Is it on the reading board?"

"Here's my copy," said Forsyth. "Take a look at this." Forsyth chuckled as he handed the cable to Nate. As Nate started reading, Gable appeared behind Forsyth.

"Has Tommy Fuckfaster read the traces?" said Gable. He too was laughing. Nate didn't look up and continued reading:

> 1. Traces on subject ref indicate confirmed status as SVR Corporal in possibly Directorate I (Computer and Information Dissemination). Approximate SVR EOD date 2007–08. Graduate of Foreign Intelligence Academy (AVR), 2010. Probable family connection to SVR First Deputy Director Ivan (Vanya) Dimitrevich EGOROV. Subject posting to Finland not reflected in Russian Federation Foreign Ministry lists, suggesting TDY status and/or specific operational assignment of limited duration.
>
> 2. Headquarters Comment: Reference contact is of interest to Hqs. Subject's family tie to SVR leadership arguably provides her with unique access and represents an opportunity for significant recruitment.
>
> 3. Applaud Station diligence in aggressive spotting and developmental activity. Encourage Station officer to pursue subject for additional assessment and development. Hqs standing by to support Station ops plan as required. Regards.

Nate looked up from the cable at Forsyth and Gable. "You can't get a better trace response than that," said Forsyth. "This could work out to something big if you can take it all the way to recruitment."

Nate could feel cement filling his legs. "This feels wrong, Tom; she's not plugged in, she's too junior. Remains to be seen whether she's recruitable. There's something distant and closed up about her." He looked at the cable again. "Women haven't been allowed into the Academy for the last fifty years. I could waste six months trying to develop her for nothing. I think I should concentrate elsewhere."

Gable leaned farther into the room past Forsyth's shoulder. "That's right, think it all through." He laughed. "Are you fucking kidding me? A knockout like that, plus a close relative to someone on the fourth floor of the SVR? You better check it out, good and hard. Never mind going after someone else. This is a fucking ripe plum just waiting to get plucked."

"I get it, I get it," said Nate. "It's just that she doesn't seem like the type who's an SVR operator. Dour and scared, at least that's my assessment." He shrugged and looked at the other two.

"Well, assess away, kiddo. You got yourself a solid developmental prospect," said Gable as he left the office. "Let's talk ops plan when you're ready," he said over his shoulder. Forsyth turned to leave, gave Nate a wink.

Nate looked at Forsyth and nodded. *Okay, let's see where this goes,* he told himself. *A waste of time. C'mon, get motivated.* From right now, Dominika Egorova was something more than a beautiful face. She was his development target.

Up the road from the US Embassy, in the Russian Embassy, Rezident Volontov was haranguing Dominika on the slow progress of her operation.

"Corporal Egorova, you have made a good start, but your progress has been too slow. General Egorov has sent three requests for updates since you arrived. You must redouble your efforts to move your friendship with Nash forward. More frequent meetings. Ski trips. Weekend trips. Be inventive. General Egorov once again recommends that you cultivate in Nash an emotional dependency on you." Volontov sat back in his chair and ran greasy fingers through pomaded hair.

"Thank you, Colonel," said Dominika. Her uncle, Simyonov, and now this smelly throwback. "Can you tell me, please, what Director Egorov means by 'emotional dependency'?" Her level gaze dared him to suggest she seduce the American.

"I'm sure I cannot speak for the Deputy Director," said Volontov, swerving away from the washed-out bridge of their conversation. "All you need to focus on is to move the relationship forward. Develop bonds of trust." Volontov waved his arm in the air to illustrate what "bonds of trust" might mean. "Most important, get him talking about himself."

"Of course, Colonel," said Dominika, getting up from her chair. "I will push forward and keep you informed. Thank you for your valuable guidance."

After her session with Volontov, Dominika was deflated. He operated in a puerile, slimy world full of sly hints, insinuations. "Bonds of trust," "emotional dependency." Sparrow School. Would she have to deal with that her entire career?

Walking home, Dominika thought furiously. *Snap out of it.* She was on assignment in a foreign country, living in her own apartment in a fairy-tale little city. It was wonderful. She had an important job to do, against a trained American intelligence officer. Well, he did not seem dangerous, but he was a CIA officer, and that was enough. Tonight she'd get him to talk more about himself. She'd ask him what he thought of Russians—he had not yet admitted he spoke the language. She would get him to talk about Moscow. He had to admit to his posting there. As she walked quickly down lighted streets toward Yrjönkatu, unaware that her limp was more pronounced, she looked forward to the contact.

Walking toward Yrjönkatu himself, Nate was thinking hard, so preoccupied that he realized he was oblivious to the street, that he was ignoring his six. *Wake up, sport,* he thought, *this is the first night of your new case.* He used a red light to cross the street and change his directional flow, to catch a look as he watched for traffic. *No hits, no casuals. Walk three more blocks and do it again. No repeats. This is no longer a splashy fun romp with a blue-eyed Slav in wet spandex.* No, if she was an SVR officer—and he still doubted it—he'd have to pay attention and do some more assessment. God, he'd rather be working that drunk Tishkov. At least he'd have access to documents and the minutes of private meetings. That would be a real scalp, something that would start a buzz back home.

Also lost in thought, Dominika likewise neglected to check for surveillance until she was three blocks from the pool. To atone for her inattention, she did a preposterous reverse in an alley—the *pensionerki* would have howled—and felt ridiculous. As both of them absentmindedly flailed away on the street, they turned different corners and arrived at the front door of the swimming hall at the same time. Dominika's breath quickened, Nate's pulse increased, but they both remembered what each had to do to the other, and got down to work.

Dominika leaned back against the wooden partition of the booth. Long fingers slowly twisted the stem of her wineglass. Nate sat across from her, legs extended and crossed at the ankle. He was dressed in a V-neck sweater and jeans, she in a blue cable-knit top and pleated skirt. She wore dark tights and black low-heeled shoes. Nate noticed she bounced her foot under the table.

"Americans never take things seriously enough," said Dominika. "They are always making fun."

"How many Americans do you know?" asked Nate. "Have you been to the United States?"

"There was a foreign student, an American boy, at ballet school," said Dominika. "He was always joking." She did not mind mentioning ballet, it was part of her legend.

"But was he a good dancer?" asked Nate.

"Not especially," said Dominika. "The program was very difficult, and he did not apply himself."

"It must have been lonely for him," said Nate. "Did you show him around Moscow, go drinking together?"

"No, of course not, it was forbidden."

"Forbidden? Which part? Drinking or making him feel welcome?" said Nate, looking at his wineglass. Dominika looked at him for a second, then averted her eyes.

"You see, always making jokes," she said.

"It's not a joke," said Nate. "I just wonder what he will remember about Russia, about Moscow. Will he have fond memories of the city, or will he remember only being lonely, unloved?" *What a strange thing to say,* thought Dominika.

"What do you know about Moscow?" she asked, already knowing part of the answer.

"I lived there for a year, I think I told you before, working in the American Embassy. I lived in the housing compound next to the chancery."

No interest, *no inflection.* "Did you like it?" she asked.

"I was always busy, not enough time really to explore the city." He took a sip of his wine and smiled at her. "I wish I had known you, though; you could have shown me around. Unless it was forbidden."

Innocent little boy, she thought. *What an act.* Dominika ignored the comment. "Why did you leave after a year? I thought diplomats stayed longer than that." His answer would be the lead sentence of her report.

"There was a sudden vacancy in Helsinki," said Nate. "So I made the change." *Very smooth,* thought Dominika. She noted that the purple around his shoulders did not change when he did not tell the truth. Very professional.

"Were you sad to leave?" asked Dominika.

"In some ways, yes," said Nate. "But I felt sad for Russia as well."

"Sad for Russia? Why?"

"We finished the Cold War without blowing each other up, came close a couple of times. Whatever you thought about the Soviet system, it was over. I think everybody hoped Russia would see a new day, freedoms, a better life for its citizens."

"And you think life is not better in Russia now?" said Dominika, trying to tamp down the indignation in her voice.

"In some ways, yes, of course," said Nate, shrugging. "But I think people still struggle. The cruelest outcome is seeing a new age dawning, but nothing coming of it."

"I do not understand," said Dominika.

Let's see if she takes the bait, he thought. "Don't take this the wrong way, but I think that your current leaders are creating a system as notorious as the Soviet system of the past. But it's not as evident. It's more modern, telegenic, plugged-in. The new weapons are oil and natural gas, but behind the scenes there's just as much cruelty and repression and corruption as before." Nate looked at Dominika sheepishly and raised his hands. "Sorry. Didn't mean to criticize."

Despite all the training and practice, Dominika had never before engaged with an American in such a discussion. She had to keep in mind that he was an intelligence officer, was adept at saying provocative things to elicit comments from her. She told herself to relax. This was no time for her to lose control. Still, she had to respond. "What you say is not correct," said Dominika. "This is the sort of anti-Russia attitude that we are constantly aware of. It is simply not true."

Thinking about the renegade KGB officer poisoned by polonium and the journalist shot in her elevator, Nate finished his wine. "Tell that to Alexander Litvinenko or Anna Politkovskaya," said Nate.

Or Dimitri Ustinov, thought Dominika guiltily. But she was still furious with him.

SPANISH EMBASSY TORTILLA ESPAÑOLA

Cook seasoned, medium-sliced potatoes and chopped onions in abundant olive oil until soft, then remove and drain. Add beaten eggs to potatoes and onions and return to oiled pan on medium heat until edges and bottom start to brown. Place plate over skillet, invert, then slide tortilla back into pan and cook until golden brown.

11

Nate sat in the Station staring through the slats of the venetian blinds on the window in his office. He absentmindedly batted the cord of the blinds, making the plastic handle hit the wall and bounce back, click, click, click. Last night had been another National Day reception at some embassy. The half dozen calling cards on his desk amounted to squat, and there was a knot between his shoulder blades.

The thought of swimming reminded him of Dominika. He had looked hard at her, they had been out several times, but he still thought the case was going nowhere. She was a believer, way committed, no doubts, no vulnerabilities. He was wasting time. The plastic at the end of the cord clicked against the wall. The cards on the desk mocked him. A single paper—his latest cable on contact with Dominika—lay in a metal tray on his desk.

Gable stuck his head into his office. "Jesus, the fucking Prisoner of Zenda in the tower," he said. "Why aren't you out on the street? Take someone to lunch."

"I struck out last night," said Nate, staring out the window. "Four National Days this week alone."

Gable shook his head, walked to the window, and yanked the slats of the blinds closed with a snap. He sat on the edge of Nate's desk and leaned close.

"Bend over, Hamlet, I'm about to give you a pearl of wisdom. There is a perverse element to this HUMINT shit we do. Sometimes the harder you try to find a target, to start a case, the farther away it gets from you. Impatience, aggression—in your case, desperation—gets in the air like a whiff of sulfur, no one wants to talk to you, no one will dine with you. Sulfur in the wind. You smell like rotten eggs."

"I don't follow you," said Nate.

Gable leaned closer. "You got performance anxiety," he drawled. "The longer you stare at your pecker, the softer it's gonna be. Keep trying, but ease off the accelerator."

"Thanks for the graphic image," said Nate, "but I've been at Station for a while and I have nothing to show for it."

"Stop, or *I'll* start weeping," said Gable. "The only guys you have to please are me and COS, and we ain't complaining . . . yet. You got time, so keep going." Gable picked up the cable in Nate's in-box.

"Besides, this Russian sugar-britches is gold waiting to be mined, your professional assessment notwithstanding. Get to work on her, for Christ's sake. I have an idea how we can blow air up her skirt for a better look."

Gable suggested they direct the small Station surveillance team on Egorova to get a sense of what she was doing in Helsinki. Putting surveillance on her struck Nate as overkill. He had been trying to tell Forsyth and Gable that Egorova was a low-level target, an admin type with no access. Surveilling her was a waste. "Let's agree to disagree," Gable said. "In other words, shut the fuck up."

Forsyth held up his hand. "Nate, since you're the action officer with Egorova, why don't you handle the team while they cover her? Useful experience, and you can provide input. They're an interesting old couple. They're both sticklers for tradecraft."

Great, thought Nate. Gable had made the suggestion to employ surveillance to kick-start the operation, and Forsyth assigned him to run the team to focus him on the case. Forsyth and Gable worked well together, real pros, they knew how to motivate their officers.

Gable slid the file to him, daring him with a look to say anything. "Here's the file on ARCHIE and VERONICA." He paused for a beat. "These two are legends. They've been working since the 1960s. Worked some shit-hot ops over the years, including Golitsyn's defection. Tell 'em I said hello."

Twenty-four hours later, after a two-hour vehicular SDR that took him north for an hour on the E75 and then west on secondary roads to Tuusula and back into the city on the 120, Nate ditched his car in public parking at the Pasila train station and walked into Länsi-Pasila, a district of high-rises and commercial buildings. He found the right one, a modest apartment block of four stories of brick and glass, with enclosed angular balconies. He pressed the intercom button marked RÄIKKÖNEN and was buzzed in. Nate rang the bell at the door of the fourth-floor apartment.

"Come in," said the elderly woman who opened the door. Spry. In her seventies. VERONICA. Her face was narrow and patrician, with a straight nose and firm mouth that hinted at what must have been considerable beauty in her youth. Her ice-blue eyes were still striking, her skin was pink with good health. Her thick white hair was in a bun and a pencil stuck out of it. She wore woolen pants and a light sweater. Reading glasses hung from her neck, and there was a pile of papers and magazines on the floor beside a chair. "We've been eager to meet you," she said. "I am Jaana." She grasped Nate's hand and shook it firmly. She radiated vitality and energy. Her grip, her eyes, the way she stood.

"Would you like a cup of tea? What time is it?" She checked her watch, which she wore with the face on the bottom of her wrist, a classic tell of a street surveillant, thought Nate. "It's late enough to contemplate something stronger," said Jaana. "May I offer you schnapps?" All this was said in a flurry of movements, gestures, smiles, twinkling eyes.

"Marty Gable sends his regards," said Nate.

"How kind of Marty," said Jaana, clearing a space on a cluttered coffee table. "He's a dear. You're lucky to have him as a supervisor." She was shuttling back and forth from the kitchen with glasses and an unidentified clear liquid that seethed in an oval bottle. Schnapps. "We've seen some strange chiefs over the years," she said, "on both sides. Of course, the Russians were uniformly worse, beastly clods trying to survive in their beastly system, bless them. They certainly provided us with interesting times."

Jaana Räikkönen poured two glasses of schnapps, raised her glass in a Scandinavian toast, looking him in the eyes while taking the first sip. The living room was small and comfortable, with overstuffed furniture and bookshelves lining the polished wood walls. The house was filled with the smell of vegetable soup.

"Is your husband home?" asked Nate. "I hoped to meet him too."

"He won't be long," said Jaana. "He was out on the street covering your arrival." She shrugged. "I'm afraid it's a habit with us." Nate chuckled to himself. He had run a two-hour dry-cleaning route looking for a tail and had missed the old guy hanging around outside his building. *That's how they've operated for so long,* he thought.

Just then a key rattled in the lock, the front door opened, and Marcus Räikkönen walked into the room. ARCHIE. He led a tan dachshund on a leash, which, after sniffing briefly at Nate, trotted over to his bed and flopped down. His name was Rudy. Marcus was tall, over six feet, and broad across the shoulders. He had clear blue eyes under bushy eyebrows. Muscular cords stood out on the side of his neck, under a sharp jawline. He moved easily, athletically. He was balding and wore his remaining hair in a buzz cut. His handshake was firm. He wore a dark-blue tracksuit with black training shoes. There was a small Finnish flag on the left breast of the suit.

"Across the street in the courtyard?" asked Nate. "The bench near the steps?"

"Good," said Marcus. "I didn't think you noticed." He smiled and picked up the third glass of schnapps. "To your good health," he said, draining the glass while looking Nate in the eyes.

Nate remembered the summary file on them. ARCHIE and VERONICA had been the core of Helsinki Station's unilateral surveillance team for close to forty years. Both were retired pensioners now. ARCHIE had been an investigator in the Finnish Tax Administration, VERONICA a librarian. They were effective simply because they mixed different looks on the street with an instinct about what the rabbit was going to do next. Of course, they knew the city and its Metro system intimately, they had grown up as the city had grown. Dogged, discreet, with the patience and perspective of a lifetime, they could work on a target for months without being burned. Their style of coverage was what Gable had called "more of a wife's caress than a doctor's finger."

Nate and the Räikkönens drafted a surveillance sked on Dominika, who they would cover irregularly but at carefully selected times—evenings after work, weekends—when something interesting was likely to occur. From afar Nate watched them work. Knit caps, mittens, and parkas one day, business suits and umbrellas the next. Bicycles with ting-a-ling bells and Rudy on a leash. An indistinct gray Volvo compact, a motor scooter with a basket. Sometimes they walked together, holding hands, sometimes apart. One day

Jaana followed Dominika into a store using a walker. ARCHIE and VERONICA did it all—trailing surveillance, static, leading, crossing, parallel, leapfrog.

Nate met them again at their apartment after the first two weeks. They had taken a few photographs. Marcus summarized the results so far. His report was crisp, precise. Jaana would occasionally interrupt with observations. "First," said Marcus, "we are quite sure that up until now she has not detected or suspected surveillance." He shrugged his shoulders. "She is young, but we see considerable skill on the street. She does not resort to the usual tricks and she moves well, takes advantage of her surroundings. I would say she is significantly above average on the street.

"She knows her way around already. We observed her using specific tradecraft only once," said Marcus, looking at Jaana. "She waits in the mezzanine of the Torni Hotel across the street from Yrjönkatu Swimming Hall to watch you arrive. She waits for a few moments after, then enters."

"Marcus disagrees with me," said Jaana, "but I think she is not operational. She is not handling agents and is not involved in operational support to the *rezidentura*. She does not have a job to do." Jaana looked over to Marcus, waiting for the rejoinder.

"Of course she has a job to do," said Marcus. "It's just that we have not seen it yet. Give it time."

"One thing is for sure," said Jaana, ignoring Marcus. "She is lonely. She goes straight from the embassy to her little apartment. She buys groceries for one. She walks alone on the weekends."

"Have you seen any hint of coverage *on her*?" asked Nate. "Is anyone from the *rezidentura* keeping tabs on her?"

"We think not," said Marcus. "She is clear. We will keep looking for any indication that they are watching her."

"I'm going to have more encounters with her," said Nate. "I'll need you to help cover some of our meetings outside the swimming hall."

Marcus nodded. "As you see more of her it will become interesting. Especially what she does immediately after your meetings. That is when they always run to the phone or rendezvous with an embassy officer. As much as you can, let us know your plans. If you wish, we can make some suggestions for places to meet her," Marcus said.

"One last thing," said Jaana, pouring another glass of schnapps. "If you would forgive me, she looks like a nice person, a sweet girl. She needs a friend." Marcus looked at her and back to Nate with arched eyebrows.

Nate reviewed ARCHIE and VERONICA's reports with Gable. "Good, keep an eye on her, especially if she's got anybody from her embassy supporting her," said Gable. "If we see she's got backup, then it's possible she's operational, maybe even she's working on you."

"Not in a million years," said Nate. "No way."

"Glad you're so sure. Anyway, go after her, hard. Take your time, in a hurry."

Nate set a goal of seeing Dominika at least once a week outside of the swimming. He scoured the city for places to meet without being seen. They met after work at basement bars, for coffee on Saturday mornings, lunches on Sundays at remote cafés. Put her in the chair with her back to the room. There were embassy Russians all over Helsinki, and Nate wanted to avoid a chance sighting. Build a friendship, stay clandestine, always arrive separately, leave apart. Stay off the phones, vary patterns, build a relationship. A waste of time.

Dominika applied her own tradecraft. She checked for coverage as she walked through the city to their meetings. Finns would stare at the beautiful dark-haired girl walking up the escalator, or slipping into a snowy alley, or leaving a store by a back entrance, unaware she was looking for coverage, or that she was watching from across the street as Nate arrived at their coffee shop, counting heads, looking at faces, marking hats and overcoats.

They were getting to know each other. Over the last few meetings they had talked, really talked, a natural evolution after spending time together. Dominika assessed Nate as honest, natural, intelligent. He was not *nekulturny.* He was, well, just American. His comments about living in Moscow were evasive, of course they would be, he was hiding the fact that he had been handling a Russian mole. Dominika didn't much care for his comments about Russia, even though she knew she felt mostly the same way. *Come on, get going,* she told herself. She had to spend more time with him, continue concentrating on his patterns. She had to determine when he was operational.

She felt the pressure. If there was no breakthrough soon, with the Center and Volontov bearing down, would she contemplate a physical approach? *Nelzya!* she thought. No, never. He was attractive, his openness and humor appealing. But forget it.

How many meetings had there been? Nate felt the anticipation of seeing Dominika again, but he wasn't convinced that he could persuade her of anything. She was unbending. Facing a hundred surveillance cars in Moscow didn't faze him, but he fretted over how to determine what motivated her. If she had an operational agenda, Nate couldn't identify it. It almost seemed as if she were in Helsinki just to get experience, and that didn't make sense. The SVR connection was important, the aspect that made her a worthwhile recruitment target. He had to get a handle soon or Forsyth would grow impatient and Gable would kick his ass.

One thing. He could look at her face for hours. *Jesus, listen to you. Concentrate on the developmental, on the assessment, what makes her tick.* They talked more easily now, even though they disagreed. She got hot and fussy whenever he pinged on Russia, he could see that, but he also had a sense that she grudgingly agreed with him at times. She didn't believe all the propaganda. Maybe an opening. Maybe not.

He looked into the mirror and combed his hair. This Sunday he had suggested lunch at a little ethnic restaurant in Pihlajisto, a crossroads community on the Metro line northeast of the city. Dominika had agreed to meet him there. Weeks before, ARCHIE had suggested it as out-of-the-way: "We will not encounter any Russian friends there," he said. "One of us on the train watching her, the other covering you." Nate threw on an oiled field coat over a V-neck sweater and corduroy pants. He wore ripple-soled walking shoes. He left his apartment and walked a stairstep route through the swept streets of Kruununhaka, then along the frozen waterfront, then kicked off his real dry-cleaning route.

Across town, Dominika was also looking in the mirror, her blue eyes wide. She did not use perfume, but combed her hair for the tenth time with the tortoiseshell talisman. She got ready to walk out of her apartment to take the Metro, taking a slantwise look through the curtains of her front window to the street below. She looked forward to this, talking to him, sparring, learning a little more each time.

She wore a turtleneck sweater and tweed jacket over woolen pants for warmth. She also wore sensible shoes. She tied a scarf over her head like an old babushka and left her apartment, locking the door. She went down to the basement of her apartment building, walked through the storeroom, and pushed through to the boiler room. A small corridor led from the room to a heavy iron-barred window high on the wall that Dominika had discovered several weeks ago. It looked as though it had been a coal chute, long since converted. It had taken her almost an hour to pick the padlocked grille two nights ago; the damn things weren't easy, especially since she had only an improvised torsion wrench fashioned from a hairpin. Dominika stacked boxes under the window, boosted herself up, and wormed through the window. *Some start to a date,* she thought, thinking about seeing him again.

Dominika eased the window shut and stepped out into the alleyway, looking up at the curtained windows. Nothing. She walked quietly up the alleyway, squeezed between a parked truck and a Dumpster, boosted herself over a low brick wall and out onto a city street. She was already a block away from her apartment building. Her coat collar was turned up and the scarf hid her features. She walked west for another block casually, checking for repeats whenever she crossed the street and looked both ways for traffic. She entered the Kamppi complex, walked through the mall, stopped at a bookstore, checked for faces, then down into the Metro entrance. She stayed still on the slowly descending escalator, using the reflective bounce on the fashion posters on the walls. No silhouettes. Dominika was halfway to the platform level as a slight elderly lady dressed in a raincoat and floppy hat stepped on the escalator at the top and started down behind her. She was holding a bunch of flowers wrapped in green paper and a string bag with two apples. VERONICA hoped that one day she could speak to the dear girl about how predictable she had been, using the mall and its integral Metro station so close to her apartment.

Nate's surveillance instructor a hundred dim years ago was named Jay, a former physicist who wore a Van

Dyck beard and long sandy hair and looked, well, a lot like Van Dyck. "*Get it out of your heads, stop being heroes,*" he had said. "*If you detect surveillance, your night is over, you will abort.*" He had drawn a horizontal line on the chalkboard. "*Your SDR is to compel surveillance you have not seen to show themselves. It is not designed to lose anyone. All surveillance has a breaking point,*" he had said, intersecting the line with a vertical stroke. "*This is the point when the bad guys must choose between staying undetected and losing the eye.*" He brushed his hands of chalk dust. "*If you can force them to show themselves without breaking their hearts, you have succeeded. For that night only. Then you have to start all over again.*"

Fuck breaking their hearts, thought Nate. If he had coverage they'd have to show. He slid down an embankment near the rail yard behind the central station, climbed a chain-link fence in an alley, and dodged traffic as he crossed the E12. He wondered what she would be wearing. Along his route, Nate would look for ARCHIE, but he was wasting his time. The old man was a ghost on the street, protoplasm, smoke around dry ice. ARCHIE was countersurveilling Nate, looking for repeats using time and distance. Forget coats, forget hats, ARCHIE was looking at the way people walked, their gaits, the sets of their shoulders, the shapes of their ears and noses. Things surveillants cannot change. And shoes. They never change shoes.

Three hours after climbing through half of Helsinki, and seeing ARCHIE—finally—with the duffel in his right hand (you're clean), Nate was confident he was black. The modest country restaurant was owned by an Afghan family. Nate entered the small whitewashed dining room decorated with rugs on the wall and colored cushions on the chairs. Each table had a candle. A dial radio on a shelf played softly. The place was deserted, only one other couple—young Finns—at a corner table. A wonderful smell of warm spices and stewed lamb came from the kitchen. Nate was seated at a corner table facing the front window. In two minutes ARCHIE and VERONICA walked arm in arm by the window, looking straight ahead. VERONICA flicked the side of her nose with a finger. All-clear signal. ARCHIE thought it idiotic but she was implacable. He looked at her and rolled his eyes, then they disappeared.

A minute later, Dominika pushed through the door, saw Nate, and walked to the table. Cool, confident, composed. He held her chair but she shrugged her coat off by herself when he made to help her. Two glasses of wine came. Nate's bad knee was throbbing from when he had rapped it on a fence post an hour ago. His left hand was scraped after a controlled slide down the rail embankment. Dominika's jacket sleeve had a rip at the shoulder from when she had caught it on a corner of the Dumpster behind her house. A woolen sock and shoe were wet. She had gone ankle-deep in a slushy puddle crossing the street after getting off the train at Pihlajisto.

"I'm glad you were able to find the place," said Nate. "It's a little out-of-the-way, but a friend said the food was excellent." He looked at the light on her hair. "I hope it wasn't too far to come."

"It was an easy trip, there was hardly anyone on the train," said Dominika.

If you only knew, thought Nate. "I hope you like the restaurant. Have you tried Afghan food?"

"No, but there are several Afghan restaurants in Moscow. They are supposed to be good." His halo was rich and full, and Dominika thought of her father.

"Because, you know, I worried about inviting you to an Afghan place, I worried you would think I was being provocative," said Nate, smiling. He wanted to turn the corner, get her to relax.

"I do not think you are provocative. You are an American, you cannot help yourself. I am beginning to understand you, perhaps a little." She dipped a piece of hot flatbread into a little bowl of chickpea paste drizzled with oil.

"As long as you can forgive me for being an American . . ." Nate said.

"I forgive you," said Dominika, looking straight at him. Mona Lisa smile and another bite of bread.

"Then I'm happy," said Nate, leaning on his elbows, watching her. "What about you, are you happy?"

"What an odd question," said Dominika.

"No, not right now, I mean are you happy generally, with your life?" said Nate.

"Yes," she said.

"It's just that sometimes you seem so serious . . . sad, even. I know your father died several years ago, I know you were close." Dominika had mentioned her father to Nate.

Dominika swallowed; she didn't want to talk about this, about herself. "My father was a wonderful man, a university professor, kind and generous."

"What did he think about the changes in Russia? Was he glad to see the Soviet Union disappear?"

"Yes, of course, as we all did, I mean welcome the changes. He was a Russian patriot." She took another sip of wine, wiggled her wet toes in her shoe. "But what about you, Neyt?" She wasn't going to let him hijack the conversation. "What about your father? You told me you are from a big family, but what is your father like? Are you close?"

Nate took a breath. They were going back and forth, trading question for question.

A week ago, Nate had confided to Gable that

he felt he was going nowhere with the Russian girl. She was too tight, too guarded, he couldn't see that he was making any dent in her armor. "Whattya expect?" said Gable. "You want to bang her right away? She's young and nervous, a little Russian-nutso, she doesn't have fucking supervisors as sensitive and helpful as you got." Nate noticed for the first time that Gable had a 1971 Laotian calendar on his office wall. "Throw her some bones, show some petticoat. Just don't bullshit her, see if she'll relax."

"My father is a lawyer," said Nate. "He is very successful, owns his own practice. He is influential in the law and politics. He is close to my two older brothers, both work with my father. The law firm has been in my family for four generations."

Close to his older brothers, she thought. Dominika went straight at the question. "And why did you not go into the law with your father? You could be a rich man. Don't all Americans want to be rich?"

"Where did you get that impression? I don't know, I suppose I always wanted to go on my own, to be independent. Diplomacy appealed to me, and I like to travel. So I thought I would try something else first."

"But your father, was he disappointed that you did not follow your brothers?" Dominika asked.

"Sure, I suppose so," said Nate. "But maybe I was getting away from people always telling me what to do. You know what I mean?"

Images flashed behind Dominika's eyelids. Ballet, Ustinov, Sparrow School, Uncle Vanya. "But is it enough to have just run away from your family? Don't you have to accomplish something in the bargain?" She was going to press him, she decided.

"Running away is not exactly how I would describe it," said Nate, a little nettled. "I have a career, I'm contributing to my country." He saw Gondorf's face floating above the table.

"Of course," said Dominika. "But how exactly do you contribute?" She took a sip of wine.

"Lots of ways," said Nate.

"Give me an example," said Dominika.

Well, as an example, I handle the CIA's best asset, a high-level penetration of your frigging monolithic service, to thwart the worldwide evil designs of the Russian Federation and your lupine president for life, he thought. "I've been doing some interesting economic work lately, working on timber exports from Finland," he said.

"It sounds interesting," Dominika said, blinking at him. "I thought you were going to talk to me about world peace." Nate looked up at her. The purple mantle behind his head and shoulders blazed.

"I would, if I thought Russians knew what world peace was." He looked around the little dining room. "With *Afghanistan* and all."

Dominika took another sip of wine. "Next time I will take you to a *Vietnamese* restaurant I know," she said. They sat there looking at each other, neither willing to look away. *What the fuck is going on?* Nate thought. She had gotten under his skin a little. He remembered that VERONICA thought she didn't have a job to do. Was she working him? Her blue eyes were steady across the table.

"It's all right," Dominika said, reading his thoughts. "Just don't dismiss Russia all the time; we deserve some respect."

Very interesting, he thought. "We'll think back and remember this as our first fight," he said.

Dominika bit into a piece of flatbread. "How do you say, I will cherish the memory," she said.

Their food came. Dominika had ordered a rich lamb stew with lentils, which arrived steaming in a large bowl. A dollop of thick yogurt spread out over the top. Nate had ordered *bowrani,* dark caramelized pieces of sweet pumpkin in meat sauce with yogurt. It was delicious, and Nate made Dominika try a forkful. They finished their wine and ordered coffee.

"Next time I will pay the bill," said Dominika. "We should go to Suomenlinna before it gets too warm and there are crowds."

"I'll let you arrange it all," he said, and she nodded, looking at him through her eyelashes.

"You know, Nate," said Dominika, "I think you are honest, and funny, and kind. I like having you as a friend." Nate braced himself for what could be coming. "I hope you consider me a friend."

She wants to be friends now, thought Nate. "Of course I do," he said.

"Even though I am from Russia?"

"Especially since you're from Russia."

They sat in the fading light looking at each other, each thinking where this was leading, how each could bring the other along. Forty-five minutes later, they stood on the Metro platform—it was an aboveground station this far out. It was getting dark, cold but not freezing. Nate didn't offer to drive her back into the city, and in any event Dominika would not have accepted. Nate wasn't going to risk a chance sighting of Dominika in Nate's diplomatic-plated car by another Russian from her embassy.

The fat, glass-nosed train whizzed into the station and slowed. There was no one else on the platform, and the lighted interior of the train was empty. "Thank you for a wonderful afternoon," said Dominika, turning toward him. Their eyes met and she shook his hand, the proper SVR gladiator. He had decided he was going to test her a little, so he held her hand, leaned forward, and kissed her on the cheek. *Very charming,* she thought, but she had seen somewhat more in her short career. The musical horn sounded and she stepped into the carriage unsmiling, a faint limp when she turned and waved as the doors hissed shut.

As the train picked up speed, Nate saw through the accelerating windows an old lady in a parka sitting in the next car with a basket of knitting on her lap. The train was flashing by almost too fast for Nate to see VERONICA flick the side of her nose. The platform had been deserted, so how did she manage to get on the train?

During their respective journeys back into the city both Dominika and Nate should have been cataloguing their impressions, remembering details and composing tomorrow's contact reports in their heads. But neither of them was. Rather, Nate remembered how her cheek had felt and how she had stepped onto the train through the open doors with the slightest catch in her stride, and Dominika thought about his hands, one scraped red and raw, and how he had blinked in surprise, followed by delight, when she had thrown Vietnam back in his face.

KADDO BOWRANI—AFGHAN PUMPKIN

Deeply brown large chunks of peeled sugar pumpkin, cover liberally with sugar, and bake covered in medium oven until tender and caramelized. Serve over thick meat sauce of sautéed ground beef, diced onions, garlic, tomato sauce, and water. Garnish with sauce of drained yogurt, dill, and puréed garlic.

12

Through the open office door, Forsyth watched Nate work on the cable covering the last developmental lunch with Egorova. Nash was pushing the development now, but skeptically. It was slow going with the Russian, and Nate's confidence was still shaky. He was desperate to log a success, but banging your head against the wall took its toll. Inevitably, the stakes were getting higher. With every contact with Egorova, Forsyth knew that Headquarters would push harder, offer outside assessment, begin asking for ops tests. If Nate brought her to recruitment, they'd insist on interviews and a polygraph. The most recent Headquarters response to Nate's contact reports was, as Gable said, "already a fucking harbinger of things to come in the future."

> 1. With receipt of this cable please confine reporting on this case to restricted handling channels. Subject ref has been encrypted GTDIVA. Please establish Station BIGOT list and relay to Hqs.

> 2. Headquarters continues to applaud Station and case officer's diligence in developmental effort against DIVA. We find especially significant DIVA's continued willingness to meet with c/o (certainly unauthorized) and to discuss personal thoughts. Urge c/o to continue to probe for professional details and determine extent subj will

respond. Officer's elicitation efforts have paid off to date. Look forward to future progress. Kudos.

3. In light ref developments, solicit updated Station ops plan and ops tests contemplated for future DIVA contact. Please advise next scheduled meeting and security measures planned. Hqs standing by to consult on possible next steps.

Forsyth knew the signs. The last line presaged interference from Headquarters if the case really started taking off. The buzzards would be circling, but a stampede of visitors wouldn't start until the weather turned warmer, thought Forsyth. He called Nate into his office at the end of the day. "Have a seat, Nate. Your last cables on DIVA were really first-rate, objective, with good case-officer assessment," said Forsyth.

"Thanks, Chief," said Nate. Privately, he wasn't so sure. He knew the growing audience who saw his cables would read them with an increasingly critical eye.

"Your tradecraft is tight, keep it that way. MARBLE's a priority, of course, but after that make sure your pursuit of DIVA is undetectable to her embassy." Forsyth thought for a moment. "That translator you met, what's his name, Tishkov, he was an interesting nugget. But working two Russians in the same embassy probably is not a good idea, especially since DIVA is coming out to play. Maybe you can save Tishkov for later."

Nate thought that if he didn't recruit Dominika, all the Tishkovs in Helsinki wouldn't help him. Too many expectations. And Forsyth pointed out another danger. "This case is on Headquarters' scope now, big-time. Everyone's nose is going to be in it. If you recruit her, all the heat-seekers will come out of the woodwork.

"Right now you have to figure out whether DIVA has the inclination to doubt her system. Is she willing to listen to you and let you lead her to make the big decision?" Forsyth sat back. "Not a bad job, sitting with a beautiful Russian, trying to convince her to spy for you. Okay, get out of here and have fun. Door's open anytime you have a question."

Gable took him to a little bistro owned by Greeks and made him try the scrambled eggs, fluffy and laced with onions and tomatoes. Over eggs and multiple beers that night, Gable tried to lighten Nate's mood about the DIVA case. "Don't try to get her in bed before you recruit her. She will correctly conclude that you fucked her to get her to sign up. Recruit her first, then you'll be able to enjoy two of life's singular pleasures: Running an SVR officer, and eating breakfast in bed with cunty fingers." Gable threw back his drink and ordered two more for them.

"Golly, Marty, I feel I'm really growing under your coaching," said Nate, rolling his eyes. "All I know is I have to get her to relax, to like me. What happens if this starts getting emotional?"

Gable looked over at him with a face. "Please. There's no such thing as a case officer falling in love with an agent. It's not allowed. It cannot be done. Get it out of your head. Go ahead and bang her if you must, but love?"

The large main room of the SVR *rezidentura* in the Russian Embassy in Helsinki was dotted with plain wooden desks, set up in vaguely staggered rows. None of the desks had a terminal, but most had electric typewriters with odd lacquered turquoise covers sitting on small metal typing tables. These were specially produced JAJUBAVA typewriters manufactured in Moscow under license for the SVR and FSB, and securely pouched to overseas *rezidenturi,* to ensure the machines were not tampered with.

The low-ceilinged room was harshly lit by overhead fluorescent tubes also imported from Moscow for the same reason. They hummed and blinked and reflected milk-white off the scratched glass desktops. Along the exterior walls, the small dormer windows—the *rezidentura* was on the attic level of the Russian Embassy—were secured first by exterior bars, then by bolted steel shutters, then double-paned glass, and finally by heavy gray curtains, the hems of which trailed ragged on the floor. Worn deer trails in the bare carpet ran between the desks. The shabby room smelled of stale cigarettes and cold black tea in paper cups.

At one end of the room there were two offices. One was glassed in—the classified file room—with the clerk sitting at a desk in a circle of light from a gooseneck lamp. The room was lined with tall safes, some of whose drawers were open, others closed and secured by irregular yellow wax seals, as if someone had been throwing fried eggs at them. The other office was totally private, the windowless office of Rezident Volontov.

The half dozen officers in the SVR *rezidentura* kept their heads down over their work as Volontov's voice came through the closed door of his office. It was obvious that he was dressing down the newly arrived junior officer from Moscow, Egorova.

"Moscow has been hectoring me for progress reports," yelled Volontov, leaning over his desk. "They want to see more results against the American." The orange cloud around his head was like smoke, swirling and unsettled. *He's feeling the pressure,* thought Dominika.

"I *am* making progress, Colonel," said Dominika.

"We have had a dozen encounters, all of them discreet. He has made no indication that he has reported the contact to his superiors, a significant development."

"Don't tell me what's significant and what isn't. I directed you, the Center directed you, to document each of the meetings with Nash. Why aren't you drafting telegrams for my review and dispatch to Yasenevo?"

"I *have* drafted telegrams. You yourself told me to combine several messages in summary format. I cannot write about contacts until they actually materialize."

Volontov slammed his desk drawer shut with a bang, and the orange smoke swirled. "You'll do well to be respectful and leave the sarcasm for another time. Now I want you to accelerate this slow waltz with the American. You'll remember that the ultimate goal is to elicit information that may lead to the identification of a traitor. It is urgent, paramount, that you do."

"Yes," said Dominika, "I understand the ultimate goal. I drafted the operational proposal in the first place. Everything is progressing."

"That includes observing whether he seems to be preparing for an imminent operation, whether he is going on a trip, whether he is nervous, or distracted, or apprehensive."

"Yes, Colonel, I know all these things. I am confident I will be able to discern changes in his schedule." Dominika wasn't sure she could; their relationship was stuck, it seemed.

Volontov pretended to look thoughtfully at Dominika. His eyes flitted from her chin to her waist and in between. "Many of the indicators we are looking for," he said, sitting back, "are perhaps most discernible the better one knows the target. *In my experience,*" said Volontov, "the more intimate the relationship, the more intimate the conversation." *In your experience with Moroccan tea boys,* thought Dominika. She tamped down a cold rage as she looked at the warts on Volontov's neck.

"Very well, Colonel. I am to meet the American again next week. I will remember your guidance concerning intimacy, and I will report progress. I will propose additional meetings in the hope we can discover his work schedule. Does that meet with your approval?"

"Yes, yes, it's fine. But do not underestimate an emotional dependence. Do you understand?" Orange haze swirling around his head, nerves, fear.

The words came out before she could stop them. "Why don't you just come out and say it?" said Dominika, coming out of her seat. "Why don't you just order me to get on my back? I am an officer of the Service. I serve my country. I won't let you talk to me that way." Her body was trembling with rage and frustration. Before the scowling Volontov could react, Dominika wheeled and walked out of his office, slamming the door behind her. *If it had been any other junior officer,* Volontov thought bitterly, *I would have followed him into the outer office, stripped the hide off him with a birch branch, then shipped him home under escort to the Lubyanka basement. Let this one go for now,* he thought. *With her pedigree, it's safer this way.*

Eyes watched Dominika burst out of Volontov's office and make her way red-faced to her desk in the corner, hard against the angle of a dormer. She sat gripping the edge of her desk, head bowed. *This is some hothead,* thought her colleagues. They had heard Dominika's voice raised. Was she some kind of fool? Best to keep away from this *samoubiystvo,* this suicide waiting to happen, they all thought. All except one.

The conversation with Rezident Volontov festered inside Dominika for the five days before she was to meet Nate again, this time for dinner at a local restaurant. At night, in her apartment, she looked at her reflection in the dark glass of the window, the lights of Punavuori showing through the treetops. *Who are you?* she asked herself wearily. *How much will you take?* How she longed to wipe the eye of the beast, to puncture the desiccated self-importance of these users and falsifiers. To do so publicly was suicidal. No, better a secret revenge, undetectable, something delectable she could hold inside her, something *she* knew that *They* did not know.

Volontov was just the latest *nadziratel* in a procession of hoggish overseers in her life and career, but he was here and now, and she wanted to damage *him,* to extinguish the grimy orange halo around his warty face. She had to put her building rage into a box and calculate. The operation against Nate was critical to Volontov; he feared failing the Center. She could get back at him—at Them—by ruining it. *How to do it without destroying yourself?* Later that evening, she stopped with the toothbrush still in her mouth and looked at herself in the mirror. *You could give the American a surprise, drop your cover, let him know you're SVR.*

Izmena. Treason, that was what it would be. *Gosudarstvennaya izmena.* High treason. But it would ruin Volontov's case, put the Americans on guard, would rock Nate back on his heels. It would be interesting to see his surprise when he learned that she was an intelligence officer. He would respect her for that, he would be impressed. He would respect her.

Come on, are you insane? Have you forgotten discipline? Responsibility to the Rodina? But this was not an act against Russia. She was getting back at Them, knocking over their dominoes, not selling state secrets. She would be in control, she would determine how far was far enough. No, it was madness, and trouble, and impossible. She would have to find her satisfaction elsewhere. She brushed her hair and looked at the tapered handle of the brush, imagining it seated firmly between Volontov's buttocks. Then she turned off the light and went into her bedroom.

At the end of the week, Nate and Dominika were sitting in the ersatz Ristorante Villetta in Töölö at a corner table. The restaurant was classic Italian in Helsinki. A plastic canopy with Italian colors jutted out from the first floor of the apartment block in which it was located. Inside, the requisite red-and-white tablecloths and runny candles completed the décor. The weather was still cold, but winter would break soon, a few more feet of snow, then the short spring would give way to delicious summer, with the harbor full of sails and the ferries running. Dominika and Nate had arrived separately, as usual. Under her winter coat she wore a black belted knit dress and black wool stockings. The dress clung to her as she hung her coat over the back of her chair.

Nate wore a suit, but he had stripped off his necktie, and his shirt, in a blue pencil stripe, was open at the neck. He had left the embassy two hours before and had driven up the E12 until Ruskeasuo, cut west, and come back south on surface streets, entering Töölö only after having seen ARCHIE parked on a side street with the left-hand visor down. All clear.

Nate had huddled with Gable the day before. "Get her talking about work," Gable had said. "She's an SVR officer, that's her guilty secret." Nate nodded. He squirmed, agonizing over the need for a breakthrough moment. Forsyth had praised him, Gable was nothing but encouragement, but Nate was getting antsy. He needed to turn a corner, and right now.

They chatted for a minute while looking at the improbable oversized menus. "You are quiet tonight," said Dominika, looking at him over the top of the menu. *Same majestic purple. He never changes,* she thought.

"Hard day at the office," said Nate. *Keep it nonchalant.* "I was late for a meeting, left figures out of a cable, my boss was not happy and told me so."

"I cannot believe you are not excellent in your work."

"Well, I feel better now," Nate said, ordering two glasses of wine from the hovering waiter. "You look nice tonight."

"Do you think so?" He was paying her a compliment. How confident he seemed.

"Yes, I do. You make me forget my boss and work and the lousy day."

His boss. She wondered what he really thought. Dominika looked back down at the menu, but she had trouble focusing on the print.

"You are not alone, Nate. My superior also scolds." She could feel her heartbeat in her ears. She took a swallow of wine, felt it light up her stomach.

"So we're both in hot water. What did you do?"

"It's not important," Dominika said. "He is an unpleasant person, *nekulturny*. And ugly. He has warts." *How many* rezidents *in Helsinki have warts?* she thought.

"What's that, *nekulturny*?"

As if you don't know, thought Dominika. "He is a peasant, no culture."

Nate laughed. "What's his name? Have I met him on the dip circuit?"

She had changed her mind five times in the last two days, had ultimately decided to steer clear of silly games. She looked at Nate across the table. He was munching *grissini*, grinning at her. No! *Izmena!* Treason!

"His name is Volontov, Maxim," she said, hearing her own voice through someone else's ears. *Bozhe moi, my God,* she thought, *I've said it.* She looked at Nate closely. He was scanning his menu and did not look up when she said the name. The halo around his head did not change.

"Nope, I don't think I've met him." Nate felt the hairs on his arms stand up. *Holy shit. What's she doing? She just declared herself.*

"Well, you are fortunate, then," Dominika said, still staring at him. Nate looked up from the menu. Had Dominika made a mistake and let the *rezident*'s name slip out? She looked back at him evenly. No. She had deliberately said it.

"Why is he so bad?" asked Nate.

"He is disgusting, an old Soviet bastard. Every day he stares at me; what is the expression in English?" Dominika kept looking at Nate evenly.

"He undresses you with his eyes," said Nate.

"Yes," said Dominika. No reaction from him. Had he missed what she just said? My God, had she gone too far? Then, suddenly, she knew she didn't care. She had slid down the slope, and now was custodian of a mortally dangerous secret. *Are you happy now,* durak, *you little fool?*

"He sounds horrible . . . but I can understand why he stares." Nate looked at Dominika and smiled a boyish grin. *Jesus,* he thought, *this came out of the blue. Is this a signal to me? Is she being coy?* He looked at her unwavering blue eyes. Her chest rose and fell under the wool dress. Her fingertips gripped the edges of the ridiculous enormous menu.

"Now you are being *nekulturny*," she said. Did he already know? Was he so good, to hide his reaction?

"Well, it sounds like we both have trouble at work. We can commiserate."

"What does 'commiserate' mean?" asked Dominika. Blue-eyed stare.

"Crying on each other's shoulders," Nate said. Purple, steady and warm.

Dominika didn't know whether to laugh or scream. *Stay professional.* "Crying we can save for later. I am hungry, let's order," she said.

It was a Monday morning when a restricted-handling cable from Headquarters was passed to Nate, informing the Station that MARBLE had communicated via covcom that he would be arriving in Helsinki in two weeks as part of a Russian trade delegation participating in a two-day Scandinavian/Baltic economic summit. MARBLE relayed that he was using the delegation as cover for travel. He would stay under Line KR's radar that way. He was further covered by being operational, in town to attempt to bump the senior member of the Canadian delegation, Assistant Trade Minister Anthony Trunk, who the SVR thought was a valid recruitment prospect based on the minister's predilection for men in their early twenties.

A senior Canadian official and a *pidor,* to boot. The Americas Department had primacy, and MARBLE was the logical candidate to travel to Helsinki to sniff at Trunk's cologne-scented personage. The trip was approved by the Center. As MARBLE knew would happen, instructions were issued to exclude the Helsinki *rezidentura* from both the conference and the operation. MARBLE had subsequently signaled in his satellite burst transmission that he would be able to meet with CIA handlers late at night after the daily sessions and celebratory dinners concluded. Risky, but possible.

A Headquarters Russia analyst would arrive two

days before the start of the conference to help prepare current intelligence requirements for the meetings. A long list of follow-up questions generated by MARBLE's previous intelligence reports was cabled to Station. At the bottom of the list, as always, the softly phrased counterintelligence questions: Do you have knowledge of any moles in the US government? Are you aware of the compromise of any US classified material? Do you know of any intelligence operations being directed against US persons or systems? Mild, opened-ended questions designed to open the furnace door and look inside.

They went down the checklist. Replenishing commo gear was impossible—MARBLE would go through customs on his return from Helsinki. A universal contact plan would be updated. Forsyth vetoed the addition of two senior officers from Headquarters to participate in the debriefings. Nate was MARBLE's handler and he would do the job.

Now there were preparations no one else could make: Nate receded into the background, went out onto the streets, dropped from sight. By night he cased dark alleys, angled walls, loading-dock stairways—Brief Encounter sites—near the neoclassical splendor of the Kämp Hotel, where the summit would be held and delegates housed. He wandered past cafés, restaurants, the City and Sculpture Museums, pacing distances, measuring angles, determining flow and screening—these would be the Brush Pass sites—all within easy walking distance of the Kämp.

Lastly, during a night of driving rain with sheets of water pouring off the monoliths on the façade of the train terminal, Nate went up the side steps and, just inside the doors, felt the hand, then the heavy weight of the hotel key in his pocket. A thin-faced man, a nonofficial cover officer, an NOC from Europe, had taken a room at the Hotel GLO for a week with a throwaway alias. Every night during the conference, Nate would wait in the hotel room to meet MARBLE when he could get away, wait for the minute scratch at the door, wait to begin the long conversations in the overheated room with the shades down and the television turned up, into the early morning hours, while the city slept and the changing traffic lights reflected endlessly off the wet, empty streets. By the time MARBLE stepped off the plane in Helsinki, the Station was prepared to spend as much time as securely possible with him, without remotely showing an American hair on the street.

It was early evening, after work, and Dominika stood by a window on the mezzanine level of the Torni Hotel across from the swimming pool, waiting for Nate to show. They swam together now at least three days a week, but Nate had not been at the pool for six days straight. Strange, she thought, feeling a little jilted. A week ago, on a windy spring Sunday, they had met for coffee at the Carusel Café on the water in Ullanlinna. There was a growing forest of swaying rigging in the harbor as halyards clanked against aluminum masts and clouds moved across a rare blue sky.

Dominika had taken a bus, then the Metro, and finally two taxis to get to the marina. She argued with herself as she walked along the Havsstranden, but in the end had dabbed a little perfume behind her ears. He came on foot, walking across the road, and there was a spring to his step. Nate was his usual charming self, but there was something else. His purple halo was hazy, faded. He was distracted, something was on his mind. When previously they would have spent four, five, six hours together, Nate after an hour said he had another commitment—it was unexpected work, nothing social, he assured her, but he had to go. They had walked a little ways together, and when

Dominika suggested that next weekend they might take the ferry to Suomenlinna and spend the day exploring the old fortress, Nate said he would love to, but two weekends from now would be better.

Trees along the street were budding, they could feel the sun on their faces. At a quiet street corner they stood and faced each other. Dominika was heading home, Nate was going the other way. Dominika could feel him; he radiated nervous energy. He was waiting for something to happen, she thought. "I'm sorry I'm such a pill," said Nate. "It's just a lot of work. So we go to the fortress in two weeks together?"

"Of course," she said. "I will look for you at the swimming pool. We can arrange Suomenlinna when we see each other." She turned to cross the street. What, she asked herself, had possessed her to use perfume? Nate watched her walk away down the sidewalk of the leafy neighborhood, registering the slight hitch in her stride. Her lean dancer's legs bunched at the calves and she swung her hands easily as she walked.

Then he thought about MARBLE's imminent arrival. He still had to find an all-clear signal site near the Hotel GLO so MARBLE would know to come upstairs. He took off.

GREEK STRAPATSADA EGGS

In heated olive oil reduce peeled, chopped tomatoes, onions, sugar, salt, and pepper to a thick sauce. Add beaten eggs to the tomatoes and stir vigorously until eggs set into a small, fine curd. Serve with grilled country bread drizzled with olive oil.

13

It's been too long. *Where is he? What's he doing? Does he have another target,* another woman? Did he break contact because she dropped her cover? She let it go another day, standing in the Torni Hotel across from the swimming pool each evening, waiting for sight of him. She knew he wasn't coming again tonight. *This is it, this is what I was sent here to do.* She fought off the image of Uncle Vanya in his office, the suety face of Volontov looking at her each day. She would have to report in the morning.

Walking to her apartment, Dominika barely registered the streets or the lights in the windows. She thought about what would happen tomorrow in the *rezidentura.* Her report about Nate's weeklong no-show would be forwarded by immediate cable to the deputy director, Eyes Only. In Line KR, an urgent request to the travel office would produce a list of all Russians traveling to Scandinavia, for six months previously and six months in the future. Diplomats, businessmen, academics, students, officials, even flight crews. The list would be finite. The patient wolves in KR would start eliminating names based on age, profession, history, and, most critically, access to state secrets. The pared-down list of leading suspects might contain a dozen names or a hundred. It wouldn't matter. The SVR would then start watching them in Moscow, covering their mail, monitoring their phones, searching apartments and dachas, dispatching informers to get close.

The search would surely extend to Helsinki, she thought. A Directorate K surveillance team might be deployed to cover Nate for two or three weeks, a month, to observe his activities. Unexpected and invisible—the Directorate K team was referred to in whispered awe—they would record their observations, then the endless watching would begin once back in Moscow. It was inevitable. At the end of the process, if the agent was indeed a Russian, he or she would be arrested, tried, and executed. The Gray Cardinals would have their way again.

Her footsteps were loud in the night air; the city was quiet. Who was Nate's agent? she wondered. Why was he betraying Russia? Was this man or woman decent? Venal? Treacherous? Noble? Crazy? She wanted to hear his voice, watch his face. Could she ever sympathize with his motives? Could she ever justify his treason? She thought about her own pettish transgression. *You rationalized that easily enough, haven't you,* zagovorshchitsa, *you great conspirator?*

Dominika closed her eyes and leaned against the wall of a darkened building. Right now she was the only one who suspected—no, *knew*—that Nate would be meeting his agent, the mole, and she felt light-headed. What if she said nothing? What if she denied Them the knowledge and the power to win this gambit? Could she be this disloyal?

She thought of how her foot had been ruined by that tart Sonya. She remembered the green-agony scream in the shower room at the AVR. She flashed to the orange overhead light as a helpless Delon withered before the thugs, and remembered the taste of Ustinov's blood in her mouth. And she saw Anya's milkmaid face choked blue.

Let them wait, she decided, determination welling up inside her. This would be horribly dangerous, potentially fatal. Her resolve was fragile, exquisite, forbidden—the power she would wield over Volontov and Uncle Vanya would be real. Her mother was always telling her to control her temper, and now the icy bite in her throat was exhilarating.

She began walking again, her heels clicking on the sidewalk. There was something else, a realization that surprised her. She knew enough about the Game to know that Nate would be destroyed, his reputation obliterated, if he lost his agent. She replayed their time in Helsinki. She would not do that to him, thinking how much Nate was like her father, how much she liked him.

The next morning, sick to her stomach, she showed her pass at the embassy front door, walked across the courtyard, and climbed the marble steps to the attic, steps worn smooth by countless officers who had served before her. *Sluzhba Vneshney Razvedki*, the Foreign Intelligence Service. At the top of the stairs was the massive vault door on massive hinges, then the day door with the cipher lock, then the privacy wire gate with the electric keypad. She put her purse down on her desk, nodded to a colleague. Volontov stood at his office door, beckoning.

Dominika stood in front of his desk, unable to take her eyes away from his doughy hands. "Any developments to report, Corporal?" asked Volontov. He was cleaning his nails with a letter opener. Her heart was racing and the pounding in her head would not stop. Did it show? Did he know something? She heard her voice in her head, as if someone else in the room were speaking.

"Colonel, I have discovered that the American seems to favor museums," said Dominika. Her voice sounded wooden. "I have invited him to the Kiasma art gallery soon. I plan to have dinner afterward . . . in my apartment." What was she saying? The very thing Volontov wanted to hear. Volontov looked up from his manicure, grunted, then stared at her breasts.

"It's about time. Make sure you entertain him so he will want to visit you again," he said. "You haven't seen anything out of the ordinary?"

Three words—*Yes, I have*—and the machine would take over, her responsibility would be over. A simple sentence—*He said he is busy the next two weeks*—was all that would be necessary. The roaring in her ears grew louder and the edges of her vision clouded. Dominika could barely make out this hog behind his desk, wrapped in his dingy orange haze. Her throat closed and she was amazed to feel her legs tremble, knees actually knocking, quite extraordinary, and she resisted leaning against the desk, willed herself to stop. Volontov continued looking at her chest, a wing of pomaded hair sticking out from the side of his head. In the last millisecond, Dominika decided.

"There's nothing to report at this time," she said, heart pounding. She had stepped across the line separating being guilty of an infraction to committing treason against the State. They would find out, they would send men with ice picks to stab her to death like Trotsky. They would roll her mother into a furnace. Volontov looked at her for a moment, grunted again, and waved her out of his office. In a flash, Dominika knew he suspected nothing. She was sure of her instincts and felt the ice in her veins, tingling.

Dominika returned to her desk, sat heavily in her chair. Her hands were damp and shaking, and she looked around the room at the officers and secretaries at the other desks. All had their heads down, reading, typing, or writing. Except Marta Yelenova, sitting at a desk two across from Dominika's. Marta was holding a cigarette, staring at her. Dominika smiled thinly and looked away.

Marta, Dominika supposed, was the closest thing she had to a friend in the Embassy. She was the senior administrative assistant in the *rezidentura*. They had spoken in the office occasionally, had sat next to each other during a dinner for some unknown embassy colleague. They had met one rainy Sunday for a walk along the harbor and among the fresh food stalls in Market Square. Marta was elegant, aristocratic, about fifty, with thick brown hair that she wore down to her shoulders. She had dark, prominent eyebrows over the most striking hazel eyes. Her fine mouth tended to turn up at the corners in a wry smile that hinted at an unshakably cynical view of the world. She was one of those with strong color about her head and body, a deep ruby red of passion and heat, a red as when Dominika listened to music.

Dominika thought that Marta must have been a beauty in her youth. She rounded on any man in the office who made even the slightest comment about her Junoesque figure, now a little thick around the waist, sending him scuttling for the exit. Marta was not in the least fazed by Rezident Volontov, characteristically telling him that he would get the *voucher,* or the *accounting,* or the *monthly report,* when she *finished it.* Volontov could not dent her Olympian aplomb.

Dominika previously knew nothing about Marta's life, but if she had, she would have been amazed to learn that Marta Yelenova had, in 1983, been conscripted by the KGB to attend State School Four—Sparrow School—in the forest outside Kazan. She was twenty years old. Her father had fought in the Great Patriotic War, then became an NKVD guard at the Leningrad headquarters, a party member, a loyal vassal of the State. Marta's heartbreaking beauty had been noticed by a KGB major from Moscow making an inspection tour, and he arranged for her to be hired into the Service as, he originally hoped, his special assistant.

Marta's father, who knew the game but nevertheless hoped for a better life for her, said nothing, and sent his only daughter to Moscow to live with his sister and to begin work in the KGB's Second Chief Directorate (internal security), Seventh Department (operations against tourists), Third Section (hotels and restaurants). The Seventh Department alone employed two hundred officers and sixteen hundred part-time informants and agents.

Now in Moscow, it was inevitable that Marta would be noticed by an SCD colonel, who outranked the major, and who assigned her to his staff. She was subsequently noticed by an SCD general, who outranked the colonel, and who made her his adjutant, even though Marta had no idea what an adjutant's duties entailed. She found out when the general one afternoon forced her down on the divan in his office and put his hand under her uniform skirt. Marta hit him on the side of the head with a (typically Soviet) steel water carafe. The resultant scandal in the strangely puritanical KGB was exacerbated by the fact that the general's wife was the sister of an alternate Politburo member. Marta was hurriedly transferred to State School Four. She had no choice. Marta was going to learn to be a Sparrow.

Marta had the rare combination of a sublime allure and a superior intellect. The former quality served to attract hapless foreign diplomats, journalists, and businessmen. The latter gave her perspective and a keen eye for making influential friends. At the end of her nearly twenty-year career, Marta was known as *Koroleva Vorobey*, Queen Sparrow. She had participated in scores of SCD honey traps, among which were included the recruitments by the KGB of a sex-crazed Japanese billionaire, a philandering British ambassador, and a reptilian Indian minister of defense. At the apex of Marta's career, she was the bait in the legendary seduction, compromise, and recruitment of a cipherine, a female code clerk working in the German Embassy, the suborning of whom enabled the KGB to read German and NATO encrypted traffic for an uninterrupted seven years. It was the only time Marta worked against another woman, but the recruitment was still taught at KGB Higher School as a classic operation.

Over the years, Marta's nonoperational romances included discreet affairs with two members of the Politburo, with a general in the First Chief Directorate, and with various sons of influential officials in the Collegium of the KGB. Many bushy-browed old bosses remembered her with affection. Thanks to these "mentors," Marta was bulletproof and was given an SVR major's pension on retiring from Sparrow operations by grateful if exhausted benefactors. Marta decided to enjoy life and see a little of the outside world, so she requested and was readily granted an overseas assignment, to Helsinki.

At first Marta did not know whether Dominika was SVR clerical or administrative. She certainly was very young to be assigned overseas. The last name explained much, but the fact that Dominika had no steady duties in the *rezidentura*, came and went as she liked, and spoke directly and privately with the *rezident* suggested that she was in Helsinki under a special charter. Dominika's clothes were new, she must have been provided a wardrobe. Office gossip accelerated when it was discovered that this beautiful newcomer had been assigned a private apartment outside the block reserved for all embassy personnel. To Marta, that had a familiar ring to it.

In the *rezidentura* she was correct, reserved, did her work quickly and well, with an uncommon intensity. On the street, Marta saw how Dominika's eyes flitted from people's faces to the doors, along the sidewalk, across the street, using normal movements to mask her constant glances. When they were sitting together at a café, there was the flash of gratifying intuition, a hint of playfulness, the brilliant smile. Marta knowingly identified Dominika's nearly unconscious use of her beauty—eyes, smile, body—in her interactions. And when they talked, Marta recognized how Dominika used techniques of conversation and elicitation.

Quite a creature, thought Marta, *and in operations!* Beauty, brains, tradecraft, and incandescent blue eyes. It was apparent that she knew her duty, loved her country, but there was something beneath the surface, an underground spring bubbling unseen. Pride, anger, disobedience. And something else, hard to define, a secret side, an addiction to rebellion, as if she courted risk. Marta wondered how long it would be before this young woman, with her discerning eye and natural instincts, would realize that the Center's work was *pokazukha,* something done solely for effect, for show. Rezident Volontov was an extreme example of the work ethic, the type of functionary who had run the KGB and the Kremlin for the last seventy years.

They began walking out of the embassy at the end of the day, stopping at a local bar for a glass of wine and a sinful slice of caviar pie oozing crème fraîche and cheese. They spoke of family, of Moscow, of experiences. Dominika did not mention Sparrow School. Marta laughed and made Dominika laugh, and they walked arm in arm down the sidewalk at the end of the evening.

One night in a bar, after smoothly telling a disgusting German to leave them alone, Marta told Dominika her life story, about her career as a Sparrow. She was proud of having served her country; she didn't think about the beastly years of the KGB. She was not in the slightest ashamed of who she was or what she'd done. Dominika's lip trembled and she looked at her friend and began silently weeping. It was a long evening after that, but Marta knew everything about Dominika in the end. The assignment to pursue Nate, Uncle Vanya, Sparrow School, the Frenchman Delon, even Ustinov. The words came out of Dominika in a flood. There was no thought about elicitation or manipulation. The two women thereafter were, simply, friends.

Evening after evening, cool and collected, Marta listened and thought, *My, how the* vlastiteli, *the bosses, have wrung quite a lot out of this girl in such a short time.* But Marta saw strength in Dominika, and something else. Marta suspected Dominika's exposure to the easygoing young American CIA officer was creating deeper reactions as well. To have said so would have been to imply that Dominika could not operate correctly, so Marta said nothing.

"I don't know," said Dominika. "He's arrogant, he's facetious, he doesn't like Russia, or at least he doesn't give us much credit. Uncle Vanya believes he is a desperate operative."

"He sounds unpleasant," said Marta. "But it should make it easier to work against him—even to sleep with him—to get what you want." She lit a cigarette and looked at Dominika leaning back in the booth. They were on their third glass of wine.

"Not so much unpleasant as frustrating. But nice." She sighed. "I am supposed to tell Volontov when I think he's operational, distracted. They want to catch him with his agent." Dominika was feeling the wine.

"And do you know him well enough to do that?" asked Marta. "Will you be able to know?"

Dominika brushed a lock of hair off her forehead. "I think I already have—I mean, I already do," she said.

"And you ran right in and reported to Colonel

Volontov," said Marta. She already knew what was happening.

"Not exactly," said Dominika. "I told him I would keep watching."

"And you positively did not report that you suspected your young American was becoming busy."

"He's not my 'young American,'" said Dominika, her eyes closed.

"But you suspect it's so, and Volontov asked you outright, and you didn't say a thing, correct?" asked Marta, leaning toward Dominika. "Open your eyes, look at me."

She opened her eyes. "Correct. I didn't say anything." She closed her eyes.

Marta sipped her wine, noting with some detachment that Dominika not only had committed treason against the *State*—saying *treason against the Duma* sounded ridiculous—by not reporting and lying about it, but also had that evening made Marta likewise guilty of treason for having heard about the crime. She reached out and squeezed Dominika's hand. "You must be careful," she said.

Marta had devoted her life to the State, had for years ignored its excesses and personally contributed to the downfall of men whose only sin was to succumb to the pleasures of the flesh. But inside, she had long since broken with the bastards. She knew what a situation Dominika was in. *The beasts,* she thought, *they will utterly empty this beautiful, intelligent girl, then cast her aside.* And if what she was doing even remotely thwarted Vladimir Putin, it would be mortally dangerous. Dominika's knowledge was like a knotted bag of snakes—safe for the moment, but don't bang it against the wall.

MARBLE's short visit to Helsinki was a triumph in multiple ways. First, MARBLE himself met and made significant progress with Trade Minister Trunk, thus incontrovertibly establishing the continuing need to pursue the flamboyant Canadian. Second, three nights of midnight-to-dawn meetings in the Hotel GLO with Nate had already produced eight highly graded intelligence reports (with notes for a possible thirty-seven more) on SVR operations in Europe and North America. Third, MARBLE provided the name of an assistant commissioner in the RCMP's Strategic Policy and Planning Directorate who was meeting a Russian illegal (whose day job was as a dancer at the Bare Fax in Ottawa). Last, the old agent repeated from memory—he did not normally have access to China reporting—the gist of three superb SVR reports from Beijing detailing the power struggle still smoldering within the Politburo Standing Committee fully two years after the removal of Bo Xilai in early 2012. MARBLE's "source comments" regarding President Putin's interest—"significantly obsessive," he called it—in Chinese Communist Party disunity were highly valued by analysts.

That was just the positive intelligence from MARBLE. The most explosive item was a hint MARBLE had picked up that there was a "Director's Case" being run out of the fourth floor of Yasenevo, an asset in the pay of Russia so important and so sensitive that SVR leadership were running the case exclusively. To CIA counterintelligence, this special handling could only mean a megamole. Some government, some country, had a big problem, was gravely penetrated, and they all looked at one another and wondered if it was in Washington. That intel tidbit was compartmented from the rest of MARBLE's reporting and handled separately.

No one had to tell the old spook what to do about this. *He* told *them* what he would do. He knew how to pull the string with his fingertips, how to be the spider sitting on the web, waiting for the tremble of the radius threads. He would collect—softly, softly—more information when he could. Meanwhile, the words *SVR mole, Director's Case,* and *Yasenevo* went on the office whiteboards of a dozen counterintelligence analysts in CIA headquarters. They were good at waiting, they would wait for months, even years, to fit more pieces into the mosaic.

The last evening, MARBLE told Nate that Anthony Trunk would within the next six months attend an economic conference in Rome as well as the UN General Assembly in New York, providing two future opportunities for MARBLE to travel out of Russia with plausible cover provided by the SVR's pursuit of Trunk.

Headquarters was pleased with this round of MARBLE meetings and with Nate's performance. A bonus was deposited in MARBLE's secret fund account, and Nate was awarded a Quality Step Increase amounting to a salary bump of $153 per pay period, after taxes. "Wicked good," said Gable when he heard about Nate's QSI. "One hundred and fifty-three dollars. Just as long as they don't fucking devalue your contribution. You realize you also get a voucher for six free car washes?"

At the end of the meeting series, before MARBLE returned to Moscow, Nate pushed gently about the general's security. MARBLE rather nonchalantly acknowledged that since he and Nate had narrowly missed being rolled up on the snowy Moscow street that one night—it seemed like a hundred years ago—there was a serious mole hunt going on inside SVR headquarters in Yasenevo. His old comrade First Deputy Director Egorov was convinced someone senior in the Russian service was spying for the CIA. "In other words . . . me," he said with a laugh. Nate's concern showed on his face.

"Look," said MARBLE, "I am used to the risk. I know how my Service works. I know how that *zhulik*, that old fraud Egorov, thinks and operates. There's no cause for alarm." He thought to himself about fourteen years as Langley's agent, of wakeful nights listening to footfalls in the stairwell, or feeling the tightness in his chest when called back to Moscow "for consultations." He remembered the inexpressible wave of relief on seeing a full conference room after being summoned to a meeting. Others before him had entered an empty meeting room with the *ubijca*, the thugs, waiting behind the door.

The old man humored his intense young handler, and they reviewed their contingency plans for the biggest high-wire act in denied-area operations. Exfiltration. Smuggling someone to freedom. From inside Moscow, under hot pursuit, with family or with the mistress, curled tight in a car trunk or brazening it through passport control. After forty minutes MARBLE held up his hand. "Nathaniel, enough for tonight, I think. You are very thorough." Nate blushed in self-conscious embarrassment and they said good night.

Now MARBLE was safely home and Nate was pleased to read effusive praise from Headquarters for the secure and productive meeting series with the agent. A cable had characterized Nate's reporting as "well received *at the highest levels,*" cablese for the White House and the NSC.

Forsyth tapped him on the shoulder for a good job, and Gable bought him a beer. "All the kudos you're getting, no one's thinking about the agent," said Gable. "It's your responsibility never to forget him. You got that?"

The glow faded with Nate's pressing problem. Dominika. Where was the case going? What did her admission that she worked for the *rezident* mean? If there wasn't some progress soon, there would be complaints from Headquarters.

"Screw Headquarters," said Gable, starting on another beer. "Just take it easy for a couple of weeks, bask in the glow of your recent scary-good performance, then we'll decide what you can do next."

Nate knew Gable well enough by now. "You really mean, *Get out of this chair and hit the street before I kick you out the front door,* don't you?" said Nate.

"Yes, yes, in fact I do," said Gable. "Go to the swimming pool. Find your SVR corporal. Bring her flowers. Tell her you were miserable without her, that you missed seeing her. Take her to dinner."

"To tell you the truth, Marty, I *did* sort of miss seeing her," said Nate, looking down at the carpet. He looked back up at Gable.

"Jesus wept," said Gable, and walked out.

CAVIAR TORTE

Blend sautéed shallots, crème fraîche, and grated Neufchâtel cheese and pour mixture into a springform pan. Sprinkle with chopped boiled eggs. Spread a thin layer of small-gauge caviar (Ossetra or Sevruga) on top of torte and chill. Unmold and spread on blinis or toast points.

14

Marta conspired with Dominika in little ways. She helped her pad attendance and work logs to show activity, and together they talked out how Dominika could write contact reports that showed hopeful progress, while at the same time being sufficiently anodyne not to rouse the sleeping bear in the Center. She wrote of pleasant but inconclusive sessions with the American at a museum, a lunch, a coffee, veiled references to his almost languid unresponsiveness. "It makes him sound horrid," said Dominika, "and it makes me sound horrible too. We'll be two old maids, you and I!"

"You think so?" said Marta, lighting a cigarette. "Perhaps we'll be like the two girls buying sausages. The butcher has no change, so he gives them an extra sausage. 'What are we going to do with the third sausage?' whispers one girl. 'Quiet,' her friend says. 'We'll eat that one.'" Dominika started laughing.

Volontov was constantly hovering, feeling the pressure from Moscow and passing it downhill. He saw the obvious friendship between the two women, the aging former Sparrow and her young friend. And Egorova was clearly abetted by Yelenova. Yelenova's already chronic lack of respect and compliance was increasing and becoming more apparent daily.

It was a stormy day with sheeting rain coming in waves from the south, from Estonia. Dominika was out of the embassy when Volontov called Marta into his office. Marta sat without being bidden, squared her shoulders. "You wanted to see me, Colonel?"

Volontov looked at Marta without speaking. His eyes traveled from her legs to her face. Marta looked him in the eye. "What is it you wish, Colonel?" Marta repeated.

"I have been noticing your close friendship with Corporal Egorova," said Volontov. "You and she seem to be spending a fair amount of time together."

"Is there anything wrong with that, Colonel?" asked Marta. She lit a cigarette, lifted her head, and blew the smoke toward the ceiling.

Volontov watched her like a farm boy. "What have you been saying to Egorova?"

"I'm not sure I understand the question, Colonel," said Marta. "We go out for a glass of wine, we talk about family, travel, food."

"What else do you talk about?" Volontov asked. "Do you speak about men, about boyfriends?" The light from the fluorescent tubes in his office reflected from the sheen of the lapels of his Bulgarian suit.

"Excuse me, Colonel," said Marta, "what is the reason for these personal questions?"

"*Sookin syn!*" Volontov slapped his hand on his desk. "I don't have to give you a reason," he bellowed. "Whatever you have been saying to Egorova, I want it to stop. Your well-known cynical attitude and jaded views are affecting her. Her productivity has dropped. She is falling behind in her assigned work. Her written reports are unsatisfactory. Leave her alone. Or I will take measures."

Accustomed to and unaffected by the phlegmy bellows of Soviet officialdom, Marta calmly leaned forward and stubbed her cigarette in the ashtray on his desk. His eyes flicked down to the opening in her blouse. She put her hands on the edge of his desk and leaned farther to give him an even better look. "Colonel," Marta said, "I must tell you something. You are repulsive. It is you who should leave Egorova alone. Don't sully her with your disgusting manner. She has done nothing wrong."

"Who do you think you're talking to?" yelled Volontov. "You're nothing but an overripe whore, *blyadishcha*! I can have you sent home tonight, trussed up like the sow you are. You'll be manning a regional travel office in Magnitogorsk, where you can check travel permits all day and suck toothless Metallurg hockey players all night."

"Ah, yes, Colonel, all the familiar threats," said Marta. She knew this species of toad, this kind of coward. "But what about *this* threat, Colonel? I'll go over your head. I'll create so much trouble for you in Moscow that it will be *you* on *your* knees in Magnitogorsk. Vanya Egorov will not be pleased to hear that your *rezidentura* is a *svalka,* a trash heap, and your accomplishments are nonexistent. He will be quite interested to hear how you leer at his niece and dream of putting your face between her legs. Bastard. *Mudak*."

This was colossal insubordination. This was treason. Volontov stood behind his desk and screamed at Marta. "Pack your belongings. I want you out of here by tomorrow night. I don't care how: train, boat, plane. If you're not gone by tomorrow night—"

"*Zhopa!* Asshole!" said Marta, who turned her back on Volontov and walked toward his door. Trembling with rage, Volontov tore open the desk drawer, scrabbled around in it, and brought out a small Makarov automatic, the pistol he'd had with him all his career. He had never fired it in the field, never fired it in anger. Now, with shaking hand, he racked the slide back to chamber a round. At the door, Marta heard the sound and turned. Volontov's pistol was raised, pointing directly at her. "I'm not Dimitri Ustinov, Colonel Volontov. You and your kind cannot destroy every single thing you don't control." Marta's heart was beating; she didn't know if Volontov would pull the trigger.

Ustinov? The murdered oligarch? Butchered in his penthouse, buckets of blood, rumored Mafia vendetta? Volontov had no idea what this bitch was talking about, but the 1950s-vintage Soviet vacuum tubes in his head heated up. His water-bug instincts told him there was something lurking under the surface, perhaps something very important. He lowered his pistol. Marta turned the knob on his office door and walked out. Colleagues were gathered in the hallway; they had heard the shouting.

Inside his office, Volontov smoked a cigarette and tried to calm down. He reached for the secure, crème-colored telephone labeled VCh for *vysokochastoty*, high-frequency. "Get me Moscow," he said to the operator. After a thirty-second wait he was speaking to First Deputy Director Egorov. Two minutes later he had been given instructions. These included: Ignore what Yelenova had said to him, repeat it to absolutely no one, and do nothing more. Volontov was about to protest that this sort of insubordination would undermine his authority. Over the scratchy line, Egorov told him to pay attention.

"*Yest' chelovek, yest' problema. Nyet cheloveka, nyet problemy,*" said Egorov. A chill ran through Volontov. He knew that one by heart. One of Comrade Stalin's aphorisms: *If there is a person, there is a problem. If there is no person, then there is no problem.*

Nate and Dominika sat on the couch in his apartment. Lights from the harbor filtered through the window and the bass note of a ship's horn came from the darkness beyond the islands in the bay. A sweep team had checked Nate's apartment so he could invite Dominika for dinner. Neither knew, at this stage, who had the operational advantage. Neither knew where his or her respective developmental efforts would lead. Neither fully understood the stakes of the Game. All either of them knew was that they looked forward to seeing each other. Nate's little living room was dimly lit with two lamps. Music played softly, Beny Moré ballads.

Nate had cooked for Dominika, *vitello picatta,* veal scaloppine with lemon caper sauce. Dominika had stood leaning against the kitchen table watching while Nate lightly sautéed the wafer-thin medallions of meat in oil and butter. She moved closer to the stove as he poured wine and lemon juice into the pan to deglaze the *fond,* added thin lemon slices and capers, then pieces of cold butter. He put the pieces of veal back into the pan to warm them. They ate dinner on the couch, the plates on their laps. Dominika finished her wine and poured herself another glass.

They had picked up their relationship after the break of several weeks ago, had spent time together since then. On a chilly Sunday, walking around the old fortress, they had started the familiar argument.

"You lived in Moscow for a year, for goodness' sake," Dominika said. "But you don't know Russians. Your view is black-and-white. You haven't learned anything."

Nate smiled and offered his hand to help her over a grassy parapet, part of the castle walls. Dominika did not take it and trudged up the mound on her own. "Look, nationalism is fine. You've got a lot to be proud of," said Nate. "But the world is not populated with your enemies. Russia should concentrate on helping her own people."

"We do very well, thank you," said Dominika.

They continued squabbling in the apartment after dinner. "I'm just saying that Russia hasn't fundamentally changed from the old days, that she is missing the great opportunities before her. That the familiar bad habits are all back."

"What bad habits?" asked Dominika. She was drying a plate at the sink.

"Corruption, repression, imprisonment. Soviet behavior is the default, it's strangling democracy in Russia."

"You almost seem pleased to repeat the list," said Dominika. "I suppose there is none of that in America?"

"Sure we have our problems, but we don't let dissidents die in jail, or murder political opponents." Nate saw Dominika's face change. "There are people who value humanity, who believe that all humans have rights, it doesn't matter what country they're from. And then there are people who don't seem to care about their fellow man, who have no conscience, like some of the people in the former Soviet Union, in the old KGB. Some of them never went away."

Dominika could not believe they were having this conversation. For the first part, it was insulting to sit here being lectured by this young American. For the second part, Dominika knew that much of what he said was correct, but to admit it would be unthinkable. "Now you're an expert," she said, putting the plate down and picking up another, "on the KGB."

"Well, I knew one or two of them," said Nate.

Dominika continued drying the plate without pausing. "You knew KGB men? Impossible. Who were they?" she asked. *And what will you do if he tells you?* she thought.

"Nobody you would know. But in comparison I greatly prefer knowing SVR officers. They're much nicer." That grin again, deep purple.

Dominika did not react, but looked at her watch and said it was getting late. Huffy. Nate helped her into her coat, pulling her hair free of the collar. Dominika felt his finger brush her neck as he did so.

"Thank you for dinner, Nate," she said. She had her temper in a box, just barely.

"May I walk you home?" he asked.

"No, thank you," said Dominika. She walked to the front door and turned, offering her hand, but he was right behind her and he put his hand on her shoulder and kissed her lightly on the mouth. "Good night," she said, and went out into the hallway, her lips tingling.

NATE'S VEAL PICATTA

Pound small medallions of veal paper-thin. Season and quickly sauté in butter and oil until golden. Remove and cover. Deglaze pan with dry white wine and lemon juice, boil to reduce. Lower heat, add thin lemon slices, capers, and cold butter. Gently simmer to a thick reduction (do not bring back to a boil). Return medallions to sauce to warm.

15

Past midnight now, the Helsinki snow had given way to the rains of emergent spring, which spattered on the pavement, dripped off the bare limbs of the trees, and rattled against the windows. Nate tossed in his bed. Twelve blocks away, Dominika lay awake hearing the rain and felt the lingering tingle of Nate's good-night kiss on her lips. She was glad she had saved him, and she would do it again, she decided.

Thank God for Marta. Not only had her friend's support helped her with the decision, but also Marta's wry commentary on life had crystallized her thinking, especially about keeping a secret from the Service. Marta did not believe in blind devotion. She told Dominika not to be a *tricoteuse,* to be true to herself, to owe allegiance first to herself, then, if there was room, to Russia. Dominika tossed in her bed.

Five blocks to the east, Marta Yelenova eased open her apartment door in the residence block reserved for Russian Embassy employees. Cooking smells of boiled beef and cabbage were heavy in the corridor and reminded her of apartment blocks in Moscow. She shook the rain off her overcoat and hung it on a hook next to the door.

Her apartment was small, with a separate kitchen nook, beyond which was the tiny bathroom. The apartment had been used by generations of Russian Embassy employees and was dingy and worn, the furniture scarred and wobbly. Marta stumbled as she took off her wet shoes. She giggled to herself. She was tipsy after a long night alone in a small café. At some point during the evening she had ordered *pytt i panna*, a popular Scandinavian hash of beef, onion, and potatoes. She had left the bar and walked home in the rain. It had been some time since her blowup with Volontov, and the expected recall to Moscow, the reprimands, the firing from the Service had not come. The *rezident* studiously ignored her, but absolutely nothing had happened.

Marta saw that Dominika in the last days was trying to schedule more frequent operational meetings with Nathaniel, primarily because that was what kept Volontov happy, but also, Marta observed, because Dominika looked forward to contact with the young American. Volontov had called her into his office as well, and Dominika returned to her desk, giving Marta a wink. "He was very calm, almost apologetic," said Dominika over wine after work. "He encouraged me to keep working, to try to pick up the pace if I could."

"I don't trust that jellyfish," said Marta. "My advice, Domi, is to keep telling them you're working very diligently, progress is slow, but you're encouraged by developments. They all want to report success to the Center, so Volontov will keep up a good face." Later that night, walking home, she tipsily told Dominika that if either of them had any sense, they'd both defect. Scandalous.

Marta went into her bedroom. She sat heavily on her bed, peeled off her damp clothes, and let them fall in a heap to the floor. She put on a short silk pajama shirt. It was from India, light beige, billowing, and embroidered with green and gold thread. Matching green knotted buttons ran from throat to hem. She stood in front of a wall mirror with its cracked corner and looked at herself. The shirt had been a present from a GRU general who had been posted to the Soviet Embassy in New Delhi. He had met Marta during the honey-trap operation against the

Indian defense minister. They had had a torrid affair for eight weeks, but in the end he stopped it. Having the Queen Sparrow as a Moscow diversion was one thing, he said, but settling down with "someone like you" was another.

Someone like me, Marta thought, looking at her reflection. She opened the nightshirt and looked at her naked body in the mirror. Several years past fifty and she was still holding together, she thought. A little more waistline, some lines around her eyes, but her breasts had not completely fallen, and, turning slightly and holding the material aside, she saw that her backside still had the swoop and curve that had been, in large part, responsible for making the young French intel officer in 1984 forget his duty and spend a month of Sundays in a Leningrad hotel room with her. She thought about him sometimes, for no reason.

Marta padded barefoot into the kitchen to draw a glass of water. It would clear her head so she could sleep. She returned to the bedroom and felt an arm snake around her neck from behind. She had heard nothing. The man held tight against her throat. She grabbed his arm with both hands to relieve the pressure. The person behind her didn't feel big; in fact, he felt somewhat thin. The breath on her neck was steady; he wasn't scared. He did not overly tighten his grip on her throat—he was just holding her. Marta thought maybe a pervert, a molestation? She got ready to reach behind to twist his testicles off.

It wasn't until he had frog-marched her sideways to stand in front of the mirror that she knew this wasn't a Finnish delivery boy with a wet spot on the front of his apron. She smelled ammonia and sweat. Then something else. A voice in her ear like a beetle walking across rice paper. One word in Russian. "*Molchat.*" Silence. In a horrified flash she knew. It was Them.

There was a creature looking out over her shoulder into the mirror. Their eyes met. More specifically, her eyes met his single eye. The other, a chalky marble in its socket, stared obliquely. In the dim light of her bedroom, Marta could not see his body, just his disembodied arm and pocked, scarred face behind her, floating over her shoulder. His voice started scuttling again.

"Good evening, Comrade Yelenova. May I call you Marta? Or perhaps 'my little Sparrow'?" Marta's nightshirt was slightly open. The gold highlights in the shirt were vibrating, picking up the trembling in Marta's body. Her pubic delta was visible between the folds of the slightly opened shirt. The monster pulled her a little straighter, Marta was lifted to her toes. "My little Sparrow," the man whispered. "What have you been doing?" He moved her, still up on her toes, a step closer to the mirror. Marta looked in the mirror and saw her own terrified eyes looking back at her.

"Will you share your bed with me, little Sparrow?" the man said. "I have come a long way." A second hand, black-gloved and holding a two-foot-long knife with a curved handle, came from behind and crossed her body. The man flicked one side of her shirt farther open with the tip of the knife. Her breast was heaving in fright. The floating head behind her smiled, tucked his chin into the crook of her neck, and tightened his grip. Marta's vision of herself in the mirror was going gray at the edges. A rushing noise in her head grew louder. She heard the devil say, "*Ya tebe pokazhu gde raki zimuyut*." I will show you where the crayfish spend winter. She knew this phrase, its deadly portent. Then the rushing noise got louder and she passed out.

Marta regained consciousness quickly, like a surfacing rush, coming back up to the light. She was naked on her back, on her narrow, bitter little bed. She felt the pull of tape over her mouth. Her hands were tied behind her, the knots on her wrists dug into her back. The familiar bedside lamp with its faded, gauzy pink shade cast a mild light on the bedspread. Her legs were tied together at the ankles. She pulled and tested each knot, but there was no give.

She heard a noise, turned her head, and her heart stopped. It was the most terrifying thing she had ever seen. The man was wearing her India shirt. He was dancing around the little room, rocking his body forward and back. The knife was in his hand, and he occasionally twirled it above his head as he pirouetted. Marta began weeping silently.

Sergey Matorin was forty-five hundred kilometers away on a head trip to the Panjshir Valley. He contemplated the shadows cast by the little pink lamp in Marta's bedroom. He was in his Alpha Group's sandbag bunker built into the hill with the hissing gas lantern casting green light into the corners of the shelter. Marta's trussed-up body became the body of the wife of the village headman, taken hostage during a dawn raid as punishment for sheltering insurgents. The Helsinki rain pattering against the window was the howling Hundred Nights Wind that carried the sands of the northern desert up and over the Kush in billowing clouds and shook the bunker's corrugated tin door. "Khyber" was home again.

The Afghan woman had died sometime in the early evening, too much excitement, or too much handling by a succession of his troopers, or perhaps the ammo belt around her neck, stapled to the plywood wall, had gotten too tight across her throat. She was upright against the wall, chin up as if in pride, held by the collar, her dead eyes flashing green from the lantern. She kept Khyber company. He was sitting, swaying to tinny Afghan music from a tape deck, but the batteries were fading and the music kept slowing down and speeding up.

Marta thrashed from side to side hoping to loosen one arm, get her legs free, to be able to fight him. Her movement attracted his attention and he climbed on the foot of the bed and on hands and knees started inching toward her. The shirt billowed around his body. He hovered over her, looking down, pressing his weight on her. She kept straining her arms, the cords in her neck standing out. Matorin lowered his face inches from hers and looked into her eyes, listened to her huffing breaths. He ripped the tape from her mouth and savored her labored, panicked breathing. "*Bozhe,*" she whispered.

His eyes searched her face as his unseen hand shivered the tip of the Khyber knife at a shallow angle up under her diaphragm nearly nine inches, completely through her heart, and up into her throat. Marta arched her back, convulsing. Her open mouth could make no sound and her body bucked against the ropes. Matorin rode the tremors in her body, felt her hoarse breaths quicken, and watched, watched, watched the light go out in eyes that partially rolled back inside her head. A trickle of blood oozed from one nostril and out of the corner of her mouth. It took Marta three minutes to die. She didn't hear Matorin whisper, "*Bozhe?* No, God could not be here tonight."

Dominika entered the *rezidentura* the next morning and looked over at Marta's empty desk. *Probably a long night of aquavit,* she thought.

When Marta had not come in by midmorning, Volontov stuck his head out of his office and yelled, "Where is Yelenova this morning? Has she called in sick?" No one knew where she was. "Corporal Egorova, call her at her flat. See if you can reach her." Dominika dialed several times but no one answered.

Volontov called the security officer and told him to go over to her apartment, pound on the door, use the office copy of her key to get in. He returned an hour later to say that the apartment was empty but looked perfectly normal. Clothes in the closet, dishes in the sink, bed made.

"Draft a short cable to the Center," barked Volontov to the security man, who looked at Volontov like a Rottweiler waiting for hand signals. "Inform them that Administrative Assistant Yelenova, Marta, has not reported for work, whereabouts unknown. She has not called in sick. Inform them we are searching for her and also filing a request to the Finnish National Police to search for her. Call your contact in the police. Tell them the embassy demands immediate action and utmost discretion. Go."

Volontov called his counterintelligence referent into the office and shut the door. "We may have a problem," he said. "Marta Yelenova has not reported to work." He checked the SVR-issue wall clock above the door. "It's been almost five hours," he said.

His Line KR man, an unimaginative beast of burden formerly from the KGB Border Guards Directorate, looked at his watch, as if to confirm Volontov's estimate of the time. "Get over to SUPO," Volontov said. "Ask for an appointment with Sundqvist. Tell them about Yelenova, that we think she's been kidnapped. Ask them to check all the terminals: air, rail, ship."

"Kidnapped?" asked the CI man. "Who would kidnap Yelenova?"

"Idiot. We're not going to tell Finnish intelligence we think she defected. Just get them to start checking. They'll have visa photos of her. Tell them utter discretion is imperative. And keep your mouth shut."

In the next six hours the police had made no progress, but SUPO had retrieved a photo of a woman vaguely resembling Yelenova at the Haaparanta border-crossing station at the Swedish border on the Gulf of Bothnia. The woman was wearing a scarf and dark glasses that concealed most of her face, but the nose and chin were right. SUPO said the woman was processed through immigration control with a Finnish passport in the name of Rita Viren, a name the Finns were tracing. She was in the company of an unidentified man with sunglasses and a baseball cap.

"That confirms it," said the CI man. "It was the Americans. She defected to the CIA."

"Imbecile. How did you arrive at that?" said Volontov.

"Look at the ball cap, Colonel," said the CI man, pointing at the SUPO security-video photos that had been faxed to the Russians. "It says New York on the cap." Volontov told him to get out.

The office was afloat in rumors. A murder? A kidnapping? The word no one dared utter. Defection? Everyone knew Marta and Volontov had had a screaming match several weeks ago. But to run away? Dominika was beside herself. Marta would not defect, but if she did, she would not leave without saying good-bye. She had only *joked about* both of them defecting together. No. Something bad had happened. Then she froze. Did They somehow know she, Dominika, was not reporting, falsifying progress with Nash? Was Marta's disappearance a warning? Ridiculous. There was some very easy explanation. Marta had run off for a week to Lapland with a blond yoga instructor. Anything. But Dominika couldn't convince herself.

The search for Yelenova continued for days, without result. Volontov was frantic that the disappearance of one of his people would stain his copybook at the Center, an ironic fixation considering his pokey thirty-year career ledger was already liberally blotted with sloth, inattention, and careerism. The embassy protested to the Finnish Ministry of Foreign Affairs and to the Interior Ministry about the criminal kidnapping of one of its diplomatic personnel, whose security, they reminded the uncomfortable Finns, was the direct responsibility of the Finnish government. A special Moscow investigator arrived from Directorate K to interview embassy officers and the *rezident,* as well as to confer with Finnish investigators. He left after four days, solemnly concluding that Ms. Yelenova had disappeared.

Dominika suspected the truth as she lay facedown on her bed in her SVR-provided apartment and wept for her friend. She had been a true friend—a big sister she never had—and it was monstrous, inconceivable, that They would have harmed her. But why? As she ran things through her mind, the memory of her telling Marta about Ustinov came back in a chilling rush. Did They know about that? Did Marta mention it to someone? Would a slip on her part result in the disappearance of a colleague, an officer of the Service, from sleepy little Helsinki, in the twenty-first century, in a sane, civilized world? She closed her eyes and felt the bed spinning, and she was in Ustinov's love nest, on his blood-soaked revolving bed. Thinking back, she remembered Volontov's face had shown fear, his orange halo was ragged with it.

She got up, walked to the window, and looked up at the night sky. She scorned herself. Trained intelligence officer. A real operator. Relentless seductress. They used her, were using her still, as a little chess piece, a little pawn. Whoever it was that Nate was handling, she could understand that person a little better now, appreciate the hate that must sustain him.

Dominika more than ever was confirmed in her decision not to report on Nate. It had been like a draft of cold air sweeping across her. But her little games were passive, weren't they? She saw Marta's face in the glass. How could she make Them atone for what They had done to her? How could she destroy them, Volontov, Uncle Vanya, all the others?

Tears ran down her cheeks. She cried for Marta, for her father, perhaps for herself too. She cried for Russia, but she knew she no longer believed. She turned away from the window, eyes closed. Something broke loose inside her and she swept a little ceramic bud vase—Marta had bought it for her at the Sunday market—off a side table with her arm, her teeth clenched and fists bunched.

Back in the *rezidentura*, filled with dread, Volontov was waiting for official censure in some form. Instead he received a sympathetic call on the "Vey-Chey," the VCh phone, from Vanya Egorov, who commiserated that service in the field, on the front lines, was not without risk. There had been defectors in the past, there will be defectors in the future. We deplore them, he said, and we must be vigilant, but it's impossible to prevent all of them. Egorov asked Volontov to concentrate on managing secure operations, and especially to focus on the "special project" with his niece and the young American. "Of course, General," said a relieved Volontov. "I believe we are making good progress on that front."

Chush' sobach'ya. Bullshit, thought Egorov, and ended the call. Vanya knew that his niece must have mentioned at least part of the Ustinov story to this Yelenova woman, a serious mistake, but one he had to overlook for the time being. It was actually a stroke of luck that Yelenova subsequently let it slip in front of the mouth-breather Volontov, who blessedly had the wit to call him. It was only a matter of dispatching Matorin, then a relatively simple *imitatsiya* to send the investigator for show, to wrap up all the loose ends. God, if the president had gotten wind of this breach—Egorov didn't want to think about it.

On the Finnish-Russian border three kilometers west of Vyartsilya, Russia, through an uninhabited tract of dense pines and rolling hills, the Soviets after World War II had established an infiltration route past the towers, border wire, and plowed strips. The Finnish side was always lightly patrolled. For decades, cleared KGB border guards periodically were assigned to the area to allow agents to pass through unmolested. The more techniques changed, the more they stayed the same: Routes through the minefields in 1953 were marked by stakes driven into the snow with cloth strips tied to them. Since 2010, the correct route through the field was marked by plastic pylons fitted with infrared strobes visible only with night-vision goggles.

A week earlier, Matorin had infiltrated Finland using this route, was picked up by a Directorate S support illegal on country road number 70, and was driven four hundred kilometers south on Rural Route 6 and finally into the city on state highway E75. The Spetsnaz killer had gone directly to Yelenova's apartment, killed her at midnight, and put her body in a rubber military body bag. He had sanitized the apartment, then signaled the illegal, who, in the early morning hours, drove Matorin and Marta's body back north to the Vyartsilya bolt-hole. The illegal then returned to Helsinki. The next morning, using real Finnish documents, the illegal and his lightly disguised wife left the country at Haaparanta, ostensibly for the start of a nice vacation in Sweden. They would never return to Finland, further complicating the investigation into what had happened to Marta Yelenova. The entire operation had taken a little less than forty hours.

The sunlight was rising through the pinewoods of

Vyartsilya, casting long, delicate shadows that crept up the snow-covered hills. Guards from the Federal Security Service stood in elevated tower B30, watching the tree line with binoculars. The sun came up behind the tower, over the tops of the pines, bathing the whole area in golden light. "*Vot,*" said one of the men. There. A single thin figure came out of the trees. He was dressed in a white snowsuit with a hood, and wore snowshoes. The guards saw he moved steadily through the drifts, his long shadow stretched out behind him. He dragged a small equipment sled on a tether. An oblong shape lay on the sled, shrouded in white nylon. Marta Yelenova had returned to the *Rodina.*

MARTA'S LAST MEAL—PYTT I PANNA

In foaming butter, separately and aggressively brown cubed beef, potatoes, and diced onions until crisp. Incorporate ingredients in the skillet with additional butter, season and reheat. Form a well in the mixture, and break a raw egg into it. Stir the egg into the hash before serving.

16

Nate sat with Gable in the India Prankkari in Kallio, at the back, looking out the windows. The restaurant was nearly empty. Gable had insisted on ordering *rogan josh*, fragrant, spicy, oily vermilion lamb stew. They ate it with soft bread, a fiery relish of tomatoes and ginger, and copious amounts of beer. Gable compared his first spoonful to a Nepalese *rogan josh* he had tasted around a campfire in Dhahran a hundred years ago, waiting at the airstrip beside the Pilatus that had infiltrated the four Tibetans into China.

"Fucking Scandinavians cannot prepare Indian food," he said, chewing. "With them it's all reindeer and punk berries in cream sauce, boiled potatoes. Chef reaches for parsley and they have a stroke." As usual, food was disappearing into Gable's craw at a prodigious rate.

"Four little guys, sherpas, tough as nuts, trained 'em for a month, going to pop in and pop out, splice a relay on a PLA trunk line running along the border, literally in the shadow of Everest and Kanchenchunga. The fucking end of the world. They flew in over the mountains, were supposed to walk out . . . but they never came back. Chicom patrol probably got 'em." He was silent for a minute, then waved for more of the relish, and they started talking about the DIVA case, how to kick-start it. Nate couldn't pin her down, he couldn't turn the corner with her. She wasn't softening, he was wasting precious time. Gable stopped chewing and stared at him when Nate admitted he had grown to like her.

"She's willing to come out, to engage, we debate stuff, but there's no give," said Nate.

"You ever think she's working on you, not the other way around?" said Gable, chewing.

"Not impossible," said Nate. "But there's no handle she's been working on. No career bullshit, no money, nothing."

"Yeah, and what would you do if she showed up with nothing on under her raincoat? Think you'd call that a recruitment peg?"

Nate looked at Gable, nettled. "I don't think she'd go with that kind of approach. Just a gut feeling."

"You wish. Well, it sounds like you guys are stuck. I suggest you think of something to unstick the case. Shake her up, rattle her, upset her equilibrium." He emptied his beer and called for two more.

"She's not going to go with the standard canned pitch, Marty," said Nate. "I've been trying to get her to talk more about Russia, about the problems, not pushing her, just giving her openings. Something there in her eyes, but not yet."

"You have to look for another handle. The good life in the West. Luxury items. Bank account."

"Wrong direction," said Nate, "that's not who she is. She's idealistic, a nationalist, but she's not a clunky Soviet. She grew up with ballet, music, books, languages."

"You talk about the Kremlin? All the shit going on behind the walls?"

"Sure I did," said Nate. "But she's too gung-ho. She looks at it all at the level of the *Rodina*."

"Hell's that?" said Gable.

"The whole national myth—the Motherland, the soil, the hymns, chasing Nazis across the steppes."

"Oh, yeah, some of those Russian Red Army girls were hot," said Gable, looking up at the ceiling. "Those tunics and boots, they looked—"

"Is this your idea of operational coaching? Are we discussing DIVA?"

"Well, you have to find something to jolt her out of her defensive position." He leaned back in his chair, rocking slightly, hands behind his head. "Don't discount her feelings for you," said Gable. "Maybe she'll want to help you in your career, a gift. It won't feel to her like she's committing treason. Or maybe she's a thrill freak. Some agents drink adrenaline."

Nate's doorbell rang that night. Dominika stood at the door, her face pinched, eyes red. She was not crying, but her lips trembled and she put her hand over her mouth, as if to stifle a sob. Nate checked the hallway quickly while pulling her inside the door. She was leaden, she didn't resist his tug. He took her coat. She was wearing a white stretch top and jeans. He lowered her gently onto the couch. She sat at the edge of the cushion, looking down at her hands. Nate didn't know what was wrong or what to do. She was being sent home short of tour, she was in trouble. That would be a first. Exfiling an SVR officer *before* recruitment.

Got to calm her down. Whatever it is, she's upset, vulnerable. A glass of wine, scotch, vodka? Teeth chattering against the glass as she took a sip.

"I know you speak Russian," Dominika said suddenly in Russian, her voice flat, exhausted. Her head was still down, her hair hung on each side of her face. "You're the only one I can talk to, a boy from the CIA, it's mad, isn't it?"

A boy from the CIA? thought Nate. *Fuck's going on?* He sat still, made himself blink. Dominika took another ragged sip.

She started talking slowly, in a low voice. She told him about Marta, about her disappearance. When Nate asked why, Dominika told him about Ustinov. When Nate asked how, she told him about her training. *Those rumors about State School Four,* he thought. *Jesus.*

She looked at him then, trying to gauge his reaction on hearing she'd been to Sparrow School. There was no pity, no disdain, his eyes met hers. He was always that way. The purple mantle around his head pulsated. She wanted desperately to trust him. He poured her another glass. "What do you need?" he asked in English. "I want to help you."

She ignored the question, switched to English. "I know you're not an American diplomat working in your embassy's Economic Section. I know you're a CIA officer. You know very well that I work in the *rezidentura* in my embassy as an officer of our state security. At least you should have realized it when I told you Volontov was my chief. I suppose you also know my uncle is Vanya Egorov, First Deputy Director of the Service." Nate tried not to move.

"In Moscow after the AVR, I worked in the Fifth Department in an operation against a French diplomat. It was unsuccessful. Then I was assigned to Helsinki." Dominika looked up at Nate. Her face was puffy. She looked at him searchingly, and he reached out and held her hand. It felt cold to the touch.

"Marta was my friend. She served loyally all her life, they gave her medals, a pension, an overseas posting. She was strong, independent. She had no regrets about her life, she enjoyed everything. In the time I knew her, she showed me who I am." She squeezed Nate's hand slightly.

"I don't know what happened to Marta, but she's gone, without a word, and I know she's dead. She never did anything to them. My uncle is afraid of exposure. He would protect himself. There's a man, a *koshmar,* a nightmare creature who belongs to my uncle. He would use him for such a thing."

"Are you in danger?" asked Nate. His thoughts were racing. She was talking about past operations, a political assassination, liquidation of one of their own personnel, scandal at the top of the SVR. She was dictating at least a half dozen intel reports right there, from the couch. He didn't dare take notes, he had to keep her rolling.

"You were involved in the Ustinov affair," said Nate, "so your uncle may be nervous about you."

She shook her head. "My uncle knows I cannot hurt him. My mother is in Moscow. He uses her as a *zalozhnica,* a hostage, like in the old days. Besides, he trained me, put me through school, sent me abroad. I am as much his creature as that monster of his.

"I was sent to Helsinki to meet you, to develop a friendship with you," Dominika said. "My uncle says he considers me one of his operations officers, but he looks at me as his little Sparrow, right out of the 1960s. They have been impatient with the progress I have been making with you. They want to hear how I took you to bed."

"I'm willing to help you there," said Nate. She stared back at him and sniffled thinly.

"You are pleased to continue joking," she said. "Perhaps you will not think it is so funny when I tell you that I am supposed to find out about your former activities in Moscow, about the mole you meet. Uncle Vanya sent me to watch you, to see if you become operational, active, like you did for two weeks last month."

The mole you meet? Nate felt like the child standing beside the tracks as a fast freight roars by, inches from being swept away. He tried not to react, but he knew Dominika saw it in his face.

"I did not say anything to that slug Volontov," said Dominika. "Marta was still alive then. She knew what I had decided." Nate was trying to concentrate on her words while numbly contemplating the close call with MARBLE. They had had no idea of the danger. Dominika's decision not to report most probably saved his life.

"Since I bumped into you at the swimming pool, I was trying to establish a friendship with you," said Dominika. "In many ways, we were doing the same thing to each other. I know you were trying to identify my weaknesses, my *ujazvimoe mesto,* what is the word, *vulnerability*?

"Your charming pursuit ensured only that we would spend more time together. I suppose that was Uncle Vanya's plan all along. What surprised me was that I continued to let you work on me because—it dawned on me—I *wanted* you to continue to work on me. I liked being with you."

Nate sat motionless, still holding her hand. Jesus Christ, she *had* been working him, just like Gable thought. The SVR were hunting for MARBLE. Thank God she had decided the way she had. *And,* thought Nate, *God bless Marta, wherever she was.*

He knew Dominika was already out of the starting gate, the critical stage. Her flat voice was a distillate of anger, fear, her desire to lash out. She had already told him enough to cook her three times over. Now came the infinitely delicate moment when she would pull back and go away, or she would make the decision that she would become a CIA source.

"Dominika," he said, "I already told you I wanted to help you. I already asked you what you needed. What do you want to do?"

Dominika took her hand out of his, her cheeks flushed. "I don't regret anything," she said.

"I know you don't," said Nate. There was no sound in the room. "What do you want to do?" he asked softly.

It was as if she could read his mind. "You're very

clever, aren't you, Mr. Neyt Nash?" she said. "I came here to cry on your shoulder, to tell you about my mission against you, to tell you I helped you."

"I am grateful for all that," said Nate, not wanting to show how scandalously relieved he was.

Dominika could see it in his face nonetheless. "But you're not asking me to work with you to avenge Marta, nor to get back at my uncle, or Volontov, or the rest of them, nor to try to reform my beloved country."

"I don't have to tell you any of that," he said.

"Of course you don't," she said. "You're too careful for that." Nate looked at her without saying anything. "All you do is ask me what *I* want to do."

"That's right," said Nate.

"Instead, suppose you tell me what *you* want me to do."

"I think we should begin working together. Stealing secrets," Nate said immediately, his heart in his mouth.

"For revenge, for Marta, for *Rodina,* for—"

"No, none of those," interrupted Nate. Gable's words came into his head. Dominika looked at him. His purple halo had spread like the rays of a rising sun. "Because you need it, Dominika Egorova, because it helps you feed that temper of yours, because it'll be something you own, for once in your life."

Dominika stared at him. His eyes were steady, open. "That's a very interesting thing to say," she said.

The best recruitments are the ones where the agents recruit themselves, his instructor had bellowed at the Farm. *Remember that, no surprises, a natural evolution,* he had said. Well, this was hardly a natural evolution of the phased recruitment. Nate felt as though he had just run Class Four rapids in a bathtub.

It was an hour later and Dominika had never actually uttered, *Yes, I will do it.* No agent makes the decision with a handshake and a signature. Instead Nate just got her to start talking about it. He had told her, "Whatever you decide, I promise we will work safely," which is the standard catechism when addressing agents. You mean it, but everyone—case officer and agent alike—knows that long-term survival for an agent, especially inside Russia, is unlikely. But the bland comment got a reaction.

"To do this work correctly we cannot avoid risks. We both know that," said Dominika archly. *She said "we,"* thought Nate.

"And we'll start slowly, carefully . . . if we decide to start at all," he said.

"Exactly," said Dominika. "*If* we decide."

"And we'll proceed as quickly or as slowly as you want," said Nate.

"Your side can examine my *motivatsiya* at their leisure. If our collaboration turns out to be unsatisfactory, I will tell you and we will agree to the *okonchanie*, the termination of our relationship." They apparently had the same agent-handling cant in the SVR.

She was through the first stage. It was getting late. Dominika stood and reached for her coat. Nate helped her, watching her eyes, the corners of her mouth, her hands. Was this going to stick? They stood looking at each other for a moment. She turned to him at the door, offered her hand. He took it and said, "*Spokoinoi nochi,*" good night, and she left quickly, making no sound in the stairwell.

After Dominika left his apartment, Nate stayed up, jotting notes, remembering what she had told him. He resisted the idiotic urge to walk to the embassy, wake up the Station, begin writing cables to Headquarters. *Recruitment. SVR officer, Sparrow cadre, her uncle runs the whole outfit, assassinations. It's a spy movie, for Christ's sake.* He couldn't wait to get into the Station tomorrow.

His high spirits evaporated. He tossed in bed, throwing the bedclothes off. The Dead Sea fruit turned to ashes in his mouth. He had to secure the recruitment, make sure of her commitment; she could back out, a lot of agents did. When he put her in harness, he'd have Headquarters breathing down his neck. What's her motivation? How much salary? What's her access? What do you mean, she didn't sign a secrecy agreement? This was very sudden. Is she a provocation?

Production. They were going to want results, fast. They would ask first for the best information she could get, and that would be dangerous. The little men in the little offices with the little beady eyes would want to validate her as a bona fide asset. Everything would be a test, they would not be satisfied until her information was corroborated, until she was "boxed," passed a polygraph. Push her too hard, or push in the wrong direction, and they'd lose her, Nate knew that. And if he lost her after claiming a recruitment, there would be the knowing looks from Headquarters. Case was bogus from the start.

That was just the beginning. If Dominika was caught, the SVR would kill her. It didn't matter how she was caught: a mole in Headquarters, a mistake in handling, hostile surveillance, or simply bad luck, the lights coming on with her standing in front of an open safe drawer with a rollover camera. Nate turned over in the bed.

There would be an interrogation and a trial, but they wouldn't care about the facts. Uncle Vanya wouldn't save her. They'd walk her, barefoot and wearing a prison smock, to the basement of the Lubyanka or Lefortovo or Butyrka. They'd push her down the hallway lined with chipped steel doors into the room with a drain in the sloping floor, and the hooks in the ceiling beams, and the stapled, waxed-cardboard coffin standing upright in the corner of the room. They'd shoot her behind the right ear even before she was halfway into the room, no warning, and they'd look at her lying facedown on the floor before picking her up, wrists and ankles, and dropping her into the cardboard coffin. That simple. That final.

ROGAN JOSH

In a mortar, roughly grind chopped onions, ginger, chili, cardamom, clove, coriander, paprika, cumin, and salt into a smooth paste. Add bay and cinnamon. Add heated clarified butter. Cook until fragrant. Add cubed pieces of lamb, stir in yogurt, warm water, and pepper. Bake in medium oven for two hours. Sprinkle with coriander.

17

The recruitment of Dominika was not in any sense normal. She was a trained intelligence officer, but she now had to learn how to become a spy. It wasn't a natural transformation. *Cement the bond,* Forsyth had said.

Station's first move, therefore, was to make extremely discreet inquiries into the whereabouts of Marta, to demonstrate their concern. Gable arranged a meeting with a cooperative liaison officer from SUPO. No trace of the Russian woman. The security video of a possible crossing at Haaparanta was inconclusive. A tearless Dominika thanked Nate for trying.

They kept the BIGOT list way down, the registered tally of officers cleared to read into the operation, though they couldn't do much about the Headquarters end. The case was already in Restricted Handling channels, which was bullshit, said Gable, because only about a hundred people read the cables. They still tried to limit distribution. Forsyth and Gable had done this before, knew the more carefully they started the case the longer the intel stream would last. Nate felt his resolve building—protect her at all costs. Do not fail, do not fail *her*.

Nate found a two-bedroom in Munkkiniemi along the Ramsay Strand and the marina inlet, and the rat-faced NOC came back and rented it for twelve months as a Dane, a business flat, he'd be coming and going at all times. The gratified landlord couldn't have cared less.

A night of spring rain, headlights reflecting on the

pavement. Dominika was backlighted as she stepped off the green-and-yellow No. 4 trolley at Tiilimaki. Nate caught up to her after two blocks, put his arm in hers. Not even a hello, in strict SVR operative mode, back straight, nervous. Her first safe-house meeting as an agent, grappling not so much with fear as she was with the shame. They walked wordlessly down narrow lanes, behind apartment blocks, silver light from the television game shows in all the windows. They hurried through the main door, cooking smells, boiled reindeer and cream sauce, up two flights, walking quietly.

The first night of the rest of their lives. A couple of lamps on, and Gable was waiting and crowded her, took her coat. Dominika could not stop looking at Gable's wire-brush hair. She liked his look, his eyes, the purple behind them. *Another solid* purpurnyi, she thought. Forsyth came out of the kitchen, glasses up on his forehead, wrestling with a cork. Elegant, wise, calm, the air around him was azure. *Lazurnyj*. He would be sensitive. Dominika sat on the couch and looked at the three men moving around the room. They were natural, unaffected, yet they looked at her and she knew she was being assessed.

She knew it was for real, with them in the room, filling it up. Nate was a young officer, all she had known of the CIA up till now, but these other men were calm, serious, you could feel the years, like General Korchnoi back home. Then Gable raised a glass and massacred *zdorov'e* and Dominika suppressed a smile, stayed serious and correct.

No business tonight, that was how good they were, just talk, and they let Nate do most of the talking, that was how good they were, and they listened and heard everything. At the end she left first—standard tradecraft for them too, she registered—and walked along the strand; not all the boats were in the spring water yet, and she didn't feel ashamed like before. That was how good they had been.

The second meeting, Dominika had time to look around. The galley kitchen had a two-ring cooktop, enough to boil water, and a refrigerator with rubber trays to squeeze the ice cubes out of. In the nature of furnished safe houses, the couch and chairs and tables were thin and cheap and garish, avocado and harvest gold, still the rage in Scandinavia, said Gable. The cheap prints on the wall were crashing waves and elk in moonlight, the throws on the floor were straight Lapland. One bedroom had a double bed that touched the wall on either side, and you'd have to crawl onto it over the footboard. The second bedroom was empty save for a hanging fixture of bright red glass. The bathroom had a tub and the requisite bidet, which Gable one night mistook for the toilet, and Dominika had tears in her eyes and started calling Gable *Bratok,* dear brother, from then on.

Running a trained intelligence officer as an agent is more difficult than directing a sweaty banker desperate for the euros because he's got King Kong for a wife, a two-year-old BMW, and Godzilla for a mistress. Dominika was an AVR grad. They argued, wryly, over tradecraft ("I cannot believe you think this is a suitable site") or security ("No, Domi, the rug on the railing when it's *safe,* didn't they teach you *positive* signals?"). Nate wondered how many times he had to say, "Let's do it my way," and cringed every time she said, dramatically, to get under his skin, "It is my head if you're wrong."

The CIA men quickly recognized that Dominika had extraordinary intuition. She finished their sentences, nodded quickly at discreet suggestions, had an uncanny sense of when to listen. An intelligent woman, trained as an intelligence officer, thought Forsyth, but there was something else he had never seen before. *Clairvoyance* was the wrong word, but it was close.

A part of Dominika watched the process from afar. She saw how they respected her, valued her training, yet took nothing for granted. She knew they were testing her in little ways. Sometimes they deferred to her, other times they insisted on doing it their way. They were very thorough, she thought.

The weekly meetings at the safe house, her work with them, all began defining her. The torment of the decision forgotten, her recruitment by the CIA became the burning gemstone in her brain. She walked around with it, savored it. It was especially sweet when talking to Volontov. *Can you guess what I am doing?* she thought as the sweaty *rezident* droned on about her work. Nate had been right. This was something she owned, hers alone.

Forsyth came back when it was time to discuss, with infinite care, what secrets Dominika could steal from the *rezidentura*. They built the igloo, big blocks on the bottom, starting with what papers she personally handled, then what she could safely steal, then what treasures she knew existed but didn't have access to. They told her to take it easy. Trained spooks as agents always initially push too hard, try to do too much. Dominika asked whether they would give her a camera and commo gear. She wanted to show them how much ice and edge she had, but it only rang bells in the CIA men's heads. Dominika saw their faces and their halos change, and understood she had made a misstep. Let's talk about equipment a little later, Forsyth said, and wrote a cable the next day asking for an examiner; they might as well get it over with.

Polygraph. The Flutter. Nate sat in the little bedroom listening to the muffled voices from the living room, one deep, the other sweet. Dominika was in a white ash chair answering yes or no to a thick-fingered examiner with a mustache whom Gable knew from other polygraph sessions and disliked. "Guy hit bottom twenty years ago, then started digging," Gable said. Dominika knew this was an important test for her and she willed herself not to read the man, not to get cute, not to play with him. She concentrated on his questions, which drifted, colored, past her cheek.

Nate sweated for an hour, then went out to the living room when he heard them wrapping up. Dominika gave him a nod, but Big Fingers didn't bat an eye. They never do, they withhold results till they "review the charts," coy as virgins. In the end Forsyth got him back to the Station and sat him down and told him he didn't give a fuck, he wanted a preliminary up or down, because this was important. Fussed, the examiner declared himself satisfied that Dominika was who she said she was, held the rank of corporal in the SVR, and most important, was not a double agent dispatched by the SVR to disinform the CIA, or to identify clandestine service officers, or to elicit current US intelligence requirements.

Now a confidant, the examiner did note privately to Forsyth that the charts showed a mild galvanic spike whenever she responded to a question in which the recruiting case officer, Nash, was mentioned. It required another series of rephrased questions, he said gravely, before he could confirm this was not evidence of classic Czech or Cuban polygraph countertechniques—there had been no controlled breathing, no bunched fists or clenched anus. Gable, when Forsyth related the examiner's comments about Dominika's reaction to Nate, simply said, "Orgaspasm," and left the room.

With a test result of "no deception" in their pockets, the operation could move forward, and they had to talk about managing her security, about cover, behavior, comportment, pacing.

"You have to keep your profile normal," *lazurnyj* Forsyth said. "You have to keep reporting your contacts with Nathaniel to the Center, keep showing modest progress. Once a month, not so good. Every two weeks, every week, better. It's what gives you the freedom to move."

"I know I must do this," Dominika said. "I have telegrams already written in my head. From now until winter."

"You have to write them on your own," said Forsyth. "We can help you, but they must be your reports, in your words, with your details." Dominika nodded her head. *She knows the Game,* thought Forsyth. *She's at home with it.*

"I will paint a picture of Neyt. Vain, boastful, but cautious. Easy to manipulate, but suspicious, distracted." She turned to look at Nate, raised an eyebrow.

"Hard to believe it will take you till next winter to figure all that out," said Gable, sitting on the couch next to Nate, who flipped him a middle finger.

"I don't know how long we can roll this out. Yasenevo is going to lose patience sooner or later," said Forsyth. He already was thinking about the day Dominika would be recalled to Moscow. Would she be ready to operate inside? Could they get her ready in time? It would be the calendar that beat them, he thought, not her.

"There is one way to prolong the contact, keep my collar loose. Something that will persuade Yasenevo to invest more time," Dominika said. "Uncle Vanya expects it."

"What is it?" asked Forsyth.

"In time, if I report that Neyt and I have become lovers, Moscow will be gratified; it will satisfy their expectations. It will make sense to them—they will remember State School Four."

Gable heaved himself up from the couch, a look

of pain on his face. "Lovers? Jesus Christ, I couldn't ask anybody to do that with Nash. It's too much."

A blustery Sunday, and the little skiffs and day-sailers snubbed against the pontoon docks in the inlet. In the safe house Dominika spoke a little of Marta but stopped and told Nate her news. The monotreme Volontov had recently realized he was without an administrative assistant and solicitously had asked Dominika to assume some admin duties. She wanted to tell him no, to discredit him in the eyes of the Center, but she thought now about Nate and Forsyth and *Bratok,* and had replied that she would be willing to help out. Her gemstone secret was burning deep now. She was learning to look for opportunities to feed her mounting appetite.

They gave her *rezidentura* officers' time cards and filing of operational accountings. The latter came with an added benefit, could Nate guess? Each expense must be referenced to a case report or to an operational telegram describing the activity. "Volontov and his officers should do it themselves, but they just toss everything on my desk," said Dominika. "No one but the *rezident* may read others' cables, there is strict *razdelenie,* compartmentation." Dominika's blue eyes blazed. "Except that they need me to reference the expenses." She stretched it out. "So . . . Volontov has given me access to the operational traffic. All of it."

The intelligence started coming in bits and pieces, and they watched it, Forsyth firsthand, the arthropods back in Langley long-distance, for any false note, anything too pat, too clever. She was prodigious in remembering details, recalling one story line, which triggered another, then another. She began to take cryptic notes, they checked her on it, and she was sound.

She memorized nearly the complete text of the

Line N referent's monthly support activity report, blowing up three Line S illegals in Helsinki, sleepers who had lived in Finland as Finns for decades. One had already exited the country at Haaparanta as a smoke screen after Marta's disappearance. The other two lived in the nearby municipality of Espoo, but they left them alone to protect Dominika.

Next meeting, she scared them when she unfolded an *original* document plucked out of Volontov's in-box. She had stuffed it crumpled into a pocket instead of taking it to be shredded with the rest of the dross. *Sovershenno Sekretno,* Top Secret, from Line PR, four pages on the Estonian and Latvian Parliaments. They were NATO allies now, so Langley took that intel downtown, to the NSC and the Oval. Gable yelled at her never to do that again.

Headquarters agreed with Gable. No more pinching documents, give her a concealed camera. Nate didn't like it, as risky as it gets, but Forsyth said they had to get her used to it, he thought she could handle it.

"I'm not sure she's ready for that," said Nate. Any spy gear trebled the risk and he didn't want the case blowing up, didn't want to put her in any more danger.

"Well, you better get her the fuck ready," said Gable. "If they call her home tomorrow, the case ends."

"Speaking of which, it's time for a little Moscow internal ops training," said Forsyth to Nate. "Your specialty."

Dominika's education in denied-area tradecraft began. Summer had settled on the peaked roofs and copper domes of Helsinki, and perpetual twilight replaced dusk, and scores of drab Finns rode the escalators down to the Metro platforms. Dominika in a scarf, Dominika in a beret, Dominika in a coat, counting the paces, funneling with the crowd toward the turnstile. She got through and at a corner of the passageway she brushed by him, through the crimson air, she could smell him, feel the sleeve of his sweater as she held a cigarette pack firmly between two fingers against her waist. He palmed it—a perfect Brush Pass—and was gone into the crowd.

Summer rain, fresh and light, traffic slow and sluggish, lights reflected off the pavement. She checked her watch by the light of a display case. No tickles behind her, she felt good, and she knew she would hit the timing window. When Nate had described what they were going to do, she had laughed. "We do not resort to such drama," she had told him, and he said, "That's because SVR operates in democracies," and she had huffed but listened carefully.

She walked tight beside the granite wall, cars hissing past on the wet street. She turned the corner and stopped in the shadow of a scaffolding, in the covered pedestrian walkway. Nate's car had come around the corner at thirty-eight minutes after the hour, random and quick, the car rolling and the passenger-side window down, and she stepped off the curb and stuck her hand in the window, letting the plastic bag drop on the seat, and took the replacement cassette from his hand, and stepped back under the scaffolding and he had driven on. He hadn't looked at her, but she had seen his hand pulling on the hand brake, no brake lights, the Moving-Car Delivery. *Such drama,* she thought.

They were hitting their stride, all of them, and inevitably the Headquarters heat-seekers started circling. She was a controlled asset, well-placed inside an SVR *rezidentura,* they had written, and they wanted to "explore other possibilities." Forsyth kept them off for weeks, but then they made it an order, and Gable wanted to get on a plane and go back there, but Forsyth told him to stop.

The madness began. The engineers in the Directorate of Science and Technology wanted DIVA to download the entire *rezidentura* computer network, attack the crypto systems, emplace audio and video inside the *rezidentura*. The S&T techs blithely admitted that some of their devices *might, repeat, might dim the lights of southern Helsinki,* and in one instance required DIVA to install a *radioactive source* on the roof of the Russian Embassy. Headquarters then advised that the "Rule of Sixes" that governed the development of all new technology would, however, delay deployment of any equipment to the field: R&D for the device would take *six more years,* it would cost an additional *six million dollars,* and, based on breadboard bench testing, one device would weigh *six hundred pounds*. Madness.

As the clandestine side of the operation expanded, Nate and Dominika continued their dilatory public contact for Volontov and the Center's benefit. Dinners, trips to the country, concerts. Nate provided personal details about himself, something the Center could check independently, to illustrate how well Dominika was prying open the oyster. But as Forsyth predicted, Volontov wanted more and faster progress, so with Gable's enthusiastic assistance Dominika drafted the much-anticipated contact cable reporting the beginning of a physical relationship with Nate, to buy more time. Gable wanted to write an "erectile dysfunction angle" into the script, arguing that would build in even more delay, but a red-faced Forsyth overruled him. Nate flipped Gable the bird.

Dominika commenced taking photographs of classified Russian documents from within the *rezidentura* using a variety of concealed cameras installed in purses, key fobs, lipsticks. She was discerning in photographing only the best documents, flexible enough to know when to wait. Gable praised her but Nate was perpetually worried and gloomy at the risks Dominika was taking.

One Sunday afternoon in the safe house, Dominika had heard enough. "Are you worried about me, or about this case and your reputation?" she asked. The room fell silent and Gable cleared his throat.

Nate turned slowly toward her, embarrassed and angry. "I'm intent about preserving the intelligence," he said, and watched her face harden. "I just think you should slow down."

"If that's what you think," said Gable, "you're gonna love the next round."

The cable from Headquarters ran five pages. They wanted her to insert a specially prepared thumb drive into a *rezidentura* computer, preferably the machine in the file room, but the one under Volontov's desk would do. Fourteen seconds of downloading and Langley would be able to access the clear text behind all encrypted, "point-to-point" SVR cables, Yasenevo–Helsinki, transmitted over commercial telephone lines. Reading messages *en claire* was a lot easier than trying to crack ever-changing encryption algorithms. But this was the riskiest thing yet. Forsyth saw Nate's face and told him to skip the meeting at the safe house. Gable would run her through it.

Two days later, Dominika pushed the wire trolley with the wobbly wheels loaded with files and burn bags and ledgers into the file room. Thank God she could hold on to the thing, because her legs were trembling. The file-room custodian looked up expectantly, a middle-aged man named Svets, who wore enormous glasses and a wide wool tie that came only to the middle of his belly. He looked forward to watching Egorova replace the files every evening at close of business, especially when she stretched to reach the higher safe drawers. His compound beetle eyes followed her as she horsed the trolley through the door.

She had practiced it in pantomime with Gable, he said don't stop, make it flow. She caught the trolley on the corner of the clerk's desk, let it go over, cascading paper across the floor, and Svets got up, all fussed, and she was on her knees beside his desk and there was the port with a winking green light, and she made sure the pins were the right side up and felt it go in, and started counting while she kept picking up paper, nine, ten, eleven, and Svets was straightening up and Dominika pointed to another file on the floor in the far corner, twelve, thirteen, *fourteen,* out came the thumb drive, and she was up on her feet, brushing her hair behind her ear, the piece of plastic in her skirt pocket thumping like the Tell-Tale Heart. She tidied the files and put them back in the drawers, and let him look at her on tiptoe, lifting one foot for effect.

Two hours till the end of the day and every eye seemed on her, every person seemed to know. Then the lobby and the impatient grumbling line of embassy employees stacked up at the double front doors, beside which was a table with two Volga boatmen behind it, embassy security with brown clouds around their heads, checking purses and pockets. *Dear God, random bag check and I pick today.* A rivulet of sweat went down her back, she could feel it all the way down, and she was caught in line, she couldn't retreat back upstairs, they watched for that, and she held her coat close in front of her and slipped the thumb drive under the waistband of her skirt and down the front of her underwear. The security man reeked of vodka and his red eyes knew, *had to know,* she had the thing in her panties, but he stirred the contents of her purse and slid it to the end of the table and waved her through.

She told them about it that night, the adrenaline of the risk still hot in her belly, with Nate standing apart, in the door of the little kitchen, and Forsyth listening quietly with his glasses up on his forehead. Gable opened a longneck and tipped it back in one swallow. "I guess now we know why it's called a thumb drive," he said, and pushed past Nate and started making cheese fondue, for Christ's sake. Dominika had never tasted it, didn't know what it was, and when it was ready they sat around the table and dipped bread into the sharp, melted cheese, smelling the wine in it, and talked and laughed a little.

Forsyth and Gable left after dinner. Nate poured two glasses of wine and they walked into the living room. "What you did today was too risky. I should have never let you try it," said Nate.

"It came out all right," said Dominika, turning to face him. "We both know there are risks."

"Some risks are acceptable, a few of them unavoidable, most are stupid."

"Stupid? *Glupyj?* Don't worry, Neyt," said Dominika, "you won't lose your star spy." The word *stupid* had lit her fuse. His was already smoldering.

"It's just that you should learn to get high on something other than adrenaline," he said.

"You mean like wine?" she said, and threw the wineglass against the wall. "No, thank you, I prefer adrenaline." The drip of liquid was the only sound in the room.

Nate crowded her, and grabbed her arms above the elbows. "What is wrong with you?" he hissed. They glared at each other, their faces inches apart.

"What is wrong with *you*?" she said in a whisper. The room was out of focus for her. Nate was purple and hazy. She looked at his lips, daring him, willing him to come closer. Another second, and the moment disappeared into the slipstream. "Please let go of me," she said, and he dropped her arms and she picked up her coat and without looking at him opened the door—taking the automatic, precautionary glances into the hallway and stairwell—then went out, closing it softly behind her.

Nate stared at the closed door, his tongue thick in his mouth, his heart pounding in his chest. Jesus, all he wanted was to keep the case running smoothly. All he wanted was to keep her safe. All he wanted . . .

GABLE'S CHEESE FONDUE

Reduce white wine and crushed garlic, add grated Gruyère and Emmentaler cheese, whisk over medium heat until melted. Stir in cornstarch slurry, more wine to taste, and reheat (do not boil) until fondue is creamy and thick. Serve with lightly toasted, cubed country bread.

18

Short-sleeve weather now, and Finns on the sidewalk waiting for the pedestrian light to change all had their faces turned to the sun, like sunflowers, eyes closed. The broad lawns and benches of Kaivopuisto were dotted with lunchtime secretaries sunbathing in their bras, chins up, drinking in the light.

The note was taped to his door, and Nate walked into Forsyth's office and sat down. Gable was sitting on the couch. Forsyth handed him the short Headquarters cable announcing the availability of the new Director of the CIA, recently confirmed, to travel incognito from Copenhagen to Helsinki for six hours, for a controlled meet and greet with DIVA to express the Agency's appreciation for her service so far. Nate looked up at Forsyth, and then over at Gable.

"How can he travel incognito?" asked Nate. "He was all over the news."

"He'll be in Copenhagen for the NATO thing," added Forsyth. "How he'll slip away from the Danes beats the hell out of me. Allen Dulles used to do this, Angleton too, get on a plane, not tell anyone, show up unannounced."

"Yeah, in fucking 1951," said Gable. "And those guys traveled solo, and you walked down the steps of the Constellation across the tarmac into a taxi, and checked into a hotel by signing the register. Those pillbox hats on the stewardesses, though . . ."

Forsyth ignored him. "I sent a polite no-thank-you response last night, and Chief Europe called me on the green line half an hour later and chewed my ass. Not a request. Director wants to get involved."

"There's another inflated balloon, fucking Chief Europe," said Gable. "Thinks he's a ship's captain at Trafalgar. Ever read his Christmas benediction to the troops?"

Forsyth continued to ignore him. "We can control things only from the minute he gets off the plane. VIP gate, drive him around, dry-clean him, stash his security guys in a van downstairs, get him up there, shake her hand, then get him out. Just pray FAPSI—Russian SIGINT Service—doesn't pick up his flight plan." Forsyth looked at the cable again. "They must have briefed DIVA to him recently. Well, at least it's good PR for the case."

"PR? He's going to get her killed," said Nate. "It'd be safer for us to put her in a car trunk and run her over to Sweden for a long weekend. Why don't we tell him she's not available?"

"No," said Forsyth.

"Tell him she refuses."

"No. Get her primed, tell her to smile. Those blue eyes will do the rest. Let's get some food up there, some drinks."

"A bug-out car, parked close," said Gable.

"What about Dominika?" asked Nate. "Who eats the shit sandwich if something goes wrong?"

"You do," said Gable and Forsyth.

Footsteps on the landing, and the door opened and Dominika stood up as the Director of the Central Intelligence Agency shrugged off his coat and came across the room and pumped her hand up and down, saying how glad he was to meet her, then pumped Nate's hand too, told him he was doing a great job with this young lady, a beaming smile in her direction, and they both could be proud of what they were doing for the United States. Dominika tilted her head a little at that, and they sat down, Dominika and the

Director on the couch, and he opened the charm spigot from his legislative days and he tapped her knee to make a point, and sometimes his hand stayed on her knee, a habit from the Senate cloakroom and the pages.

He was tall, and thin, and squirrel-eyed, with sunken cheeks and shiny hair dyed black. Dominika decided he looked like Koschei, the mythological evildoer her father used to read to her about when she was a little girl. Dominika looked hard at him, but his aura was faint, a pale green glow around his face and ears. *Green,* zelenyj, *emotional, not what he appears to be, an actor,* thought Dominika. So different from Uncle Vanya, but the same, different services, the same *yashcheritsa,* the same lizard.

He was asking Forsyth about the "operational ambient" in Scandinavia, and they all knew that was nothing to be discussing in front of an agent, so she got up and brought out a plate of *pelmeni,* steaming dumplings just fished out of the pot, stuffed with savory ground meat and spices, slathered with sour cream. Dominika had insisted on making something, a Russian way to honor the guest. Nate thought they should have served dry näkkileipä crackers and warm cream soda.

"Quite excellent," said the Director, clotted sour cream at the corner of his mouth.

The Director wiped his lips and patted the cushion so Dominika would sit back down beside him. Nate and Gable and Forsyth sat in chairs close by, angled to watch Dominika, to give her support, while the Director asked where she was from, as if to check if she were a constituent. Gable thought of long ago and desperate late nights in stinking hotel rooms with sweating agents, little men running unspeakable risks, spinning up their nerve to go out again, intently listening to Gable speaking slowly and without pause, watching his face, pouring the vodka, or the maotai, or the arrack. That was long ago. Here, in the sun-splashed apartment, they were having a jolly old agent meeting.

For a Russian, talking about future success is inviting bad luck. Better to shut up about it. The Director moved closer to Dominika but she didn't lean away. *Good show,* thought Nate, *she would know how to handle that, wouldn't she?* The Director was saying that they all *applauded* her efforts, that he was taking a *personal interest* in her activities, and that she should *not hesitate* to contact him directly at any time *of the day or night.* Nate was tempted to ask for his home telephone number in Bethesda. Forsyth read his thoughts and scraped his chair to tell him to shut the fuck up.

Bottle-green and prattling, Director Koschei was saying something about a covert bank account. A sum of money had been put in the account for Dominika as a *recruitment bonus,* more money would be deposited *each month.* The account was completely under her control, but of course withdrawals and *profligate* spending were inadvisable. He continued that additional funds would be deposited when she began work *in Moscow.* Dominika looked up at Nate, and turned to look at Forsyth. Both their faces were expressionless. Koschei continued remorselessly.

At the end of two years' *internal* service in Moscow, he droned, an additional bonus of *a quarter million dollars* would be deposited in her account. Finally, on the *mutually agreed-upon* date of her retirement from service, the CIA would resettle her in the West in a location selected with her *security* in mind and would provide her with a retirement home of not less than *three thousand square feet.*

The room was quiet. Dominika's face had changed and she looked at each of them, then turned back to the visitor. She smiled her incandescent smile. Nate thought, *Oh, fuck.*

"Sir, thank you for coming such a long way to meet me," said Dominika. "I have told Mr. Forsyth, and Mr. Gable, and Mr. Nash"—she gestured to each of them as she mentioned them—"that I am committed to helping your service any way I can. I am committed to trying to help my country, to help Russia. I appreciate all you have offered me. But please excuse me. I am not doing this for money." She looked evenly at this *nekulturny* scarecrow.

"Oh, of course you're not," said Koschei, patting her knee. "Although we all realize how *useful* money can be."

"Yes, sir, you are right," said Dominika. Nate saw she was upset, there was a flush at her collarbones. Forsyth saw it too. Gable started gathering coats, moving around the room.

"Mr. Director, we unfortunately have to spend another half hour driving out of here before getting you back to the plane," said Forsyth, getting to his feet.

"Fine, fine," he said. "It's been a pleasure meeting you, Dominique. You're a courageous woman running terrible risks." *Jesus, tell her how long she has to live,* thought Nate.

"Remember," the Director said, giving her a hug, his arm across her chest, "call me anytime in case of need."

Yeah, so he can take you by the hand and lead you across the plowed strip at the border wire, between the bounding antipersonnel mines and two minutes ahead of the dogs, thought Gable.

Forsyth bundled Koschei into his coat and hat while Gable went downstairs to alert the security detail. The Director followed. Forsyth stopped at the door and winked. "Talk to you soon," he said, and disappeared. Dominika and Nate stood in the doorway of the apartment like newlyweds saying good-bye to a grumpy uncle who had come to Sunday dinner.

Nate softly closed the door. The safe house was dead still, they could hear car doors chunking, then the sound of them driving away. "Well," said Nate, "did you like the Director?"

It was twilight and running lights ghosted along the inlet, and happy voices came over the water through the open window. Two glasses of wine stood untouched on the table as they sat in the dark, Dominika on the couch, Nate in a chair. The ambient light caught her hair and the eyelashes on her right eye. She had worn a summery dress for the day, tight in the bodice, with heels, like for a job interview. She didn't feel like talking, and Nate didn't know what to say, worried that their arguments and now this visit had broken her back, that she was going to tell him she was backing out. Nate was her handling officer. It was his responsibility to keep the case going.

Fuck, he thought, *lots of pitches get turned down, agents are lost in the CI grinder, there's bad luck, or bad timing, you miss a train by thirty minutes and it changes everything. But who loses an agent because she thinks we're all shitheels?* He could imagine the heads bent forward in the Headquarters cafeteria. Yeah, it was Nash, in Helsinki. Hall file was right after all, usually is. Langley would cable, *Time for a CONUS tour, sit a spell, let's talk about your future.* His father would write, *Welcome home, son, all is forgiven.* A pitch-black mine shaft, steep and airless. He registered that she had stood up and was walking toward him.

The dark room affected her, a cocoon, invisible, she didn't know, but she stood in front of him, looking down at him. The usual deep purple of his background was there, and strangely she could feel a heat emanating from it, still and steady. She knew he was suffering, the too-serious professional worried about the equilibrium of his career, but there was vulnerability under the professional seriousness. Whatever he thought about her personally—she wasn't sure—his fretting and worry were endearing. She realized that she herself was feeling the strain, living constantly with the ice-cold secret. Goaded by anger at first, she had fallen into her new role, a different role. She had pushed herself for the Americans because she trusted them, they cared for her, they were professionals.

But especially for Nate. Part of what Dominika was doing was for him, she realized. If he had asked her, she would have told him she had no thought of quitting. She was determined and focused.

But right now she needed something more than the rush of deception, of the knowledge that her will was stronger than all others', that she was besting the Gray Cardinals. She needed to be needed. By him. She could feel her secret self open the hurricane-room door and step outside. Dominika put her hands on the arms of Nate's chair, bent over, and kissed him on the lips.

She hadn't foreseen this. (She knew *he* certainly had not.) In her service as well as his, Dominika knew it was *zapreshcheno,* strictly forbidden, to become physically involved with an agent. Emotional complications are death to a clandestine operation. It's not for no reason they whisk the Sparrow from the room after the honey trap and "Uncle Sasha" takes over, all business, because passions get in the way, you can't get anywhere with an agent who is thinking about his *khuy,* the old instructors used to say, cackling and trying to get her to blush.

She was in his arms, kissing him, not frantically, but slowly, softly; his lips were warm and she wanted to drink them in. She felt a pressure building in her body, inside her skull, in her breasts, between her legs. His hands pressed on her back and she felt sweet and edgy, as if they were childhood friends who years later had discovered each other as adults. He breathed deep purple heat into her ear, and she felt it down her spine.

"Dominika," he said, wanting to slow down. They had argued days before, it was folly to become involved like this, the stability of the case required—

"*Zamolchi,*" she whispered, shut up, you fool, and she brushed her lips along his cheek and held him tighter.

His head was spinning, from indecision, from alarm, from an unbidden lust growing in his guts. Nate knew he wanted her; it was insane, reckless, forbidden. He couldn't remember what happened next.

They were naked and feverish in the little bedroom, and Dominika raked her nails lightly between his legs to make him follow her—she thought she must have just invented a new come-along technique—and they were climbing ridiculously over the footboard onto the bed wedged between the bedroom walls. She kept her hand on him, fixing her fingernails a little tighter, and she laughed, her mouth dry with desire. Feeling his skin for the first time, trailing her lips across his stomach, was unreal and dizzying. He looked at her in surprise as she pushed him back, her hand on his chest. Prurient and tender and shy and slutty, she tasted him, and savored the mouthfeel of him, and it was as if they had been lovers since forever. There was never a thought of Sparrow School, or numbered techniques. Dominika simply wanted him.

It was becoming more urgent, her secret self was expanding and filling her head and constricting her throat, and just in time Nate blessedly flipped her on her back and she pointed her quivering toes at the ceiling and the light of a bloated moon rising over the harbor islands came through the window and got in her eyes. She was night blind and moon blind, and Nate was only a silhouette above her, then a crushing weight. Dominika felt a sudden, excruciatingly sweet expansion, and the moonlight was rocketing around behind her eyelids, and she hoped he could keep her heaving body from blowing away like a piece of paper. She felt the hollow rush expand inside her, and then a rogue wave rose up from the deep, bigger than the others, hanging, curling, and she said, "*Bozhe moj,*" from way back in her throat, and a white-eyed state of grace rolled through her like the wind bends a wheat field.

They lay side by side in the crushing moonlight. Dominika waited for her thighs to stop quivering before turning to look at his moon-wet body. "*Dushka,* you are very good at agent handling," she whispered.

The night air had not yet dried their bodies when they heard a key turn in the lock of the safehouse door, and they rocketed out of the bed, and Nate pulled on shirt and pants and shoes, Dominika grabbed a handful of clothes and ran into the bathroom. Nate walked into the living room to see Gable in the kitchen, leaning into the open refrigerator.

"Thought I'd come back to do damage control after the Director's tour-de-force performance," said Gable. He turned back to look into the refrigerator. "Any more of those dumplings left?"

"On the bottom shelf," said Nate. "Yeah, I talked to Dominika about all that shit. I think she understands the diff between us and the suits."

"I was laughing my ass off when she got pissed at the old peacock. She's got spirit," Gable said. He put a container of dumplings on the counter. "So you calmed her down okay?" he asked.

"Yes, *Bratok,*" said Dominika, coming out of the bathroom, "I am calm now." She was completely dressed, hair combed and features composed. Nate watched Gable's face. "Let me reheat the *pelmeni* for you," said Dominika. She lit the burner, rattled a pan. "They are best the second time," she said, "especially like this." She poured the boiled dumplings into the skillet with butter and fried them until lightly brown on all sides. "But now this way they are best with vinegar," she said.

The deadly domestic prattle continued as they stood around the kitchen counter eating out of bowls. No one spoke, and Gable occasionally looked from Dominika to Nate and back again. Nate studiously looked at his food, but Dominika returned Gable's look unperturbed, reading the bloom around his head. Finished eating, Gable ran water in the sink as Dominika put on her coat and said good night. She didn't look back at Nate as she went down the stairway. Nate closed the door, turning with dread to face Gable, who was walking to the living-room couch with two glasses held between his fingers, a bottle of scotch in the other hand.

"Well, Priapus," said Gable, setting the glasses down on the table, "run your fingers around the rims while I get the ice."

PELMENI DUMPLINGS

Roll two-inch discs of wafer-thin dough made from flour, egg, milk, and salt. Mix ground beef, ground pork, minced chicken, grated onion, puréed garlic, and water. Place a dot of filling in center of each disc, moisten edges, fold closed, and crimp. Bring bottom corners together, pinching to attach. Boil in salted boiling water until dumplings float to the surface. Serve with sour cream.

19

"It got away from you?" said Forsyth, leaning over his desk. "You are handling, by Headquarters' reckoning, one of the most promising Russian cases in the Operations Directorate in the last decade, and you lack the discipline to stay out of her bed?"

"Chief, I know it was a mistake, I didn't plan it, it just happened. She was freaked out about the Director. He called her Dominique. It's been building up with her, she needed a connection, she's been under a lot of pressure."

"She needed a *connection*?" said Gable from his usual seat on the couch behind Nate. "Is that what your generation calls scrogging now?"

Forsyth's normally kindly, patrician face was dark; his eyes held Nate's until the younger man looked down. "Then you address her needs, you talk her down, you give her support. But you don't—"

"Go at it like minks," said Gable.

"Yeah, minks," said Forsyth. "What happens if your relationship hits a bump? What if you have a fight in four months and she decides she can't stand you?"

"Easy to see it happening," said Gable.

"Is she going to keep working for the CIA? Or is she doing all this because she's besotted with your—"

"Macho gazpacho," said Gable.

"What the fuck are you talking about?" said Forsyth, looking at Gable slouched on the couch. He turned back to Nate, who had laughed at Gable's comment.

"C'mon, Nate," he said. "Despite the intelligence

she's provided to this point, and despite her poly, DIVA is a new asset. We need to see her operate productively before we know your recruitment took. Does that mean we don't trust her? Yes and no; you never totally trust any agent.

"Russians get morose, they get dramatic, they get homesick. They get nutty. Remember Yurchenko waving good-bye on the steps of the Aeroflot flight? DIVA's strong, but we all know she's temperamental, impulsive." He held up his hand to stop Gable from making a puerile comment.

"Your job as a case officer is to collect the intel, ensure her security, sublimate your personal emotions, and make DIVA the best agent you can."

"Sublimate," said Gable. "That means no fucking."

"You've been moping since you came to Station about making a big recruitment, about not losing the case, about your hall file. Well, goddamn it, start running this Russian like a pro. Run her with a cool head—"

"The one on your shoulders," said Gable.

"And consider what a love affair could do to the operation, to her. We've got to start thinking about her return to Moscow. We don't know the timing. She could flat refuse to work inside, so start her thinking about that grind, prepare her for it."

"Yessir," said Nate, looking back up at Forsyth.

"Are we clear?" said Forsyth, bearing down a final time.

"I know, I know, *I know,*" said Nate. "I'm all over it. Thanks for the pep talk, I'll get it back on track."

"That's good to hear," said Gable, pushing up from the couch. "Now I can yank the four nanny cams out of the safe house." Nate looked over at him, eyes wide. Forsyth was keeping a straight face.

"Just kidding, Romeo," said Gable. "I couldn't bear watching the replays."

What prevented Forsyth and Gable from further kicking Nate's ass over the affair was a signal from Dominika the next day: Nate studiously did not jerk his hand away when he touched the slick smear of Vaseline on the underside of his car door handle in the morning. She had wiped it on during the night. *Emergency signal,* he thought, *plus twelve hours.* The night was chilly, Scandinavian fall had arrived, with hoarfrost on windshields, steam dribbling from the vents. They were waiting at the safe house, reviewing the emergency contingencies. Was she on the run, was this a hot pursuit situation? Nate had researched the air and ferry schedules. Gable's SUPO guy was on standby. ARCHIE and VERONICA were sitting by the phone. All three CIA officers dealt with the waiting, the stomach feel. No one checked his watch—they were too good for that.

Nate stood up when her key turned in the lock, and they knew it was okay because her ice-blue eyes were sparkling and her cheeks were flushed—from not only the SDR, but also something else.

Gable fetched a cup of steaming tea and she blew on it while she told the story, quickly and well, details up front because that was how they all were trained. She wanted to rock them a little, impress them. The day before, an unidentified man had come to the Russian Embassy, asked to see the "security man," and had given him an envelope with block printing on it: DELIVER UNOPENED TO M. VOLONTOV. The man slipped out of the embassy before the bovine security officer could get his name, but the security officer instantly took the letter upstairs to Rezident Volontov, who found a second envelope inside the first. Volontov had bellowed for Dominika to come in and had hovered and fumed in a dusty orange cloud while she translated the English-language note. Printed in block letters, it said that the bearer was offering a classified US technical manual to the SVR for the sum of $500,000, and proposed to meet in five days at the Kämp Hotel.

Dominika looked from Nate to Forsyth to Gable, sipped her tea, kept going. There was a second page in the envelope, with three torn strips as if yanked out of a three-ring binder. TOP SECRET/UMBRA top and bottom of the page, boldface title **US National Communications Grid**, an upper corner trimmed diagonally. Volontov was nervous, made her read the warning notice under the title to him twice: "Unauthorized distribution," "If found, return to Office of Coordination," "Misuse subject to prosecution."

Volontov's face was gray, he barked at her to make a copy. His Soviet sycophant juices were flowing, and he puffily told her he was going to pouch the original title page directly to First Deputy Director Egorov, top priority, more secure that way. Forsyth looked at Gable, and Gable was standing up, throwing on his coat, when Dominika lifted her sweater and pulled a folded piece of paper from her waistband and slid it across to Forsyth—she'd made a second copy. The Americans clustered around; Gable tapped the torn diagonal corner and muttered, "Fucker's cut out the serial number," then looked at Dominika and said, "I thought I told you never to do that again," then leaned over and kissed the top of her head and went out. The Station's NIACT cable would be in Washington in thirty minutes. Gable liked sending night-action cables and waking the doughnut-eaters in Langley.

Volontov had been in torment the rest of the day, said Dominika. He had called her into his office half a dozen times, an orange Ferris wheel of anticipation around his head. Even he realized that this could be a colossal intelligence windfall. Near the end of the day he decided that he would call Vanya Egorov directly to inform him of the sensitive and potentially spectacular development, and to alert him to the incoming pouch. Let the deputy director see how he, Volontov, personally was handling the operation.

Volontov shut his door to make the call on the VCh phone, and Dominika had heard the gratuitous laughter and the servility in the repeated, barked "*Da, da, da,*" a real *l'stets,* how do you say it, she asked, buttock-kisser? Close enough, said Forsyth. Volontov summoned her for the tenth time that day and archly informed her that the deputy director of course had ratified Volontov's suggestion that Dominika, and only Dominika, would assist the *rezident* in this operation. She would prepare the funds—she was told to draw only $5,000. She was directed to rent the room at the Kämp. She would translate during the meeting with the American. Start now, he said, dismissing her with a wave.

Unbeknownst to Dominika, Volontov also called in his Line KR referent, the former Border Guards prodigy. "I want you to countersurveil a meeting I'm having at the end of the week. In the lobby of the Kämp Hotel. Just sit and watch."

"A meeting?" said the counterintelligence officer. "How many men will we need? Of course we'll be armed."

"Idiot. Just you. No weapons. Just sit in the lobby. Watch me meet a contact. Stay there. Then watch me leave. Is that clear?" said Volontov. The KR man nodded, but he was disappointed.

Nate hustled Dominika out of the safe house after an hour. Moscow Rules from now on: No unnecessary meetings. No daytime meetings. Look for surveillance, *assume* surveillance. Curtail ostensible social contacts. Stay close to the embassy until after the Kämp Hotel rendezvous was complete. Volontov would be on edge, jumpy, might draw in the strings, watch everyone. They would take no chances, no risks. "There's a cobra in the toilet bowl," said Gable back in the Station. "We have to proceed very carefully. Anything happens to blow the meeting, anything—this shithead American gets arrested, the SVR doesn't get the manual—Dominika is the only other person in the SVR who knows about the volunteer."

Forsyth sent a restricted-handling cable reminding Headquarters of the risk to DIVA. Chief Europe for one was shocked, *shocked,* to read Forsyth's recommendation that Station simply identify the traitor and let the FBI settle his hash after he returned to the United States. Chief Europe could not *countenance* a plan that would result in the grave loss of national security information—not as long as his hand remained *at the tiller* of Europe Division.

When the Legal Attaché of the American Embassy, a fifty-two-year-old Special Agent of the FBI named Elwood Maratos, barged into Forsyth's office to coordinate the "takedown," they knew Headquarters had briefed the walk-in all over Washington. Maratos had distinguished himself during a twenty-five-year career as a bank-robbery investigator in the Midwest, and he put his feet up in the office, showing the soles of his shoes to Forsyth and Gable, and said this was a clear case of espionage committed by an American citizen, and therefore under the strict purview of the FBI.

"Fucking guy," said Gable when Maratos left, "thinks *espresso* means 'nonstop train' in Spanish."

It was a certainty that, if they let them, a dozen FBI Special Agents would descend on Helsinki wearing cargo pants, tactical boots, and New York Yankees ball caps. All the Station could do would be to try to keep the FEEBs under control. Forsyth told Nate to have the exfiltration plan for DIVA spun up and ready. They might have to get her out if there was a flap and the Russians started looking for reasons why.

Then something happened in Headquarters. There must have been a big meeting, and they started paying attention to the danger to DIVA. Some later said it was Simon Benford, Chief of Counterintelligence, who threw one of his well-known histrionic fits, warning that inattention to the counterintelligence threat to this agent would ensure "a pig's breakfast." The result was two cables that arrived on the third day, two days before the meeting at the Kämp. The first was tagged *From Chief Europe, direct for COS.* The second had been drafted by Benford with characteristic economy bordering on rudeness. That cable proposed an operational gambit that astounded even Marty Gable, an old whore who had an ashtray in his office made from a human skull from either Cambodia or Miami—he claimed he could not remember which.

The first cable read:

```
1. Please confine future traffic on
reference information to this chan-
nel. Appreciate ref. Hqs assigns top
priority to preventing the potential
illegal sale to SVR of US classified
material. Station directed to coor-
dinate with Embassy FBI representa-
tive, who has been briefed by FBI
Hqs in Washington. Hqs confirms to
Station that FBI has primacy in all
investigatory and law-enforcement
matters involving threats to the na-
tional security and Amcits suspected
of a federal crime, per Title II of
the Intelligence Reform Act of 2004
and Executive Order 12333 and 50 USC
401.
```

2. Request Station fully support FBI investigation as required. Hqs of course is concerned that any arrest could affect security of Station asset GTDIVA. Submit Station should increase measures to vouchsafe DIVA's operational security.

3. Please report developments by immediate precedence cable, including NIACT. Hqs standing by to assist as required. Fair winds and smooth sailing.

The second cable read:

1. Reference GTDIVA report received. DIVA developing into exceptional source.

2. Please express Hqs compliments.

3. Concur that even slight misstep in dealing with ref volunteer will put scrutiny on DIVA. In event worst-case outcome, please ensure exfil contingency plan is in place. Hqs prepared for defector processing and resettlement.

4. FBI law enforcement equities notwithstanding, Hqs goals are to identify volunteer, affect his arrest without alerting SVR, and permit rpt permit SVR to take receipt of manual without raising Russian CI suspicions. FBI will be briefed on covert action opportunity and will follow Station direction to achieve CA goals.

5. For Station background, separate DoD compartmented program last year produced modified manual (GTSOLAR) identical to copy offered for sale in Helsinki. Exact nature modifications classified, will result in technical disinformation and misdirection.

6. Iden OSWR researcher couriering SOLAR manual departing Washington evening 17th expected arrival morning of 18th. Please meet and accommodate.

7. Submit asap operational proposal to substitute SOLAR manual by immediate precedence. Disregard guidance in previous cable.

They worked it out, called in the techs, called one more meeting with DIVA on the night before the contact. They showed her the drawings, copied her hotel room key, ran her through the steps. Made her look at the drawings again. It's all right, Neyt, she said. An edge to her voice, nerves showing. Talked about the risk, her exposure, but she didn't want to hear it. Her blue eyes searched his face when he rolled out the map, marking the corner where they would pick her up if she was on the run. She heard the concern in his voice.

Was this about her, she thought, or about the operation? Nate the handler was back, his aura unchanged.

Things were too serious, so they broke for a late dinner, and it was Forsyth's turn. He didn't cook much, but Dominika gaped at him in an apron, bathed in blue, wearing oven mitts, pulling a *saucière* out of the oven. He knew one dish, a *soubise,* buttery braised rice and caramelized onions. In case of disaster, and so they wouldn't starve, Gable had bought lamb kebabs from a take-out place. They ate without talking. Then a look at the clock; she'd better get home.

She didn't open the door, waited a beat, pulling up her collar. "Good luck tomorrow," she said. *And she's the one under the blade,* thought Nate.

"You too," said Nate. "This is going to be fine."

"See you in a couple of days," she said, pulling on a pair of gloves, ready to open the door. Waiting. Sound of dishes in the sink. Looking at him, Mona Lisa smile.

"I want you to be careful," he said. She looked over his shoulder toward the little moon-blasted bedroom, but he didn't blink, and her heart fell a little.

"*Spokoinoi nochi,* Neyt." She never made a sound going down the steps.

They walked around putting out the lamps, getting ready to go home. It was already tomorrow. Forsyth was talking as they buttoned up the apartment. "No ripples, no hovering, no heroics, is that clear?" Gable was drawing the curtains, flicking off the light in the bathroom.

"Got it," said Nate.

"I mean, if we hit a bump tomorrow, we don't launch in specwar mode," Forsyth said.

"Right, I understand," said Nate, knowing what was coming, trying not to patronize his chief.

"If there's trouble, what we do is assess the trouble. Then we make the decision to act. But it is going to be critical that Dominika play out her role in the exchange, to sell the swap. If she stumbles, no matter what the reason, the operation is gone."

Gable came back into the room. "By this time tomorrow the SVR has got to be jerking one another off that they got away with the authentic goods. No doubts, sheer joy in Moscow." They were all pulling on their overcoats. What had to be said, had to be said now, because once outside on the street they walked away in different directions, no good-night hugs.

"So what I'm hearing is that we let her walk into a shitstorm to sell the con," said Nate, trying to keep his voice even.

"'Sell the con'?" said Gable. "This ain't Las Vegas. We're gonna protect her every way we know how. But you gotta get on board, nugget. Get your head straight, this is as big as it gets."

The three of them split up in the frosty air. Nate took the long walk around to his car, trolleys weren't running that late. He felt a little of the Vaseline still left under his door handle, and he got into his car and stared at the dashboard, and his vision tunneled, and he was parking in front of her apartment, and pounding on her door, and she was in his arms, her nightgown clinging and thin over her body, and she was showering him with kisses, and his cloudy vision popped and he shook his head clear and started his car and drove home, looping around the fringes of the city, watching his mirrors.

FORSYTH'S SOUBISE

Boil rice in salted water for five minutes. In separate French saucière, lightly caramelize seasoned onions in butter. Stir in rice, cover, and cook gently in medium oven, stirring occasionally, until golden. Before serving, stir in heavy cream and grated Gruyère.

20

Forsyth, Nate, and a tech named Ginsburg perched gingerly on red velvet Empire chairs in an elegant room in the Kämp Hotel. They looked skeptically at the flocked silk wallpaper and satin canopy over the bed. Traffic noise on Norra Esplanaden came faintly through the sheers across the tall French doors. The three CIA officers sat around a low gilt side table, which was covered by two laptops, a cell phone, a miniature signal receiver, and an encrypted Motorola SB5100—the bulky radios were more secure than cell phones, especially in the likely event that the Russians were monitoring all channels during the hotel-room meeting. The laptops displayed two images: Number one was of Dominika's room at the Kämp, essentially identical to the one in which they were sitting. It was, in fact, the room next door. Laptop number two showed the interior of that room's large adjoining bathroom. Both images were from an upper corner, near the ceiling, a bird's-eye, 270-degree view.

Per Volontov's instructions, Dominika had rented the room several days in advance, which gave the techs time to do an entry. The Station had worked overnight to install two wireless cameras, one mortised into the ornate plaster ceiling molding of the bedroom, the other secured inside a forced-air vent in the bathroom. The cameras transmitted an encrypted signal to the receiver that then was displayed on and recorded by the laptops. Each remote-head camera—the size of a Zippo lighter—also contained a miniature digital microphone that provided audio.

Gable was on the street in a parked van at the

front of the Kämp with LEGATT Maratos and three other Special Agents from the FBI's counterespionage office in Washington. To Maratos's barely concealed fury, Forsyth had vetoed any FBI presence in the hotel room, partly to contain and control the FEEBs, but mostly to prevent them from seeing Dominika. They were not going to expose her as an asset to the FEEBs.

The FEEBs had played hardball in Washington. They refused to agree to permit the volunteer, whoever he was, to depart Helsinki and return to the United States before they popped him. Too many things could go wrong, they argued. What they really meant was that they couldn't survive the political blowback if the UNSUB, the unknown subject, got away. Cake-eaters in Headquarters therefore agreed that the FEEBs would wait till the Russians had cleared the area before taking him down. They said, "Sure, sure," when the CIA insisted that Forsyth, and only Forsyth, would give the go-ahead to arrest.

"Everybody understands the sequence of events, right?" said Forsyth in his office the day before. He was looking pointedly at Maratos.

"Yeah, yeah we got it. This isn't our first bust," said Maratos. "Just be sure you call us when you find out the little cocksucker's name."

"Elwood, I want to stress that you have to wait for my go signal. You'll put my source's life in jeopardy if you go in too hard too soon," said Forsyth.

Maratos looked up at Forsyth in annoyance. "I said I got it, Jesus. I got it."

Gable had told Nate that his job for this operation was to shut up and listen, but Nate spoke up anyway, looking directly at the FBI man. "If you guys fuck this up, better have your wife start your car every morning." It was a howling breach of etiquette.

"You little shit," said Maratos. "Is that a threat against a federal officer?"

Nate had been about to respond when Forsyth snapped, "Shut the fuck up, both of you." Maratos thought to say something else but kept his mouth shut.

The radio on the table clicked twice, the signal from Gable in the van that Volontov and Dominika had entered the hotel lobby. Three minutes later, laptop one showed the door opening and Volontov, Dominika, and a short young man entering the room. Dominika carried a briefcase. The volunteer was dark-complexioned, had an unruly shock of black hair, and heavy eyebrows. He wore a blue Windbreaker and carried a black duffel bag slung over his shoulder. What the camera did not record was what Dominika saw. The air around him was suffused with a soiled yellow cast, like a fever wind or the sky before a tornado. She knew what Volontov was going to do to him—Dominika knew the young man was lost. They sat in chairs around a low table. The audio picked up Volontov speaking in Russian and Dominika translating. It was eerie to hear Dominika's voice coming out of the laptop.

At Volontov's insistence the young man identified himself as John Paul Bullard, a midlevel analyst in the National Communications Service. He described his work and his need for money. He patted the duffel bag and repeated his demand that Volontov pay him a half million dollars for the manual, the cover sheet of which he had already provided. Volontov spoke again and Dominika asked the young American how they could be sure it was genuine.

Bullard zipped open the duffel and handed Dominika a bound manual the size of a thin telephone book. She handed it to Volontov, who spent three seconds riffling the pages before he handed it back to Dominika. He said something to Bullard that Dominika translated. They would have to examine the document privately before determining its exact value. Bullard said, "It's genuine, all right, it's the real thing."

At Volontov's nod, Dominika got up from her chair with the document and the briefcase and walked into the bathroom. Per his detailed instructions the day before, the *rezident* wanted the manual in the false bottom of the briefcase as soon as possible in case this was a Western provocation, a trap. The windowless bathroom was the place to secure it.

Forsyth whispered into the radio, "All okay, hold." Laptop two showed the bathroom door opening and Dominika's head filled the screen. She closed the door, placed the briefcase on the bathroom vanity. Moving quickly, she bent to the floor and pushed the kick plate of the vanity, which opened inward on three piano hinges. Dominika pulled an identical-looking manual, modified under a microscope by a score of eggheads and meticulously prepared—down to the missing cover page—out of the concealment cavity and pushed Bullard's original manual into the space. The hinged kick plate swung closed. Dominika pressed two rivets in the lid of the briefcase. With the pressure, the inside lining of the briefcase opened to reveal a false bottom, into which Dominika put the modified replacement manual. She snapped the concealment cover closed, and shut the briefcase lid with a click.

Dominika paused to look at herself in the mirror, patted her hair, and then looked up at the vent and into the invisible camera. Nate, the evening before, had told her they would be monitoring the switch to ensure everything went smoothly. Dominika stuck her tongue out at the camera and, with a last look at herself in the mirror, went back out into the bedroom.

"Jesus Christ," said Forsyth, "unbelievable. What kind of operation are you running?" he said, looking over at Nate.

"Can I get her number?" said Ginsburg the tech.

"Shut up, both of you," said Forsyth.

Dominika sat down again as Volontov dug into his coat pocket and took out a fat envelope. He placed it on the table and slid it across to Bullard. Dominika told Bullard that they could pay him only $5,000 until they had verified the authenticity of the manual. Bullard's look of astonishment was met with stony-faced silence from Volontov.

"What's he gonna do," said Ginsburg, "go to the authorities?" A sharp look from Forsyth shut him up. Dominika told Bullard that they would leave first and that he should wait in the room for five minutes before exiting the hotel. The young American sat back in his chair, gobsmacked. Volontov stood up, buttoned his coat, and walked out of the room, Dominika following him. Alone now, the American leaned forward with his face in his hands.

Forsyth was whispering into the radio, repeating Bullard's name twice. "Party's over. Guest still upstairs. No one move. No movement." Two clicks of acknowledgment came back. Suddenly Bullard straightened and stood up. "Sit the fuck down," Forsyth said to the screen on the laptop. "Stay put, you little bastard." Bullard walked to the door and left the room. Forsyth grabbed the radio. "Guest is moving. Blue Windbreaker, black duffel. All still hold. Do not move."

Volontov and Dominika walked out of the hotel and into an embassy car waiting at the curb. The FBI men watched them go and made to get out of the van. "Sit tight, you guys," said Gable. "No go yet from upstairs."

"Fuck this," said one of the FBI agents. "The Russians are gone. Let's take this prick down." Gable grabbed the arm of one of the agents.

"No one is going anywhere till we get the okay," he said.

"Get the fuck out of the way," said Maratos as he slid the van door open. The FBI agents piled out of the van and ran into the hotel. The elevator doors opened and Bullard walked out into the lobby in his blue Windbreaker and into the arms of the three FBI agents, who forced him to the ground, wrenched his arms behind his back, and slapped on a pair of cuffs. A crowd of hotel guests and tourists gathered around as the FBI agents pulled Bullard to his feet and frog-marched him out of the lobby. In the commotion, no one noticed the KR man from the Russian Embassy standing in the back of the crowd. He turned and left the hotel by a side entrance.

Forsyth packed up the equipment as Nate retrieved Bullard's manual from the meeting-room bathroom and the tech hurriedly removed the cameras from the corner of the ceiling and the bathroom vent. They all met back at the Station.

"Goddamn it!" fumed Forsyth. "I'm going to rip Maratos's nuts off. It was too soon! Too goddamn soon!"

"You'll have to wait till he gets back to town," said Gable. "They headed straight to the airport. They had a G waiting to fly the guy right back to Washington. Those assholes all had woodies, they were so excited. They were already thinking about their promotions."

"You think the Russians had anyone covering the lobby?" said Nate. He was fighting down the dread in his guts.

"Impossible to tell," said Gable. "There were a lot of people watching the arrest. If it were me, I'd have somebody hanging around."

"Great," said Nate. "I'm going to the safe house to wait for Dominika. Call me if you hear anything." He got up to leave.

"Hold it," said Forsyth. "Sit down for a second."

Nate sat down. "I want you to keep calm, you understand? No going over to her apartment. No phone calls, not one. No putting up signals, no checking her sites. If I see you within five blocks of the Russian Embassy I'm going to tear your nuts off right after I do Maratos." He looked at Nate for a long beat. "Do you understand me, Nate?"

"Yes. I'm going to the safe house to wait. That's all."

"This is just the kind of situation we discussed. We don't know what, if anything, the Russians saw. I'm sending a cable right now to Washington with the entire picture, and I hope they assign Maratos to Topeka cataloguing safe-deposit-box signature cards for the rest of his career."

Nate stood to leave, his face showing his anger and fear.

"Sit down, I'm not finished," said Forsyth. "Now comes the hard part, waiting for word that your agent is safe. If you move too soon, you might jeopardize her even if they suspect nothing. We have to let this play out."

"How about putting ARCHIE and VERONICA on her apartment?" asked Gable, a suggestion more for Nate's benefit than anything else.

"No, I don't want to risk even that," said Forsyth. "But, Marty, I do want you to have your SUPO boy hang around the lookout on Tehtaankatu Street to keep an eye on the Russians. Anything strange coming in or out of that embassy, he should call; promise him a bonus."

Nate stood to leave. "Stay cool," Forsyth said.

The instant he stepped into the safe house, Nate could smell Dominika in the air, a whiff of soap and powder over something more elemental, woody and sharp. For a minute he thought she had already arrived at the apartment, but there was nobody there. They had told her to stay away for a day and a night. Volontov would be flying high, sending cables and making calls. He would need her near him. Nate walked into the bedroom and lay on the bed. He fell asleep in his clothes, waking in the middle of the night to drag the bedspread over him. The smell of her on the bedclothes filled his lungs. The sunlight woke him up.

Gable was in the kitchen making coffee. "Everything's cool," he said. "Nothing strange, nothing out of the ordinary. One thing, don't tell Forsyth, but I sent VERONICA to ring her doorbell late last night. No one's home. Looks like she didn't sleep there. The Russkies probably pulled an all-nighter."

Nate went to the sink and splashed water on his face. His chest felt tight. The container with a single dumpling was still in the refrigerator. He looked at the crimped pocket of dough that she had made with her fingers. Gable was making an omelet on the stove, but Nate was too edgy to eat.

"No one knows how to make a real omelet," said Gable. "It's not just cooking eggs and folding them over. That's bullshit. You have to shake the pan and stir to get the curds small—are you listening?—get them smooth, then form them in the front of the pan. Like this." He gathered the cooked eggs lightly with a fork, reversed his grip on the skillet handle, tapped it on the stove, and inverted the pan over a plate. Gable's omelet was a pale-yellow teardrop of softly cooked eggs. "And the fucking center still has to be runny," Gable said, cutting it open with a fork. "Want some?"

"Jesus, Marty," said Nate.

"Look, all we can do is wait to see what happens. Not a peep from our side. No movement." He ate a forkful of omelet. "Let me ask you a question. What's the most important aspect about this clambake?" he asked.

"You mean the manual, the substitution?" said Nate. "Fuck the manual, what about our agent? They might have Dominika in a chair in the basement right now, and you're eating omelets."

"I want her safe as much as you do," said Gable, "but we wait to see if the Russians believe they pulled off stealing the manual. We wait to hear them slapping themselves on the back. The Fort is looking in real time at the *rezidentura* traffic. Dominika's thumb-drive download took; it's giving us everything, and NSA is reading it all. Total radio silence, but that could mean they're being extra careful."

"And if we lose the agent? Is it worth it?"

"You figure it out. We make the Bolshies waste seven years planning cyber attacks against what they think is our infrastructure, for nothing. What's more important?"

Nate looked over at Gable, who was staring back at him. "Enjoy your fucking omelet," said Nate.

Forsyth looked up from his desk in the Station at midday. Gable had just heard from his guy who had spent the morning watching from the OP. Nate didn't like the way Gable's face looked. "A van left the Russian Embassy at nine o'clock this morning. DIVA and two others. They were carrying a diplomatic bag, and headed to the airport."

"There's an Aeroflot flight to Moscow every day at noon," said Gable, looking at his watch. "That's in ninety minutes."

"That's it?" said Nate. "What are we going to do about it?"

"What we're going to do is absolutely nothing," said Forsyth. "The van going to the airport is normal. The first thing they'd do—all last night—is copy the damn thing and prepare the pouch. Now they're bringing the original back in the bag on the noon flight. Dominika and two escorts. Volontov would do something like that, send her, to kiss ass and get the credit."

"We don't know that," said Nate. "What if they're escorting her back? What if she's in trouble?"

"Even if that's true, what do you suggest?" asked Forsyth. "That manual is going to get to Moscow."

"Let me go to the airport," said Nate. "I won't fuck around. I'll just scope it out. Maybe we'll get a feel for what's happening. We'd like to know what the situation looks like, wouldn't we, we'd like to be able to report the details, right?"

"No fucking way," said Forsyth. "You'd be like Romeo yelling for Juliet to come out on the balcony."

Nate looked over at Gable.

"I can't stand this," said Gable. "Any second this dickhead is going to start weeping. Tom, I'll go with him. I won't let him step on his dick. We might see who she's traveling with, get an indication of what's going on." Gable looked at Forsyth and nodded.

When Forsyth didn't say anything, Nate and Gable threw on their coats and pounded down the stairs. With Nate at the wheel, the drive to the airport was on two wheels. They walked along the glassed-in observation mezzanine that overlooked the departure hall. Gable spotted Dominika sitting close to the Aeroflot gate. She was dressed in the same navy suit and white shirt. Her hair was tied with a ribbon. An embassy official sat on either side of her. The yellow canvas diplomatic bag was on the floor between one of the officials' knees. Dominika looked small and quiet, dressed like a good little functionary, returning to Moscow and the Center.

Gable grabbed Nate by the collar and hustled him behind a broad pillar. "Just stand there. No waving. No movement. If she sees you, we don't know how she'll react. If you fuck up, you could kill her."

Dominika sat between the *rezidentura* security man and an embassy admin flunky who, when told he was getting a free round-trip home, packed his suitcase full of tinned salmon and music CDs to sell to his neighbors and friends in Moscow. He didn't even know who the busty young bonbon sitting next to him was, and he didn't care. The security man on the other side had received whispered instructions about this trip. He was told only that Corporal Egorova would be met at the airport by officials and that he was to turn over the bag directly to the same officers. He was to get a signed receipt for the bag and was granted two days' leave before he returned to Helsinki. Period.

Dominika was enveloped in the overpowering double wash of the security man's cologne and the gagging smell of cooked cabbage from the admin sloth. Something caught her eye and she looked up at the observation mezzanine. Standing beside a column in the glass wall was Nate. He stood looking down at her, his hands by his sides, the glass tinted purple. Her breath caught in her chest; she willed herself to stay still. Their eyes met, and she gave an imperceptible shake of her head. *No, dushka,* she willed her thought to reach him through the glass. *Let me go.* Nate looked down at her and nodded.

GABLE'S PROPER FRENCH OMELET

Beat eggs with salt and pepper. When butter in pan over high heat has stopped foaming, pour in eggs. Violently stir eggs while shaking pan until eggs begin to scramble. Tilt pan forward to pile eggs at the front. Run fork around edges to fold into the still-wet center, ensuring ends of the omelet come to a point. Change to underhanded grip, tap pan to bring omelet to lip of skillet, and invert pan onto a plate. Omelet should be pale yellow and creamy inside.

21

Volontov didn't look at her when he told Dominika he wanted a summary translation of Bullard's manual, but the air around his head was suffused with a dark orange cloud. Deception, mistrust, danger. She could feel it. She would have to stay in the embassy overnight, she could sleep on the couch in the dayroom next to Records. The *rezident* KR thug kept her in his sight the whole time. She was unaware that he had observed the flurry of men pulling the volunteer Bullard to the marble floor of the Kämp lobby, tourists milling, but her intuition told her something was seriously wrong.

Volontov looked at her from across the room, and she felt the acid of the old days, the look of Stalin's hangmen Dzerzhinsky, Yezhov, Beria, the blank, bloodless look that sent men and women to the cellars. Dominika knew something had happened, she fought a rising surge of panic. They were keeping their distance, always a bad sign, the machinery of distrust had kicked in. Dominika resolved to act as if nothing had happened, to assume an air of innocence. She thought about the safe house, about Nate and *Bratok,* then she told herself to stop thinking about them, to prepare for what was coming. She began bricking up her mind, burying the secrets as deeply as she could. They mustn't get at her secrets, no matter how deep they dug.

Two gray men met them at Sheremetyevo, standing shoulder to shoulder in the middle of the terminal. They took the dun-yellow canvas pouch from the security man, who then left the terminal in a separate car. They told her she was required at an interview, walked on either side of her to the waiting car. She rode in silence from the airport in the late afternoon light to a nondescript building in the eastern end of the city. It was off Ryazanskiy Prospect was all she could see, a creaking lift, a long corridor painted green, and she sat there as daylight faded to night. She had not eaten and she had worn the same clothes for two days. A man with glasses opened a door and gestured her to enter a room that was made to look like a private office, but it was unlived-in, a stage set, down to the bowl of roses on the sideboard.

The man had thin hands, pianist's hands. He was bald, with a dent in the side of his head, as if from a trepanning that, remarkably, also bent and distorted the yellow bubble around his head. *Zheltyj,* the familiar yellow of treachery and betrayal. He welcomed Dominika back to Moscow, it was always good to return to Moskva, was it not? They were pleased, he said, with her work in Scandinavia, especially with the handling of the volunteer. No, not *zheltyj,* but *zheltizna,* the man was yellowness itself. This was deception, this was danger, mortal danger, she could smell it.

She had to hit the right attitude—curious, a little puzzled, tired from the trip. Above all, for God's sake, no hint of fear, no hint of desperation. Was there a problem? she asked. Was she permitted to know his name, rank, and directorate? She assumed he was a colleague from the Service. Colonel Digtyar, Directorate K, yes, of course, from the Center. Digtyar. *Ukranian,* she thought. *The overhead lights cast a shadow on the hollow of his skull.*

She related the timeline of the operation, from the walk-in to the hotel meeting. No, she was unaware that there had been an incident, she knew nothing about an apparent arrest after she and the *rezident* had departed the Kämp. Rezident Volontov had not mentioned anything was wrong. Digtyar did not take notes, did not refer to any file. They were taping it all, looking at her face, watching her hands. She resisted the urge to look for where the cameras could be. *Don't look, don't think, no one can help you, you have to do this yourself, this is your journey to make alone.*

They took her passport and let her go home that night. Her mother came to the front door in her dressing gown, initially surprised, but it took less than a second for her face to close down, her eyes to become blank.

"Dominushka, what a surprise, come in, let me look at you. I did not know you were coming home," her mother said flatly. Caution.

"It was an unexpected trip," said Dominika in as normal a voice as possible. "It's good to be home, Mama, it's good to see you again." Danger. Mother and daughter hugged, they kissed each other's cheeks the requisite three times, and hugged again.

Dominika did not dare clutch her, she could not break down. They might be watching, listening. Mother and daughter stayed up and Dominika prattled on about the Finns, about life abroad. She had to sleep, she had work in the morning. Another kiss, and her mother stroked her cheek, then shuffled off to bed. She knew.

They picked her up in the morning and deposited her back at Ryazanskiy, and she told the story again, this time to three men sitting at a table with the bowl of roses in front of them, probably an audio pickup tucked among the flowers. No one spoke, but they turned the pages in an unmarked file—had that pig Volontov sent in a report that quickly? They filed out and left her alone, then filed back in and she told the story again, just the same. They were looking for changes, contradictions. Dominika had never been stared at like that in her life, worse than in ballet school, worse even than the men looking at her at Sparrow School. She felt her throat constrict, felt the rage coming, but resisted and returned their stares with unflinching eyes. She did not let them near the icy secret in her breast.

All day it lasted, then she was permitted to go home. Her mother had *shchi,* a rich meat stew, in the oven, the smell of dacha and vegetables and memories of snowy mornings filled the apartment. Dominika's hand shook as she ate, her mother not eating, sitting across from her, watching. She knew.

Her mother had not played professionally in fifteen years, but got up and came back to the kitchen with a case. It was a common violin, nothing like her Guarneri, but she sat close to her daughter at the table and put it under her chin and played slowly, Schumann or Schubert, Dominika didn't know. The violin vibrated, the notes thick and rich and red-purple, like long ago in the living room with Batushka.

"Your father was always very proud of you," said her mother as she played. Was she consciously playing to defeat any microphones? Impossible. Her mother? "He always hoped that your enthusiasms, your patriotic duty, would sustain you." Her eyes were closed. "He was desperate to tell you how he felt, he who had succeeded in the system. But he did not dare. He did not speak because he wanted to protect you." She opened her eyes but continued playing, as if in a trance, her fingers firm and sure on the fingerboard. "He despised them, he would tell you now, in your time of trouble." What had she guessed, how did she know? "His whole life. He wanted to tell you. Now I will tell you," her mother whispered. "Resist them. Fight them. Survive." With the last word she stopped playing and laid the violin on the table, got up, kissed her daughter on the head, and walked out of the room. The music lingered in the air, the violin was warm where it had rested beneath her mother's chin.

The next day a succession of offices, with one man or two or three, or a woman in a suit with her hair in a bun, cloudy black and evil, who came around the desk to sit close to her, or Colonel Digtyar with the yellow caved-in skull asking her to describe the pattern of the rug in the room of the Kämp Hotel, and the doors sometimes closing softly behind her, sometimes slammed with a bang that shook the frame, *We don't believe you.* Then the unbelievable, the monstrous, the impossible, the inevitable.

A poisonous, swaying ride in the closed van and the echo of the underground garage and they were in a prison, it had to be Lefortovo, not Butyrka, because this was political. She was pushed down an ill-lit corridor into a stinking anteroom. A man and a woman watched her step out of her skirt, shuck off her shoes, and reach behind to unclasp her brassiere. They expected her to hang her head, to turn away from their stares, to cover her nipples and mons, but she was Sparrow-trained and a graduate of the AVR. They could go to hell. Stark naked, she stood straight and stared back at them until they tossed her a stained cotton prison smock. It rasped against the mattress ticking in the dark cell, no windows, two cots, and she thought about her mother waiting for her with dinner, and silently called out to her father and then, surprising herself, to Nate.

They walked her down the corridors, but they never let her see another prisoner, to starve her spirit. Guards clicked their stamped steel crickets, and when two crickets clicked, silver barbed click-*clack,* click-*clack* at the same time, they shoved her into a wooden closet, one at the end of each corridor, wedged tight, black and heavy with the smell of prisoners long gone, until the other prisoner went by. A skylight showed inky black, or pale yellow, night still followed day, but the overhead lights in her cell never stopped humming and the Klaxon screeched on a regular basis.

Her father walked by her side and a smiling Nate was waiting for her in each of the different rooms, some hot, some cold, some dark, some bright. She shook her hair out of her eyes when they threw water on her and turned the blowers on. Nate sat beside her and held her hand, strapped to the arm of the chair, while she shivered. They didn't speak to her, but it was enough to know they were with her, to feel their touch.

The investigators screamed or they laughed, very close to her face, and they asked about foreign contacts—the Frenchman Delon and the American Nash. Was she working for the Americans? It was no problem these days, by the way, détente and all. They said they wanted to hear her side of the story, then slapped her to shut her up and told her Marta Yelenova was dead, that Dominika had as good as killed her, men would be sent to do the same to her mother. They slapped her so her face was mottled and sore, all little Sparrows like a bit of that, don't they?

They varied the days and the nights, and the screaming interrogations, and sometimes they strapped her flat on the stainless steel tables. It didn't matter whether she was upright or whether her head hung down over the edge of the table. Dominika resisted with all her strength, all her will. It wasn't hatred, because that would be too brittle. She cultivated *disdain,* she wouldn't succumb to these beasts, she refused to let them exert their will on her.

They didn't look smart enough to find all the nerve bundles—at the base of the coccyx, or above the elbow, or on the soles of her feet—but the light, questing fingers never missed, and the screaming pains rocketed up her body into her head, and she heard her own ragged breath in her throat.

The nerve pain was different from the tendon pain, which was different from the pain of a cable tie cinched tight around her head, across her open mouth. Dominika found that the *anticipation* of pain, waiting for what was next, was worse than the agonies they could generate. The glob of conductive lanolin slathered between her buttocks scared her more than the first nudge of the rounded aluminum peg they pushed into her, scared her more than feeling the electrical current, the bitter, pulsing pain, involuntary, back-arching pain, that left her limp when the current stopped.

One female jailer indulged in personal sport while conducting official business. Her strong hands and thick wrists were splotched by vitiligo, they lacked pigment. Strapped to a steel-and-canvas chair, Dominika watched the pinkish hands scuttle endlessly over her body, pressing, squeezing, pinching. The matron's eyes—they were oval like a cat's—watched Dominika's face. One Appaloosa hand lingered low on Dominika's belly, and the matron's lips parted unconsciously in agitation.

The matron leaned close—her face was inches from Dominika's, her eyes questing, looking for revulsion, or terror, or panic. Dominika kept her face still and looked back into the darting eyes, then opened her thighs.

"Go ahead, *garpiya,* harpy," whispered Dominika in her face. "Go ahead and wet your sleeve."

The matron straightened and slapped Dominika across the cheek. *Sorry to ruin your soggy little game,* Dominika thought.

The crickets clicked and she was shoved, thumping against the back of the cabinets at the ends of the corridors, and the lights stayed on in the cell until she could feel the sand under her eyelids, and the screeching hailer sounded like Schumann or Schubert, she couldn't tell which. A sallow girl with bruises on her legs and a crusted sore in the corner of her mouth was thrown into her cell, face-first onto the floor, and she wanted to talk all night, a frightened cellmate sobbing about how she hated them, she hadn't done anything wrong. The little yellow-winged *kanarejka*, the canary, wanted a friend. The girl licked the sore on her mouth and looked at Dominika on her cot and put her hand out and whispered she was lonely. Dominika turned her face to the wall and ignored the raspy voice.

They didn't know anything. They were looking for something to come adrift, something to pull on, but she held on tight to her secrets. They came back to the Americans, they wanted to know about her assignment to get close to Nash. Did you fuck him? Did you wrap your little Sparrow beak around his *khuy*? Every day there would be two hours without the straps, or the screaming, or the slaps across the face that brought her head left and right and blurred her vision. A nameless colonel—in formal uniform with powder-blue shoulder boards that matched his halo, sensitive like Forsyth, an artist—sat across a table. She had to be careful with him, stay alert.

He spoke quietly, evenly, at the start of each session asking why she had betrayed her country. She replied she had done no such thing, and he continued as if not hearing her, asking mildly what were the *reasons* she had decided to do it, what was the *exact point in time* that she had decided.

The colonel was so mild, so assured in his manner. His questions were drawn from a premise—her guilt—that began to become a reality. Let us talk about life's disappointments, he would say, those disappointments that compelled you to do these things. Logic and fantasy and misstatements all began to invade her exhausted mind. Would you like to read the transcripts of Sinyavsky's trial? She didn't know who that was, a dissident, in 1966. Read how denial evolves into acceptance, how it can liberate, said the colonel. His voice was soft, modulated, his blue bubble seemed to envelope her. *Stay awake.*

The ancient, poisonous, and dispassionate transcripts mesmerized her; it was as if she were physically present during the show trial. She felt herself slipping. The wearisome act of denying individual accusations brought her closer to agreeing with the colonel's overarching assumption of her guilt. It was simple, really, he said, they simply had to establish *how* she had strayed, *when,* and *how badly.*

He almost broke her, the moderate colonel in his pressed uniform, but she refused to be drawn down into their black hole. Her name was Dominika Egorova. She was a ballerina, an officer in the SVR, a Sparrow trained to bend others' minds. She loved and was loved in return. She closed her eyes and flew high above Moscow, tracing the river, high above the fields and the forests, and dipped her wings over Butovo and the slit trench that held the body of Marta Yelenova, the ground frozen solid above her.

Marta gave her strength and she wrenched her mind back from the abyss, she retreated inside herself, used everything they gave her to resist them, including the hallucinations, Dominika welcomed them. She lay in her cell and it was the bed in Helsinki, and the hot light in her eyes was the Finnish moonlight, and she lay still and felt him on top of her. The fever and the chills were his caresses. Her infected eye shed tears of love, which he kissed away. She turned on the mattress, her fists bunched under her stomach to stop the ache.

Even as her arms went numb from the straps, she felt herself getting stronger. She touched the secret inside her, it had been buried deep, but she could feel it again. The secret that lived in her soul, the secret that she had stuffed away out of their reach, was rekindled, began to burn again. She could think about it, knowing they could not get their hands on it. Her mother had told her Resist, Fight, Survive. They were getting weaker, she was getting stronger. Their individual colors were stuttering on and off, as if a fuse were loose.

She told them, kept telling them, she did not do anything wrong, she couldn't tell them anything because there was nothing to tell. The louder they screamed, the happier she became. Yes, happy—she loved these men and women who tormented her, she loved the turquoise-painted colonel. They knew they could not keep on indefinitely, they were running out of time. Unless they forced a confession, they had nothing.

Far above the crenellated roof of Lefortovo and Lubyanka and Yasenevo the ether was filled with sly messages, queries and responses, precedence and deadlines. Information was coming out of Washington about the Bullard affair. The Washington *rezidentura* had its feelers out, contacts were being taken to lunch, cooperative Americans were being met in underground garages, or on the C&O Canal Towpath, or on darkened cobblestoned streets in Georgetown or Alexandria. A rumor circulating out of the US Justice Department held that Bullard had been under suspicion *for a year* before he contacted Russian intelligence in Helsinki. His arrest in Washington had been planned, but his unexpected travel abroad had forced their hand.

Official US sources downplayed the loss of the

manual—not much made it into the public record, but a leak from a "high-placed government source" described the incident as a "grave loss of national security information." Congressional calls for an accountability investigation followed. The dithering, and recriminations, and accusations were all a part of variegated deception, assembled and propagated via scores of unwitting sources and assorted blabbermouths, orchestrated by CI Chief Simon Benford, with the sole goal to reassure the Russians that the manual they had acquired was genuine. If an ancillary benefit was to protect the agent DIVA—if she was still alive—all the better.

SVR Directorates R (analysis) and X (science) submitted reports. Preliminary analysis of the US National Communications Grid document passed by Bullard concluded with the assessment that the document was authentic and unique. Directorate T officers, FAPSI communications experts, and scientists from the Saint Petersburg University of Information Technologies began studying the manual in consultation with the Ministry of Defense to identify exploitable vulnerabilities in the vast US network. Funding had been requested from the defense budget for developing software, cyber applications, and other tools for potential use against the assessed weakest spots in the system.

Because they wanted to believe, a consensus was reached among the Kremlin *knyaz'ki,* the princelings. The material was authentic, a significant windfall, even if the Americans knew of its loss. Obtaining Bullard's information from under the nose of American intelligence was a tactical triumph, a demonstration of Russian mastery in tradecraft. That the volunteer Bullard had been arrested was his misfortune, obviously a result of his stupidity, sloppiness, and greed. The Kremlin couldn't care less about his fate. He was the Americans' concern now, for three consecutive life sentences.

A commendation from the Duma recognized Rezident Volontov and the Helsinki *rezidentura.* In a late afternoon ceremony in the gilded Andreyevsky Hall of the Grand Kremlin Palace, double eagles over the doors where red stars had once hung, SVR First Deputy Director Egorov was awarded a second star as lieutenant general. President Putin himself handed Egorov the oblong felt box with the two-star clusters, bussed him on three cheeks, and gave him a trademark crocodile smile that from the president was an exhilarating gesture of approval. The promotion ceremony coincided with the weekend and delayed Dominika's release by two days.

On Monday, after breakfast, Vanya Egorov finally made the calls. To KR, to the Internal Investigations Directorate, ultimately to the FSIN, the creeps in the Service for the Execution of Punishments, the demon offspring of the gulags. He identified himself using his new star, *Lieutenant General* Egorov, to tell them all to finish it up. It was beginning to look bad, she was his brother's daughter, for God's sake. No, he did not want them to go to Level Two. No, he did not authorize administering drugs, or a course of sensory deprivation, or more severe electric shock. *What the hell is wrong with you people? These measures are for bastard traitors, like the mole still out there,* he thought. *If she hasn't confessed, there is nothing to confess,* though the devil knew what had happened in Helsinki, with that *sliznjak,* that garden slug Volontov running things. Clean her up and send her back to me, her mother is worried, I want her back on the job, he said with fatherly concern.

Colonel Digtyar himself brought the cardboard box with her clothes to the cell, stood there while she undressed and returned the smock—State property—and dressed in front of him, her shins and thighs mottled blue-black, her fingernails purple, her ribs showing. They had accomplished all that in such a short time. They walked her upstairs to the grilled door and she stepped out onto the snowy street, with the traffic noise and the smell of exhaust from the buses, and she walked gingerly on the ice for a little way, just to feel the ground beneath her feet, her breath in clouds rising above her head. Her ballet limp was more pronounced now, and her foot throbbed, but she concentrated on swinging her arms and walking away from the walls with her back straight. The marks on her wrists were visible from under the cuffs of her overcoat.

Dominika dreamed about prison, in her bed, or sitting in a chair in the living room while her mother washed bedsheets sour from the poison that was leaving her body. She backed into the hall closet and closed the door on herself and stood wedged in the dark to relive the cabinets—smell and sound, click-*clack,* click-*clack*—and for the pleasure of knowing she could come out into the light whenever she liked. She wrapped her wrists together with panty hose and strained the knot tight with her teeth, to feel her pulses. After all the edgy urges left her, she cried silently, tears wetting her cheeks. Her mother played the violin every day now, a half hour at a time, while Dominika sat on the floor and stretched, and lifted her legs until her stomach screamed, and pushed up from the floor until her arms shook. Her mother washed her, sitting in the tub the first night, but now Dominika stood in the bath alone, seeing the marks disappear, watching herself heal. She nodded to herself in the mirror. She was getting better, and with the feeling of redemption the coda of a vermilion fugue, a red fury, repetitively welled up around her. It was a deep rage, one easily enough controlled, one that would last, one on which she could feed.

Dominika Egorova sat in a chair in front of the paperless desk of her uncle in his office on the executive fourth floor of SVR headquarters in Yasenevo. Outside, the snow-blasted pine forest stretched out of sight, beyond them the bare fields and the flat horizon. Sunlight streamed through the picture windows, illuminating half her uncle's face but plunging the far side of it into shadow. Half his beastly yellow aura was mottled, the other half sparkled in the sunlight. Vanya Egorov sat back, lit a cigarette, and looked at his niece. She was dressed in a plain white shirt buttoned at the neck and a blue skirt. Her dark hair was carefully combed. She looked thinner and pale.

"Dominika," Vanya said, as if she had just returned from a cruise on the Volga. "I was gratified to hear that the unpleasantness is over. The investigation of the Helsinki matter is concluded."

"Yes," she said, staring at a point on the wall behind him.

Vanya looked carefully at her. "You must not be concerned. Every officer who is active in operations will at some time in his or her career be involved in an investigation. It is the nature of our business."

"Is it the nature of our business to be tied dripping wet in front of an air conditioner for four hours every day?" She said it calmly, without inflection.

Vanya looked sourly at her. "Animals," he said. "I shall order a review."

A review of your own promotion prospects, thought Dominika. She nodded at the new plaque on the wall.

"Congratulations, Uncle, on your promotion," she said. Vanya looked at the citation and ribbon, and fingered the rosette on his lapel.

"Yes, thank you very much," said her uncle. "But

what about you? What shall I do with you?" As if she were being given a choice, she thought. But she had something in mind.

"Now that I have returned, I am ready to report wherever you wish to send me. It is your decision, of course, but with respect, I would very much *not* like to return to the Fifth. Would it be possible to resume the place offered me in the Americas Department by General Korchnoi?"

"I will ask him," said Vanya. "I'm sure he would agree."

"There is something else," Dominika said. She thought of them all and her prison cell and felt the tightening in her throat and knew her face and neck would be flushed (*No. 47, "Infuse the neck and face to authenticate emotion, or the advent of climax"*). Vanya waited.

"I want to continue working on Nash," she said suddenly, holding his eyes in hers. Vanya sat back and looked thoughtfully at her.

"Quite a request," said Vanya. "You know Colonel Volontov thought your progress against the American was too slow."

"With respect, Colonel Volontov is a beast of burden," said Dominika. "He has no appreciation of an operation. He is doing nothing to further your interests or those of the Service. Now that I'm away from his lecherous stares, I no longer care about his opinions."

Vanya turned and looked out the plate-glass window. "And what about Nash?"

"I developed a close friendship with the American," said Dominika. "We saw each other frequently, just as you envisioned. Before I left Helsinki we had become . . . intimate."

"And you believe you could have determined his activities?" He continued staring out the window, his yellow crown increasing in intensity. *He's going to agree,* thought Dominika. *It's too important for him.*

"Without a doubt," said Dominika. "Despite Colonel Volontov's unhealthy interest, Nash's *pylkyi,* his ardor, was growing." Dominika did not take her eyes off her uncle. "Unfortunately, prison and my interrogation somewhat derailed our romance."

Vanya considered the whole idea. He desperately needed some action on the matter of the mole. His niece knew Nash better than anyone else did, and she certainly seemed motivated. But she was different in a way—the Lefortovo experience certainly had affected her—she seemed obsessed, driven now. Was she sweet on Nash? Did she want to spend more time outside Moscow, in the West, did she . . . ?

"Uncle, I was cleared," prompted Dominika softly, reading his thoughts. "They told me I was reinstated, my record is clean. I'm the best officer, the best chance, to engage the Americans and identify the Russian traitor. This operation is a challenge for me now. *I want to go up against them again.*"

"You seem quite sure," said Vanya.

"I am. And you should be. It was you who created me," said Dominika. She saw how Vanya swelled up at that, his vanity was like a yellow balloon above his head.

"And how would you proceed?" asked Vanya. Dominika knew she had one thread to pull, gently.

"I would rely on your advice and guidance, and that of General Korchnoi."

"In this matter, General Korchnoi has not been briefed," said Vanya.

"I assumed that his department would be the logical place from which to work," said Dominika. "If you have another idea . . ."

"I will consider bringing Korchnoi in," said Vanya.

The peppery uncle considering something he already has decided on, thought Dominika.

"Whatever you decide, we would keep it strictly *razdelenie.* I would clear operational steps directly with you or whomever you designate."

"You know Nash is concluding his assignment in Helsinki?" said Vanya. He searched her face for a reaction, found nothing.

"I did not know," said Dominika. "But it does not matter. There's nowhere he can hide."

Gossip channels in Yasenevo started humming. Word was out that Egorov's niece was back in the building, back from Finland; that was where the Service just scored a big success, very hush-hush. Did Egorova have anything to do with that? Rumors about an investigation? The usual malfeasance or something else? She looked the same, but different, thinner. Something in the way she looked back at people, crazy unblinking eyes. Now working in a private room in Korchnoi's Americas Department. Special job for the deputy director's niece, no surprise, but not just *semeystvennost'*, not just the expected nepotism. Just look at those eyes, nutcracker eyes—not the ballet.

She had petitioned General Korchnoi, asking his permission to join his department. He had paused and looked at her from under bushy white eyebrows, his purple mantle majestic. "I commend you for your fortitude in Lefortovo," he said quietly. Dominika flushed. "We will speak no more of that," said Korchnoi.

That afternoon Korchnoi had sat with the deputy director and sipped brandy and was briefed on Vanya's operation to reestablish the relationship between Dominika and the American in pursuit of the mole. Korchnoi showed he was impressed, asked Vanya to approve bringing Dominika to the Americas Department. “It is the best place from which to work the problem,” said Korchnoi.

“Volodya,” Vanya said, the depth and length of their friendship apparent in his use of the affectionate diminutive, “I need your imagination on this problem. I need something new.”

“Between us, I will be surprised if we cannot come up with something,” said Korchnoi. Vanya refilled their glasses. “And strict secrecy on all of this,” he said, sipping cognac. “We don’t want to alert the mole to the noose tightening around his neck.”

SHCHI—RUSSIAN CABBAGE SOUP

Boil cubed beef, chopped onion, celery, shredded carrots, and whole garlic in water for two hours. In a separate pot, cover sauerkraut and heavy cream with boiling water and steep in a medium oven for thirty minutes. Boil cubed potatoes, celery root, and slivered mushrooms until soft. Combine all ingredients; season liberally with salt, whole peppercorns, bay leaves, and marjoram and boil for twenty minutes. Cover pot with cloth, set in low oven to steep for thirty minutes. Serve with sour cream and dill.

22

Nathaniel Nash walked aimlessly down a light-green corridor of CIA Headquarters. The hallway was empty, stretching into the waxed-floor distance of D Corridor past where it transitioned into E Corridor and the DI. To an operations officer, passing through Directorate of Intelligence territory was like walking in a mysterious jungle. Heads would peer around corners and jerk back, doors would open an inch and slam shut. A braying laugh, a howler monkey in the forest canopy, the booming notes from across the river of a hollow teak log being struck with sticks.

Helsinki was a memory, a torment. Dominika had been swallowed up, disappeared, status unknown, welfare unknown, "contact with agent broken," wait till she comes out again, perhaps a station officer meets her at a dip party halfway around the world, maybe in ten years, maybe never. Or wait till another agent hears how she was sent to *lagerya*, the camps, or when the Moscow watchers read in *Pravda* how she died. The ongoing tap on Helsinki *rezidentura* communications revealed nothing of her fate.

A month after Dominika's recall, Nate had asked Forsyth if he could go LWOP. He artlessly said he thought he'd travel to Moscow, privately, to see if he could find out what had happened to her. The usually unflappable Forsyth lost his temper.

"You want to go to Moscow?" Forsyth raved. "An officer of the CIA with knowledge of Moscow operations wants to enter Russia as a private citizen, without diplomatic immunity? A CIA officer the SVR *knows* was active in their capital committing espionage? Is that what you're telling me?" Nate did not reply. Gable, hearing the shouting, came into the office. "What's your plan, Nate?" said Forsyth. "Do you plan to storm the Lubyanka, blow her cell door, shoot your way up to the roof, and hang-glide to the West?"

"It would be too far to hang-glide from Moscow," said Gable. "Otherwise, it's a wicked good plan."

"I'm going to tell you this once," said Forsyth. "You do not have my permission, or that of the Central Intelligence Agency, to go on leave without pay, to leave this duty post, or even to remotely contemplate travel to the Russian Federation. We do not know whether DIVA is in trouble, nor do we know her current location or status. We wait for word. We collect intelligence." Nate slumped in his chair.

"If she's in trouble, we'll eventually hear," said Forsyth. "You are not responsible for this; you did not put a foot wrong. DIVA was an agent, we protect agents, we run risks, we run them, the best ones we run against horrendous odds. And sometimes we lose them, despite all the tradecraft and all the precautions. Do you understand me?" Nate nodded.

"The long and short of it, Nate," said Gable later in his office, "is shut the fuck up. We have lots to do. Get to work, for Christ's sake. Stop mooning around. It's like a Jane Austen novel."

In Headquarters, it made sense for Nate to be reassigned to CE/ROD, which stood for Central Eurasia/Russian Ops Desk, the "Hot RODs," the elephant's graveyard for officers returning from Moscow, still feeling the yips from constant surveillance. There were also officers who had swung and missed at a Russian in Malaysia or Pretoria or Caracas, and there were the first-tour cherries who were in the pipeline for Moscow, all puffed up and serious, never having tasted the asshole-shrinking fear of having an agent's life depend on how well you use your mirrors.

Chief ROD sat in his Langley office, a small corner space with a sealed, double-paned window looking out onto the triple-vaulted roof of the cafeteria between the Original and New Headquarters Buildings. C/ROD was in his fifties, a slight man with liver spots on his cheeks and thinning white hair combed across the top of his nearly bald head. A wiry white mustache and heavy-rimmed glasses gave him the look of a professor; the rack of pipes on his desk added to the fiction, for C/ROD was anything but a donnish academic.

He was an old whore, with a dozen foreign assignments under his belt. He had made his bones working the Cuban target and had shifted in midcareer to the Russian target when it was revealed that the entire stable of the CIA's Cuban agents—half a hundred of them, recruited and handled and producing intelligence for three decades—had with two exceptions been double agents controlled all along by the General Directorate of Intelligence in Havana. The revelation so demoralized a dozen veteran officers who had devoted their entire professional lives to Cuban operations that the DGI could not have destroyed the CIA's Cuban Section any better if they had blown it up.

Now C/ROD was busy managing Russian cases around the world. Running existing agents, a score of the best ones solid producers. MARBLE was still the sine qua non of ROD's stable, but there were other potential acquisitions coming up, developing nicely.

Every morning he would read the "daily board"—historically a three-inch stack of printed telegrams, now a cascade of ops cables scrolling luminously down his screen from young officers in Stations around the world about their "developmentals." A global palette of events from Rio or Singapore or Istanbul, descriptions of contacts, budding friendships, drunken evenings spent knee-walking with Russian second secretaries or attachés or, most exhilarating, with suspected intelligence officers from the SVR or GRU.

A recent cable made him remember. The young and convivial wife of a CIA case officer posted to a dusty African capital had shared her grandmother's recipe for fried cheese pancakes with the new bride of a quite formal GRU major. The women bonded as the young Russian wept over the platter of golden cakes. She was homesick and thinking of her own grandmother. *Feed her enough pancakes and he may flip,* thought C/ROD.

Against this backdrop, once, or twice, or five times a year, somewhere in the world, there would be a recruitment. A human in a state of need would say *da* to the offer, whether gentle, oblique, fraternal, or simply a business proposition. And then cable traffic would increase as Headquarters and the Station in question plunged into the arcana of production, validation, tradecraft, and, in a few delicious, exceptional cases, internal handling on the asset's return to Moscow.

There were problems, as always. Recruitment targets lost their resolve in the light of a hangover dawn. Others could not—could never—summon the nerve to brave the wrath of their system. A few escaped the pitch simply by reporting the Americans' offer to their superiors, to be hustled back to Moscow, out of reach, on the next available Aeroflot flight.

And there was the dark side of the Game, a reminder that the opposition was not always in defensive mode. The bombshell cable, one a year, sometimes a rash of them, reporting that a young CIA officer somewhere around the world was himself or herself the object of a Russian recruitment attempt, usually because the Center was making a point or was trying to exploit a perceived vulnerability. The last flurry had come the year CIA salaries had been frozen by Congress, and the Russians were asking around, "Who needs money?" or "Who is disillusioned?"

To this world of ebb and flood, C/ROD had another, immediate problem. He had been wondering how he could open the door to the zoo cage and get Nate Nash the hell out of the office and back to the field. The covcom message that came in last night provided the answer.

C/ROD liked Nate, was thoroughly familiar with his record. He saw the inner fire, guessed at the emotional component, recognized firsthand the personal doubts of the thinking case officer, doubts that refracted successes and caused brooding over setbacks. He knew about the DIVA case and how it colored Nash's days and nights. C/ROD stood and went to the door of his office, leaned against the jamb. Marty Gable would have bellowed for Nash. C/ROD was quieter than that. He waited till Nash caught his eye and gestured with his head to come see him.

"MARBLE signaled," C/ROD said, putting a cold pipe into his mouth. "He's coming to New York, UNGA, for a couple of weeks." Nate sat up in the chair, a bird dog on point. "It's been some time since we've seen him; there'll be a lot to cover. You free right now to start prepping?" C/ROD was amused at the look on Nate's face. "Go introduce yourself to Simon Benford in CID before you go. He'll want you to cover the CI leads carefully, not to mention MARBLE's current security situation." Nate nodded and rose to leave the office.

"Hold on," said C/ROD. "When you see Benford . . . don't say or do anything stupid, okay? Try really hard. I talked to him about this upcoming session with MARBLE. I'll quote him directly. 'Tell the case officer to *scare me* with his brilliance in managing these meetings with MARBLE.'" Nate turned to look at him.

"You get the message?"

Nate nodded again and left. C/ROD saw his face had, for the first time in months, cleared.

POTATO CHEESE PANCAKES

Coarsely grate onions and potatoes, drain and squeeze out absolutely all moisture. Add shredded Gruyère, flour, and puréed garlic to beaten eggs, then incorporate potatoes and onions to create a thick batter. Fry three-inch rounds of batter in oil until golden brown, then flip and finish. Serve with dip of seasoned spinach poached in heavy cream and mixed with sour cream.

23

MARBLE was too sensitive an asset to involve the Station in New York. ROD bypassed the local New York COS, an ill-tempered, short-legged sycophant known exclusively for his ability to slap backs and cadge any sports ticket in town. He was excluded, clueless. MARBLE would meet Nate at night, after his UN meetings concluded.

Moscow, Helsinki, New York. They picked up where they'd left off; there was never time to get reacquainted with internal agents, you just began talking. Nate was sitting with MARBLE in a small Midtown East hotel suite. A desk, two chairs, the bedroom beyond, their coats thrown on the bed. It was nighttime and the faint buzz of traffic from the FDR came up through the window. Two lamps were lit and the men had drawn two chairs to the small table. MARBLE gripped Nate's hand affectionately.

Nate poured a glass of water from a carafe with his free hand and offered it to MARBLE. "You look well," he said, priming the pump. There was a tray on the sideboard with plates of sandwiches, a small salad, a container of vinaigrette. They had not touched the food.

MARBLE smiled and shrugged. "The work progresses," he said. "In the Center we claim successes to please one another. We play the *myshinaya voznya,* the mice games. Few of them are really worth the effort." He let go of Nate's hand, sat back, took a sip of water, and looked at his watch. "I do not have more than a half hour tonight. I will probably be free in two more nights. There are some interesting developments, however, let me tell you," he said. "I think Directorate S is running an illegal in the United States. He is being handled out of New York but I think he is operating in New England because there are meetings in Boston. I am not supposed to know about the case, but they just started coming to me for advice on meeting locations. The case is well established, the illegal has been in place for some years—five, I estimate."

"Are there any other details to identify him?" asked Nate.

"None. But there is something else that might be related. It is just a guess," said MARBLE. "There is a new reporting stream that has begun. The GRU is very interested. Someone is inside your ballistic submarine program."

"A new stream? What kind of information? What can you guess about the source?"

"It appears to be someone involved in maintenance. There is information about rebuilding the older boats. Poseidon—no, Trident—class. Some information is very dense."

"Dense. You mean detailed?" said Nate.

"Yes. I have read a reporting summary. The source is inside the program, by the look of it." MARBLE took another sip of water. "But there is something strange. As chief of the Americas Department, I am unaware of any active source in my area providing military information. Judging by their interest, the GRU is not running the asset either. The information is new to them."

"What does that tell you?" said Nate.

MARBLE ticked off the points on his fingers. "There is a new stream of reporting. I myself am not aware of any registered source to explain this. An illegal exists. So I think perhaps this illegal, run by Directorate S, could be the submarine source," said MARBLE.

"The reports just began, but you said it's likely the illegal has been in this country for five years," said Nate.

"Precisely," said MARBLE. "For five years he has been careful and built his legend, and he has finally developed access and has now begun actively reporting. It would be the perfect combination, an invisible and well-placed mole who has eased into a position of importance," MARBLE said. Nate nodded, writing in a small notebook.

"What about the Director's Case you mentioned in Helsinki?" asked Nate. "Is there any more on that?"

"Nothing. I know how important this could be, so I am listening and looking every day. There is one thing that might be related. I was in the Director's office one day, sitting at the back of the room. Egorov came in and told the director, 'There is something new from LEBED.' He didn't know I had heard."

"SWAN?" asked Nate.

"Yes, *lebed*, swan."

"The cryptonym for the mole?"

"Precisely," said MARBLE.

"Anything else? Any other clues?"

"Just what I have told you. SWAN must be very high up in someone's government, to be run as a Director's Case. There are no indications anywhere in my department about such a case. No handling protocols, no operational cables."

"What do you think?" asked Nate. "What do you conclude?"

MARBLE took another sip of water. "What I conclude, *dorogoy drug,* my dear friend, is that this wouldn't be a Director's Case if it were not in Washington, inside your government."

"You think SWAN's here?" MARBLE nodded. "How do we find him?"

MARBLE shrugged. "I will redouble my efforts

to identify him. In the meantime, you might look at Rezident Golov in Washington. He would have the stature to meet someone senior. And he is a *britva,* as sharp as a razor on the street."

He got up and walked to the window to look out over the street. "So many games," he said to the city below, "so many dangers. I will be glad to see an end to it."

"As long as we're speaking of dangers," said Nate, "what is your status? Are you secure? What are they doing to find *their* leak?" Nate avoided the word *krot,* mole, with all its connotations.

"I will have to save that for our next meeting," said MARBLE, looking at his watch. "There's nothing urgent, so it will keep."

MARBLE turned, walked to the bed, and put on his overcoat. Nate straightened the old man's twisted collar, patted him on the shoulder. They no longer had to worry about *metka.* MARBLE looked at him affectionately. "We can discuss the most fascinating subject—me—in two days. The conference ends at midday. We can have dinner and talk all night." He looked out the window again. "I love this city. I would like to live here someday."

"And someday you will," said Nate, thinking it was unlikely that MARBLE would be permitted to relocate here. It would depend on the nature of his retirement, specifically if he was alive to retire. MARBLE walked to the door with his arm in Nate's arm. Nate desperately wanted to ask whether MARBLE had heard something—anything—about Dominika, but he could not. Per the strict catechism of compartmentation, he had never told MARBLE about Dominika's recruitment, nor her mission to unmask the mole through Nate. Agents simply didn't know other agents.

Instead Nate said, "We're hearing that Vanya Egorov recently was promoted."

"Vanya is reckless," said MARBLE. "I've known

him for twenty years. He wants to run the Service but does not have enough support yet in the Kremlin, with you-know-who. He needs an operational success to please the *oboroten,* his werewolf master. If he does well with SWAN, perhaps it will help him, but he needs something more, something dramatic."

"Such as?" asked Nate.

"To catch me, for instance." MARBLE laughed. "I don't wish him luck." MARBLE grasped Nate's hand warmly. Something was on his mind, Nate could sense it.

"Is there anything else?"

"I have a request, a message that I would like you to pass along," said MARBLE.

"Of course," said Nate.

"I would like to speak to Benford, if he has the time to come to New York in two days' time. I must discuss something with him." MARBLE looked into Nate's eyes.

"Do you want me to pass him a message?" Nate said.

"Nate, I do not wish you to feel offended, but I must speak directly to Benford. Do you understand?" MARBLE searched Nate's face but saw nothing other than affection and regard.

"Of course I do, Uncle," said Nate. "He will be here."

MARBLE opened the door; Nate saw the instinctive, undetectable beat as the old man checked the corridor. "*Spokoinoi nochi,*" said MARBLE.

"*Spokoinoi nochi,*" said Nate. "Sleep well."

A change of hotel at Benford's insistence, and Nate waiting in Bryant Park to pass MARBLE the room number, the basalt-and-gold battlements of the former headquarters of the American Radiator Company bathed in milky footlights against the city night glow. A bear hug at the door, it had been four or five years, and they sat, and the radiator rattled, and the Manhattan taxi horns came up from West Fortieth through the window glass. A bottle of brandy half-full and two glasses filled and refilled. They were not quite *old friends,* but Benford had followed MARBLE for fourteen years. Once a year he had read the file, watching it expand, like a swimming pool filled from a garden hose, fat with contact reports describing the precious outside meetings each year, twice a year, in Paris, or Jakarta, or New Delhi.

The MARBLE file was the well-thumbed chronicle in twenty volumes of the life of an agent, a wife's death, a widower's sadness, the unexpected trips out to the West, the hurried arrangements to meet. CIA medals presented, three of them, and taken back, saved for a rainy day. Thank-you notes from handlers and chiefs and directors, and the implausible certificates commending MARBLE for "preserving democracy around the world." Problems over the years solved, big and small, and the deposits to the retirement account, the yellow flimsies bookmarking each six-month chapter of the odyssey.

The file captured a chronology of CIA Russia Division chiefs, some prodigious, some less so, who claimed MARBLE's successes as their own. It likewise documented a genealogy of CIA directors, some formerly admirals or generals who unconcernedly wore their uniforms and ribbons among the spooks in the building that Allen Dulles built, and who carried MARBLE's occasionally stunning intelligence to the White House, presenting it as the unmistakable fruit of their tenancies. And the file listed the names of the young men and women, MARBLE's handlers, case officers of the snowy streets and the flyblown lobbies and the ringing stairways, all moved on, some upward, some not.

As was his custom, Benford had read the file annually over the years for the signs of tradecraft fissure, listening for the tapping of the deathwatch beetle in the woodwork. Cynically, Benford looked for signs of the turning, the flip, the falloff in production, the photographic exposures more frequently out of focus or out of frame, the coincidental loss of access. There were no indications of trouble. MARBLE was the best Russian case in the CIA not only because he had survived so long, but also because he kept getting better.

"Nathaniel has told you what I have reported?" asked MARBLE.

"Yes," said Benford. "We're going to be busy."

"The illegal, the submarine matter, the Director's Case, this SWAN?"

"I read his summary this morning," said Benford.

"I'm sorry to say that the end of the Cold War has not diminished our leaders' inclinations to do mischief. In many ways the old Soviets were easier to understand." MARBLE poured two more glasses of brandy, lifted his glass, and sipped.

Benford shrugged. "We're probably just as bad. Besides, if we stopped, we'd all be out of a job."

"Which is what I want to talk to you about," said MARBLE.

"Volodya, are you telling me you want to stop?" said Benford. "Is there any reason for the timing?"

"Benford, do not misunderstand me. I do not want to quit. When it is time, I would very much like to retire calmly, to move to America, to let you buy me an apartment in this city."

"You will have all that and more. Tell me what you are thinking."

"How long I can continue working with you, and the precise nature of my retirement, whether voluntary or kinetic, remains to be seen," said MARBLE.

Benford thought he had never heard an agent refer to the possibility of his arrest and execution as a "kinetic retirement." MARBLE continued. "One thing is certain. I have two or three years left in the *normal course* of my career, given Vanya Egorov's aspirations and the general direction of the Service."

"You could still become a deputy director," said Benford with conviction. "You're respected in Yasenevo, you have friends in the Duma."

MARBLE took another sip of brandy. "You would have me in harness for another ten years, then? Among the politicians? Benford, I thought we were *zakadychnyi drug,* comrades. No, my friend, my time is finite. And with some boasting may I say that when I stop working, the intelligence will stop, and the loss will be felt?"

"Correct," said Benford. "No false modesty need intrude. It will be a grave loss. You cannot be replaced."

"And then will come the frantic cries of alarm from your masters, the calls to replace the intelligence, the wrong candidates considered, the rush to recruit."

"A time-honored process, it keeps people like me young," said Benford. "Volodya, what are you driving at? I can hardly wait for what we call the 'payoff.'"

"I propose to provide my successor, a replacement to continue the work."

Benford had seen too much over the years to be surprised, but he did lean closer. "Volodya, with respect, are you telling me you have a protégé? Someone who knows the work we do together?" He thought briefly of the lead sentence of a CI memo documenting *that.*

"No, she has no idea of our work together. This will come with time, when I train and prepare her."

"'*Her*'?" said Benford. "You propose to replace

yourself, a general in the SVR with thirty years of experience and in charge of the Americas Department, with a woman? I do not object to the gender, but there are no senior women in the Center. I am aware of only one woman ever sitting on the Collegium in the last thirty years. There are junior officers, administrators, clerks, support staff. What kind of access will she have?"

"Calm yourself, Benford, such a person exists."

"Pray, tell," said Benford.

"Dominika Egorova, the niece of Vanya Egorov," said MARBLE.

"You're not serious," said Benford, face dead, eyes unmoving, steady hands pouring another brandy. Lightning thoughts one after the other in that wire-snare mind. *Jesus H. Christ, she's alive. The two agents have met. They're working together. Please God they have not shared their respective secrets while eating borshch in the cafeteria. Young Nash is going to be busy.* And finally, in a hot flash: *This could fucking work.*

"Tell me why," said Benford with immense skepticism. "Please, Volodya, before the brandy runs out and I start to sober up."

MARBLE tapped the little table with his forefinger. "Benford, I want you to open your ears. This is a perfect *konspiritsia,* an opportunity as good as you have ever had in the history of your service." He tapped the table with each point he made. "She is the perfect solution to our problem. I have considered it carefully. Her last name gives her something of a pedigree, at least until Vanya retires or is purged, but by then she will be on her own way. She is a graduate of the Foreign Intelligence Academy, the AVR, and she graduated with honors. She is intelligent and has spirit." Looking down, Benford turned the stem of the glass in his hand. MARBLE knew what he was doing.

"You and I know that a good record is not

enough," continued MARBLE. "She has the motivation, a mountain of resentment. Her father died, she was expelled from dance academy, her *svin'ya* uncle used her in the elimination of a Putin rival. He traded her silence for a slot at the Academy, then broke his word and sent her to Sparrow School. You know what that is, I presume." Benford nodded.

"And then there was Helsinki, I assume you know she was there. Then an operational flap, not her fault, but there was trouble, and they brought her back and sweated her for two months. *In Lefortovo,* can you imagine, like the old days. I can tell you she will not soon forgive them that.

"I'm saving the best for last," said MARBLE, sitting back in his chair. "I know what you're thinking, that her career prospects as a woman are doubtful, that she is on the bottom rung of the ladder, that she will never, ever be able to develop any access. I propose to accelerate her career, to ensure her success, and she will never have to sit on a single general's lap, mine included."

"I see," said Benford. "And how will you accomplish this, to catapult her to stardom?"

"Vanya Egorov is obsessed by the almost-certain knowledge that there is a spy in the Service." MARBLE pointed to himself and laughed. "He in fact directed Egorova to Helsinki to get close to Nathaniel to generate some clue, or a name, about who the spy is. Did you know Nathaniel was targeted in Helsinki?" Benford kept his face shut down. MARBLE continued.

"Vanya's plans have been delayed by her security investigation, but she is out, and cleared, and frankly this test of her, this Lefortovo episode, gives her more allure, more *losk,* more luster."

Only Russians can think like this, thought Benford.

"I have taken her into my department," said MARBLE, "to give her a foundation. Vanya has informally asked me to reopen the operation using Dominika against Nate, and this will establish her as my close subordinate. We will choose our best moment, you and I, Benford, then make young Egorova a heroine, a star in the Service, her career assured, from whom no advancement will be denied."

"The payoff, Volodya," said Benford. "It's getting late. How are you going to make her a heroine?"

"It's quite simple," said MARBLE. "Dominika will discover I am the spy and turn me in."

They wanted the noise and the people and the distance from the UN, away from the other Russians, in the Village, on West Fourth Street. It was MARBLE's last night. The restaurant had a red canopy, with steps down from the street, and drawings of dancers on the walls, and high-backed wooden booths that screened well and let them talk. Benford made MARBLE order *pasta con le sarde,* Palermo-pungent with *finocchio* and saffron and raisins and *pinoli,* and they sat shoulder to shoulder at the table, so they could hear each other.

Benford was worked up, talked a blue streak, was even a little frightened. He had thought about it for two days, from every angle, and it was monstrous, impossible, exorbitant. Things weren't that desperate; if they had to suffer a break in the intel stream, then so be it, it was the nature of things. But to contemplate giving yourself the chop simply to establish a successor—it cannot happen, he said. MARBLE said of course it could happen, it *had* to happen.

"If I am caught—who knows how the mole hunt will end?—it all stops instantly, no retrieving anything. We cannot afford to let things fall apart, and if you doubt it, then think about the faceless illegal crawling around the inside of a submarine, or whoever is SWAN, reporting to Yasenevo from Foggy Bottom or Capitol Hill or the White House. We can't afford to wait."

And Benford, running out of room, said there was no guarantee that Dominika would even get the boost she needed and MARBLE's gesture would have been wasted, to which MARBLE said, Don't be a *shutnik,* are you kidding? A young officer, a woman in the new-age Russian Service, covetous for a place in the new millennium, with a counterintelligence coup like that, they'll make her a colonel overnight. Benford looked at MARBLE and ordered two more *grappe,* and MARBLE said, Look, Benford, if I told you I have cancer and they give me a half year, would it make more sense to you? and Benford said, You have cancer? And MARBLE said no, and Benford said, Now who's being the *shutnik*? Benford was down to his last card and said, rather pathetically, What about retiring to New York? MARBLE smiled and said he never really expected he would, he really couldn't finish it like that, and put his hand on Benford's arm and said, Let's play it forward a step at a time, to see how it shapes up, and Benford, surrendering, said, On one condition: We don't tell anyone—not even Nash—until we're sure, and MARBLE said, Two conditions: We don't tell Egorova either. And they drank the grappa as the voices of the late-night crowd swirled around them, secure in their conspiracy.

PASTA CON LE SARDE

In olive oil sauté chopped onions, slivered fennel, saffron, golden raisins, and pine nuts. In the bottom of the same skillet melt cleaned fillets of sardines and anchovies. Add a splash of white wine, season, cover, and simmer until flavors mingle. Toss with pasta of substance such as bucatini or perciatelli.

24

MARBLE's reports about illegals and moles were restricted to a few senior managers in ROD. The real gerents of the information were the fussy introverts in the CIA's Counterintelligence Division, the cave dwellers of the fourteen-hour days in the wilderness of mirrors, the balmy men and women who at home had train sets in their basements and pruned bonsai trees. They began to read Nate's reports, dissecting the information, starting the research.

On his return from New York, Nate was summoned again to Benford's lair. CID occupied an entire floor of Headquarters, a series of interior rooms bisected with hallways and warrens that, unlike the normal Headquarters suites, were equipped not with the usual cubicles, but with individual offices. All the doors were closed, each had a combination dial above the doorknob. There occasionally was a door without a knob, the keyway painted over. What were these rooms, and what did they contain? A bland secretary whose left eye twitched intermittently sat at a desk outside Benford's office. She looked at Nate carefully, blinked, got up, and knocked on the door, but did not open it. She listened carefully, then knocked again, gingerly. A voice from inside, and she opened the door a crack, uttered Nate's name, and stood aside, motioning for him to enter.

Benford's office looked like the atelier of a dissolute professor at a forgotten midwestern college. A torn and faded couch along the back wall was completely covered by stacks of files, some of which had fallen to the floor, where they lay fanned out like spilled poker chips. At the other end of the room, Benford's desk was a riot of overflowing in-boxes, stacked three high. A pile of newspapers leaned precariously on the opposite corner. On the walls were small framed photographs—grainy, black-and-white—not of wife, children, or relatives, but rather of bridges, tree stumps, wooded country lanes, and snowy alleyways between derelict warehouses. Nate realized that these were photographs of infamous sites, long-ago signals, drops, and car pickups. Benford's children. Behind Benford's desk was a framed photograph of the Neo-Baroque All-Russia Insurance Company building in Moscow, otherwise known as the Lubyanka.

"Have a seat," said Benford, his voice gravelly and low. Benford was short and paunchy, with a high forehead and uncombed salt-and-pepper hair, a wing of which stood out from the side of his head. He looked at Nate with large, deep-brown cow's eyes through long lashes that were nearly feminine. Jowly cheeks framed a small mouth that displayed in its constant tics and frowns Benford's utter disgust, or at best his contemptuous dismissal, of the matter at hand. "I read your final reports from New York," he said. "Grammar notwithstanding, they were satisfactory."

"Thanks, I think," said Nate. He had carefully moved a few files and perched on the edge of the couch.

"Do you like MARBLE?" asked Benford. "Do you trust him?"

"I call him Uncle, if that's what you mean," said Nate. "We're close."

"I didn't ask if you engage in frottage with him," said Benford. "I asked you whether you trust him."

"Yes, I trust him," said Nate. "He's been spying for us for fourteen years." Benford's mouth turned down in impatience at being told something he already knew.

"And do you think the nature of his new information, these clues and hints and traces about illegals and moles, is authentic?"

"It seems like it to me," said Nate, instantly regretting it.

Benford puffed his cheeks with annoyance. "Seems like it, or you believe it is?"

Nate took a deep breath. "I think his information is authentic. If MARBLE were being fed a barium meal, the leads would be more distinct, more identifiable." Nate waited for the next series of frowns and pouts.

Benford's head came up slowly. "Barium meal, indeed. Where did you hear that, have you been reading history?" His gaze drifted to the far wall. "Do you know who that is?" he asked, pointing to a small black-and-white photograph of a square-jawed man in gig-lamp glasses, hair slicked close to his head.

"That's Angleton, isn't it?" said Nate.

"James Jesus to you," said Benford. "For ten years he thought every Soviet agent was a double, every volunteer was dispatched, every piece of information was disinformation. He was charming and poisonous and paranoid and utterly convinced that his night sweats were reality. He might have been right. I keep his picture to remind me not to rebuild his asylum. Now, about MARBLE. I believe him too." Nate nodded. His eyes drifted to the other side of the room, to a bookshelf overflowing with papers and books. Five leather-bound volumes were unevenly stacked on the top shelf. Benford followed his gaze. "Those are the *Wind in the Willows* books: full of rats and moles."

Benford stared at Nate for a few seconds, his face working, whether in mounting distaste or in deep thought, it was impossible to tell. Nate kept his mouth shut, the only possible course of action. This misanthrope. Twenty years of mole hunts, double traps, and triple crosses. Networks disrupted, attic radios silenced, spies arrested. Black-and-white newsreels of shrunken men being led out of courthouses with jackets over their heads, hands manacled at the waist. Benford's battlefield.

He was clairvoyant, they said, a savant who relished the Byzantine world of deception and doubles and false trails. Nate took in the twitchy hands, long fingers running through his hair, the brain perhaps running too hot for its own good. Nate could see that MARBLE's recent report about moles and illegals was to Benford what a sack of rats was to a terrier.

"I suspect he'll draft you to work with him," C/ROD had said. "Good luck with that."

"I want you to work with me on MARBLE's information," Benford said. "Starting today. Move your belongings up from ROD. Don't tell anyone what you're doing. We're going to find the illegal."

"Do I tell C/ROD?" asked Nate. "Should I tell him how to reach me?"

"No one. I'll let him know if he asks. But he won't. We're not going to tell anyone about these leads. No Boston or New York Station, no tight-ass FBI, no interior decorators in DIA, no NSC, no congressional committees. No fucking fuckers in Washington fuck-starting this fiesta with their fucking leaks. It's just you, me. I trust that meets with your approval?"

Nate nodded.

Becoming Benford's acolyte is either a distinct honor or a prison sentence, thought Nate, but it didn't matter much. His career path after Helsinki had stalled. Benefactors like Forsyth and Gable were still in the field, but unable to support him. Nate looked at the brilliant, twitchy Benford and decided. Nate was good at internal ops, he knew Russia, and he could contribute. Benford could hardly be viewed as a patron—someone this misanthropic and sour would never be a willing mentor to anyone—but Nate decided to throw in with him, to immerse himself in counterintelligence, to learn about the fog-shrouded world in which Benford thrived. Maybe he could salvage his rep. In any case, for the first time since the Farm, Nate stopped worrying about the future.

Nate was quietly installed in a disused office in the corner of the Counterintelligence Division. It was utterly quiet in the hallway. Were people in there, working? Or would Norman Bates's mother's desiccated skeleton swivel grinning in her chair to greet you? "Here you are," said the secretary, giving him a wink, or perhaps it was her twitch. Ambiguous conundrums, Benford had said, get used to it.

His new office was windowless, nude, and stale. Pushpins dotted the walls . . . what must they have held up for display? A desk drawer that squealed when pulled open was filled with fingernail clippings, hundreds of them, thinly covering the bottom of the drawer.

The office next to his belonged to Alice LNU (last name unknown). In her forties, or fifties, or perhaps sixty, she was square, with apple cheeks and a fleshy nose, russet hair cut tight to her head and combed forward on the front and sides, like Napoleon's. She wore prison matron's shoes and walked splayfooted and fast. She spoke to Nate, as to everyone else, by tilting her head and leaning forward, as if to share a confidence or a secret, which of course she never did—no one in CI ever did.

In the first days, colleagues drifted by slyly to tell him that Alice was a "plank owner" in the division. She's been here forever, they said. She's the one who really killed Trotsky, they said. She *fucked Allan Pinkerton,* they said as they fled back to their offices.

CID, the Island of Broken Toys. Nate checked behind his door for Boo Radley flattened against the wall.

Benford had told Alice to help Nate. She had sat at her desk—her office was actually sunny, a fern and geraniums flourished on a file cabinet—her sensible shoes propped up and squeaking. "You don't know much," she had said. "Let's review: We have an illegal, we have submarines, we have New England, and we have meetings in Boston and New York. MARBLE mentioned submarine maintenance and five years. Okay," she said, "where would you start?"

"Navy personnel lists?" said Nate.

"Nope," Alice said swiveling in her chair. "Lunch."

They sat on the upper level of the cafeteria. Nate played with a salad, Alice spooned soup. Alice's friend Sophie arrived, huffing from climbing the mezzanine stairs on massive legs. She worked in OSR, where they still counted the rusting, radioactive nuke subs, the Oscars and Typhoons and Akulas in Olenya Bay and Polyarny, it still mattered, she said, thin-lipped, never mind what the Seventh Floor said. She was fifty and had jet-black hair, big hair, and black eyebrows, a profile off a Knossos frieze. She wore black tights and a black billowing dress and black therapeutic shoes with ski-jump toes. A black scrunchy was wrapped around her wrist for emergencies.

She set a Sailor Moon lunch box on the table and unpacked plastic boxes and containers, chopsticks and tasting spoons that stood up on their own, and a cruet of salad dressing. Sophie looked at Nate's salad and poured some of her dressing on top. "Try this, homemade." The dressing had a balsamic sweetness cut with Dijon and a hint of heat, unlike any vinaigrette he had ever tasted. He said so, and Sophie beamed.

Alice told them to stop fooling around and told Sophie what they needed to know, and she ate her curry and reeled it off, eyes closed in the remembering, or in the pleasure of the eating, or both. New London, Connecticut. Portsmouth, New Hampshire. Brunswick, Maine. Only three bases. Subs were big. Only one place repairs them, they're getting old, being refitted all the time, like the Akulas in the late 1980s, Schukas they called them, really, a *lot quieter,* and Alice got her back on track. Electric Boat Works, big shipyard in Groton, Connecticut, across the Thames River from New London. Start there, Sophie told them.

Back in Alice's office, the CID link was cathode-tube-archaic and the names inched down. Security-clearance databases, employee roles, US Navy active duty and contractor rosters. Alice's mannish finger ran down the screen; nope, nope, longer than seven years, less than three, nope. Senior management at Electric Boat and General Dynamics, of course not. Alice was fast, she looked at a name, scanned the info, and moved on. She had been pulling at names on lists for three decades. They had two piles of papers and Nate stopped arguing about "possibles" because Alice was so fast. She had her "first string," her Lovely Eleven, she called them, and started going through the holies: employment, salary, taxes, residence, phone, Internet, vehicle, banking, mail, marriage, education, children, arrests, divorces, travel, parents, ethernet or cable, straight or gay. "How well did you prepare our little illegal? How far back did you go? As far as me?" whispered Alice to the screen.

Three days later, Nate and Alice brought Benford the list, and he tapped the end of his pencil on each name as he glanced at the profiles, tap, tap, tap, and tossed the pencil aside and handed Nate the paper. "It's Jennifer Santini," Benford said with a yawn, the casual savant with unruly hair. Alice nudged Nate—*See, I told you*—and cackled.

"Let's do a deep dive, but I'm sure she's our boy," said Benford. He looked at Nate. "Now we go to New London and look around."

SOPHIE'S VINAIGRETTE

Combine puréed garlic, dill weed, dried oregano, dried pepper flakes, Dijon mustard, sugar, salt, pepper, and grated Parmesan cheese with one part balsamic vinegar and three parts extra virgin kalamata olive oil and emulsify.

25

Despite the splendid summer weather, New London was drab and depressed, past its commercial and cultural prime (which had concluded when the whaling fleets disappeared in the 1860s). The once-teeming Thames River waterfront, which during World War II had seen gray hulls rafted three-deep, a forest of masts and antennae and funnels rocking gently on the tide, was now a brackish moonscape of tilting, oil-soaked piers and rusted-out warehouses with collapsed roofs. Two- and three-story clapboard houses, mostly double-family units, covered the residential hills above the river. The black tarpaper roofs were separated by the width of two outstretched arms, clotheslines stretched between second-floor balconies. Waist-high chain-link fences and swingy gates pitted by the salt air marked tiny front yards and weedy back lots.

Across the river in Groton, the Electric Boat shipyard stretched along miles of the riverbank, a city of cranes, steam plumes, and arching factory roofs. Occasionally visible from the seaward end of a massive floating dry dock, itself the size of a cruise ship, was the impossibly big cigar shape of a matte-black nuclear submarine, high and dry on blocks, its seven-bladed propeller shrouded in heavy plastic, hidden from Russian spy satellites.

Nate did not know what to expect. They took the train up—Benford did not drive—and they stood on the station platform like two Bulgarian swineherds in Sofia for the weekend, not mole hunters looking for a Center-trained illegal. It was not clear whether Benford was parsimonious or crazy or simply operationally deluded to insist, mystifyingly, that they share a turret room at the Queen Elizabeth Inn, a B&B in a creaky Victorian halfway up a leafy hill. And the constant walking—casing, he called it—five, six, twelve hours a day, during which the quirky, brilliant cockatoo talked to Nate about the OGPU and the NKVD and the Cambridge Five, a primer of Cold War history.

Day One: They worked up and down the hill, uphill in the morning, downhill in the late afternoon, looking at the houses, at the cars parked solid along the curb, the weeds coming up on the sidewalk, and the lace curtains in the front windows. They looked for likely signal sites, cache sites, nearby parks, the geography that could support an illegal. They had nothing.

Day Two: They walked past Santini's house at different times to mark the positions of her window shades, to see if the empty geranium pot on the front steps was moved, which could be a safety signal. They were careful at night, walked by the darkened house only once, dim lamplight behind the shade of an upstairs room. Was she sitting in the dark, looking out at the street? Did she have another apartment, rented in alias, for meetings with her handler? They had nothing.

Day Three: They casually asked about her at the faded mom-and-pop store on the corner. No one knew her, no one cared. *How the fuck we must look,* Nate thought, *this counterintelligence mystic and his young sidekick,* and he tried a joke but Benford told him if he didn't pay attention he'd send him home, and Nate said, "Pay attention to what?" while they were jerking off in New frigging London, Connecticut. They had nothing.

They were working on the margins; Benford was

determined to keep this out of the gun-and-badge clutches of the FBI. "If she's a Center-trained illegal, she'll smell trouble long before anyone drives up to the front of the house. She'll bolt ninety seconds after she sees or hears something she doesn't like. It's their training." They had to do this solo.

Day Four: They did it all over again. That night, a summer thunderstorm rocked the trees and moved the shutters on the turret room, and the electricity went out and a battery radio played downstairs. Nate awoke to a flash of lightning and saw Benford in a chair sitting at the window, staring at the storm, seriously creepy. He was seeing the faces of the *twelve* Russian agents the CIA lost in one year, 1985, the Year of the Spy, all victims of Ames, and Hanssen, victims of inexplicable treachery that fed them all to the belching blast furnaces of the Soviet Union.

And meals with Benford were the real test, the challenge. It wasn't just the bumper-car conversation, but also the lobster bibs and hot sauce and oyster crackers and rating the clam chowders—too creamy, too many potatoes, too brothy, not enough sand, you needed a minute amount of grit—and discussing the difference between cod and scrod and what did and did not belong in a New England boiled dinner. "No cloves. Ever. There are rules that cannot be violated," said Benford the mole hunter.

With little of substance to go on, Benford on Thursday night over dinner announced that it was time to do an entry into Jennifer Santini's house the next morning. "An entry?" said Nate across the table. They were dining at the Bulkeley House on Bank Street near the harbor. "Benford, what do you mean, 'an entry'?"

Benford was sawing at an immense rare piece of prime rib, head turned sideways, the better to slice the flesh. Nate put down his knife and fork.

"Compose yourself," said Benford, chewing. "By 'entry' I mean the extralegal breaking and entering into the private residence of a presumed innocent American citizen against whom there is no evidence of wrongdoing by two unauthorized officers of the Central Intelligence Agency who are, incidentally, currently engaged in an uncoordinated and thus illegal counterespionage investigation which in the *domestic field* is the purview of the Federal Bureau of Investigation as stipulated by Executive Order 12333." He looked back down at his plate and slathered more creamed horseradish sauce onto his beef. "That's what I mean," he said, then added, "This horseradish sauce is excellent."

Day Five: A quiet Friday morning. They waited until ten and walked bareheaded and with empty hands through the little gate to the back of Santini's two-story house. The windows of the houses across the street were empty. The backyard was unkempt. A rusted washtub lay upside down on the bare earth next to a tilting shack. Benford walked up the wooden steps and tried the back door. It was locked and he peered through the chintz curtains. No one home.

"Can you pick the lock?" asked Nate, standing behind Benford looking through the curtain.

"Be serious," Benford said. He still had an eight-track tape deck at home.

"Should we pop the window?"

"No. Second story," said Benford, who unlaced his shoe, walked over to a rubber utility cable stapled to the side of the house, and knotted the shoelace around it, leaving a loop hanging free.

"Prusik knot," said Benford, and he showed Nate how to stand up in the loop with one foot and slide the friction hitch upward, a foot each time, to climb the cable until he could reach the unlocked second-story window. *Where the fuck did he learn that?* thought Nate, as he signaled that he was in.

The upper room was an empty, disused bedroom. Nate walked to the door and looked down into the house. He whistled for the dog, but nothing stirred. He imagined a Russian illegal would have a Doberman or Rottweiler silently guarding the house.

Nate crept silently down a wooden staircase, the thick mahogany banister creaking as he descended. Tiptoeing through a 1950s-style kitchen that smelled of wheat and seeds and oil, Nate unlocked the back door and let Benford in. "The place feels empty," Nate said. He and Benford walked through the downstairs rooms silently. The feeling of risky trespass enveloped them. The house smelled like a health club. Liniment and dusty radiators, no air moved, incongruous for a bright summer day.

The house had two front rooms, dining and living rooms, with windows that looked out onto the street. Chintzy, lacy curtains were drawn across all the windows. Spidery sunlight dappled the threadbare throw rugs laid on dark-stained hardwood floors. The furniture was heavy, dark, overstuffed furry pieces with doilies—actual doilies—on the arms and backs of the chairs and sofa. The mantelpiece above a sooty fireplace was lined with Bakelite mugs and figurines—a sea-captain mug, a Spanish girl with a mantilla. One lampshade had a pom-pom fringe around the lower edge. A wrought-iron fireplace poker set stood beside the hearth. Benford's mouth worked as he surveyed the décor. "She must have cleaned out half the Portuguese antique shops in Fall River to decorate."

Off the living room was a small office with a desk and a low bookcase stuffed with magazines and newspapers. On the desk was a small pile of utility bills and a white and blue porcelain schooner with *Ahoy* painted on the bow.

"Check the desk," said Benford. "I'm going upstairs to look around." Nate registered the ridiculous feeling of not wanting to separate from Benford, but nodded and pulled out the drawers one by one. Empty. As he closed the bottom drawer he felt resistance and heard the crunch of paper. He pulled the drawer all the way out and saw a rolled-up piece of paper at the end of the recess. He reached and pulled it out, unrolled it on top of the desk. It was a blueprint, a single sheet, with cross-sectional drawings of parts and electrical connections. The page was labeled *Section 37, fasteners and brackets.* Submarine parts? Santini worked in supply and procurement at Electric Boat. Was this a classified document? Why did she have it at home, stuck at the bottom of a drawer?

Benford meanwhile had gone upstairs into the bedroom. A four-poster bed was made with a quilt in a floral pattern with three large pillows at the head with lacy pillowcases. The single closet had blouses and slacks hanging uniformly on hangers. Several pairs of shoes on the floor, all sensible and made for walking, were lined up neatly. No pictures, no mementos, no personal items, a house that could be abandoned in ninety seconds. The bathroom was neutral, the medicine cabinet nearly empty. A toothbrush, bottle of aspirin, a twin pack of saline Fleet enemas. The pervasive smell of liniment.

Returning to the bedroom, Benford pulled out the single drawer of the bedside table. No books, porn, vibrators, or lube. Under a piece of felt he found a piece of paper with a long list of handwritten dates and times. June 5, 2100; June 10, 2200; June 30, 2130. Transmission schedule. She probably carried the laptop and encryption card with her. Standard meeting sked with a handler from the Russian Consulate in New York. A penetration of the submarine program.

Benford closed the drawer and started downstairs to tell Nate.

Nate had just finished checking the backs of the other drawers again, but found nothing. He rolled up the blueprint to take upstairs to show Benford. Walking out the door, he stopped. Jennifer Santini was standing in the living room looking at him. A duffel bag was on the floor at her feet. Nate realized that they had never actually seen her before. *Huh. She works out. With weights. On steroids.* She apparently had just gotten home from the gym. Why wasn't she at work?

Jennifer was in her late thirties, of average height. She was dressed in skintight spandex shorts stretched by tree-trunk legs, calves and quadriceps bulging. Her arms, shoulders, and neck were corded with muscle, her jawline bulged. She wore a tight tank top that covered not feminine breasts but dinner-plate-sized pectorals with nipples. She had brilliant green eyes, the whites bluish with health and vitality. Her face was etched around her mouth and a sharp, straight nose. Her forehead was deeply creased by the frown splashed across her face. She wore her red hair slicked tight to her head, pulled back in a ponytail, a bullet, a torpedo, an assembled action figure, a cross-over SUV with the parts cobbled together.

In that final instant of appraisal, Nate noticed that she had beautiful feminine hands, with manicured nails painted a light pink. She was barefoot and her feet likewise were pretty and delicate, with painted toenails in the same soft color. The sound of Benford clumping down the stairs triggered Jennifer to move, blindingly fast, toward Nate. With hideous power she swatted a lamp off a side table at him as she closed the distance in two long strides. Nate ducked the lamp, which smashed against the wall behind him, but straightened to find himself face-to-face with her, a rock-hard forearm against his throat, pushing him back against the living-room wall, while taking thunderous, sweeping clouts at him with her free arm. Nate put both hands on her forearm and pulled. Nothing.

Nate hammered on her arm, but she stayed with him, crushing against his throat with those Schwarzenegger arms and Grace Kelly hands. Nate threw an overhand punch at her face, his fist glancing off her cheek with no apparent effect. Her face was inches from his, and she bared her teeth with the effort. Nate expected her to bite his lips off. As she continued hitting him with looping punches, insane, disjointed thoughts ran through Nate's mind: (1) His luck he has to corner the one Russian illegal in the world who isn't the bird-watching accountant; (2) What in Christ the men in her office must think about her as she sits at her desk every morning; and (3) What, if anything, does this cyborg do for sex? Then, absurdly, Nate thought about what Dominika was doing at this very moment; where was she? An inexpressible sadness swept over him as he thought that Dominika might be dead, and his head bounced off the wall and his throat constricted and he thought that this freak was part of the machine that killed her.

Benford appeared at the bottom of the stairs and stood in shocked immobility. Jennifer looked for a second at the tubby, rumpled man—he would be dessert after the main course—and Nate raked her shin with his shoe and stomped on one pretty, Lolita-pink foot, which made Jennifer ease up an inch, and Nate slid sideways away from her pinioning arm and kicked the spandex bulge between her legs with his instep as hard as he could. Jennifer grunted like a man, held herself with both hands, and thumped heavily on the floor, then fell over on her side, doubled up.

Benford looked at Nate, then back at the beast on the floor. Nothing in his thirty years of mole-hunting, spy-catching, illegals-baiting was ever like this. Especially not when Jennifer suddenly sat straight back up like an unstoppable serial killer at a lakeside summer camp. She picked up the glass-and-wood-topped coffee table in front of the couch and threw it across the room at Benford standing on the bottom step of the staircase. Benford called upon some hidden burst of speed—perhaps held in reserve from his two years as equipment manager of the Princeton Varsity Heavy Eights in the late 1960s—and pounded back up the stairs just as the coffee table hit the very spot on which he had been standing, smashing wood and glass and knocking out two sturdy balusters. Benford did not stop moving up the stairs, and disappeared above the second-floor landing.

Jennifer turned back to Nate, who now stood in the middle of the living room. In the last seconds, he had moved a few steps and had taken the iron poker from its stand near the fireplace and was holding it by his side. Her ponytail swinging, Jennifer rushed at Nate again, her bare feet lightly slapping the wooden floor. Nate bizarrely remembered his hand-to-hand instructor's name was Carl, took a half step forward, snapped his wrist, and hit Jennifer on the side of the neck with the poker, like in close-quarters training, the brachial plexus. The shock of the impact ran up Nate's arm. It was like hitting the trunk of a holm oak.

A surprisingly feminine shriek came out of Jennifer as she was catapulted sideways into the couch, which overturned backward, doilies flying. She rolled three feet along the floor until she came to rest against the far wall, her face against the baseboard. Breathing hard, his arm tingling and numb, Nate held on to the poker, rounded the corner of the overturned couch, and knelt beside her. One of her legs twitched slightly and the simian muscles in her bottom fluttered. Nate pulled her over to flop her on her back. One of Jennifer's eyes was open, sightless; the other, mismatched, was rolled up into the back of her head. Her mouth was open but Nate could detect no breathing. Those fucking pink nails against the dark wood floor. One of Jennifer's pedicured feet lay on top of a doily, like an éclair in a display case.

The stairs creaked and Benford came up to stand beside Nate. The living room was devastated, broken furniture and ceramics littered the floor. Benford looked down at Jennifer's lopsided face. "Jesus," he said.

"She's like a fucking Bond villain," said Nate. "Where do they find these people? I think I bent the poker." He reached down to feel for a pulse on her neck, but her head flopped over to the other side too loose, too wobbly.

"Don't bother," said Benford. "The cervical neck flexor is gone. The strike tore the spinal cord loose. Avulsion."

"What the fuck are you talking about?" said Nate, whose hands were starting to shake.

"Avulsion. You separated her neck."

Nate wiped his face. "Terrific. Stop me before I kill again."

"Are you okay?" asked Benford.

"Yeah, thanks for the backup. The diversion of you running up the stairs gave me the opening I needed." Nate stood up and let the poker drop to the floor. "Now what do we do?"

"I found a transmit sked," said Benford. "We have to find her laptop and encryption card. Look in her bag. She probably communicated via secure Internet link. That and personal meetings. You?"

"Some sort of parts blueprint in a desk drawer. We should take this place apart."

"Fuck that," said Benford. "Collect what we have, we can call the FBI in now. Let them search this place with tweezers and baggies. They can go right ahead and explain how they didn't catch an illegal operating right in their backyard. They can stuff their primacy up their asses."

BENFORD'S CREAMED HORSERADISH SAUCE

Cook a medium béchamel; incorporate butter, Dijon mustard, and grated fresh horseradish to taste. Season with ground black pepper and red wine vinegar. Chill and serve.

26

The Moscow summer was coming; the sun actually felt warm on her face. Dominika had started work on the "special project" in the Americas Department under General Korchnoi. Soon after her transfer, the general took her aside and told her they—the general and Dominika—would be taking an operational trip. The general said they were bidden to the First Deputy Director's office within the hour to discuss it.

Dominika knew she was deceiving General Korchnoi, using the operation as cover to travel overseas so she could recontact the Americans. She liked and respected the general—he was professional and helpful—and she reflected that she was now taking advantage of someone decent, just as she had been taken advantage of by others. The muck of the cesspool had begun to stick on her haunches too. There was nothing to do about it, she told herself. She would have to betray his trust.

Back upstairs to Uncle Vanya? She would look him in the face and enjoy it. Her secret had not been discovered by the interrogators at Lefortovo. Dominika Egorova was a CIA penetration of the SVR, and none of them knew it. She had manipulated Uncle Vanya to put her back on the case against Nate. Now she would report early success, arrange more contacts, more foreign travel. The clandestine agent, reactivated.

What was this fever in her body? The Americans understood her. They had recognized right away the *zhazhda,* her thirst for owning this secret, for the power it gave her. Nate's purple cloud, and *Bratok*'s purple cloud, and Forsyth's azure halo, all intense and precious—they knew her better than her own countrymen did.

She did not know what, exactly, were her feelings for Nate. Thoughts of him while she was in prison had helped her survive the cabinets at the ends of the prison corridors. She tried not to think about their one night together, and she wondered if he thought about her. He had treated her mostly as an asset, a commodity. Did he ever see her as a woman? Did he care for *her,* Dominika?

She had to see them, all of them, the Americans, but especially Nate. Sending a message to them from Moscow would have been a frightful risk. Directorate K almost certainly would be watching her periodically, checking. They always did with the rehabilitated. With overseas travel imminent, she could wait.

It was time to go upstairs. They rode the elevator together in silence. She liked the white-haired spy beside her, the small space was filled with his deep purple spirit, comforting and steady. She knew that beneath the paternal smile was operational brilliance, a keen intellect, unbending patriotism. How had such a decent, thinking man lasted this long in the Service? From where did he draw sustenance? Dominika had no illusions that this old professional wouldn't be able to detect any misstep on her part. She would have to be careful around him.

They walked together down the carpeted hallway Dominika knew so well, past the gallery lined with the airbrushed portraits of the Directors. The Gray Cardinals stared at her as she passed. *You escaped this time,* they seemed to be saying to her. *We'll be watching,* they called as she walked past them, their eyes following her.

Korchnoi studied her face as they arrived at the executive suite and opened the door. He had seen the emotion in her, could feel her bristling. *How to harness this?* he thought. They entered the office, and Vanya was waiting for them, bluff and bald and backlighted canary-yellow, his ugly, ambitious color, against the windows, a hearty clap on the shoulder for Korchnoi, a sugary welcome for his niece. Dominika knew that the more sugar he spooned out, the more vinegar would fill her mouth.

Now down to business. The target was still the American, the CIA officer called Nash who held the name of the traitor in his head. Dominika must succeed, for time was of the essence. The general and Dominika would have been surprised that their silent thoughts during this fulsome performance were very nearly identical. *Khvastun*. Boaster, bouncer, blowhard.

General Korchnoi spoke, quietly, thoughtfully. This project will require Corporal Egorova to make periodic foreign trips. Is there a problem with that, considering her recent—and highly lamentable—investigation? Uncle Vanya spread his arms as if in benediction. No, of course not. Everything to be left in your capable hands. Getting to the American, *recontact,* is the point. See to it, then, and let it be done excellently. Vanya winked at her.

They were walking back, along the broad corridor of the ground floor, Korchnoi speaking easily, making lists for her, directing her to begin filling the folder with details, schedules, gambits. Dominika saw that he was pleased, and gratified, and not at all suspicious or worried. Why should he be? Dominika was an excellent protégée. Betraying him was difficult, but it was necessary. That was how it had to be.

Coming toward them in the corridor along the opposite wall was Line F executioner Sergey Matorin. He seemed not to recognize her. Dominika's vision started to narrow. She felt fear, then an aerosolized rage that had her measuring the distance between her fingers and his eyes. Could the general sense the woolpack of her hatred? Did he not see the trail of bloody footprints, or the black shroud that billowed around Matorin? Could he not hear the musical note of the chine of his scythe as he dragged it behind him? Matorin's milky white eye passed over her as he continued down the corridor. As he walked he hugged the wall like a ray swimming over a sandy ocean floor, trailing thick, elemental black smoke, like blood in the water. Looking after him, Dominika shuddered at the thinning hair on the back of his skull, and at his empty fingers that grasped and ungrasped, waiting to hold a knife.

Eight o'clock, and a rainy night. Vanya Egorov was driven through the Borovitskaya Gate in the western corner of the Kremlin, tires drumming over the slick cobblestones, past the Grand Palace and the Cathedral of the Archangel, and left past Building Fourteen to a yawning, deserted Ivanovskaya Square. His official Mercedes eased through the narrow gate to the inner courtyard of the mustard-yellow Senate building and pulled to a stop under a dimly lit porte cochere. The last time he had been inside these walls was to receive his second star. Tonight he had to show he deserved to keep it.

An aide knocked once, opened the door, and stepped aside. The president's office was relatively small and richly paneled. A green marble pen set was the only object on the surface of his desk; the lights in the wall sconces were dialed low. The president was in a dark suit and white shirt with no tie. Egorov tried not to notice that Putin was in his stocking feet, his shoes pushed underneath his chair. The president was sitting at a small inlaid table in front of his desk, his hands folded in his lap. No papers, no news wires, no television. Egorov sat down at the little table.

"Good evening, Mr. President," he said. Putin's face as usual was a mask, but tonight he looked tired.

"General Egorov," said Putin, who looked at his wristwatch, then fixed his electric eyes on Vanya's face. *Go. And keep it brief.* Egorov modulated his voice.

"The communications manual acquired from the Americans continues to be a rich source of critical data and cyber opportunities in the future." Putin nodded once, blue eyes unblinking.

"Our sensitive asset in Washington, SWAN, is providing comprehensive technical information on US military space vehicles. The Kosmicheskie Voyska, the Space Forces, rate the intelligence as excellent. My *rezident* in Washington—"

"You mean *my rezident*," said Putin.

"Of course; your *rezident*, General Golov, is handling SWAN with utmost care," said Egorov, telling himself to watch it, with him in this mood.

An aide knocked and brought in a tray with steaming tea in delicate filigree *podstakanniki,* silver spoons balanced over the rims of the glasses, a sugar cube in each. The tray was placed on a nearby conference table in the corner of the room, along with a silver salver of madeleines. Both were out of reach and remained untouched.

"Go on," said Putin after the aide had left.

"We continue to search for a mole run by the CIA, probably in the Service. It is only a matter of time before we unmask him."

"It is important that you do so," said Putin. "More evidence that foreigners, the Americans, are working to disrupt our government."

"Yes, Mr. President. It's doubly important. The mole threatens the security of our assets—"

"Like SWAN," said Putin. "Nothing must happen to her, no *komprometirovat,* no international flaps, no failures." Egorov noted with interest that the president correctly knew the gender of SWAN. He knew *he* hadn't mentioned it before.

"We have identified the CIA officer who handles this mole. I am initiating an operation against him to obtain the name of his agent."

"Fascinating," said Putin, a former KGB officer, "but you do not need my approval to conduct such an operation."

"It is a complicated *sekretnaya operatsiya,*" said Egorov, circling around the subject. "I intend to direct one of our officers to engage the American, to compromise him. I want the name of his agent."

Putin's mask shifted slightly, whether from discomfort or vicarious pleasure, Egorov could not tell. "I want discretion, and moderation. I do not condone the physical abduction of this CIA officer. This is not done between rival services. The consequences would be unmanageable." The president's voice was silky, the cobra flaring its hood. A porcelain Fabergé clock on a side table tinged the half hour. The tea across the room had grown cold.

"Of course. I am taking all precautions, Mr. President. Apart from my direction, a senior officer is supervising the action in the field against the American."

"And the younger officer—a woman, correct?—was recently cleared in a counterintelligence investigation?"

"Yes, sir," said Egorov, looking at the liverwurst lips as they moved.

"And do I remember correctly that this young woman is your niece?" He looked Egorov in the eyes. "The daughter of your late brother?"

"Family is the best security," said Egorov lamely. This was a show of omniscience, of strength, designed to shock, then awe subordinates. Like Stalin used to do. "She will follow my directions."

"Have her engage the American, but I do not condone active measures. It is out of the question." Putin obviously knew the option had been discussed.

"As you wish, Mr. President," said Egorov.

Nine minutes later Egorov's footsteps were ringing down the grand staircase as he scurried to his waiting car. He collapsed in the backseat, contemplating the disasters that lurked in the career of ambition. As his Mercedes flashed under the Borovitskaya archway, Vanya did not see another official car, less grand, heading toward the Senate building he had just left, carrying his Line KR counterintelligence chief, the diminutive Alexei Zyuganov.

KREMLIN MADELEINES

Make a genoise batter by mixing eggs and salt until thick, then add sugar gradually, and vanilla extract. Fold in flour and beurre noisette to form a thick batter. Pour into greased and floured madeleine molds and bake in moderate oven until edges are golden brown. Unmold and cool on a wire rack.

27

United States Senator Stephanie Boucher (D-California) was not accustomed to driving or parking her own car, or to walking down a corridor unescorted, or even to opening her own doors. As vice chair of the Senate Select Committee on Intelligence, she had a phalanx of interns and staffers to carry her in a sedan chair if she wished. She could have used some help right now: The front bumper of her car kissed the bumper of the car ahead of her with a quiet crunch. This motherfucking parallel parking. Senator Boucher twisted the wheel and touched the gas. Her rear wheels hit the curb, the front of the car still sticking out into the street. Boucher banged the steering wheel with the heel of her hand. She eased forward to get a new angle. A car behind her honked. *Take the spot or move on.*

Senator Boucher rolled down the passenger-side window and screamed, "Fuck you," at the other car as it squeezed by. Boucher knew she should be more discreet; she was a known face—a celebrity, even—on the Hill, but that cocksucker was not going to honk at her and get away with it. On the fourth try, Boucher managed to ease into the space. It was early evening on a dark and leafy N Street in Washington, D.C. As she locked the car, she saw that her left rear tire was up on the curb, but the hell with it. She turned and walked along the sidewalk past the elegant brownstones, their Georgian doorways lit by beveled glass lanterns.

Boucher was forty years old, short and thin, with a boyish figure, her legs toned and slim. Piercing green eyes and a button nose were set off by shoulder-length blond hair. Her mouth was her only feature that was not consistent with the image of vibrating energy and corporate power. It was small and frowny and thin-lipped and pinched—a mouth that would as soon bite down as pucker up.

Boucher was ascending the power chain on the Hill, young to be a senator, but she knew she had earned her position on the Select Committee on Intelligence with fierce preparation and hard work. She sat on other committees as well, but none were as prestigious as SSCI. Twelve years ago she had been elected to Congress after a hardscrabble campaign in a Southern California district replete with defense and aerospace contractors. She became adept at appropriations and at holding the bag of money over people's heads to get what she wanted. Ascending to senator had been the next logical step, and now, in her second term, as newly named vice chair, she had a hand in legislation, appropriations, and oversight within the Department of Defense, Department of Homeland Security, and the Intelligence Community. Abrasive, impatient, and abusive during committee hearings, she tolerated Defense for the commerce it brought to her home state. She recognized the political unassailability of DHS, which she privately thought was a collection of third-stringers operating in a world they scarcely understood, trying to do brain surgery while wearing catchers' mitts.

But it was for the Intelligence Community—the conglomerate of sixteen separate agencies—that Boucher reserved her most bitter, thin-lipped excoriation. Defense Intelligence organs—DIA and DH—did not concern her. They were career soldiers thrashing over their heads in the foreign intelligence milieu when all they really wanted was a clear photo of the next bridge beyond the next hill. The Department of State's INR had some brilliant analysts, but State rarely collected secrets anymore. Their analysts needed to get out in the sun more, get some vitamin D. The FBI were the reluctant brides, forced into a domestic intelligence role they neither understood nor welcomed, inevitably reverting to their button-down cop roots, preferring to run stings on Arab teenagers in Detroit rather than build networks of long-term sources.

But these were just the crowd. Senator Boucher really had the wood for just one agency, the CIA. She loathed the intelligence officials who sat before her in the committee room, slouched in their chairs, at turns earnest and evasive. Boucher knew they were lying to her every time they spoke, confident, slick, smiling, and knowing. She knew the briefing papers they carried in their zippered security bags were so much wallpaper, concealing the real story. "The hard-working men and women of intelligence," they'd say, "the National Clandestine Service," they'd puff, "the gold standard of intelligence collection" they'd announce. These were the familiar phrases that drove Boucher up the wall.

It was during her first term as a freshman congresswoman that Boucher had met seventy-five-year-old Malcolm Algernon Philips, an on-again, off-again lobbyist, lavish party-giver, and behind-the-scenes power broker in Washington. Philips knew everyone in town and, more important, knew (in Washington parlance) who was spanking whom, with what, and why. His many admirers would have been scandalized to learn that the silver-haired, impeccably dressed Philips had since the mid-1960s been a talent spotter for the KGB, recruited as a young socialite when Khrushchev was still premier. Though the Russians paid him well, Philips was in it for the sheer joy of gossip, repeating secrets, breaking confidences, and wielding the power that came along with it. He cared not a whit about what the Russians did with his information. The Russians in turn displayed an uncharacteristic patience with Philips. They did not push him to elicit secrets or pay bribes or filch documents. They were content to let him spot candidates for recruitment from within the maelstrom of official Washington. He had been doing it for nearly forty years, and he was very good at it.

During a winter dinner party at his Georgetown home, Philips's finely tuned antennae detected in the junior congresswoman from California something in addition to the usual Capitol Hill cocktail of ambition, ego, and greed. A private lunch with Boucher six weeks later confirmed his suspicions. Philips told his KGB handler that he might have found the perfect engine for their needs. Stephanie Boucher was, Philips assessed, utterly devoid of a sentient conscience. Notions of right or wrong did not occupy her thoughts. Neither did patriotism, nor loyalty to God or family or country. She was concerned only about herself. If it suited her, Philips reported, Stephanie Boucher would not think twice about the *morality* of spying for Russia.

She grew up in the South Bay, in Hermosa Beach, every day wearing cutoffs and surfing and smoking and fending off the smooth golden boys. Her father was pathetic, letting her mother whore around; she grew to despise her parents. Then her father surprised them both. She was eighteen when her father shot her mother, at the time in the arms of a FedEx deliveryman. Stephanie broke down for a while, but she rallied and made it shamefacedly through the University of Southern California, then graduate school, then drifted into local politics with a growing conviction that friendship was overrated and that relationships were worth it only if they could be exploited for personal advancement. Some of her mother's DNA stuck, however, and along with serial misanthropy, Stephanie progressively discovered she liked sex, a lot, the kind with no commitment. She had to control herself as her political career blossomed, but it was always there, right beneath the surface.

The *rezidentura* in Washington did careful research on their recruitment target. A picture slowly came together, and everything the SVR saw and heard was consistent with what Malcolm Philips had reported. A recruitment operation was initiated and a progression of SVR officers and influence agents continued to vet the senator. But it was not until Washington Rezident Anatoly Golov—urbane, soft-spoken, and charmingly ironic—made contact that Boucher got a first peek behind the treasure-room door.

The stock philosophical blandishments of recruitment made little impression on the young woman's mind. She was not interested in the concept of Amity between Nations, nor in the desirability of a World Balance between modern Russia and the United States. Golov could see all this and did not waste time. He knew what she wanted—a career, influence, power.

Golov commissioned a series of thoughtful global backgrounders drafted by Service I, which he then shared with the senator "for discussion." International relations, the global politics of oil and natural gas, developments in South Asia, Iran, and China. These specially prepared briefs on intelligence, economics, and military matters quickly made the senator an expert on her committee. The chairman, impressed by her fluency and scholarship, offered her the vice chair of SSCI. It was not lost on the senator that bigger things were possible.

As the relationship developed, Boucher never remotely struggled with the notion of espionage. She discussed SSCI hearings and issues during dinners with Golov, a matter of give-and-take, natural for a Washington politician. Golov elicited the information from her as if he were deveining a shrimp. The increasingly frequent payments from him "for expenses" Stephanie considered her due. Boucher had long since passed the point of no return, but it was not necessary to remind her of it. In her mind she was building her advantage, preparing herself for advancement, working toward her goal. The SVR had a member of Congress as an active source. SWAN.

Anatoly Golov waited for Senator Boucher in the small garden dining room at the rear of the Tabard Inn on N Street. Tiny lights were threaded through the branches of potted trees in the narrow garden closed off by a tall brick wall. Traffic noise from nearby Scott Circle could have been the murmur of gentle nighttime surf. Golov had been Washington *rezident* for a year, was personally handling SWAN. He had vast prior experience in operations, and recognized that SWAN could conceivably be the most valuable American source Russia had ever run.

Even so, he disliked the agent and he disliked the case. In truth, SWAN scared him a little. He thought back to the early days when agents were recruited because of their ideology, their belief in world communism, their commitment to the dream of a perfect socialist state. *Now it's all* sharada, *a charade,* thought Golov. SWAN was a greedy, uncontrolled sociopath.

He shot the cuffs of his shirt. Golov was imperially tall, his thinning gray hair combed straight back. A long straight nose and delicate jaw hinted at Romanov, but that didn't matter anymore, not even in the SVR. Golov was dressed in a sublime two-button dark Brioni suit, with a razor-starched white shirt and silk navy tie from Marinella with tiny scarlet dots. He wore black Tod Gommino loafers over charcoal-gray socks. Perhaps he was an elegant European count, perhaps on vacation in the United States. The only jarring note was the plain gold signet ring worn on his little finger. On Golov it was mysterious, hinted at a hidden history.

Golov was finishing his dinner of an egg-lemon lamb fricassee, red kale sautéed in balsamic vinegar, and *pommes de terre aligot* as good as he remembered having in southern France. Though he normally did not drink when operational, he needed to fortify—or did he mean numb—himself when meeting the senator. He finished his second glass of Chardonnay and ordered a *doppio* espresso.

While the table was cleared, Golov reminded himself once again that SWAN was too important an asset to waste time and technique on trying to mollify, or discipline, or control. What Stephanie wanted, the SVR would give her. She had been passing minutes of SSCI closed sessions, hundreds of digital pages of testimony by defense and intelligence officials on weapons systems, intelligence operations, and US policy the likes of which the Center had never seen, never knew existed. In return the SVR had settled on salary payments in amounts unheard of in the annals of the chronically parsimonious Russian intelligence service.

Her value elevated her above the status of agent—she was a supermole, a potential agent of influence, a Manchurian candidate. Golov had begun directing, assisting, coaching her, preparing her further for important career advancement. It was not new. Over the years the Russians had done it before, obliquely, for other members of the US Congress. Unfortunately, most of those debauched legislators eventually drove into lampposts, or caught air before splashing into the Reflecting Pool, or skidded off bridges into tidal estuaries. Compared with those cirrhotic bumblers, SWAN had no such vulnerabilities. Better yet, none of them had had the potential of SWAN. The Center envisioned Boucher as a cabinet member, as Director of the CIA, perhaps even as vice president.

Her production was astounding, and the best was yet to come. SWAN was on the threshold of tapping into the most sensitive, current SAP in the Pentagon, the Special Access Program devoted to the development of an advanced Global Orbiting Vehicle (GLOV).

Initial intelligence already provided by SWAN astounded the Russians. GLOV would be a hybrid platform capable of collecting SIGINT and ELINT while providing GPS support. It could protect itself in orbit from killer satellites. More alarming for Moscow was GLOV's anticipated ability to launch weapons from space against targets on earth. Directly. No warplanes, no refueling, no radar, no stealth technology, no antiaircraft missiles, no lost pilots, no warning. Pinpoint strikes on the surface of the planet from three hundred miles in space. US Air Force project briefers had called it the Finger of God.

The billion-dollar SAP was contracted exclusively to, and managed in a strict compartment by, Pathfinder Satellite Corporation of Los Angeles, located in the high-tech corridor along Airport Road and the LAAFB in El Segundo. This coincidentally also happened to be Senator Boucher's former congressional district. *Yes, indeed,* thought Golov, *the best is yet to come.*

Senator Boucher walked briskly through the small English country-house lobby of the Tabard Inn, squeezed past people in the narrow picture-lined corridor connecting sitting rooms and lounge, before coming out to the garden. She saw Golov at a table in the rear and strode over to him. Golov stood up, offered his hand, and bent in the European fashion to bring the lips to within inches of the hand. Golov did not actually touch the senator's hand with his lips. He recalled early assessment reports about her social habits and what she liked to do with those hands.

"Stephanie, good evening," said Golov, choosing his words. He used her first name to create familiarity and to avoid using her title, striking a chord between courtesy and intimacy. You never knew what kind of mood she would be in. Golov waited for her reply as she sat down.

"Hi, Anatoly," said Boucher. She put her elbows on the table. "I'm sorry to get right to business, but did you receive an answer from your people?" The senator fished a cigarette out of her purse. Golov leaned forward to light it with a pencil-thin gold Bugatti lighter.

"I passed along your request, Stephanie," said Golov, "along with my recommendation that they should agree without hesitation. I expect a reply within the next few days." He sat with his hands resting easily on the tablecloth. His coffee arrived, and Stephanie ordered a whiskey and soda.

"I feel so good that you recommended they pay, Anatoly," said Boucher in her committee voice. "I don't know what I'd do without your support."

What an insufferable woman this is, thought Golov. But he knew the Center would pay. They would pay five times her asking price for the information. The first discs she already had provided from Pathfinder Satellite SSCI briefings had amazed Russian researchers. Additional discs, manuals, and software from future Pathfinder and DoD briefings would be priceless. "Stephanie, you know you have my support always. Don't worry, the Center will agree, and gladly." Golov resisted the impulse to pat Boucher's hand across the table.

"That's good, Anatoly, because today we were briefed that Pathfinder is close to completing the first stage of bench testing for some of the navigational and targeting circuits. I've insisted on regular progress reports. I'm visiting Pathfinder in Los Angeles once a quarter. This project will be funded for another decade." Boucher blew a stream of smoke straight up. "So, if your *comrades in Moscow*"—this last said altogether too loudly, thought Golov, like a threat—"don't want to pay, then okay, we're finished and I'm done."

Golov noted once again that it was a measure of Boucher's sublime arrogance, of living in a world devoid of consequences, that she was incapable of contemplating the certainty that the Center would never let her "quit," that the choice was not hers. Golov tried to imagine the meeting at which Boucher would be told that she would be required to continue spying for Moscow or be exposed.

"Of course we're going to continue our collaboration," said Golov soothingly. "Don't even suggest anything else. We will continue safely and securely, you will continue to amaze and astound our people, we will continue to remunerate you for your efforts, and your career will flourish." Golov had long since discarded the temptation to add ideological blandishments. A simple recitation of the facts sufficed. You pass us secrets, we pay you for them.

"I want to continue our discussion from last time about your security," said Golov. "I know you don't think it's necessary, but I must insist that you listen to me. I'm doing this for you, Stephanie, no one else. It's rather important." Golov sipped his espresso and looked at Boucher over the rim of his cup. Boucher blew cigarette smoke in a huff of fatigue.

"You are a well-known personage in Washington," Golov said softly. "In certain circles, I am also recognizable as a senior Russian diplomat. Our continued public meetings are extremely inadvisable. Moscow is worried. I am worried. We have to do better." Golov kept his voice steady, offhand. They had met too frequently. He was stretching his luck. Boucher blew more smoke into the air.

"Are we going to have this conversation again?" Boucher said, flicking cigarette ash off the table. "We discussed all this before and I thought I made myself clear."

"Of course we did, Stephanie, but I insist that you reconsider. To start, we have to meet in more private locations, out of the public eye. In addition, the frequency of these personal meetings must also be reduced in favor of impersonal communications." Golov looked into Boucher's narrowing eyes.

"Listen, Anatoly, I told you before. I'm not going to root around under some infested tree stump in Great Falls Park at midnight looking for a package from you. I'm not going to accept one of your clunky transmitters that will start smoking in my purse and set off the alarms in the Dirksen Building." She held up a hand. "Don't tell me about your technology, I know all about spy gear. Your Russian gadgets aren't half as good as ours." Boucher bared her teeth. "And I *emphatically* am not going to begin meeting with some first-tour officer from Abkhazia with manure on his shoes." Before her SVR briefings, the senator did not know that Abkhazia existed, much less where it was located. "Why do we keep having this discussion?"

Golov knew how to handle agents, but this was different than any other case he had run, ever. He knew Egorov in Moscow was nervous about security. Golov was nervous as well. But to slow the operational tempo when the intelligence was so spectacular was not possible. "Stephanie, I understand how difficult all these precautions are. Let's agree to this: You and I will continue to meet. If you agree, I will arrange for hotel rooms outside Washington for our meetings. Because we will have lots of time, I suggest we meet less frequently. This will be a lot safer."

"Outside Washington?" said Boucher. "Are you serious? It's hard enough to get a free night in town. You expect me to get away from my staff, my schedule, and drive to a ridiculous rural Sheraton off the highway to huddle with you over a bag of chips? Like where, Baltimore, Philadelphia, Richmond? That's not going to happen, Anatoly, not even close."

Golov looked at SWAN smoothly. He was not going to insist on anything. This case was too big. He smiled at her. "Stephanie, you are too logical. Observant. Practical. I ask you to agree on one element. Let us continue, but not in public. Every month we will meet in a Washington hotel. In a suite. At your convenience. Even this little place has rooms, but they are small. We will innovate, accommodate, be flexible. Your safety is my only concern."

Senator Boucher, distracted, nodded. "All right, but let's start with a room here. This little inn does something for me, I don't know." She looked over at Golov and inclined forward so he could light another cigarette. Golov summoned thirty years of discipline to hide his revulsion. "Oh, and Anatoly," she said, "I still want the number to my account in Liechtenstein. Ask them to pass it along."

"Stephanie, we have discussed this subject also, several times. It is against Center procedure to grant access to this account. The sole consideration is your security. Believe me, the money is there, the deposits all have been made. You have seen the balance figures."

"Anatoly, you're a dear man," said Boucher. "But would you mind very much if I play the prima donna and insist? Humor me." Boucher got up and dropped her cigarette into her whiskey. Golov rose from his seat and wished her good night. As she turned to leave, Boucher reached into her purse, took out a disc in a black paper sleeve, and flipped it casually on the table. "Minutes of a committee hearing last week about Pathfinder," she said. "I was going to keep it until your pals in Moscow paid up, but I like you too much, Anatoly. Good night."

He watched her march into the hotel, her blond hair swaying with her stride. Golov casually put the disc into his suit coat pocket and sat down at the table. The garden was empty and quiet. He ordered a brandy and began composing the cable to Egorov in his head.

GOLOV'S EGG-LEMON LAMB STEW

Vigorously brown cubed chunks of lamb with diced bacon and onions; moisten with white wine and stock, season with salt, pepper, and nutmeg, and simmer for one hour. Remove lamb chunks. Beat lemon juice, egg yolks, and minced garlic, and whisk vigorously into stock without boiling. Season egg-lemon sauce again with salt, pepper, and nutmeg, and pour over lamb garnished with finely julienned lemon zest.

28

Vanya Egorov read Anatoly Golov's cable from Washington describing SWAN's continued refusal to accept more exacting tradecraft in the relationship. He swore under his breath and considered ordering Golov to slow the case down, perhaps even to put it on ice. He changed his mind when he began reading the second page of Golov's cable, summarizing the contents of the disc SWAN had passed at the last meeting. It contained a verbatim transcript of a closed-session briefing of the SSCI by Pathfinder Satellite Corporation and US Air Force managers on the GLOV project, timelines, Gantt charts, evaluation criteria, production parameters, subcontractor requirements. It was all there; the information was spectacular. Line T was already working on an executive summary for the Kremlin, the Executive Committee of the Duma, and Defense. He would present the summary himself; it would look very, very good.

But this intelligence windfall was at serious risk. Security was inadequate and the case vulnerable. The unflappable and experienced Golov improved the odds somewhat, and his handling of the little blond harridan was masterful, but nothing they could do, no regime of tradecraft or technical tools, could guarantee SWAN's safety indefinitely. Egorov lit a cigarette with hands that shook slightly.

There were two points of vulnerability: Golov as *rezident* of course could be followed constantly, monitored electronically, beaconed, bugged, and buttoned. But he was too good, too cautious to lead surveillance to a meeting. He moreover had a dedicated

Zeta Team of countersurveillants who followed their chief as a hostile surveillance team would, at the same distances and using the same techniques, both to detect and impede opposition coverage on the *rezident*. SWAN herself posed the larger problem. She could go crashing around Washington without a thought of staying anonymous and accidentally be seen with Golov, or bring attention to herself unnecessarily. No tradecraft could control that.

But if someone noticed a leak, or if there was a tip, then the American mole-catchers would indeed come out of their holes and never stop searching. And where would such a leak originate? For one, from the son-of-a-bitch SVR traitor who was being handled by Nathaniel Nash, American CIA officer, that's who. Egorov slammed his fist down on his desk. Someone in this building. Someone he likely knew.

There were a half dozen high-level officers outside the restricted list who had indirect knowledge of SWAN and who supported the case. Vanya mentally listed them now: the owlish Yury Nasarenko, director of Line T (Science and Technology), and the chiefs of Lines R (Operational Planning and Analysis), OT (Tech Support), and I (Computer Service). These officers knew they were supporting an exceptional case, they could infer where it was being run. They did not know the identity of SWAN, but they had access to the raw reports, and much could be gleaned. Despite their ranks and positions, they would all have to be vetted, and for that distasteful task Vanya had the dwarf, Alexei Zyuganov, director of Special Service II, Counterintelligence, Line KR.

Egorov knew the prospect of an internal investigation against his own professional colleagues would bring Zyuganov as close to a state of *upoenie,* sheer ecstasy, as was possible in this life, possibly with the exception of his work in the basement of the Lubyanka. Vanya had given the dwarf full authority for his internal investigation and the little man with the big ears and the bland grin went away happy, his mind brimming.

Egorov looked out the window of his executive suite. Who else could jeopardize SWAN? The Director, of course. Probably a half dozen or more in the Executive Secretariat, the President's Office, the Office of the Minister of Defense. But there was little Egorov could do about people out of his reach. Who else? The only other senior officer worth considering was Vladimir Korchnoi, director of the First Department (America and Canada), who, although he was not cleared for SWAN, was finely attuned to what was happening operationally on his turf. They were good friends, addressed each other with affectionate, village diminutives. Volodya Korchnoi was of the old school. He was trusted and liked by officers in the Service. He also had connections throughout the Service, allowing him to hear a lot of gossip. And he was currently directing the operation to get to Nash.

Egorov thought how seldom he saw or spoke to Korchnoi these days. His friend was getting old. Several more years until retirement, perhaps. By that time Egorov would be at the top of the heap, he could choose a loyal protégé to take over the Americas Department then. Even though Vanya knew in his heart that it was unlikely—impossible—that treason resided in the First Department, he decided to add Korchnoi to the list for art's sake. He would attend to the Service first, then attend to the American Nash. *Za dvumya zaitsami pogonish'sya ne odnogo ne poimaesh,* he thought. If you chase two rabbits, you will not catch either one.

Chief of Directorate T Yury Nasarenko waited at the threshold of Egorov's office like a serf waiting to be invited into a barn. Tall and gangly, even at the age of fifty, Nasarenko wore thick wire glasses that were bent and pitted with years of absentminded misuse. He had a big head, a jutting forehead, wing-flap ears, and exceptionally bad teeth, even for a Russian. He was a nervous man who twitched, and jerked his head, and bent his thumbs, and touched his sleeves in a constant marionette show of movement. He had a large mole on the left point of his chin, which Egorov used as an aiming point when speaking to Nasarenko to avoid looking at the quivering entirety of the man. Despite his outward habits, Nasarenko was a brilliant technical mind, someone who understood the science of a problem and could also apply theory to operational need or intelligence production.

"Yury, come in. Thank you for coming so promptly," said Egorov, as if Nasarenko had had a choice of appointment times and dates. "Please sit down. Have a cigarette?" Nasarenko sat down, shrugged his shoulders, clasped his hands in his lap, and bent his thumbs twice very fast.

"No, thank you, Ivan Dimitrevich," said Nasarenko. His eyebrows lifted and fell and Egorov fixed his gaze on his chin.

"Yury, I want to tell you that you are doing an exceptional job with the information that is coming in about the Americans' space vehicle. The Service is being complimented at the highest levels on the work so far," said Egorov.

More precisely, *he* was receiving compliments for the SWAN case so far.

"That is good to hear, Ivan Dimitrevich," said Nasarenko. "The information is exceptional. My analysts and I are quite impressed with the brilliance of the concept." Nasarenko looked across the desk at Egorov's impassive wrestler's face. "Of course, Russian space technology is easily the equal of this project," he added with a double bob of his Adam's apple, "but the Americans' work is remarkable."

"I agree," said Egorov, lighting a cigarette. "I wanted to tell you to continue working on your analyses and assessments, but also wanted to notify you that the intelligence stream will temporarily be interrupted. The source of the information, a sensitive source that I cannot describe further for obvious reasons, is wrestling with health matters and must suspend work for a short time." Egorov let the sentence hang in the air.

"Nothing so serious as to curtail the information, I hope?" asked Nasarenko, leaning forward in his chair. His right leg and knee vibrated slightly.

"I sincerely hope not," said Egorov expansively. "An attack of shingles can be debilitating. I am hoping our source will recover soon."

"Yes, of course," said Nasarenko, "we will continue our analysis of the existing information. There's more than enough data to keep us busy for some time."

"Excellent," said Egorov. "I know I can rely on you to keep working." He rose and walked Nasarenko to the door, his hand on the other's jittery shoulder. "Acquiring this information is important, Yury, *but how we exploit it is critical.* That's where you come in." Egorov shook hands with the man and watched him walk away down the corridor toward the elevators. His head to one side, walking with a starboard list, Nasarenko looked like a Petrushka puppet in a Skomorokh show with a cut string. "If such a man is a spy," Egorov whispered to himself, "we are doomed." He turned back into his office.

Line R Chief Boris Alushevsky was no Yury Nasarenko. He tapped once on the frame of Egorov's door and walked calmly across the room, a smooth gait with no affectation. Forty years old, he seemed older and looked thoughtfully dangerous. He was thin, dark, his sunken cheeks and prominent cheekbones were clean-shaven but swarthy. He had black almond-shaped eyes, a strong jaw, and a large nose. The dense thatch of jet-black hair piled on top of his head was wavy and thick and shiny, making Alushevsky look like a Kyrgyz Central Committee member from Bishkek. He was actually from Saint Petersburg.

The chief of Line R (Operational Planning and Analysis) was responsible for evaluating all SVR operations abroad. Alushevsky's English was perfect, after years in London. After returning from Britain, Alushevsky had drifted toward planning and analysis because it suited him. He had an intellect and an inquiring mind. He was, thought Vanya, also a political naïf. It seemed most unlikely that Alushevsky could be the mole. Still, he had evaluated the Washington *rezidentura*'s procedures in handling "the sensitive source" and it was Alushevsky who suggested the use of the Zeta countersurveillance team to protect Rezident Golov during monthly meetings. Therefore Vanya would include him in his canary-trap test.

"Boris, sit down, please," said Egorov. He liked and respected Alushevsky for his work ethic and intelligence. "I have reviewed your recommendations regarding security upgrades in Washington, and I approve."

"Thank you, Ivan Dimitrevich," said Alushevsky. "General Golov is utterly professional on the street. He rarely has FBI surveillance. His assessment is that the Americans believe an officer of his rank and stature would never involve himself in agent handling. It's an advantage to us. The Zeta Team is thorough, discreet. They will provide added protection." Alushevsky accepted a cigarette from Egorov, offered from a mahogany box with a tortoiseshell lid.

"Excellent," said Egorov.

"Technical officers in the *rezidentura* likewise are listening to FBI surveillance frequencies with special care. They especially are looking for anomalies in radio procedure. A change in tactics could indicate heightened interest by the opposition," Alushevsky explained simply, not sure Egorov understood the nuances of the game.

"Boris, I would like you to continue monitoring the security situation and our countermeasures. We have a little extra time to assess the situation."

"How so, Ivan Dimitrevich?" asked Alushevsky.

"I cannot discuss the details of General Golov's case, I regret I cannot, but you surely understand," said Egorov. "It is through no lack of confidence in you, I assure you."

"Of course I understand," said Alushevsky. "Security is security." There was no trace of resentment in his voice.

"I can tell you that Golov's source has to suspend activities for a time. A matter of illness, quite serious, actually." Egorov looked at Alushevsky mildly.

"How long a hiatus will we have?" asked Alushevsky. "It will be important for General Golov not to become suddenly inactive. He must exactly mirror his previous activity levels. *Any* change in his profile could alert the opposition, and that would be doubly dangerous when the general resumes activity in the case."

"I do not know exactly how long the agent will be inactive. Recovery from heart bypass surgery can be lengthy or quick. We shall have to wait and see."

"With your permission, I will draft some additional thoughts for your consideration, and for forwarding to General Golov."

"By all means, I would like to see your ideas. Please submit them as soon as you finish," said Egorov, rising from his seat. "I repeat that I am greatly pleased with your work. Your leadership of Line R is quite satisfactory." Egorov steered Alushevsky to the door and shook his hand.

SVR Americas Department Chief General Vladimir Andreiyevich Korchnoi walked into the outer reception area of Egorov's office twenty minutes late. Egorov's personal aide Dimitri came out of his cubicle and shook hands. Korchnoi took in the fussed disapproval of the two secretaries sitting behind their desks, but he greeted them by name, and his deep brown eyes twinkled under his bushy white brows as he sat on the corner of one desk and told a story. *"There was an announcement of the highest adultery level: First place, Movie Stars; second place, Theater Actors; third place, KGB. Someone shouts: I've been in the KGB for thirty years and I never cheated on my wife! Someone else shouts: It's because of people like you that we're in third place!"*

The secretaries and Dimitri all laughed. Dimitri poured a glass of water for Korchnoi from a carafe on the sideboard. One of the secretaries was in the process of telling another joke when the leather-padded inner door to Egorov's office opened and the deputy director appeared. The secretaries quickly bent their heads to their desks and resumed work. Dimitri nodded courteously at Korchnoi, then at his boss, and retreated into his little cubicle. Egorov surveyed the outer office.

"Quite a lot of merriment out here," said Egorov sternly. "It's no wonder we cannot get anything done."

"Director, the blame is totally mine," said Korchnoi with mock humility. "I disrupted this office with the telling of a silly story, a ridiculous waste of time."

"Yes, and twenty minutes late on top of it," said Egorov. "I trust you have time to speak with me now?" Egorov spun on his heel and went into his office. Korchnoi followed him, nodding at the secretaries as he walked past. The door closed behind him and the secretaries looked at each other, smiling, before returning to their work.

Egorov walked over to the blond-leather couch at the end of his suite and sat down. He patted the seat next to him, indicating that Korchnoi should sit beside him. "Volodya, are you making time with my secretaries? I bet I know which one you fancy, and let me tell you, they're both good in bed."

"Vanya, I'm too old and too tired to sleep with anyone these days. Besides, I wouldn't want to follow your poxy ass in any way. I feel sorry for those young girls out there." Korchnoi sat back in the soft sofa and unbuttoned his jacket.

"I'm pleased that you're commencing with the planning against the American Nash," said Egorov. "I know you will manage it well. It's our best chance to discover the traitor." He got up, went to an ornate cabinet, and retrieved a bottle of Georgian brandy and two glasses. He poured two shots and handed one to Korchnoi.

"This is a little early in the day, Vanya," said Korchnoi. He reached his glass over to touch the rim of Egorov's glass. Both men tilted back their heads and returned the glasses to the table. "No more for me," said Korchnoi as Egorov made to refill their glasses.

"I insist," said Egorov with mock seriousness. "It's the only way I can get you to stay and talk with me. I need someone I trust to talk to."

"We've been friends since the Academy," said Korchnoi. "Is it something about our operation? You're not having second thoughts about your niece. Because if that's it, I can tell you I feel absolutely—"

"No, it's nothing to do with the operation. I have high hopes for it. There's something else," said Vanya. "I have something to get off my chest."

"Are you having troubles, Vanya?" asked Korchnoi. He would not go so far as to ask how Egorov's campaign to supplant the sitting Director was going. Not even their decades-long relationship would give him the license to be so direct.

"The usual headaches and skirmishes. For each success we balance a failure, the loss of a source, a defection, a recruitment."

"Vanya, you know how our business works. We will always have failures, but once every five years, ten, we will have a stupendous success. We are due another. It will come." Korchnoi sipped at the second glass of brandy.

"That's what I wanted to speak to you about," said Egorov. "Volodya, I owe you an apology. I have kept something from you when I should not have. I must continue to keep something from you for a little longer, but I want to tell you a little bit."

"I respect your judgment, Vanya," said Korchnoi.

"You are a true friend, Volodya," said Egorov, pouring another shot of brandy for them both. "I have been running an operation on your turf, in the United States, without your knowledge or consent. By rights, your department should have been managing the case. All I can tell you is that the Kremlin ordered that it be managed in this way."

MARBLE kept his face relaxed. This was it, the Director's Case, SWAN.

"It's not the first time we've done this. I have done it myself. If it's operationally expedient, then you have to do it," said Korchnoi, registering the lie.

"I knew you would consider it professionally. I meant no disrespect to you or your department," said Egorov.

"None taken," said Korchnoi. "Is Golov in Washington aware of the case?" There was a narrow window for a delicate probe. *Softly,* he thought.

"These are details we need not examine," said Egorov, evading the question. "I can tell you that the case is beginning to produce intelligence of a sensitivity and relevance to Russia not seen since 1949 when Feklisov was buying Fuchs ice cream in exchange for his notes on a working bomb." *How apt,* thought Korchnoi. *We peaked as the NKVD in the 1950s.* Egorov laughed and slapped Korchnoi on the back.

"Congratulations are in order, then," said Korchnoi. "These are the twenty-year triumphs we need." He took a sip of his brandy. "Vanya, how can I help?"

"No, no, there's nothing for you to do," said Egorov. "I need you to proceed against the American, even as we have to pause in the sensitive case we are running. When can you move ahead?"

"As soon as is required. Your niece is ready," said Korchnoi easily. "How quickly do we need to move?"

"We have a little time. If you can move now, while our source is recovering from serious eye surgery, the timing will be suitable."

"Not a problem, we will be ready to travel within a few days' time."

"Excellent," said Egorov.

"We'll have success," said Korchnoi. "You can depend on it."

"I am depending on you," said Egorov, "my most trusted *sotrudnik*, my old partner." *You old crocodile,* thought Korchnoi. He got up from the couch and looked out the enormous picture window at the pine forest below. "We've done well, Vanya, especially you. Who would have thought those two young Academy graduates would have such careers?"

"Don't get too maudlin on me yet; we have a lot of work left to do," said Egorov. "Thank you, my friend, for being so loyal, and don't be a stranger for so long next time." They walked arm in arm to the hallway door and bear-hugged briefly.

"Now I return to my office smelling of brandy and your dreadful cologne," said Korchnoi. "I build my reputation as a drunk *and* a *pedik,* thanks to you." They both laughed and Egorov watched Korchnoi walk down the hallway, thinking, *He was brilliant and fearless once, but now he's getting tired.* He turned back into his office and closed the door.

MARBLE's thoughts raced. He would pass the information immediately, a satellite-burst transmission tonight. He imagined Benford reading the note. But there was a whiff of something else. Vanya's invitation to the fourth floor was incongruous, out of character. The apology for running an operation in his territory was so much window dressing. Vanya did not have the slightest qualms about trespassing into an area of operational responsibility. Vanya did only those things that would bring maximum credit and benefit to Vanya. He had always been like that, it was what had decided him to become a bureaucrat and leave true intelligence work to others.

He reviewed the four important details Vanya had provided. The mega-source—SWAN—was a "twenty-year case," providing the best information since the atom spies. The case was being run out of the Washington *rezidentura.* Anatoly Golov was likely involved. SWAN recently had eye surgery. *More clues for Benford,* thought MARBLE.

MARBLE walked down the broad ground-floor corridors and turned into the spacious cafeteria. It was barely eleven thirty, but employees were already bringing food trays to tables to eat their lunches. His head light and stomach churning from Vanya's damn brandy, MARBLE stopped at a counter and ordered a bowl of *gribnoi sup,* thick mushroom soup swirling with sour cream. He saw the Line T chief, Nasarenko, sitting at a table alone and desperately tried to slide away from his line of sight, but Nasarenko saw him and bobbed his head in his direction. Now he would have to go over and sit with him, for as a fellow office chief not to do so would be a breach of protocol. Korchnoi steeled himself to endure twenty minutes of eating soup with the man nicknamed "the Oscilloscope" by the junior scientists in the technical department.

"Yury, how goes it?" said Korchnoi, sitting down at the table. He broke the heel off his bread and dunked it into the steaming soup.

"Too busy, too busy," said Nasarenko. He was sawing at a cabbage roll with disastrous results. Korchnoi could not take his eyes away, like looking at a bad traffic accident. "They have us working overtime. New data coming all the time, translation, analysis, drafting summaries for the fourth floor. An avalanche of discs. They're sending everything to the Kremlin."

Interesting. Discs. It must be the same case, with high-volume production. "Do you need some help? Could I send an analyst or two?" This was an unprecedented act of largesse. No department willingly offered such help. Nasarenko's head shot up, impressed and surprised.

"Vladimir Andreiyevich, that is very kind of you. I appreciate the offer," said Nasarenko, chewing half a cabbage roll. "But the work must be confined to a small number of cleared analysts. It is a requirement."

"Well, let me know if I can help you in any appropriate way. I know how it feels to be swamped with work," said Korchnoi.

"We should have a respite soon. Egorov told me there would be a temporary suspension of information." Nasarenko leaned over his plate toward Korchnoi, his Adam's apple bobbing as he puffed his cheeks out. "The source has had a bout of shingles, he's incapacitated." Nasarenko was committing a serious breach of security, but Korchnoi was a fellow department chief, after all, a clandestine operator with a well-respected record.

MARBLE felt an icy finger trace his spine. The cafeteria walls closed in on him, the voices in the room became a dull roar. He made himself take a spoonful of the soup. "Well, that's certainly good news for you. We take all the breaks we can." Korchnoi lowered his voice. "Yury, we probably shouldn't be speaking of these matters. You know about the sensitivity of this activity better than I. Let's not mention this conversation to anybody, don't you agree?"

Nasarenko's dark-brown eyes flickered guiltily when he realized what the general was hinting at. "I agree completely," he said. He gathered his plate and stood, murmuring apologies for leaving so suddenly. MARBLE sat alone, forcing himself to spoon more soup, trying to appear natural and at ease.

Was this the beginning of the end for him, was this a snare, did they suspect him specifically? Or was this a general test for loyalty? He wryly shook his head at Vanya's canary trap, variants fed to God knows how many senior managers, with his little silver spoon. *Here, little* kolibri, *little hummingbird, how do you spread your pollen?* His message to Langley suddenly became more critical than ever.

GRIBNOI SUP—MUSHROOM SOUP

Soak dried mushrooms and strain. Add soaking liquid to beef stock and boil mushrooms for four hours. Sauté finely diced onions in butter until golden and add to soup. Whisk in cornstarch, stir, and simmer until thickened. Season and serve with a dollop of sour cream and parsley.

29

Benford sat in semidarkness in his office, the covcom message alert cable on the small square of visible desk amid the landfill chaos of the rest of it. He had read MARBLE's cryptic message twice, hearing his voice as he read the words, seeing him conserving the limited characters allowable in a burst transmission. He bellowed to his secretary to fetch Nate and Alice immediately. While he waited, he read the message again:

```
One: SWAN definitely in US. V says
SWAN material best since 50s. Poss
he working out of capital city. Golov
likely handler. Nasarenko claims work
overload, discs and technical data.

Two: V running canary trap. Nasarenko
told big source suffering shingles. I
told he recovering eye surgery. Other
variants likely.

Three: V renewing op vs NN. I assigned
to direct (!) V niece in my dept, tar-
geted against NN.

Four: Anticipate travel Rome coincide
with EBES conference. Will advise when
out. niko.
```

Benford's eyes lingered on the lowercase *n* in the niko signature, which in simple terms was the "no duress" indicator, but which more specifically meant that MARBLE had not composed the message with a circle of men standing around him, one of whom was prying the little finger of his left hand straight up, close to the breaking point, as he wrote what they wanted.

SWAN was a mole in the US government. Game on. That this was considered by the Russians the best case in years suggested SWAN's intelligence had quality as well as quantity; it meant to Benford that the United States was hemorrhaging information. When Alice stuck her head in the door, Benford told her he was assigning her a single project, starting right now.

"I have the double agent thing in Brazil," said Alice bluntly. She was not afraid of contradicting Benford.

"That bullshit can wait," said Benford without looking up from his desk. "I want you to drop everything and compile a list. It'll be unlike anything you have ever done before."

"Do tell," said Alice, vaguely looking for a place to sit. She found none and remained standing in front of Benford's desk.

"It's going to be a little unconventional, but that's right up your alley, Alice," said Benford. He looked up. "I want you to draw up a Top Ten list for me. I want you to identify the ten biggest secrets in the United States government. It could be military, political, domestic, cyber, banking, space, energy, Islam, or the tattoo on Pat Benatar's ass, I don't care—"

"On whose ass?" asked Alice.

"Pat Benatar, the pop singer," said Benford defensively. "Start with the Pentagon and their hottest SAPs, military secrets, that's what excites the Russians the most. Find out what DoD considers their ultrasensitive projects. Long-term. Expensive. Strategic. Get the deputy director for military affairs to make a call to SecDef if necessary. Politely ask them to get off their asses and hurry up. Then when we see what they consider the crown jewels, we can begin reviewing the BIGOT lists." Alice moved to the door just as Nate entered. As they squeezed past each other, Alice turned to him.

"Do you know who Pat Benatar is?" asked Alice.

"Never heard of him," said Nate, clearing files off a small chair and sitting down. "Is he the FBI guy in Boston who covered the New England thing?"

"Forget it," said Benford. "Thank you, Alice, get started on that right away, will you?" Benford turned to Nate and handed him the copy of the MARBLE message. He could see Nate's cheeks color as he read about Dominika. Nate reread the message as if he could squeeze more information out of the spare lines. He looked up at Benford.

"She's alive."

"Not only is DIVA alive, but it appears she made it through the wringer," said Benford. "And now her uncle has had the inexpressible good sense to assign her to MARBLE." Benford thought again of MARBLE's succession strategy.

"Do you think she'll come out with MARBLE to Rome?" asked Nate.

"I suggest you take a cold shower," drawled Benford. "She may never be totally trusted, or alternatively she may be fully reinstated. Right now we take advantage of the fact that an agent recruited by you—DIVA—and narrowly cleared in a recent CI investigation has been assigned by an unsuspecting Center to seduce you with the goal of eliciting the name of the senior SVR officer you handle—MARBLE—who coincidentally is DIVA's new boss and who is directing her in the operation to unman you, his case officer." Benford looked at Nate from between twin towers of newspapers and file folders, the medieval alchemist who's misplaced the philosopher's stone.

"You love this shit, don't you?" said Nate.

"I expect you to deal with ambiguity. If you are not capable of it, you should leave immediately." Benford glowered at Nate.

"Well, how would you proceed?" said Benford, throwing him the bone.

Nate took a breath and tried to clear his mind of Dominika. "The message tells us that they still have no clue about MARBLE, his identity."

"And how do you conclude that?" asked Benford.

"Egorov is dangling different variations of stories about SWAN in front of various department heads. It shows he's desperate."

"What else?" said Benford.

"If Egorov has been feeding his top managers barium meals, it suggests he expects he will get results, that one of the variants will get back to him."

"And?" said Benford.

"And that suggests he has someone inside the US government who would *be positioned to hear* a variant and report back. In the Intelligence Community. SWAN?"

"It could," said Benford. "What other tidbit in the message could help us do something about finding SWAN?" Nate looked down again, then up at Benford.

"Give me a clue," Nate said.

"Nasarenko."

Nate looked at the message again. He looked up suddenly.

"We know the variant told to Nasarenko," said Nate, "so we spread that variant around, carefully, keeping track of who we flog it to. If Nasarenko's fortunes suddenly change, we have a place to start, a finite list of people."

"And Vanya Egorov's barium meal turns into a barium enema," said Benford. "In all of this, please do not forget that he's impatient and desperate. You represent a shortcut for Egorov to solve the one problem that will keep him off the bascule of the guillotine. He's concentrating on you." Nate was thinking about Dominika again, and Benford saw it in his face, and groaned theatrically.

"Enough about you, disappointing as that may be," said Benford. "Clear your mind and tell me what you would do in the immediate matter of SWAN. If MARBLE is correct, the case is being run here in Washington, by the *rezident* himself."

"If Golov personally is handling SWAN, that's a weak point for them," said Nate. "I think we should consider covering the *rezident*."

"Brilliant. But how do we work Golov? What would you do?" asked Benford, nudging Nate forward.

"We starve him for a month. We surveil him pretty close, shut him down. Look, don't get mad, but we should bring the FEEBs into this. If we're going to be playing with Golov in downtown Washington, the FBI has to be involved. The FCI guys, foreign counterintelligence, are the best, real spy chasers, and the Gs know what they're doing on the street. Awesome surveillance team.

"Total coverage, they'll make so much noise that Golov will call a dozen aborts in a dozen tries. He won't be able to meet SWAN. The Center will start getting nervous. Golov will start sweating. They'll be frantic about losing contact with their agent. And we can only guess at the effect it will have on SWAN."

"All right, so now you've made him nervous. He's still too good to make a mistake on the street," said Benford, "and he'll have CS covering him too."

"That's okay," said Nate. "One dark and stormy night we let him go surveillance-free. He'll see he's black, his countersurveillance will confirm it, and he makes the decision to make the meeting. And we have the Orions and TrapDoor up and running ahead of him. That's when we maybe get a glimpse of a nervous SWAN pacing on a street corner, or pick up the license plates of an out-of-place car parked wrong. And we keep trying till we hit."

Benford nodded approval. The kid had been on the other end, staring into the FSB barrel on the mean streets of Moskva. Benford knew what an agent's vulnerabilities were, what scared his handler. Nate was coming along, he noted with satisfaction.

Benford owned the Orions, kept them off people's screens, didn't loan them out. Who would want them, the geriatric surveillance team of retired field officers? Clunky cars, black socks and sandals, bird-watcher's binoculars. The size of the team was fluid, grew or shrank depending on personal schedules, grandchildren's visits, or doctors' appointments. It was the very nature of the Orions—slow, patient, thoughtful—that made them so effective. It was impossible to goad them with provocative counter-maneuvers. They watched, waited, faded in and out. They caressed their targets, they sniffed delicately, they flooded and ebbed like the tide. But they never stopped coming at you.

And they used TrapDoor. Only a certain kind of surveillance team could make TrapDoor work, a different kind of coverage, a philosophy, the difference between a dog chasing a car and a cat watching a bird. They had worked on it for some time. The Orions had perfected it, grease pencil on laminated maps, the overall compass vector telegraphed by a rabbit who is, after all, nothing but human. Never mind the twists and turns, the reverses and funnels, tell me where he's going, where he's *headed*.

They had brought federal surveillance experts in

to observe the Orions, wanted to train other teams to get the same results, wanted to put a label on their black magic. *Predictive coverage based on profile analysis,* they wrote. *Situational projections supporting discreet surveillance,* they wrote. *Anticipatory deployments determined by "route of march" balanced by mitigation of acceptable risk,* they wrote.

Pretty much all nonsense, the Orions said. It was about developing a feeling, making a guess, taking a chance. The feds blinked at them. Think of it this way, said the sixty-eight-year-old team member who early in his career had tapped the GRU telephone exchange from the Berlin Tunnel. We're an *amoeba.* You know, protoplasm, flexible, soft, stretching out ahead on either side, flowing along the edges. The experts smiled politely. How the hell do you put that in a field manual?

During street demonstrations, the experts looked for the Orions in the usual surveillance-team positions. They had disappeared. This isn't coverage, the target has been left unobserved, where is the team? But when the rabbit arrived at the site, the Orions were waiting, parked in the neighborhood, in the park, at the crossroads, waiting so quietly that they didn't see them. Crackpot ideas, alchemy, said the feds, thanks very much. They left the Orions to Benford.

So they began looking at Golov, and the assessment began. Quite a distinguished gentleman, still a proto-commie, smooth and unruffled. Get to know him, said Benford, and mind the CS team covering him. Stay loose, observe, stay invisible.

"All right," Benford said, "it's time to put Mr. Golov out of work for a while." The next morning the FBI Gs were outside the embassy of the Russian Federation on Wisconsin Avenue, slumped in their Crown Vics, wearing Oakleys, with *Bring it* in their faces and two hundred fifty horses under their hoods.

Closed sessions of the SSCI to discuss "intelligence matters" were held in Room 216 of the Hart Senate Office Building on Constitution Avenue. Designated HS, for "Hart Senate," in congressional directories, the building was a nine-story black-glass-and-marble tower, not at all like the more elegant neoclassical Dirksen and Russell Senate Office Buildings. Arriving alone, Benford crossed the soaring atrium lobby and took the stairs to the second floor. At Room 216, he entered the outer office, registered with the guard behind the counter, and surrendered his mobile phone. He stepped through the open gray steel vault door into the committee room. He was early for the session and the room was empty except for aides distributing folders at each position on the raised oak dais. Of course the dais was raised, thought Benford. Senators enjoyed looking down at witnesses.

Invisible behind the marble- and wood-paneled walls, ceiling, and floor of the committee room was a hatchwork grid of copper filaments continuously pulsing energy that ensured that, once the latches dogged the vault door tight against the copper finger stock around the frame, no signals could penetrate into or escape out of the room.

In the 1980s, in an attempt to eavesdrop on sensitive SSCI testimony, the Russians had mounted an operation to leave behind recording equipment in the room that could be retrieved later, a simple technique to negate the electronic chastity belt. The audacious plan had been foiled by a janitor who found the device (which had been glued beneath a chair in the audience gallery during an infrequent open session of the committee) and turned it in to the Capitol Police, who promptly passed it to the FBI. Rather than replacing it and feeding the Soviets disinformation for years, thought Benford, looking around the august chamber, the FBI had exulted in a "foreign find"—a listening device planted by the opposition—and ground the recorder to pieces under its heel, an opportunity squandered.

Benford was the only person seated at the witness table. An aide placed a small card with his name in front of him. At the members' insistence, Benford held a counterintelligence briefing every three months for the SSCI, a session that only the fifteen members of the committee were permitted to attend. Senators long accustomed to staff aides hovering nearby grudgingly complied with the requirement that no staffers be permitted in the room, which meant that few if any notes would be taken.

Members rarely missed Benford's quarterly CI brief, generally reckoned to be the most concise and informative presentation available from anywhere inside the Intelligence Community. But for a single member of the committee, the SSCI treated him with respect. Only Senator Stephanie Boucher from California seemed to harbor intense dislike for IC witnesses, specifically those from the CIA. As the members trickled into the room and sat down, Boucher looked down at Benford with a scowl. Benford ignored her and made a note in the margin of his briefing outline. The committee members were seated, the staff aides filed out, the vault door was swung shut. As it closed, a small green light came on over the door. The chairman simply said, "Mr. Benford," to indicate that he should begin.

Benford quickly highlighted developments in a Chinese cyber case on the West Coast, but referred members to COD, the Computer Ops Division in the CIA, nicknamed the "codpieces," for a more detailed briefing on the nature of the threat. Benford moved to a sensitive case wherein the CIA and FBI had detected officers of the DGSE, the French External Intelligence Service, servicing a dead-drop site in upstate New York. A joint briefing with the FBI's French Regional Ops Group, nicknamed "FROG," on French activities inside the continental United States was being prepared. Benford turned the page of his briefing book.

"Senators, the CIA, along with the US Navy and the relevant contractor, has finished the preliminary damage assessment from the Russian illegal in New London, Connecticut." Benford looked down at his notes. "While the Pentagon is still preparing a report on the long-term ramifications of the penetration of the navy program, initial conclusions are that the Russians did not acquire sufficient technical intelligence to materially degrade the operational viability of the platform—"

"Excuse me, Mr. Benford," said Senator Boucher. Her fellow senators recognized the attack display and braced themselves. "Why do you use *platform* when you can just as clearly say *submarine* when talking about them?"

"Submarine, then, thank you, Senator," said Benford. He waited for the codicil. Boucher expostulated briefly on the outmoded capabilities of US subs as compared with the Dolgorukiy class of ballistic submarines just now making their appearance in the Russian Navy. *She is well-read,* thought Benford. The senator swerved again.

"But wouldn't you say that the real counterintelligence issue, the real teachable moment coming out of New London, is that neither American intelligence nor law enforcement had the wit to detect, locate, and apprehend a Russian illegal officer operating in the United States for nearly half a decade? This illegal moreover had infiltrated the program with apparent ease, despite background and security checks." Boucher tapped a pencil on the blotter in front of her.

"Since the end of the Cold War, Senator, the classic use of illegals is extremely rare. Even the Russians acknowledge that it is a costly and inefficient way to collect intelligence," said Benford. He would under no circumstances mention how they had gotten onto the illegal in the first place.

"That's not at all what I asked, Mr. Benford. Pay attention. I asked which agency, in your opinion, is the more incompetent: the CIA or the FBI?"

"I have no opinion on the matter, Senator," said Benford. "In the aftermath of the New London affair we, unfortunately, have bigger fish to fry."

"What kind of fish?" asked Boucher.

"We have indications that the Russians are running a separate reporting source. Someone with good access. We are just starting; there's nothing confirmed," said Benford.

"Stop this tap dance," snapped Boucher. "What are you talking about?"

Benford took an audible deep breath. He closed his briefing book and folded his hands on top of the cover. He looked at the Senate seal on the wall above the members' heads. "We have fragmentary information that there is a high-level penetration of the US government with exceptional access to national security secrets currently being handled by the SVR."

"How close are you to identifying this leak?" asked the senator from Florida.

"We do not know who, what, or where," said Benford. "We're checking every possibility."

"Sounds like you don't have the slightest idea," said Boucher.

"Senator, these investigations take time," offered the senator from New York.

Boucher laughed. "Yeah, I know all about these investigations. Hundreds of people keeping busy and drawing salaries, but no one seems to catch anyone."

Benford let the members talk among themselves for a minute before raising his voice again. "As we try to develop more information, we do have an unsubstantiated report that the individual in question might suffer from an incapacitating condition—shingles. It may be useful later, as we narrow our search and begin cross-checking."

"This is all inconclusive," said Boucher, turning toward the dais. "If my committee colleagues have no objection, I must excuse myself for another important meeting of a separate committee." She turned to Benford. "I'm done for today." Boucher rose from her seat, gathered her classified folder, and walked to the door. The other senators rustled papers and fell silent as Boucher opened the massive door and left the room.

Benford did not raise his head. It was done. Fifteen of them had heard "shingles." Two days earlier three undersecretaries of defense in a Pentagon briefing had heard the same thing, and in three days so would the special assistant to the president and senior director for Defense during a brief to selected NSC staff.

As he snapped his briefcase shut in the empty SSCI committee room, Benford pictured the jowly faces in the Kremlin and thought, *You want a canary, comrades, I'll give you a canary.*

General Korchnoi had been summoned to the Director's secure conference room on the fourth floor of Yasenevo by Vanya Egorov's aide. Dimitri had called him the instant he stepped into his office, even before Korchnoi had hung his coat in the closet and sat down to review morning traffic. It sounded urgent. The general looked wistfully at the covered plate of *syrniki,* hot cheese pancakes with sour cream that his secretary had left for him and that he had planned to munch as he read. They would grow cold and rubbery before he could get back. As he left his office, he rolled up one of the pancakes and stuffed it into his mouth.

Since he had discovered that Vanya was playing games, setting canary traps, dredging for the CIA mole within the SVR, Korchnoi's double life hardened from a now-familiar baseline of danger into one of imminent, guilty dread. For fourteen years he had lived under constant pressure; he had learned to accommodate it, but there was a difference between spying undetected and being hunted.

As he pushed through the front doors of Headquarters each morning, he was never sure whether he would be greeted by stone-faced security officers who would hustle him from the lobby into a side room. Every time the phone rang on his desk, he could never know it was not a summons to a windowless room filled with unsmiling faces. Every weekend outing was a potential ambush arrest on a wooded country road or in a lonely dacha.

Korchnoi got off the elevator and walked past the portraits. *Hello, old walruses,* he thought. *Have you caught me yet?* He entered the executive conference room to see Vanya Egorov sitting on the corner of the table laughing at something Line KR Chief Alexei Zyuganov was saying. *This is the little* domovoi, *the little goblin, who stuffed rags into prisoners' mouths before shooting them in the forehead because their cries for mercy* bothered *him,* thought Korchnoi. Zyuganov watched as the general walked across the room toward them.

Egorov's big marble head glistened, and his shirt was fresh and starched. He hugged his old friend and waved him to a seat. "I wanted to meet here, Volodya, because they can set up the projector. Since you're now directing the operation, I wanted to show you some extra material." He picked up a remote control and pushed a button. Projected on the wall was a grainy photograph of Nathaniel Nash, hands in the pockets of a coat, hunched against the cold, walking along what looked like a Moscow street. "You wouldn't know this man, Volodya, but he is the CIA officer Nash, who is handling the traitor. He was posted to Moscow for less than two years and left approximately eighteen months ago."

Korchnoi wondered first whether the surveillance photo of Nate had been taken while he was on the way back from one of their meetings. Then he wondered whether this was all sarcastic drama to bait him. Would the conference-room doors burst open to admit rushing security men? Was Egorov this devious, would he be inclined to torment him this way? *No,* Korchnoi thought, *it's nothing. This is your life, breathe it in, circle the abyss, stay cool.*

"This Nash was very skillful. But for one bungled near miss, we never were able to determine even a mote of his activities." Egorov paused to light a cigarette. He offered the pack around the table. Korchnoi filed away the words that seemed to confirm he was still safe. Unless this was all Egorov's elaborate red herring.

"I personally believe that the traitor is in the Service," said Egorov, while Zyuganov looked evenly at the image of Nash on the screen. Were they playing with him? Korchnoi thought. Zyuganov easily could be this diabolical.

"It is an assumption you're making about the Service," prattled Zyuganov. "One thing is sure. The Americans would not run the extraordinary risk of meetings in Moscow to handle a low-level source."

Say something, be casual. "If you're both right, brothers," said Korchnoi, "and he's a big fish *and* he's in the Service, then the short list of candidates would be the Director, you, Vanya, and the twelve department heads, including Lyosha and me." Korchnoi saw their sour looks. What was he doing? This was exhilarating madness.

"That, of course, is not considering that it could additionally be your special assistant, or a secretary, or a communications-code clerk, or a hundred other employees with indirect access to cable reading boards, their bosses' in-boxes, and to unguarded conversations in anterooms and the cafeteria. Clerks in Records see more sensitive paper in a day than the three of us combined see in a week." Korchnoi could tell from Zyuganov's expression that he had already calculated all that. All the more people to interrogate.

Korchnoi decided to stop there. *Too much analysis, too many pat phrases.* Egorov ground out his cigarette. "You are exactly correct, Volodya. There are too many possibilities. We'll catch this *svoloch* only if we get a creditable internal lead, or if we catch him or his handler on the street. These two options could take months, even years. That's why our third option is the only one."

"*Dogovorilis,* agreed; your niece is our best chance," said Korchnoi. This scene was unthinkable, improbable, impossible. He suppressed insane, cackling laughter. He was discussing finding the spy, flushing him out, exposing him, catching him.

Zyuganov swiveled in his chair, his feet not touching the carpet. "And if your niece does not succeed in a reasonable amount of time? Perhaps we then consider other means."

Egorov turned to him quickly. "Absolutely not. I have received instructions from the highest levels. No 'active measures' in this operation. Is that clear?" Zyuganov swiveled a little more, a faint smile on his face.

"You're right," said Korchnoi. "In the history of

our Service, in the history of postwar intelligence operations, no service has ever *intentionally* harmed an officer of an opposing service. It is not done. It would create havoc." Zyuganov swiveled.

"Volodya, relax. If we wanted to try the rough stuff, I'd be talking to Line F, not you," said Egorov, laughing. Korchnoi saw Zyuganov's right eyelid twitch. "No, what I want is an elegant operation, nuanced, brilliant, that will produce quick results and will leave the Main Enemy wondering what hit them, wondering how they lost their sensitive asset and marveling at the SVR's skill and cunning."

MARBLE'S SYRNIKI PANCAKES

Thoroughly blend soft goat cheese, eggs, sugar, salt, and flour into a sticky dough. Refrigerate. Drop small balls of the dough into flour, coat well, and flatten into thin discs. Fry in melted butter over medium heat until golden. Serve with sour cream, caviar, smoked fish, or jam.

30

Korchnoi and Dominika were standing in the tiny living room of the general's apartment. The old man contemplated her unsettling beauty, and noted how smoothly she moved, how she walked with her back straight, how her eyes locked on his. The more time he spent with her, the more he was convinced that he had chosen correctly. Now he had to enlist her. Tonight would be tricky.

Outwardly she was unemotional, controlled, focused. But in her interactions, her gestures, even in her deference to him, Korchnoi saw her anger and determination. She had never spoken about Sparrow School, but Korchnoi had quietly found out most of the facts, just as he had done regarding her interrogation in Lefortovo.

She was hiding something, he knew. She daily declared herself eager to engage again with the American. But the timbre of her voice, the tilt of her head, made Korchnoi suspect that Dominika's contact with Nathaniel in Helsinki had created conflicts, sympathies, perhaps feelings for him. He would soon find out.

They had started work on the "Nash Project," as he called it. In his darkened office with the shades drawn, the general had clicked a remote, and images of Nate were projected on the white wall of the office. Out of the corner of his eye, Korchnoi saw Dominika draw in a breath. From the side, he could see her nostril flare. He went on remorselessly, minutely describing what the SVR knew about Nash, reviewing her own reports from Helsinki, watching her, weighing her inner reserves.

He had turned off the projector and looked at her sternly. This was more complicated than the previous mission in Helsinki, he told her. Dominika must travel outside Russia, and in order to make her foreign trips plausible, she would be reassigned to the SVR Courier Service in Directorate OT. She had to operate alone, in the West. She had to get close to and seduce the young American, identify the *krysa,* the rat. Could she still do that? Her dark eyes flashed, wavered. Emotion. Conflict.

It was a serious challenge for Dominika to look at Nate's image on the screen. Had the general sensed her agitation? How long could she continue to fool him? Could he tell?

That evening, Korchnoi invited Dominika to his apartment. He would prepare a simple supper, a decidedly un-Russian pasta dish in celebration of their upcoming Rome trip, and they would continue discussing the operation. There was no hint of anything improper. General Korchnoi was a distinguished senior officer, a veteran spy, not a *grubyj chelovek,* a cad. They rode the Metro, got off at Strogino in the Fourth District, and walked along a broad leafy park beside the Moskva River. Korchnoi's apartment building was the third in a line of five identical buildings, tubular high-rises in a row, streaked like candy canes from the rusting window frames. His apartment was on the twelfth floor—the dingy elevator groaned loudly as it carried them up.

The small apartment was spare but clean and comfortable, the living space of a person who lived alone, but who didn't mind. There were a few treasures. An exquisite little framed Italian oil on the wall, a silk Persian carpet on the floor; these hinted at a career of foreign travel. In the corner were a well-worn easy chair, a reading lamp, and a low bookcase with a few bound volumes. The small room had a sweeping view of the oxbow curve of the river.

Dominika saw a framed picture of a woman and a very young-looking Korchnoi standing in front of a lake. It was summer and his arm was around her waist. "That was in 1973," said Korchnoi. "One of the Italian lakes, Maggiore, I think."

"Is this your wife?" asked Dominika. "She's very beautiful."

"Twenty-six years of marriage," he said, taking the frame from Dominika and tilting it toward the fading daylight to look at it. "We traveled together around the world. Italy, Malaysia, Morocco, New York." He put the frame back down on the table. "Then she became ill. Misdiagnosed for months." They walked into the tiny kitchen. "Don't get sick at a Russian Embassy overseas." He smiled. Dominika noticed his head was bowed.

The general said he had moved into this apartment after his wife's death, he couldn't go back to their original apartment. He had traded it for this smaller one, relatively modern, relatively quiet, not too far out of town; he could enjoy the swath of green along the river. He didn't tell Dominika that burst transmissions aimed out the twelfth-story living room window had exceptionally fine line-of-sight to the American satellite.

He poured two amber glasses of sweet Moldovan wine. The kitchen had a sink, a small refrigerator that rattled when the door was open, and a three-burner cooktop on the counter. Dominika leaned against the counter and solemnly toasted to the successful outcome of their operation. The general was at ease, she saw. He radiated a warm purple glow that came from the depths of him.

In her short time in Korchnoi's department, Dominika had grown truly fond of him. Apart from his obvious technical brilliance and his uncanny instincts, he had treated her with respect and, even, kindness, as if he was sorry for what she had endured up until now. And there was his loyalty to her. At a meeting in the department, Korchnoi had defended and endorsed Dominika's comment about an operation. Actually stood up for her. *Where have you been all my life?* she thought, reminded again of her father. The double game she was playing would wound him if it came out, might even hasten the end of his career. Would he understand her motives?

As he prepared supper, Korchnoi asked Dominika about herself, her family. Outside the discipline and protocol of the office, she spoke freely, affectionately, about her parents, about her study of ballet, about her delight in discovering the West. Helsinki had been a marvel to her, she wanted to travel around the world. Talking like this to him almost made her forget how she was lying to him. She stuffed the thought under the rug.

"And yet something happened to you in Helsinki," said Korchnoi, busy at the kitchen counter. "Can you tell me about it?" She hesitated, gathering her thoughts, while she watched him dice tomatoes, garlic, and onions and sauté them in a pan of hot olive oil. Udivetelno, *remarkable, he knows Italian cooking,* she thought. The kitchen was instantly filled with the aroma.

"The American volunteer I helped handle," she said, draining her glass, "was arrested minutes after passing the document. The *rezident* was the only other person who knew about the meeting. They could not understand how it happened. They naturally suspected the worst, that I had leaked the information to the Americans." Korchnoi poured her another glass of wine.

"But they concluded in the end that it wasn't me," she said simply, ending it, not wanting to talk about it anymore, not wanting to keep lying to him.

"Yes. But I meant something *else* happened to you in Helsinki," said Korchnoi slowly. "I read your reports. Despite somewhat regular contacts with Nash, there was very little actual progress with him." Dominika heard the tone in his voice, considered his choice of words. *Be careful,* she thought, *he's just started working.*

"Yes, that's right," said Dominika evenly. "He was uninterested, avoided sustained contact. It was a struggle to get him to come out." Could he hear the lie?

"It's strange. A woman with your beauty. And a young man, attractive, single, an intelligence officer living in a foreign country . . ." Korchnoi let the thought trail off. The tomato sauce was bubbling.

Dominika watched as the general poured a splash of balsamic vinegar into the pan, stirred, and began tearing pieces of basil into the sauce. His halo was growing brighter. She was silent, watching Korchnoi's hands pluck the leaves from the stem.

He looked up at her. Neither Benford nor Nate had told him the CIA had recruited her in Finland, but he knew it was the answer. *Let's tip over the goblet,* he thought.

"You have been exceptionally lucky up to this point, my dear," said Korchnoi softly. "Even now, with the Soviet Union long gone, the *chudovishche,* the monster, is right beneath the surface."

Dominika felt real alarm; he was drawing her in, she could feel it. She hadn't been that clever with him after all. He suspected, no, this old *fokusnik,* this conjurer, knew. If she lied, continued to show him disrespect, he could take her off the operation, kick her out of his department. If she put her life in his hands and admitted everything, why wouldn't he report her instantly? Lefortovo would be mild compared to what they would arrange for her then. *Defend yourself,* she thought, *protect yourself.*

"I know about the monster," she said loftily. "I slept in the basement of Lefortovo. They forced me through State School Four, Sparrow School. I watched them murder a man with a wire; they almost sawed his head off. My friend Marta disappeared in Helsinki. They said she defected, but I know better." She realized that her voice was loud in the little kitchen.

She builds up quite a head of steam very quickly, thought Korchnoi. *A little more,* he thought. "The young American, Nash, did you like him?" he asked.

"I suppose so," said Dominika. "He was funny and courteous and pleasant. I never knew Americans were like that." *My God, I said* courteous? She thought she sounded idiotic. He was still looking at her, glowing purple, but with calmness. She felt like a bird, mesmerized, unable to move, watching the emerald-green snake glide up the branch toward the nest.

"I have the impression that you knew this young man rather better than you reported during your assignment in Helsinki," said Korchnoi. He paused and stirred the sauce slowly, the only sound in the kitchen. Korchnoi's voice was very soft. He would try it. "How did they recruit you?" he asked.

Dominika was still. She looked across at him. She opened her mouth but couldn't speak. This was where the risk, the danger that defined her secret life culminated; this was much worse than resisting the brutes in Lefortovo. Her hands shook as she put down her wineglass. Korchnoi was stirring the sauce, the kitchen was filled with his expanding purple bubble, she could feel his overwhelming will. *Protect yourself, you are the only one who can save yourself, leave, get out of here.* Then Korchnoi, the canny master, said a remarkable thing.

"Dominika, I can see it, I am giving you the *opportunity* to tell me, to trust me. I will not harm you." *My God, what an interrogator he would make,* but her intuition told her he was telling the truth, he *would* protect her; she *wanted* him to help her, to share her burden, she *needed* it.

"I started out by following orders, trying to develop him, just as he was developing me," she said, physically shaking. "It was a race to see who would recruit the other first." She still resisted, she was still hanging on to the lip of the cliff. This was an evasion, not an admission.

He wasn't going to let her slide. "Yes, of course," said Korchnoi. "But listen to me very carefully. I asked you how they recruited you."

Dominika's voice was almost inaudible, she was sleepwalking. He raised an eyebrow, and she decided, she placed her beating heart in his hand, she stepped off into space. "They didn't recruit me. I *chose* to work with them. It was my decision. So I did, on my own terms."

Korchnoi filled a pot with water from the sink, put it on a second burner, and threw a handful of salt into the water. He motioned her to come to the stove, handed her the spoon. Dominika stood over the sauce, stirring. "It wasn't a matter of love at all," she said in a small voice. "It was my choice."

Korchnoi did not reply, but she knew she was safe. She was soaring over the cliff now, the wind roaring around her, the sea below exploding against the rocks, and she was flying. *She knew she was safe with him.*

Korchnoi was satisfied. He did not view her admission as weakness or folly or stupidity. He saw how she had calculated, how she had assessed his intentions, but most important, how she had accepted mortal risk, based on her extraordinary intuition. A formidable combination. Her admission also demonstrated her trust in him. That was important. She would need to trust him in the near future.

Now it was he who had to take a chance. In fourteen years he had never slipped, but they had to be partners if this succession strategy was going to work. Telling her would be as difficult for him as it just was for her.

They stood shoulder to shoulder at the little cooking element, the gas hissing through the burners, the sauce simmering in the pan. The wooden spoon made a soft sound, almost a musical note, against the thin aluminum as Dominika pushed the thickening tomatoes around. She turned her face toward Korchnoi; up close her beauty was matchless, but she didn't use it. "What do we do now?" she asked quietly. "Are you going to report me?" She wanted him to say it, to declare it.

"I shall report you if you overcook the pasta," said the general, twisting a fistful of dry bucatini so it fell into the boiling water in a fan pattern. "And watch the sauce doesn't burn on the bottom. I'm taking off my coat and tie." He started down the little hall to his bedroom, then stopped and turned to her. *Now.*

"Perhaps you're wondering," he said. "My grief can't bring her back, but since my wife died, I have not believed in the cause; my heart was hardened toward Them forever. I did my work, but I never again became one of them. They did not earn my loyalty, nor do they deserve yours now. They warrant our contempt." It was done. He stood looking at her: her eyes were wide; her agile mind grasped the implication before he finished loosening the knot of his necktie. She spoke in a whisper.

"It's you? You are the one they are looking for? You're the—" Korchnoi put a finger to his lips to silence her.

"Mind the sauce, keep stirring," he said, turning down the hallway, leaving Dominika staring after his gray head and purple mantle.

"We assess the potential for success as good, the operational risk as minimal," said General Korchnoi. "We are ready to initiate, in Rome. I am familiar with the city."

"Go on," said Vanya. They were seated on the couch in his office. Zyuganov was in a chair to one side.

"Corporal Egorova will approach the American CIA chief in Rome. We know the address of his residence in Centro Storico. We will choose a sleepy Sunday afternoon when everyone is glued to the game on the telly. Corporal Egorova will explain she is an SVR courier with only a few days in Rome. She has run a fearful risk by coming to him. She wants to contact Mr. Nash, Nathaniel, whom she knew in Scandinavia. The COS will know what to do. He will call and Nash will be on the next plane to Rome."

"And once Nash arrives?" asked Egorov.

"It is likely that they will meet in Nash's hotel room," said Korchnoi. "Standard procedure. She will tell him she has been transferred to the Courier Service, and that she will be making regular trips to Europe, Asia, South America. The Americans, of course, will be interested in her access. The possibility of intercepting an SVR pouch will excite them. With this cover legend we can dictate the frequency and duration of future contacts. Corporal Egorova will then rekindle the relationship that was started in Helsinki."

"Very good," said Egorov.

"I will remain behind the scenes," said Korchnoi, "providing guidance as required."

"I expect positive results," said Vanya.

"May I make a suggestion to my operational colleagues?" said Zyuganov. "Why not have Nash come to Corporal Egorova's hotel room? More control, more secure." Korchnoi wondered why the dwarf would suggest this.

"A small detail at this stage," said Vanya, waving his hand. "Concentrate on positive results."

"Of course," said Zyuganov, deferring to his chief. He turned to Korchnoi. "You will, of course, keep Yasenevo advised of your status, the meetings, locations."

Korchnoi nodded pleasantly. "Of course, I will report regularly, security and tradecraft permitting."

"Thank you," said Zyuganov.

Korchnoi and Dominika walked down a corridor in headquarters. They each knew the other's secret now. It was unspoken, but each glance between them now was more knowing, the bond like leg irons—unbreakable and, perhaps, a bit uncomfortable. She walked beside him steadily, a little hitch in her walk, but really she was flying. She would see Rome for the first time, would see Nate again.

Dominika sensed the general's agitation. He was unsettled and nervous. She looked over at him as they waited at the elevator. "What is it?" Now their every interaction was significant, every question touched the towering secret they shared.

"Something is not right. We must take great care on our little Roman holiday," he said to her. "From now on you must do exactly as I say. *Likha beda nachalo.*" Trouble is the beginning of disaster. The elevator doors opened and closed, as if swallowing them whole.

In his own office, Zyuganov was on the phone. The walls of the smallish room were covered with photographs of Zyuganov and SVR colleagues, at the seashore, in front of a dacha, standing together in a delegation. Most were gone now, purged by his own hand, he was tickled to note.

He nodded his head and said, "*Da, da,*" into the phone as if receiving detailed instructions.

"Yes, sir, it is clear. I know exactly what must be done. Yes, sir." He cradled the phone and keyed the intercom.

"Summon Matorin. He is to come immediately."

Pro serogo rech', a seryi navstrechu, thought Zyuganov, sitting down behind his desk. Speak of the gray one, the gray one heads your way.

MARBLE'S RUSTIC TOMATO SAUCE

Sauté diced onions, sliced garlic, and anchovy fillets in olive oil until aromatics are soft and fillets have melted in the pan. Add tomato paste in center of pan and fry, stirring, until rust-colored. Add chopped ripe tomatoes, crushed dried oregano, peperoncino, and a chiffonade of fresh basil leaves. Season to taste. Reduce sauce until thick, add a splash of balsamic vinegar to finish. Garnish with fresh, torn basil leaves and serve over pasta or meatballs.

31

Officers in the Washington *rezidentura* brewed tea, read newspapers, watched CNN and RTR-Planeta, and occasionally peeked through window blinds last raised in 1990. Cable traffic—both incoming and outgoing—was down. Lunch dates came and went, appointments were missed, new contacts were going cold. The consecutive weeks of FBI vehicular and foot surveillance had been unprecedented, crushing, stifling. After the first month, the Center had directed a stand-down of all operational activity until further notice, and requested the *rezidentura* prepare a security assessment to explain the situation. There *were* no explanations.

Even the elegant Rezident Golov was not immune. He confirmed trailing vehicular surveillance on him *personally* twenty of the last thirty nights, and he desperately needed to get black. The backup meeting with SWAN was approaching and he could not miss her a second time. There was no telling how she would react.

Those ten nights that neither Golov nor his Zeta countersurveillance team were able to detect even the remotest hint of coverage were, perversely, the worst nights. The nights of not knowing, of not being totally certain. Did the Americans have some new technique, some new technology? The devil knew what their strategy was. But he had to get black.

Everything must be done to protect SWAN, but she was a security nightmare. She continued to refuse all reasonable proposals to improve her security—electronic communication, messaging, discreet hotel meets, prearranged alternates to cover missed meetings—she wouldn't have any of it. "If I have my ass at the meeting," she had said to Golov, "you can damn well have your ass there too." Impossible woman. Golov yearned to turn SWAN over to a low-profile illegals officer, but Moscow forbade it, especially after the compromise of the illegal in New London.

Golov therefore was confronted by one of the most classic of espionage conundrums—having to meet a sensitive asset on a predetermined night, at a predetermined site, regardless of conditions on the street. An abort was unacceptable, impossible. Tonight was the next scheduled meeting with SWAN. He *had* to make it.

That afternoon he reviewed his surveillance detection route with the Zeta Team. Golov told them he wanted to try to channel any trailing coverage into a *dymokhod*, a stovepipe, to expose surveillance and, more important, to try a breakout—escaping surveillance altogether. They designated a code number on the encrypted radios that would signal whether the stovepipe had worked. They reviewed the route once again.

Golov knew this was madness. Only an asset as valuable as SWAN would make him take these risks, but the Center was insistent. Golov had to try.

He kicked off in midafternoon, the middle car in a simultaneous departure by eight of his officers in eight cars who exited the embassy gates on Wisconsin Avenue, each headed in a different direction. FBI watchers in the lookout post transmitted *starburst starburst*, a stampede departure, designed to overload surveillance and get a few cars free. The starburst call-out was also heard by the CIA's Orion Team. They were interested only in the *rezident*, and they patiently listened for the watchers to call out Golov, who was driving his own vehicle, a gleaming black BMW 5 Series sedan. Golov headed up

Wisconsin Avenue, his Zeta Team already deployed to the west of Wisconsin. Golov crossed Western Avenue, the border between the District and Maryland, and turned south, reversing his course into the grid pattern of American University Park, using the neighborhood streets to drift sideways, reverse direction, pull up to the curb, and wait. After fifteen minutes the Zetas signaled, *No apparent surveillance.* They had missed two static Orion cars that had been in place on the margins of AU Park.

Golov stairstepped west again along residential streets while his team moved to parallel his route. They did not get the slightest whiff of the familiar swirling movement of active FBI surveillance because there was none. The Zeta Team covered Golov as he pushed west downhill to Canal Road and crossed the Chain Bridge into Virginia. This was called by a static Orion car sitting on the intersection of Arizona and Canal Roads, the single route onto the only Potomac River crossing into Virginia between Georgetown and the Beltway. The Orions were tempted to flood suburban Virginia but the team leader, a sixty-five-year-old former surveillance instructor by the name of Kramer, told them to hold. He instead directed three cars to parallel Golov's directional axis on the Maryland side of the Potomac. They were going north along the river anticipating the route. TrapDoor was in play.

One Orion—a grandmother when she wasn't tracking SVR officers—held at the parking lot of Lock 10 on the C&O Canal National Park. Another grandmother drove four miles to the Old Angler's Inn on MacArthur Boulevard, took a garden table in the waning light, ordered a sherry, and tried to guess which of the couples at the other tables were having affairs.

Kramer directed a third Orion—this one a great-aunt—another four miles north to the village of Potomac, where she ordered an early dinner salad at the Hunters Inn. As the three women waited, they recorded a score of license plates and marked a dozen loitering people. The list of possibles grew. Were any of them waiting for the black BMW? The two remaining Orion cars—the team was small that day—separated. One covered the upper reaches of River Road southeast of Potomac, the other parked at the entrance of the Great Falls Park, where American traitors like Walker and Ames and Pollard and Pelton over the years had pulled misshapen garbage bags of Russian money out of rotting tree trunks. The Orions all sat still and waited, keeping off the radios, their eyes scanning, checking, programmed to catch the profile, the gleam, the shape of the black BMW. If Golov continued into Virginia, they lost; if he headed back to Maryland but away from Potomac, they lost. They were content to wait. It was how TrapDoor worked. There would be other days and nights. All they had to do was be right once.

As it turned out, they lost. Golov crossed back into Maryland on I-495, part of a high-speed loop that enabled his Zeta Team to begin setting up on the final leg of the route, the *dymokhod,* the stovepipe, the long, meandering Beach Drive, which traced the gerrymandered Rock Creek Park in and out of the woods and creek bed south all the way to Georgetown. Hearing the distinctive squelch breaks designating "all clear," Golov exited Beach at the bottom of Rock Creek and parked on Twenty-Second Street in the West End, leaving the Zeta Team to continue south. If the FBI had managed to place a beacon on Golov's car—unlikely; it was never left unattended and was swept weekly—the feds would find it a block away from either the Ritz-Carlton or the Fairmont and about fifty restaurants along the K Street corridor. They would be welcome to check all those and more. He locked his car and walked six blocks to the familiar entrance of the Tabard Inn. It was dark now, and the interior of the inn was warmly lit.

More madness, to use the same meeting site twice in a row. At least there had been a cooling-off hiatus since the last rendezvous. Golov entered the inn and walked past the front desk, through the corridor, to the little walled garden in back. This time SWAN had arrived before Golov. She sat at a table hard against the garden wall, smoking. Golov braced for trouble. SWAN had just signaled the waiter for a replacement drink. An empty highball glass was on the table in front of her. She was dressed in a blue suit with a red blouse. A blue stone necklace at her throat matched the suit, and bright red nails matched her blouse. Her blond hair was brushed back off her face, which, in the diffused light of the bulbs in the trees, seemed older and papery.

"Stephanie, how are you?" said Golov in greeting. He extended his hand but she made no move to take it. He smiled at her and sat down. The waiter arrived with a double scotch for Senator Boucher. Golov, tired and stiff from nearly five hours in the car, ordered a Campari and soda.

"Anatoly," said Boucher with mock warmth, "I have been waiting in this stupid little garden for nearly an hour." She stabbed at a little gold lighter several times before she could light her cigarette.

"I'm sorry about that, Stephanie," said Golov, "but I was preoccupied by the necessity of not bringing the entire Federal Bureau of Investigation with me to our rendezvous."

"How very professional of you."

"We could arrange things a lot more securely if you would consider just a few small changes," said Golov.

"Not this again. It's so very comforting to hear

you talk about my security when there's a full-scale search in Washington for a highly placed Russian agent." Boucher blew smoke into the air.

"Indeed? What have you heard? We have no reason to believe your status is compromised," said Golov. "We are quite certain that neither the FBI nor the CIA has any idea about our relationship. Five people on this planet know who you are, and that list includes you and me. What is this about a search for a Russian agent? Details, Stephanie, please." This was important. Golov's scalp itched, a bad sign.

"I am glad you're so confident. How, then, do you explain the closed-session briefing I attended, listening to one of those CIA idiots? It sounded like they have leads. They're looking for someone who suffers from shingles—you know, Anatoly, the painful red lesions on your skin? Like the pain in my fanny?" She tilted her head back and finished her drink, the ice cubes clicking against her teeth. She signaled for another.

"Stephanie, you don't have shingles, do you?" asked Golov. He would have to transmit this information instantly, tonight.

She looked at him with irritation. "That's not the point. You know as well as I that I cannot jeopardize my position. I've worked too long and hard to get where I am."

Golov marveled that her colossal ego could translate this deadly serious game as a potential derailment to her career. Did she know the dangers involved? The consequences? "This is exactly why I insist we begin meeting in hotel rooms."

"I'll consider it," said Boucher. She appraised the waiter as he set her third drink down, staring at him as he walked away. "But now there's something else," she said in a flat tone, the one she used during congressional testimonies. "If *you people* make a mistake and the feds come knocking on *my* door, I will not go to prison. I won't go. So I want you to give me something . . . permanent. Something I can take."

Golov sat back in his chair and marveled. *The mention of a mole hunt has unsettled her, and now she wants an L-pill, a US senator.* Where did she hear of this? He reached forward, held both of Boucher's hands lightly in his fingers, and spoke softly. "Stephanie, that is the most amazing thing I have heard you say. You cannot be serious. You're speaking of ancient history, of Cold War myths. There is no such thing."

"I think you're lying to me, Anatoly," she said, smiling thinly as she twisted away from his hands. "Either I get one, or I dissolve our 'partnership,' as you call it. When we meet next month—you will be here next month, on time?—I expect a cute little pillbox; make it ivory or mother-of-pearl."

"I can still hardly believe it," said Golov. "I will consult with Moscow, but I doubt they will grant authorization."

As was her custom, Senator Boucher waited until the end of their meeting before she dug into her purse and slid a black disc across the table toward Golov. Before putting it into his pocket, he saw the Pathfinder logo inscribed on the side. The senator certainly knew how to play for drama, Golov thought as he watched her walk unsteadily out. Shingles.

Anatoly Golov sat in a New England–style rocking chair in a room in the Tabard Inn. The smallish room had florid purple walls, framed posters of French circus animals, was carpeted with a riotous Persian carpet, and featured an oversized four-poster bed in the corner of the room.

Since his last meeting with SWAN, there had been no abatement in surveillance on *rezidentura* officers. Instead of risking another long SDR, Golov had received the Center's approval to attempt a "trunk escape" to get black. On the morning of the meeting day, Golov had lain in the trunk of the car of the economic counselor, breathing pure oxygen from a small tank through a face mask. Three embassy wives drove, with absolutely no regard for surveillance, to Friendship Heights on upper Wisconsin Avenue. Following instructions, the thick-waisted wives parked in the underground parking garage, locked the car, and went shopping.

Another Russian spouse sitting in the garage watched the parked car for fifteen minutes. There had been no surveillance; it was clean. Carrying shopping bags, the wife simply walked up to the car, tapped lightly twice, and unlocked the trunk to let a cramped and pissed-off Golov out.

He cursed the SWAN case, and cursed Moscow, and cursed the Service, but he was black, undetected, surveillance-free. The trunk escape had worked. He left the garage and made his way south into the District by walking, getting on random buses, and hailing an occasional taxi. He avoided the Metro system with its ubiquitous cameras. He reached Dupont Circle and killed two hours in bookshops and in a little bistro. At sunset, at the height of rush hour, he walked around the Circle, south down Nineteenth, onto N Street, and four blocks to the Tabard Inn. No sign of surveillance. He had dressed casually, for a change, to blend in on the street, with a muted suede jacket over a brown crewneck, corduroy slacks, and suede walking shoes. Thank God for the good shoes. As he entered the inn he slipped on a pair of heavy-framed eyeglasses with clear-glass lenses.

Golov sat in the hotel suite and finished a plate of Aegean clams that had been broiled with oregano, goat cheese, lemon, and oil, accompanied by a bottle of chilled Tuscan Vernaccia. He was relieved that he had rented the room, using a forged US driver's license and traveler's checks, without a problem. It had been a number of years since Golov had rented a hotel room in alias—that was a young man's game—and he had relived the tense, dry-mouthed drill with cool enjoyment. Despite his foreign accent, and the fact that he had no reservation and no luggage, the oblivious clerk behind the desk was satisfied. This was a distinguished gentleman. He was shown to the small but elegant room on the second floor, where they would be out of the public eye. Privacy was paramount, especially tonight, with what he had to give her.

He finished his supper, went into the bathroom to splash water on his face, look into the mirror, and again curse the Service. Locking his door, Golov descended to the small lobby and sat in a slightly musty green baize couch facing the front door. He waited, keyed up, an unread magazine in his lap.

Senator Boucher walked into the place as if she owned it. She didn't see Golov sitting on the couch—the clear-lens eyeglasses broke up his patrician features—and passed him within two feet. Boucher walked through a room to be seen, not to notice who else was there. Golov silently caught her in the corridor and steered her up the small staircase to the second floor. No one had seen them. Golov unlocked the door and let Boucher enter first. The senator looked around the room and smirked.

"Anatoly, how cozy, I always suspected you were a romantic."

Ignoring the comment, Golov offered SWAN a glass of wine, which she accepted in lieu of scotch. "Meeting indoors improves our security, Stephanie," said Golov, "but we must choose another hotel for next time. I insist, and so does Moscow."

"How very nice for you and Moscow," said SWAN, holding out her glass for more wine. "Did you bring e my . . . vitamins? Tell me you did, Anatoly, and I l be very happy."

Golov thought of an agent he once ran in East Beirut, a Maronite Christian, who had gotten so accustomed to demanding money and gifts before sharing his information that the situation became impossible. Golov had directed a KGB Vympel team to sink his weighted body off Raouché and the Pigeons' Rocks, past the forty-five-fathom line. He looked at SWAN and daydreamed.

"I have positive news," said Golov. He poured another glass of wine and sat next to her on the small velveteen couch. He took an oblong box out of his jacket pocket and set it on the table. He opened the box to reveal an elegant pen nestled in a bed of powder-blue silk. It was a Montblanc Etoile, with a black hourglass barrel, flared crème-colored cap, and the iconic Montblanc inlaid white star at the tip. At the end of the pocket clip was a perfect Akoya pearl. Boucher reached for the pen, saying, "How lovely."

Golov gently stopped her by holding her wrist and pulling her hand back. "It's a beautiful pen," said SWAN. "But I asked for something I could take, a pill."

"There are no pills," Golov said rather brusquely. "We have consented to your quite remarkable request, and this is what we will give you." He picked up the pen and gripped the pearl in his fingertips. "You must grasp the pearl firmly," he said. "And pull gently but steadily . . ." The pearl suddenly came free. It was attached to the end of a one-inch needle that slid out of a channel on the underside of the pocket clip. The needle had a burnt coppery hue to it, as if it had been held over a flame. Golov slid the needle back into its sheath in the clip and firmly pushed the pearl past a detent into the locked position.

"What is this?" said Boucher. "I asked you for something simple."

"Be silent and I will explain," snapped Golov. He wildly fantasized about extracting the needle again and plunging it into SWAN's neck. He composed himself. "The needle is coated with a natural compound. It requires only that you break the skin, scratch yourself, anywhere, and it will take immediate effect. Ten seconds." He held up his hand to silence her. "This is infinitely more effective than a pill. Please forget what you have seen in the movies. A pill can lose potency after a period of time; there is no problem with this." He handed Boucher the pen. "Now *you* extract the needle," he said, once again putting his hand on her wrist, "*very slowly and carefully*."

Boucher's hands shook a little when she took the pen, hefted it in her hand, and pulled the pearl slowly and evenly, drawing it out of the clip. The little needle glinted dully, its menace somehow accentuated by its stubby length. Boucher carefully seated the needle back into the sheath and pushed the pearl home and locked. She turned to Golov, a bit chastened. "Thank you, Anatoly." She clipped the Montblanc inside her blouse between the buttons and threw back the last of her wine.

The gravity of the moment now past, her eyes wandered around the room and settled on the four-poster bed and then on Golov. "Even remotely interested?" she asked to his infinite horror.

GOLOV'S MEDITERRANEAN CLAMS

Mix fresh oregano, lemon juice, panko bread crumbs, olive oil, and crumbled feta cheese with room-temperature butter to form a smooth compound butter. Roll and chill. Put a round of the butter on each opened clam in its shell resting on a bed of kosher salt. Broil until butter is melted, one to two minutes. Squeeze lemon juice over clams.

32

Rome was ocher roofs and lambent marble under the eternal sun. The bumblebee buzz of *motorini* hip-tilted through traffic by raven-haired girls in crocodile heels filled the air. General Korchnoi breathed it in. This was his old operational ground, and he remembered. He ordered lunch in rusty but elegant Italian. Dominika had never heard of *spaghetti alla bottarga*, but a bowl of pasta, glistening with oil and with a dusting of golden *bottarga di muggine*, roe of gray mullet, transported her. She looked over at Korchnoi, who nodded, pleased. It was nothing like Russian caviar, she thought.

They were sitting in La Taverna dei Fori Imperiale, two tiny rooms with cloth-covered tables and pastel murals on white stucco walls, floors of polished black and white tiles. The restaurant was halfway down Via Madonna dei Monti, a narrow, ancient street in the perpetual shadow of scuffed apartment buildings with ground-floor bakeries and woodshops, the air filled with the smells of baked bread and sawdust.

Dominika had the day before approached the COS and delivered her message, leaving the number of her throwaway phone. Korchnoi carefully observed Dominika before and after the contact—rock-solid and calm—and he approved. She was stimulated on the street, her cheeks were flushed, her wide eyes reflected the splash of a dozen dolphin fountains.

Korchnoi unilaterally changed the ops plan once they were away from Moscow. He had quietly insisted that they would initially connect with the Americans discreetly on the street, and then use a CIA-rented room for conversation.

"Forgive me, but I do not trust your uncle, or that Zyuganov," Korchnoi told Dominika now as they strolled after lunch. They walked slowly past the Forum, over the *sanpietrini* cobblestones, and up a narrow walkway, looking for trailing coverage. They put a euro into a tin box and descended into the Mamertine Prison, imagining Saint Peter being lowered into the dungeon through the hole hewn into the rock of the Capitoline Hill. The prison unsettled the Russians and they left quickly, back up into the sunlight.

As they walked, stairstepping through neighborhoods, they used time over distance to ensure they weren't covered in ticks. Korchnoi talked to her, sometimes stopping her to put a hand on her shoulder. He described the Life, of working for the CIA from within Russia, undetected inside the Service. They sat on a bench near an obelisk, spooning granitas, rich coffee ices, stealing looks at their watches, and pedestrians, and parked cars, as Korchnoi told her how a spy must know the difference between risk and recklessness, and about evaluating—but not necessarily accepting—the direction of your CIA handler. "It's your life, your welfare," Korchnoi said. "You ultimately decide what to do and how to do it."

The Roman light freed her and she told Korchnoi more about Helsinki, about her activities, about how she felt with her secret, the sweet ice of it, she said, looking at the cone of frozen espresso in her hand. She spoke sparingly about Nate, for she did not know how he felt about her, or what she felt herself. Did he see her as an agent first, and a fleeting lover second? It was too hard, and Korchnoi saw it, knew it.

The general spoke of restraint, and calculation, and patience, the trinity that enabled him to survive for fourteen years as a CIA asset. It was unspoken that they would "work together," but they did not try to define their partnership further. They knew agents seldom spied in tandem. Korchnoi did not speak at all about his vision of "succession" or of Dominika's role as heir apparent.

What else they did not talk about—perhaps could not—was Russia and their sentiments about their country. This was boggy ground of betrayal and treason, and they left it alone. That would come later. Right now they just had enough time to finish the SDR and make it to the brief-encounter site and meet the Main Enemy.

MARBLE had informed Langley via satellite burst that Dominika's approach to COS Rome would signal their arrival in the city. That would trigger a meeting in twenty-four hours, ironically at a long-inactive KGB site in the Villa Borghese that MARBLE remembered from fifteen years ago. He had also transmitted a brief sentence—*She passed, she's ours now*—indicating to Benford that Dominika had, in essence, been rerecruited by him. A most extraordinary situation. Two agents, each witting of the other, a single handler, the whole case directed by a mad scientist of a CI chief, two mole hunts—and the added necessity of having to decide where to eat dinner. This was Rome, after all, MARBLE thought.

Dominika's cheap little phone trilled as they walked up a staircase to the northern limit of the Aurelian Walls, catching glimpses of blue-green trees and the biscuit-colored tiles and the golden domes. Korchnoi answered it in Italian and listened for ten seconds, then abruptly clacked the phone shut. "They're in place. Would you like to take a stroll through the park?"

They walked in the heat of the Roman afternoon, through the Porta Pinciana and into the Villa Borghese. Korchnoi wore a light gray suit with a dark shirt, open at the neck, Dominika a navy skirt and a pink-and-blue-striped shirt. She wore her hair up against the heat. Together they looked like father and daughter, prosperous Romans, walking perhaps to visit the museum in the center of the park. Korchnoi could see she was excited and nervous, her blue eyes flashing. But he also saw her darting glances, checking for surveillance, cataloguing casuals.

Of course, Korchnoi knew the park. He had been assigned to the Rome *rezidentura* as a junior. He had met agents there, had left packages for assets in buried caches, his young wife watching for him. A lifetime ago. Now he and Dominika walked down the broad gravel avenues dappled by sunlight filtering through the plane trees. Korchnoi led Dominika past reflecting pools and paused at the perfect Fontana dei Cavalli Marini, with the rampant seahorses with cloven hooves. They walked around the hippodrome of the Piazza di Sienna and down the Viale del Lago. Korchnoi had seen no repeats, no indication of coverage, despite their serpentine route. Two minutes to the site. He felt rather than saw that Dominika was becoming nervous, was tightening up. Korchnoi slipped his arm in hers and told her a joke:

"A frightened man came to the KGB. 'My talking parrot disappeared,' he said. 'This is not our case,' says the KGB, 'go to the criminal police.' 'Excuse me,' says the man. 'Of course I know I have to go to the criminal police. I am here just to tell you officially that I disagree with that parrot.'"

Dominika snorted, then covered her nose with her hand. Korchnoi watched her and knew his instincts had been correct. She would be his replacement. She could do it. Benford would realize it after ten minutes with her.

They were nearing a small artificial lake with a classical Ionian temple to Aesculapius on an island in the middle. She followed Korchnoi's gaze and saw a short, rumpled man sitting on a bench at the edge of the lake.

"Benford," said Korchnoi. "I will greet him." He nodded his head in the direction of the island. "Keep walking around the lake," he told her. "There is a footbridge connecting the island with the shore." He walked to the bench. Dominika saw the man get up, shake hands with Korchnoi. They sat down.

Dominika began walking around the small lake on legs she could not feel. Her heart was pounding, she could hear herself swallow. What would she say to him? That she missed him? Glupyi. *Stupid. Stay professional. It's not just the two of you here. There are others present, and this is the first day of the rest of your life as a spy. Stay professional.*

Beneath a willow at the shoreline she saw a dark figure standing on the little steel bridge, at the top of its graceful curve. She knew his form, how he held himself, leaning against the railing, a silhouette in shadow. She could see the halo around his head, darker than she remembered, but that may have been the shadow of the tree. He was moving now, his footsteps echoing on the steel of the bridge.

Blossoms from the willow floated on the still water. She walked up to him, offered her hand.

"*Zdravstvuy*," she said. Hello. She stood still, waiting for the bubble to pop, for him to ignore the handshake and wrap his arms around her.

"Dominika," Nate said, "how are you?" He extended his hand and she took it, feeling his grip, remembering everything. "We were worried about you, it's been a long time not knowing." Purple and glowing, like she remembered.

She let go of his hand. "I am fine," she said. "I have been working with the general." That at least was now out in the open, the secret she had been searching for.

He did not want to talk about MARBLE with her, for the rules of compartmentation made it difficult for him. He had replayed what he would say to her when they met: how he had thought about her every day, how much she meant to him, but it came out wrong.

"I'm glad you're out," he said. "We have a lot to talk about." He heard his donkey words, the words of a midgrade agent handler. Before long he would be reviewing the agent meeting sked with her.

Dominika could see him struggling—his halo was pulsing, as if slaved to his heartbeat. They looked at each other wordlessly, and Dominika tensed because she knew she would put her arms around his neck if he didn't move first in about three seconds.

They heard a soft click of fingers snapping gently, and Nate's head came up. Benford waved; he and Korchnoi were now standing. Benford pointed and started walking. Nate waved the assent, then walked after the two men, Dominika at his side.

The four of them sat in the elegant sitting room of Benford's suite at the Aldrovandi Hotel, on the opposite side of the park. Muted earth tones, a vase of flowers, a dazzling white marble floor. Turquoise swimming pool in the garden below, behind a screen of cypress pines. The breeze through the open balcony door blew the white sheer curtains in gentle spirals. A bottle of wine stood unopened in a copper bucket on the counter.

They sat in chairs around the coffee table, the curtains lifting and falling. Benford had discussed—was still discussing—the quite unique situation of MARBLE and Dominika. "It's unconscionable," said Benford. "The worst security possible. We're going to have to make adjustments immediately."

"An excellent idea," said MARBLE. "I would like

to speak with you about this very subject, Benford, privately. I fear it would be best, for the moment at least, if Dominika were not in the room. And while I appreciate that Nathaniel is responsible for me as my case officer, I'm sure he would not mind instead going with Dominika, to keep her company." The two left the room, and MARBLE turned to Benford, who was lighting a cigarette.

"She is young, and passionate, but she is smart," said MARBLE. "Ever since I placed her in my department, she has been looking at me, not speaking, assessing me. I could see her resolve. I made her admit her recruitment in Helsinki herself. I suspected as much. Were you ever going to tell me?"

Benford shrugged.

"And I told her about myself, obliquely, but she picked it up instantly. We have been talking. About risk, danger, work—about *penetrating* the Center. She listens, not a blink, not a tremor. Quite satisfactory," said MARBLE.

"That's most reassuring," said Benford dryly. "I still think that as a junior woman in your Service she will have challenges in her career. It will be years before she attains any important position, if ever."

"You know the Game as well as I, Benford," said MARBLE. "The ones who start small and grow into the role are the best, the most secure. She is perfect."

"And will she be able to turn you in? *Can she?*"

"She will if she does not realize what she is doing. It will make her performance all the more convincing, her shock will be genuine. In any case, she will follow instructions. I am sure she will."

"This is preposterous," said Benford. "We need you now more than ever. To contemplate losing you before time . . ." He stubbed his cigarette out in a crystal ashtray.

MARBLE shook his head. "We cannot calculate

time. I have no way of knowing how close they are getting to me. Vanya is active. Apart from the *kanareyka zapadnya*—"

"Translation, please," said Benford.

"—the canary trap he is running, God knows what else he and Zyuganov are hatching."

"The point?" said Benford.

"The point is that I may have much time or a little. It's critical that Dominika be prepared as soon as possible. If they catch me before she turns me in, the profit is lost."

"Pardon my French, but 'shit,'" said Benford.

"Stop complaining, my friend. We are doing something unheard-of in our game. We trade, what, a year or two of my information in exchange for positioning a new spy, with the potential for working in place for twenty, twenty-five years. It's inspired."

Benford shook his head. "This is not what you worked for, all these years, with the danger and the risk. You deserve retirement, rewards."

"My reward will be to leave things in place, to continue this work through her. It remains for us—you and I—to choose the right moment," said MARBLE.

"This Rome trip may not be the right time," said Benford, lighting another cigarette. "We do not want to wait too long, but I would like to wait long enough to observe whether there is a nibble from my little test."

"Will you tell me?" said MARBLE.

"I briefed that the American mole is stricken with shingles. It's what you said Egorov told Nasarenko."

"Poor Nasarenko. May I ask who you fed the birdseed to?" asked MARBLE.

"Fifteen members of the SSCI, officials at the Pentagon, a few staffers in the White House," said Benford. "Small-enough group that we can check if we get a sonar return on the canary trap."

"*Vsego dobrogo,* my friend," said MARBLE. "Good luck to you. I will keep an eye open and signal in the event poor Nasarenko jumps out a window."

"Very helpful," said Benford, "and if you could keep your eyes open for any other clues . . ."

"I have something in mind, but later," said MARBLE.

Nate and Dominika sat together in his room and talked quietly. He acted nonchalant, but she knew better, she could see the intensity of his aura. He repeated that he had been worried about her, they all had been waiting for some word, and they all had been relieved when General Korchnoi reported that she was safe. He blamed himself for what had happened, her recall to Moscow. But now they could restart the relationship, they would work together again. Dominika thought he sounded like a case officer handling an agent, which was exactly what he was. He had been *worried,* then *relieved. Chto za divo!* Wonderful.

Nate heard himself prattling on. He was conscious of the men in the adjoining room, conscious of the awkwardness of the moment, he knew he had to maintain control. He stumbled and stopped talking when he saw her face. She was elegant, stunning, poised. He remembered that expression, the set of her mouth. She was becoming angry. The endless months spent apart, not knowing if she was dead, and in the first hour together he was pissing her off.

Now what? she thought. They had been separated and she had built up expectations, but things, apparently, would be different. They could not return to the heady days of Helsinki, with her sneaking out of Volontov's *rezidentura* with pilfered documents under her sweater. The long afternoons in the little sun-splashed safe house, cooking on the little stove, were past. So was the little moonlit bedroom.

She was a silly *fantazerka,* a woolly-headed dreamer. All right, she could be all business and she wasn't about to make it easy for him. Dominika brutally told Nate about her recall to Moscow, about the cellars of Lefortovo, the endless days of questions, and the slaps and the purple lips, and how the cabinets at the ends of the corridors had creaked when she was shoved inside them.

His face was ashen when she told him she had kept his image in her mind and it helped her survive, bringing him along with her at her side, down the corridors and into the next room. Nate did not react but she saw it in his eyes, the purple haze behind him was intense with emotion. Rattled, he got up from his chair.

He was pouring wine at a sideboard across the room, and Dominika got up and went over to him. His hand was shaking as he filled the glasses. He wouldn't look at her. He knew that if, in that moment, they touched, he would be lost. Nate turned to face her. He looked at her hair, her lips, the fifty-fathom blue of her eyes. His eyes told her, *No, we mustn't,* but his throat closed up and his guts ached, and he took her face in his hands and kissed her, remembering the taste of her.

They kissed each other madly, as if someone were coming to pull them apart. Dominika clutched his neck and she walked him backward out onto the little marble balcony in the dying light. Doves were darting between the tips of the cypresses, black against the sky. There was no sound and not a breath of wind. She pushed him against the balcony railing and wordlessly they fumbled with his belt buckle and hitched up her skirt and Dominika was on her toes, facing him, like a five-minute tart in an alley off Kopevskiy Pereulok. She gripped the wrought iron with white knuckles, lifted one leg, and hooked her shoe on the railing. She mashed her mouth over his and moaned into his throat down to his belly. Her body shivered and she let go of the railing and wrapped her arms around his neck to hold on. All the bucking and shuddering and shaking on the little balcony made the doves in the trees jumpy, and they dipped and turned and flared among the cypress tops.

Clinging to each other was sweet and natural and logical, and the little balcony became Dominika's entire world, and Nate became the only thing in it as he trailed his lips across her mouth. His arms tightened around her waist and her legs began to convulse. She whispered, "*Dushenka,*" in his ear, and the doves swooped in the night sky.

They didn't move for two minutes, then Dominika breathed raggedly through his kiss and pulled away from his embrace, smoothing her skirt. He tucked in a trailing tail of his shirt. They went back inside. Nate turned on a lamp and handed her a glass of wine. They sat beside each other, looking straight ahead, not speaking. Dominika's legs trembled and she could feel her heartbeat in her head. It seemed that Nate was about to say something, but Benford entered the room just then to fetch them for dinner.

Sergey Matorin, the SVR's executioner from Line F, sat at a small sidewalk table at Harry's Bar at the top of the Veneto. He had a view of the front entrance of Egorova's hotel down Via di Porta Pinciana, and was waiting to catch a glimpse of her, of Korchnoi, but especially of the figure of the young American. His squirrel-jumpy brain had committed the American's face to memory before leaving Moscow. *There should have been some activity by now,* he thought. His chest felt heavy and his mouth was dry.

He was tempted to break into Egorova's hotel room, to wait in the dark, in a corner, enveloped in his own vinegar-ammonia body odor, but he had been given strict instructions directly by Chief Zyuganov, absolutely secret. No unnecessary action, wait for an opportunity, make no mistakes. Matorin was content to sit and wait.

He eyed several young women walking up the escalator from the underground Borghese Gallery, but ignored them in favor of his latest daydream of the group of Afghan women and children cowering behind the mud and rock walls of a hilltop sheep pen during the Parwan offensive. As the grenades from the GP-25s floated in lazy arcs and bracketed them, the women's screams mingled with the soft *crumps* of the explosions, until they were silent. A raucous horn from a passing car on the Veneto shook him out of his reverie, and Matorin was sorry for that.

FORI IMPERIALE'S SPAGHETTI ALLA BOTTARGA

Sauté garlic in olive oil until golden, then remove garlic. Stir in butter and a spoonful of grated bottarga di muggine roe, but do not overcook, as it will become bitter. Add al dente pasta to the oil and toss to coat. Remove from heat; add additional butter and a second spoonful of bottarga. Finish with fresh chopped parsley.

33

Rezident Anatoly Golov would have been unsettled to learn how much the Orion team had divined about him personally from studying his streetcraft. This was a maestro, they said, an intellectual, an artist. He didn't use the ponderous SVR rules of streetcraft, the punishing, high-speed surveillance detection routes, the arrogant demeanor, the offensive "provocations" at the end of a run. Golov's style reflected his many years as an operations officer in Europe and in America. His routes caressed surveillance, made peace with it, and only after many hours of gentle manipulation did he break their hearts. But the Orions had identified patterns, preferences, predilections in Golov's SDRs. He was unaware of his stylish predictability, that he telegraphed his favored maneuvers. One of these was to execute a *rybolovnyi kryuchok*, a fishhook reverse, in his route about three-quarters of the way through a normally straight and benign SDR. It was a murderously effective maneuver—he would simply disappear.

Golov's fishhook confounded the Gs, who for months had been jamming his right-rear quarter. The frustrated teams were ready to give him a spanking soon by boxing his car and taking him around the Beltway three times before letting him take an exit. The Orions, observing from the wings, were more patient. They quietly studied Golov's maneuver, they wanted to understand it, quantify it, to confirm what they all began to realize. After he dematerialized, the shank of the fishhook was Golov's true compass course; it pointed to the final destination—and his agent—as directly as the leading edge of the Big Dipper points to Polaris.

It was the math, really. Golov would have been safe if he ran only the normal five SDRs a year. But the Russian spooks in the Washington *rezidentura* were being starved out. They had work, contacts, sources to meet, Golov most of all. He had the enormousness of cosseting SWAN, and he needed to be black for meetings with her. That required two or three SDRs a week. Like the aging movie star who takes any work she can get, Golov's SDR tricks were becoming overexposed.

Sitting around a big table at a suburban Maryland Sizzler, members of the Orions enjoyed the Early Bird Dinner Special before the start of the evening. It was a small team that night, only five of them, but it made no difference. They were all old rock stars.

Orest Javorskiy had emplaced polystyrene tree stumps packed with electronics in the snow of the Fulda Gap to listen for the midnight rumble of Soviet armor. Mel Filippo had led her blinded agent out of Brasov by the hand. Clio Bavisotto had played Chopin for Tito while her husband cracked the safe upstairs. Johnny Parment recruited a Vietcong general in Hanoi under the noses of a twenty-person surveillance team. And sitting at the end of the table was "the Philosopher," goateed Socrates Burbank, nearly eighty, thrice married and thrice divorced, the Buddha who invented TrapDoor surveillance and who, from the backseat, called the shots and directed the team.

Burbank had Waltzed with the Pig, he had done it all. In his early twenties he had exfiltrated an agent and his family out of Budapest past idling tanks in Martyrs' Square. He had hammered landing beacons into the doomed beaches at the Bay of Pigs. He had sat in an overheated safe house in Berlin, coaxing the intel out of a Soviet general officer stupid with vodka, holding the vomit can between the Russian's knees. Not even Benford interfered when Burbank was running the Orions, grease pencils between his fingers, laminated street maps on his knees, Toulouse-Lautrec holding a radio, softly talking to the amoeba.

An afternoon of towering thunderheads in the west that evening culminated in a stupendous line of storms and lightning strikes that paralyzed metropolitan Washington. Tree limbs littered the flooded roads, the Beltway became an unmoving annulus, and both airports suspended operations. It was the worst night for an SDR, it was the best night for one.

Golov used the traffic to screen himself as he crawled from the embassy south through Georgetown, across the river on the Key Bridge, and then south along the Potomac, stopping variously in Crystal City Underground and Old Town Alexandria. Stops in the equatorial downpour were more than uncomfortable—by the time Golov finished desultory shopping in Alexandria he was soaked. So too was the FBI team that followed moodily in his wake.

Despite the weather, Golov was trying to sell Mount Vernon as his ultimate destination, supported by a mild and linear route in that direction. Evening concerts and colonial dinners were popular at the mansion, and no surveillance team worth its salt would fail to flood the area if a rabbit even hinted at heading that way. The FBI did exactly that, sending two cars ahead and keeping four trailing cars way back on the *rezident*. It was time for Golov's magic. His move would be covered by the traffic, the FBI too far behind. His fishhook was a quick turn onto the ramp to the Wilson Bridge, across the Potomac into Maryland and Oxon Hill, through Forest Heights, and toward Anacostia.

A puff of smoke and he was gone. Thirty minutes later, the FBI team glumly radioed that they had lost the rabbit somehow on GW Parkway south, Mount Vernon was negative, and they were retracing the route, sweeping back through Alexandria and north into suburban Virginia. Golov's fishhook was stuck firmly in their mouths, pulling them farther and farther away.

The rain stopped and traffic thinned as Golov cut north through southwest Washington, stairstepping, doubling back, parking at the curb to wait and watch. The wipers streaked his windshield in the intermittent mode. He now had only to traverse the National Mall to enter downtown. He would park his car in an underground garage in the K Street corridor and walk the dozen or so blocks to the Tabard Inn. He had seen no whisper of trailing surveillance; his years of experience told him he was black, alone, free.

Soc Burbank's grease pencil squeaked on the map. The reverse had been on the Wilson Bridge—the only explanation—and the shank was pointing downtown. He tossed the FBI brick to the side; the only things coming out of the FEEB frequencies now were profanities. His pencil squeaked some more and he built a static picket line along the south side of the Mall, three cars, one each on Seventh, Fourteenth, and Seventeenth Streets, leaving the tunnels at Ninth and Twelfth unguarded. At dusk, Clio observed Golov's black BMW ooze up Fourteenth Street. Softly she called him through, just direction and speed. She pulled into traffic and followed him as only a grandmother could, tenderly and with great concern.

The two other Orion cars converged on Golov using parallel tracks along Eighteenth and Pennsylvania. Mel and Soc relinquished the eye to Johnny near McPherson Square, where he saw Golov enter a parking garage. The team prepared to cover the Russian on foot; and it was here they really excelled. They had not used the ABC formation in a decade. Instead they swirled around the rabbit, dipped him in chocolate. They moved ahead, they walked back through, they crossed in front, they looped far ahead. If Golov happened to glance in an Orion's direction, he or she did not flinch or turn away or window-shop. Rheumy eyes met his for an instant, then proceeded with absentminded sweetness, blue hair under improbable berets, rakish fisherman caps, packages, purses, librarian eyeglasses, and a briar pipe. Golov, tall and patrician and at home on the streets of Paris or London, didn't register a thing.

They were too good, too natural, too fluid. They were invisible among the casuals on the street, especially to a senior SVR officer exhausted by the pressure, fed up with the uncompromising burdens of tradecraft, and who was working on a serious case of tunnel vision with each step closer to the Tabard Inn. The Russian was being had by five pensioners with liver spots and bad knees. If he could detect someone, he could turn away, buy a newspaper, order a coffee, head home, the meeting aborted. But he didn't see anything.

The rain had stopped, and when Golov turned down N Street, TrapDoor closed. It was the Tabard Inn, the only possibility on N, forget the Topaz Hotel. Mel and Clio were already waiting inside the lobby, shoes off, chafing their feet, exclaiming, My goodness how they hurt. They watched as Golov got a room key and disappeared up the narrow staircase.

Their discipline—and a firmly established procedure—compelled them to stay in place for a half hour, to observe activity and potentially interesting individuals. They had no law-enforcement arrest authority and loitering longer than that would alert the target. So Soc called Benford, gave him a terse report, and hung up. Then he keyed the radio and clicked them out of there.

They hadn't witnessed a meeting, they didn't have squat. They had foxed the SVR *rezident*, but there was no agent, no suspect. Patience and perspective helped them cope with the inconclusive evening. As did late-night hot dogs at the Shake Shack on Eighteenth.

A Russian intelligence officer was very likely meeting clandestinely with an unidentified penetration of the US government as the Orions ordered their dogs. Johnny's China Ops background manifested itself in sesame slaw and chilies. Orest was a purist and would accept only mustard and kraut. Mel favored onions and ketchup, Clio the classical pianist had hers with lettuce, tomato, bacon, and blue cheese. Socrates had years ago shocked them into uneasy silence by inventing the Depth Charge, the ingredients for which were available only at the Shake Shack: a disgusting schmear of pan-fried potatoes, caramelized onions, anchovies, and fiery Argentine *chimichurri* sauce. By mutual consent the Orions had agreed that they would never eat in their vehicles with Soc.

Benford was on the phone to the FBI, alternatively screaming and blaspheming, then begging them to deploy a team to cover the Tabard Inn this instant. Several calls were relayed, a shift supervisor was notified, surveillance squad members were activated. In the two hours it took for the Gs to deploy around the little hotel, Stephanie Boucher had arrived, met with Golov, and departed. It would not have been difficult to follow the senator, certainly not as challenging as it was following Anatoly Golov. It would not have been as challenging as following a flock of Japanese tourists walking along the Tidal Basin holding pink umbrellas. In fact, it would not have been as challenging as following an elephant through a rice-paper factory with a bell on its tail.

The measure of her arrogance and sociopathy was that Senator Boucher did not even remotely look for surveillance when on the street, even though she was engaged in the ultimate adventure of treason. She had parked in a loading zone on N Street, the only free space around—she counted on the inviolability conferred by her red-and-white congressional license plates. When she left the meeting with Golov, minus another Pathfinder Corporation disc, she drove straight home. The FBI missed it all.

Benford reviewed the Orion surveillance log the next day while raving at the FBI Special Agents in the room. Nate, back-benched, sat quietly along the wall.

"Forgive me," said Benford in his reedy professor voice, which Nate recognized as the first of the red swallowtail storm flags of a whole gale. "I alert you to the fact that the SVR Washington *rezident* has gone to ground after a multi-hour SDR, doubtless to meet the US mole classified as a 'Director's Case' by the Center. It takes your organization over one hundred and twenty minutes from the time of my call to deploy around the Tabard Inn, which is, roughly, one-point-six miles distant from the J. Edgar Hoover Building. Despite the empirical evidence of contact between the Russian and an American traitor, your people did not check the register, or speak with hotel staff, much less pound up the stairs and enter Golov's room. Had you entered that room and physically searched the most senior SVR officer in the Northern Hemisphere, you doubtless would have recovered classified information—in one form or another—provided *that very evening* by Golov's American agent." The FBI SAs shifted in their seats.

"Yet the FBI did nothing. In this, arguably the

biggest espionage case since 2001, you let the traitor walk out of the room, unidentified and at large."

"Suspect," said Chaz Montgomery. His tie was a Gauguin print of a lounging Polynesian girl. Benford experienced physical pain when looking at it.

"What?" said Benford, his voice rising. Nate wondered if the exchange would end with one of the FBI SAs actually shooting Benford to make him stop talking.

"I said 'suspect,'" said Montgomery. "Whoever is meeting with Golov is a *suspect*."

Benford looked around the room. "Chaz, would you send me the current curriculum of your basic-training course at the academy?" he said. "I expect to discover brightly colored pictures of ponies and flowers."

"Fuck you, Benford," said Montgomery. "You know the rules, and I'm guessing you are at least remotely familiar with the law. We need evidence, incontrovertible evidence, before we move forward to arrest anyone."

"And tossing Golov?" asked Benford.

"Ever hear of diplomatic immunity? We don't even know if there was a meeting or what, if anything, was passed. He could have been there to hand out invitations to the Russia Day reception at the embassy."

"You're not serious," said Benford.

"You know as well as I that we need to build a solid book before we act. These investigations take time. It could break tomorrow, next week, next year."

"You men are Tartars, Mongols, Visigoths, Carthaginians," said Benford, shaking his head.

"What's cancer have to do with it?" asked a young SA whose biceps were visible beneath his starched white shirt.

"*Carthage,* my learned young friend, not *carcinogen,*" said Benford. "I'd mention the name Hannibal to jog the memory of your lessons at Abilene Agriculture and Mining, but I fear you would recall only the Hannibal of fiction."

"Hannibal the Cannibal," said the SA. "Awesome movie. Bureau kicks ass in it."

"Proctor, shut up," said Montgomery, turning to Benford. "I don't have to explain it to you. If we do our homework, UNSUB's in a Supermax facility without parole, one hundred percent. We make a mistake, and he retires as a seven-figure consultant. You think you can press your legs together a little longer?"

"On one condition," said Benford, acting as if he were offended at the brusque way he had been spoken to. "I want a CIA officer to be present when an arrest is made. It's as much an intelligence matter as a criminal one."

"I can't agree," said Montgomery. "The Director won't agree. Besides, anyone involved with the investigation or the surveillance or the arrest is liable to appear in court. Unless you got a guy in mind without cover to preserve, are you willing to burn some case officer's cover for this?"

"Catching this person probably will cost the Agency a valuable asset," said Benford. "I want one of our own to be there."

"I still don't think the Director will approve, but I'll ask," said Montgomery. "Who should I tell them you have in mind?"

"Him," said Benford, pointing at Nate. "He is personally invested in this case." Sitting along the wall, Nate wasn't sure whether he should feel honored or not. His cover was pretty well shredded by now. Besides, he wasn't going to question Benford, especially not in front of a dozen FEEBs.

The Special Agent with the biceps looked over the back of his chair at Nate, trying to get a clue about what "personally invested" might mean.

"Proctor, do not fucking speak unless someone asks you a direct question," said Montgomery.

CHIMICHURRI SAUCE

With a knife or food processor finely chop a bunch of flat-leaf parsley, an entire head of peeled garlic, and one medium carrot. Add olive oil, white wine vinegar, salt, dried oregano, hot pepper flakes, and black pepper, and chop or pulse into a thick sauce. Best served fresh.

34

Vanya Egorov was in his office staring through the plate glass, anticipating the imminent collision of the operational factors swirling around him. SWAN was still producing magnificently, but her lack of discipline made it likely she would burn up eventually. Egorov dared not contemplate losing SWAN.

The news from Korchnoi, just returned from Italy, was barely adequate. Some contact with Nash, relationship renewed, he had accepted the legend that Dominika was now in the Courier Service. They established a universal contact plan. Too slow, always too damn slow.

The mole was still out there, a threat to SWAN, to other cases, to Egorov himself. He ordered Korchnoi to prepare Dominika for another trip, ostensibly as a courier. He needed results. Then his phone rang. The special phone.

"Unsatisfactory," said the president. "I trust you are moving ahead to engineer subsequent contact. No delays." From his KGB days, President Putin knew how important operational momentum could be.

"Yes, Mr. President," said Egorov, "a second trip by the officer is already scheduled. Results will be forthcoming." *Iisus*, Jesus, now he was blowing smoke up Putin's ass.

"Very good," said Putin. "Where?"

Egorov swallowed. "We are determining exactly which overseas location will be most advantageous. I will inform you the instant I decide."

"Athens," said Putin.

"Mr. President?" said Egorov.

"Send the officer—your niece—to Athens. Low security threat, we have people inside the police." Why was he insisting on Greece?

"Yes, Mr. President," said Egorov, but Putin had already hung up.

One floor down, Zyuganov looked into a milky eye and at the death's head skull. "Make arrangements for Athens," said the dwarf, and watched the man get up and leave his office. Zyuganov considered briefly that Dominika could be in danger if she were caught between this Spetsnaz maniac and his target, but that couldn't be helped.

Benford had CID researching compartmented defense projects and crunching names. He was waiting for an echo from Vanya's canary trap. The Orions were trying to fox Golov again on the streets of Washington. But he needed something right away.

They had discussed it in Rome and MARBLE knew what he had to do, despite the risk, and Benford had reluctantly agreed. Korchnoi walked down to the first-floor laboratory of Directorate T. Nasarenko was seated behind his desk, a moonscape riot of papers, boxes, and folders. A long table against the wall was chaos, and similarly covered to overflowing. Nasarenko looked up at Korchnoi, his Adam's apple bobbing.

"Yury, please excuse the interruption," said Korchnoi, walking up to the desk and shaking Nasarenko's hand. "May I speak with you?" Nasarenko looked like a sailor suddenly caught on a disintegrating ice floe, contemplating the widening gap between his ship and the ice.

"What is it?" Nasarenko asked. His face was gray and his hair—never overly combed anyway—was strawlike and dull. His glasses were smudged and cloudy.

"I need your advice on a communications matter," said MARBLE, and for the next fifteen minutes discussed a backup communication system for a Canadian recruitment target. Nasarenko, agitated and with twitching thumbs, distractedly discussed the matter.

Korchnoi leaned over Nasarenko's desk, crowding him, creating blind spots. "What's bugging you, old friend?" he asked.

"Nothing," said Nasarenko. "It's just that work has been piling up."

"If there's anything I can do to help . . ."

"It's nothing," said Nasarenko. "Just a lot of work. I'm drinking from a fire hose of data. I need translators, analysts." His thumbs bent spasmodically as he spoke. "Do you know how much information is on a single disc?" He swiveled his chair around to face a four-drawer safe, took out a lidded steel box, and shook it out over his desk. A dozen plastic bags, stapled at the top, spilled onto his blotter. Inside each bag was a disc inside a gray sleeve. He picked up several discs in shaky hands. "These can hold gigabytes of data. I have all these waiting for processing." He threw a plastic bag across his desk, where it skittered under a pile of dun-colored folders.

Korchnoi reached over to pick up the little bag. He peered at the piece of plastic as if he could not imagine so much information could fit into such a small object. He read the Pathfinder logo on the side of the discs. "Why can't they give you more staff?"

Nasarenko put his head in his hands. Korchnoi felt sorry for this *pugalo*, this scarecrow, with his straw hair and flapping arms. "Yury, don't panic," he said. "You've done too much excellent work for too many years to be treated this way." As Korchnoi reached across the desk to pat Nasarenko on the shoulder, he slipped the plastic bag with the disc into the out-of-sight pocket of his suit coat. Were the discs sequential? Were they logged in? Would Nasarenko notice one of a dozen was missing? "I could send one or two analysts from my department to assist you temporarily, if that would help. God knows we're all shorthanded, but your work is critical. Could you use them?"

Nasarenko looked up gloomily. "Your analysts could not work on the sensitive project, it is restricted."

"Maybe they can work on other projects, to give you some time. Yury, don't say no. It's settled," said Korchnoi. "I'll send over two of my analysts this afternoon, but Yury"—Korchnoi wagged a finger at him—"don't even dream that you'll steal them." Nasarenko smiled thinly.

Washington rezident Golov's cable reporting the barium variant with "shingles" was lying on Vanya Egorov's desk. A single page with a diagonal blue line across the text, it was wrinkled from repeated clench-fisted readings. The Line KR chief, Zyuganov, sat in a chair in front of Egorov, delighted beyond measure. Egorov shook his head. "I cannot believe that Nasarenko is the mole," he said. "He can barely carry a conversation in the cafeteria. Can you see him at night, meeting with the Americans?"

Zyuganov licked his lips. "Shingles. Golov would not make a mistake with this. You read his report, a direct quote from SWAN. 'The mole is afflicted with shingles.' The variant used with Nasarenko."

"He is an absentminded fool," said Egorov, not really knowing why he was defending the man. "He could have mentioned it to others, the word could have gotten back from another source." Zyuganov didn't really care. All he knew was that he would be crawling into Nasarenko's head. Now he had a job to do.

"Damn it, it's all we have right now," said Egorov. "Start immediately on an investigation. Every aspect."

Zyuganov nodded, hopped down off the chair, and headed for the door. He tried to remember where he had put his Red Army tunic, the one with the buttons on the side, the one he liked wearing during interrogations. The greenish brown material—stiff with brown dried blood spots and thick with the stable stench of a hundred bowels—looked smarter than a lab coat, though the sleeves were slightly frayed.

"One more thing," said Egorov after him. "Check him for *metka,* for tracking compounds. If he's touched an American in the last two years, something may show up." Zyuganov nodded, but he had his own opinion of spy dust.

He preferred *povinnaya*—confession, magnificent, liberating confession, the best way to establish guilt. Zyuganov had a connate sense of how to convince subjects, after the screams and separated tendons and spilled ocular fluid, to agree to confess to whatever they were required to confess to.

He still couldn't remember where his army tunic was.

They summoned Nasarenko to Counterintelligence for a "random security update." One did not need to work in the SVR for long to know that this kind of interview represented quite serious trouble, and it set Nasarenko into a panic. After the requisite inconclusive interview with the confused and weeping scientist, Zyuganov transferred him straight to the cellars, in this case to Butyrka in central Moscow. He shrugged on his tunic with anticipation.

People are funny, thought Zyuganov, fingering the lightweight truncheon. *They all react differently.* With Nasarenko it was the soles of his feet and the hollow aluminum baton—much more of a reaction than the average subject. Zyuganov was able to complete one session with the pop-eyed scientist before an inventory of his laboratory revealed that a SWAN disc was missing, and the *pytka,* the torture, stopped because this was something critical. Zyuganov authorized a course of amobarbital that unpeeled Nasarenko's memory enough for him to walk them through the recent past, reviewing staff, and colleagues, and visitors, including the brief visit by General Korchnoi to Nasarenko's laboratory. Korchnoi? Impossible. Make another sweep of the lab. There had to be an explanation. Where was the disc?

Korchnoi heard the rumors about the mole hunt redoubled, about trouble in Directorate T, about sensitive materials gone missing. He spoke to old friends in other departments, and listened to the "porcelain gossip" in the senior-officer toilets. Nasarenko had not been seen in days.

Korchnoi knew the searchers and investigators and counterespionage interrogators would start closing in. He urgently had to send Benford a note, as well as pass the disc he had shoplifted from Nasarenko's lab to the CIA instantly, via dead drop, this evening; that is, if they still let him walk out of Headquarters. He wondered if he had played it too close, whether he had enough time for Dominika to make another trip—to Athens—and blow the whistle on him.

Korchnoi walked out of headquarters on his own legs—not very much longer, he reckoned—and, once back in his apartment, composed a message. His burst transmission took a fraction of a second. Twenty minutes later Benford read the two lines of the message: *Nasarenko is in the snare. Will load DD DRAKON.*

Dead drop, thought Benford. *The old fox must have something important. And Nasarenko's in trouble. That means one of their twenty-three names in*

Washington is SWAN. He reached for the phone to call the FBI.

The night rain sheeted the street, blowing almost horizontally with the gusts of wind. The platform and stairs of the Molodezhnaya Metro stop were deserted, a few cars moving, stores closed. MARBLE flipped up the collar of his raincoat, jammed his hands into the pockets, and started walking slowly up Leninskaya Ulitsa. He had ridden three separate trains, taken a long walk along the river, before his instincts had been satisfied. There was nothing moving around him, or out on the wings, and he did not sense the presence or pressure of men on the street watching him.

Keep walking, steady pace, final approach and sloshing through the rain, water like fingers down his back. *Night creature, hug the wall, listen for the squeak of shoes behind you. Follow Leninskaya through black woods, then the dogleg curve of the road in the trees, one light from Obstetrics School No. 81 flickering through the branches. Quickly now, off the pavement and into the dripping woods.* MARBLE shivered. *Shut up, stop moving, watch and listen, especially* listen, *for the gearbox banging or the brakes squealing or the doors chunking.* Just the wind creaking the trees.

Time to move. Black water was gurgling through a metal culvert under the roadway, and MARBLE knelt and took the pouch out of his pocket, stripped the backing off the adhesive, stuck his arm in, and pressed the gray matte package hard against the inner upper curve of the culvert. *Hold for a count of ten, let the epoxy cure, and listen for the splash that doesn't come.* Satisfactory.

He checked himself again, defending the cache on the way out and all the way to the barnyard heat of the Krylatskoye Metro. There was a sodden pile of clothes on his kitchen floor and the keyboard shook in his hands and the stylus was too small, even with reading glasses. *Hell, don't they build these things for old eyes? Because no one lives that long, that's why,* and the recessed button felt hot as he released the dove into space: *HAVE LOADED DD SITE DRAKON.*

MARBLE sat back in his armchair and closed his eyes. *Come unload DRAKON, retrieve the little black disc, and God preserve the young-limbed CIA boy who will get mud on his suit, or the ponytailed embassy wife, Phonak in her ear, listening for squelch breaks from the radio cars.*

The Station heat-wrapped it twice, tight around the corners, and swaddled the box in burlap and stapled it and banded it and jammed it into the Halloween-orange K bag with the lockable zipper, and flew it home, couriered direct, because this one was from MARBLE. And the dove came back with the branch in its mouth, *DRAKON RECOVERED,* and the culvert in the woods vomited its black water but kept its secret nearly forever.

Benford sat at a conference table in the basement of FBI headquarters on Pennsylvania Avenue in Washington. The table was littered with the remains of lunch ordered out from several local restaurants. This was a working lunch, no executive dining room for them now. Benford had ordered a Thai chicken salad called larb gai, succulent ground chicken with onions and chilies, basil, and lime, so highly seasoned that he was blowing contentedly like a steam boiler while others around the table finished their more conventional Episcopalian lunches of sandwiches or soup.

The table was divided evenly between CIA and FBI, mostly senior-level officers from technical and counterintelligence divisions. When the courier from

Moscow arrived with MARBLE's pouch, Benford—even Benford—agreed to let the FBI handle the forensic dissection of the package, to ensure proper procedure. "These federal automatons," said Benford earlier to Nathaniel, "have been speaking to me about maintaining the 'evidentiary chain' as regards MARBLE's package. If he has in fact recovered an actual disc containing top-secret information, passed by hand to the Russians from SWAN, then according to our FEEBish colleagues we must begin thinking about considerations of admissible evidence and securing convictions and such things." Benford had uncharacteristically deferred to them.

Benford contemplated a metal evidence tray at the center of the table. The disc—now out of its SVR outer plastic and Pathfinder inner paper sleeve—lay in the bottom of the tray, on a sterile towel, its surface lightly coated with gray powder. FBI techs had followed procedure and staggered the tests—a ninhydrin swab to raise existing latent prints on the drive, then the spritz of calcium oxide for contrast. Seated around the table, everybody could see the three distinct, single prints on the dull surface. What would it be: a Russian lab rat's salami thumbprints, or the whorls and ridges of an American mole? Benford knew that MARBLE would not have opened the plastic envelope, he would have been too good, too careful, to touch the actual disc itself. The FEEBs had taken photos and lifts to the laboratory for enhancement. An automated search in the FBI's print archives was already under way.

Benford was in his car heading back up the GW Parkway toward Headquarters when his car phone rang. It was the deputy chief of the FBI Laboratory Services. "You might want to turn around and come back down here," the FBI man told Benford. "You are freaking not going to believe the hit we just got."

"This better be good," said Benford, looking for the Spout Run exit so he could double back.

"Oh, it's good, all right," said the FBI scientist.

BENFORD'S THAI CHICKEN SALAD (LARB GAI)

Finely hand-chop lean chicken breasts with a large knife or cleaver. Season with lime juice and rice wine and sauté until crumbly and white. Let chicken cool and fold in lemongrass, diced garlic, diced chilies, lemon zest, fish sauce, salt, and pepper. Incorporate well. Add chopped cilantro, basil, mint, and scallions. Toss well; serve in lettuce cups with rice.

35

The DNA Fingerprint Act of 2005 was in that year drafted, submitted to, and discussed in the Senate Judiciary Committee of Congress, but, for a variety of political reasons unrelated to national security, was deferred twice and taken off the docket. The bill intended to establish a national fingerprint and DNA archive for background checks, criminal and immigration registration, and identification for federal employees in sensitive jobs. Caucus leadership in the Senate had at the time mildly suggested to freshman senator Stephanie Boucher that in the interest of bipartisan comity she join a mixed group of Democrats and Republicans in support of the bill. Even though she personally opposed the notion of a national archive of identity information as an obscene invasion of privacy, Senator Boucher privately assessed that her public support of the bill would strengthen her national-security credentials and play well to the many high-tech aerospace companies in her state. She even participated in a televised bit of dumb crambo. Legislators agreed to be fingerprinted and for DNA samples to be taken in front of reporters. Senator Boucher smiled for the cameras as a technician swabbed the inside of her cheek, prompting one off-camera staff aide to wonder how many separate DNA nucleotides would be found inside that mouth at any given time.

The result of this bit of bipartisan theater almost a decade ago—long forgotten by her and unbeknownst to her SVR handlers—was that the fingerprints of Senator Stephanie Boucher resided in the FBI's IAFIS database. When a partial right thumb and smudged index and middle fingerprints were lifted off the classified Pathfinder Satellite Corporation disc taken from the SVR laboratory in Moscow, it took the automated system approximately ten minutes to identify Boucher's latents from among the more than twenty-five thousand civilian prints stored in the system.

Benford and FBI counterintelligence chiefs for the next days huddled in conference rooms on both sides of the Potomac, not so much to argue about primacy in the case, or to debate the finer points of a full-court investigation of the senator, but to determine how to keep the White House, the National Security Council, the Capitol Police, the US Senate, the California state legislature, the City Council of Los Angeles, and the California State Raisin Growers Association from leaking details of the investigation to the media. "The last thing we need is for Boucher to panic and defect to the Russians," said Charles "Chaz" Montgomery, chief of the Bureau's National Security Division.

"Nonsense," said Benford, gathering up maps after a long session to discuss surveillance. "Sending Boucher permanently to Moscow would be better than detonating a neutron bomb in Red Square."

The CIA and FBI formulated their tactical plan for blanket coverage on the street, and for telephone, mail, and trash covers. Boucher didn't know it, but she had become the flaxen-haired milkmaid walking alone on the gray moor as the first howls of the hounds came up out of the fog, from the boggy ravines, over the rocky ledges. It was already too late to run.

The California house owned by Senator Boucher was a low-slung, slate-roofed, Prairie-style five-bedroom hilltop retreat on Mandeville Canyon Road in Brentwood with a view of the Pacific on one side and the waffle-iron lights of Los Angeles on the other. A black-bottomed pool and sprawling paved deck in the center of the U-shaped house fizzed under the hazy sunlight. The sliding glass doors of the bedroom wing were open and music drifted out, languorous, careening, enticing, k. d. lang and Miss Chatelaine.

Stephanie Boucher lay on the sheets of an immense bed with an imposing black ash headboard of a certain Scandinavian severity. The slash of black contrasted with a bedroom done in beiges and creams. The senator was naked; a band pulled her hair back tightly on her head. Next to her lay a man half Boucher's age. In his midtwenties, he played either for the Dodgers or the Angels, Stephanie couldn't remember which. He was asleep, naked, an ebony baby grand glistening with morning sweat, the rippling muscles of his back like the stones in a creek bed. He lay on his stomach, feet crossed at the ankles.

Stephanie slowly moved to the edge of the bed, trying not to wake what's-his-name. It was less a matter of being considerate than it was of not wanting to stir him to additional exertions. Last night had been enough, hours of it, some of it *significantly* painful. Legs weren't designed to bend that far, certain body parts were meant to be used in only one direction. But it was the only way to fly, she thought as she slid off her side of the bed, her back and thighs and belly itchy.

She looked into the bathroom mirror and combed her hair, and saw her mother's face, in the little bedroom of the little house in Hermosa, swollen and slack and sitting up in bed sharing a cigarette with a man, sometimes old and fat, sometimes young and skinny, tattoos and mustaches and buzz cuts and ponytails, and Stephanie would close the door and look at the wall clock in the kitchen and wish, just once, her timid, frightened father would come home from work early. After the funeral, and the trial, Stephanie looked into another mirror and told herself that no one was going to help her if she didn't help herself, which was why she had called her father to come home that final afternoon.

Senator Boucher reclined on a padded steamer chair by the side of the pool and picked at a shrimp salad laced with cumin and dill. She had thrown on a white cotton cover-up to spare her assistant the discomfort of seeing her topless as they worked. This latest staff aide, a jumpy, size-fourteen nail-biter named Missy, was sitting at a table covered with papers. Missy was the senator's third personal assistant in the last twelve months. The bleached bones of previous staffers on Team Boucher littered the landscape from Washington to Los Angeles. Missy read from a folder, reviewing the senator's upcoming California schedule. There would be two speaking events in San Diego and Sacramento, a visit to Pathfinder Satellite in Los Angeles for a classified briefing, and a fund-raising dinner in San Francisco. She had to return to Washington no later than Tuesday of next week, in time for the appropriations vote on supplementals for the Pentagon. Boucher told Missy to remind her also to order a top-to-bottom review of the CIA's classified budget. She would ram unpleasant things up the CIA's fanny in the next few months.

That mental image prompted Boucher to look across the pool at the open bedroom doors. Her shortstop was still asleep, thank God. She would get her driver to take him to the ballpark or Malibu or—

Movement. Quite a lot of it. The housekeeper escorted four men onto the pool area from the main wing of the house. Three wore suits and white shirts with muted ties, laced shoes, and aviator shades; one carried a briefcase. The fourth man was Nate, dark-haired and thin. He wore a blazer over a cotton shirt, jeans, and loafers. Boucher watched them come across the deck. Her brain, overheated and mazy, registered a whiff of danger. Whoever these bureaucrats were, she would break some balls, act pissed at this interruption. They didn't give her a chance to build up a head of steam.

"Senator Stephanie Boucher," said the oldest of the three suits, "I am Special Agent Charles Montgomery from the National Security Division of the FBI." He opened a black wallet to display official identification. His two colleagues did the same, but young Tab Hunter behind them didn't make a move. "You're under arrest for espionage as an agent of a foreign power in violation of USC Title 18, Sections 794(a) and 794(c) of the Espionage Act of 1917."

Boucher looked up at the men, squinting in the sunlight. She purposely had not gathered her cover-up around her, and it hung loosely on her shoulders, slightly revealing the curve of her small breasts. "What are you talking about?" she asked. "Are you crazy? Do you think you can barge into my house without making an appointment?" Missy sat silent at the table, looking back and forth at the men and her boss.

"Senator, I'm going to have to ask you to stand up," said the FBI agent. "I need you to come inside the house and get dressed." He began reciting a Miranda warning as he gently took Boucher by the arm to lift her out of the recliner.

"Take your hands off me," said Boucher. "I'm a US senator. You fuckers just bit off more than you can chew." She turned to the plump Missy, still sitting motionless at the table. Missy was mentally reviewing how the day had begun (with a half hour of syncopated grunts and wailing from the bedroom) and how it was progressing (with the FBI arresting her boss). She wondered how it would end. "Missy, get on the phone. I want you to make three calls right away," said Boucher. Montgomery was courteously helping the senator get to her feet.

"Call the fucking attorney general this minute. I don't care where he is or what he's doing, I want him on the phone. Second, call the chairman of the SSCI, same drill, I want him on the line in five minutes. Then call my lawyer and tell him to get over here instantly." Boucher turned to the FBI men standing in a semicircle around her. "Your boss at Justice will impale you on a spit, and my lawyer will roast you over an open flame." Missy hurriedly gathered her papers, but an FBI agent gently said, "I'm going to have to take these papers, miss, sorry." Missy looked once at the FBI agent and then at her boss, and rushed inside the house.

The FBI agents walked Boucher across the deck toward the main wing of the house. In the living room, Boucher pulled brusquely away from the restraining hand on her arm. "I told you dickheads to take your hands off me," she said. "This is outrageous, you have no right accusing me. Where's your evidence, where's the proof?" She walked stiffly to the couch and sat down. There was a hairline crack in her unassailable confidence and arrogance now; she wanted to buy some time, give her lawyer time to get here. Golov's constant yammering about security, maybe she should have paid more attention. Still, the FBI didn't know squat. Golov was a pro, no way they could prove a thing. She did not contemplate the possibility that it was she, Boucher, who may have compromised everything. "I'm waiting for my attorney," she said, crossing her arms across her chest.

"Senator, we have properly identified ourselves as federal officers. We have read you your rights. Do you understand these rights?" Boucher stared at him, refusing to answer. "If you do not understand these rights, I will repeat them. If you do so indicate that you understand them, and keeping these rights in mind, do you wish to speak to us now?"

Boucher figured that any temporizing and delay would be in her interest. The calls to Washington and to her lawyer would soon result in a flurry of action that would string this out for months or years. Boucher told herself that if they had not caught her red-handed, they couldn't prove shit. Allegations, flawed conclusions, unsubstantiated associations. She knew all about this kind of trench warfare. She could brawl with the best of them. She looked up at the FBI agents and said, "I'm not answering any of your questions."

Special Agent Montgomery snapped his fingers and reached around for the briefcase. He took out a folder and laid it on the coffee table in front of Boucher. She opened the file and saw a timeline of classified briefings that she had attended at Pathfinder Satellite Corporation, and records of personal bank accounts reflecting a dozen unexplained cash deposits from unknown sources, each for exactly $9,500, totaling hundreds of thousands of dollars. She remembered demanding mad-money payments, and how Golov tried to dissuade her. The Capitol Hill instincts in her head told her this was still circumstantial, a good lawyer could create doubts, obfuscate, keep the ball rolling. Boucher looked up at Montgomery, defiant. "Just a lot of paper. Doesn't mean squat."

"Senator, please take a look at the last document in the file." Boucher flipped over the penultimate page at the bottom of the file, a brilliantly clear black-and-white photograph of a disc with the Pathfinder logo on it, white and smudged with powder. "We acquired this disc with your latent prints on it from

Moscow," said Montgomery. Boucher did not speak. The living room was quiet; muted music came from the bedroom wing, Yanni's *Out of Silence* album with John Tesh on keyboards, Missy's favorite. Montgomery cleared his throat and slid a one-page document, single-spaced, across the table at Boucher. It had an embossed FBI logo at the top.

"What's this?"

"If you have understood the rights as I have explained them to you, this is a confession of guilt to the charges of espionage. Will you sign it?"

"You think I'm going to sign a confession of guilt?" Boucher could not feel that her cotton shift was hanging open. The FBI agents tried not looking down the front of her cover-up.

"You're not being forced or coerced in any way to sign the document. I am simply offering you the option," said Montgomery.

Among her many flaws, Stephanie Boucher did not suffer from indecision. She believed in herself and had always thought that she deserved—no, it was owed her—the success, career, wealth, and lifestyle she now enjoyed. The fierce and greedy light that burned in her had long ago fired the conviction that she would not give ground, to anyone, for anything. That meant not letting these cake-eaters arrest her, that meant not losing the power and title and respect of elected office. That meant not going away forever to prison. She would not let that happen. She looked around at their faces.

"Okay, I'll sign," she said abruptly. The agents looked at one another. One stepped forward and took a pen out of his pocket. It was a white plastic Skillcraft pen with US GOVERNMENT stenciled on the side. Boucher looked at the pen and waved it off. "Missy, get my pen from the desk," she said. Missy had been telephoning frantically and now walked over to the couch with Boucher's black-and-beige Montblanc Etoile.

Boucher unscrewed the cap, leaned over the paper, and scrawled something on the line at the bottom of the document. "This do it for you?" she asked. Montgomery took the document, looked at it, and smiled.

"I'm not quite sure 'Suck my dick' would be admissible in court. We'll do it any way you like," he said mildly.

"Who the hell is that guy?" she said, pointing at Nate. A moment of awkward silence, while all heads turned toward Nate.

With the agents standing around the couch distracted, Boucher replaced the cap of her pen, grasped the pearl on the end of the pocket clip, drew out the copper-colored needle, and plunged it into a vein on her left arm. Nate was the only one who saw what she had done and he leapt forward toward the couch, batting the pen out of her hand.

None of the people in Boucher's living room had ever heard of the golden dart frog, nor did they know that the two-inch, bright-yellow leaf-sitter lived exclusively in the Pacific-coast rain forest of Colombia. An FBI toxicologist with research materials at hand could have informed them that the batrachotoxin secreted from the skin of the tiny amphibian is highly lethal to humans—a neurotoxin that locks the muscles violently into a state of contraction, causing respiratory paralysis and heart failure. It was KGB chemists in Laboratory 12, the *Kamera,* who first harvested batrachotoxin in the 1970s after they discovered that there is no antidote for the poison and that the toxicity of the compound, as on the point of a treated needle, does not dissipate when dry or over time.

The observed effects of the pinprick on Stephanie Boucher were less scientific and rather more spectacular. Her body convulsed massively, her legs involuntarily shot out straight, her toes pointed, and her limbs quivered uncontrollably. Boucher toppled flat onto the couch, her head flung back, the cords on her neck bulging, her eyes rolling white into the sockets. Nate threw himself at her to hold her down by her jerking arms. Her hands formed rigid claws at her sides and her lips were flecked with saliva. No sound came from her paralyzed larynx as she arched her back almost double. Nate cupped her chin in his hand and moved to resuscitate her. "Better not, dude," said Proctor, the young SA, eyeing the froth that had thickened around her lips. The men in the room stood looking down at her. She thrashed twice more and was still. Her cover-up had fallen open on one side, her breast exposed. Nate leaned over and covered her.

"Jesus," said Proctor, "you think it was the US government pen?" In the far corner of the room, Missy was whimpering. She now knew how this crazy day ended.

SHRIMP SALAD

Lightly boil peeled shrimp until tender-firm. Finely dice scallions, celery, and kalamata olives, cube feta cheese, and mix with mayonnaise, olive oil, cumin, fresh dill, and lemon juice. Add boiled shrimp, toss, and chill.

36

Vanya Egorov sat behind the desk in his darkened office. Shades were drawn across the massive picture windows, his cigarette burned unattended in the ashtray. He was looking at the soundless picture of a flat-screen television in a credenza to one side of his desk—a news outlet from America was reporting a development. A Los Angeles reporter with blond hair and pouty lips was standing in front of an ivy-covered gate on a tree-lined street. Behind him was superimposed the face of Senator Stephanie Boucher, a file photo from several years ago. The scrolling ticker of words along the bottom of the screen read, "CA lawmaker dead at forty-five of apparent heart attack."

SWAN. The most important asset for Russian intelligence in the last five decades. Gone. Heart attack. Nonsense. It was likely she had used the suicide pen Golov had requested and which Egorov himself had authorized. This was a nightmare. Who could have guessed that the Americans would so quickly identify her as the mole? And who would have predicted, in this post–Cold War age of celebrity agents and politician spymasters, that such a drastic, such a violent—*such a Soviet*—conclusion to the SWAN case would be played out? Egorov told himself that he had a narrow window to redemption. The CIA-directed mole was responsible for this costly loss. If Egorov could unmask him, he could salvage his position.

There were at present only two options to pursue: the technical chief, Nasarenko, implicated in the canary trap, and the traitor's CIA handler, Nash. Egorov pointed a remote control at the television to change channels. A clear color picture of Nasarenko appeared on the screen. Every second of the multiple hours of his security interviews in the interrogation chambers of Butyrka had been filmed, and Egorov was coming to the same opinion voiced by Zyuganov, that the twitchy technician was incapable of acting as a CIA internal asset. The tapes showed the beatings, the drug-induced hysterics, Zyuganov leaning over his subject wearing some sort of military jacket. *Don't ask,* thought Vanya.

The relevant portion of the tape had been marked, and Egorov ran the counter forward to the spot. Nasarenko numbly was admitting that he had spoken of the crushing backlog of work with the Americas Department chief, General Vladimir Korchnoi. Korchnoi had offered to send him two analysts to ease the workload. Nasarenko had showed Korchnoi one of the discs during the conversation. No, he had not inventoried the discs after that conversation. Yet by the investigators' count one disc was missing, misplaced. No, it was ridiculous to think Korchnoi would have taken one of the discs. Impossible.

Impossible? thought Egorov.

He had known Volodya Korchnoi for nearly twenty-five years, ever since the Academy. Korchnoi had proved himself to be a superlative operations officer, adept, bold, cunning, the sort of man who could in theory excel as a clandestine asset for the CIA and survive the dangers. His foreign assignments moreover would have presented many opportunities to connect with the Americans. *Impossible,* he thought. Nasarenko would be spluttering for months, more names, more mewling explanations, more temporizing delays. Egorov would raise the idea of Korchnoi with Zyuganov, but there was no time now. The

American Nash was the key. His niece was already on her way to Greece. They would see how things turned out.

Dominika marveled at the white light in the Athens air. Rome's sunlight was golden, softer. This Aegean light weighed down on you. The buildings reflected it, the black roads shimmered in it. Downtown traffic—taxis, trucks, and motor scooters—poured in a liquid mass down Vasilissis Sofias to part, like waves against a spile, around Syntagma Square and the House of Parliament, to recede down smaller streets toward the Plaka. Dominika left her hotel and walked downhill through the buzz of Ermou Street, past shops with two-story displays of lighting fixtures, sports bags, and fur coats. Mannequins in white fox stoles stared back at her, signaling her with tilted heads and segmented wrists. *Be watchful,* they said.

Dominika worked the street hard, crossing in midblock, entering doorways, using the mirrors in the shops and in the sunglasses stores to categorize elements on the street. Short, dark, sleeveless, mustache, dusty rubber sandals, flicking dark eyes. She smelled roasted, popping chestnuts, heard the twang of the wheeled barrel organ on the corner. *Look for the foreign face, the blue eyes, the Slav cheekbones. Look for the brown bloom, the yellow, the green, the signals of danger, deceit, or stress.*

Dominika was dressed in a blue cotton dress with a square neck and black sandals. She carried a small black clutch bag and wore round sunglasses with black frames. An inexpensive wristwatch with a black face and a simple link band was on her left wrist. She wore her hair up, cooler in the midmorning heat, a blue-eyed Russian doing countersurveillance before meeting a member of the opposition.

Dominika turned off Ermou onto a side street,

passing tiny storefronts displaying religious vestments, golden cassocks, stoles, and miters. Silver pectoral crosses hung on heavy chains and rotated slowly in the display windows. She was alone on these side streets, alone after one, two, three turns. Ahead of her was the little Byzantine chapel of Kapnikarea, sunken in the middle of Ermou Street, broad brick and slit windows and sloping tile roof. Dominika crossed the street, went down five steps—the level of the street in AD 1050—and entered the chapel.

The inky interior of the church was minuscule. Frescoes and icons in the ceiling arches were chipped and water stained, the spidery Byzantine letters came off as pale red to her, faded as if by eons of candle smoke and incense. Near the door was a sand table with long orange tapers, some tilted against each other. Dominika took a candle out of a nearby stack and lit it with the flame of a candle already burning in the sand tray.

Before she could seat the bottom of the candle into the sand, a hand appeared and tipped another wick to the flame of her candle. Dominika looked around and saw Nate standing close behind her. He had a wry expression on his face, and the purple halo around him made him look like one of the Byzantine saints on the peeling frescoes. He put his finger to his lips, gestured with his head, and slipped out the door. Dominika waited a moment, planted her candle in the sand, turned, and went out into the white sunlight and city noise.

Nate was standing across the street, and Dominika went over to him. He was very proper, businesslike, the case officer meeting his asset. Dominika remembered the intimacy of Rome the time before, and of Helsinki earlier. They had been lovers, apart from the spying, something vital and edgy and true.

For Nate, the memory of them was more complicated. He had slept with his agent, he was risking his career, her safety, an enormous misstep. He had been warned by Forsyth and Gable, men he respected, yet he made love to her again in Rome, helpless to stop, and with the transcendental Benford in the next room. He had died a little inside when she had been recalled to Moscow, and he blamed himself for what she had had to endure. Now they had a mission to complete and there was a line of dew on her upper lip and he wanted to reach out and touch her.

Dominika knew it too, with the clarity of a synesthete. She stood apart from him, not offering her hand, watching his eyes, the purple in the air around his head. She knew he wanted her to be his asset, his source, his agent, but they were more than that. He wouldn't budge, so she was determined to remain professional. They stood there in the drubbing sunlight for a second, then Dominika said, "Shall we go?" and she followed him as he turned to walk up the street.

They meandered down narrow alleys into the heart of the Plaka, turning left, then right on a seemingly aimless course, a route that would force any coverage to close up in the maze of passageways and courtyards and little open squares ringed by shops. Music drifted out of stores, yellow sponges threaded together in lumpy ropes draped the doorways, the peppery perfume of incense and sandalwood drifted in the air. Automatically, Nate stole glances over Dominika's shoulder—she fluidly looked past his ear to check the other side of the street. He caught her eye and she shook her head slightly. *Nothing that I can see.* He nodded his agreement.

As dusk fell, they walked slowly around Plateia Filomouson, ringed with chairs and canopies and umbrellas, crisscrossed overhead by strings of lightbulbs. Dishes clattered from the kitchens of the restaurants. Nate guided Dominika around a corner to a worn green door in a wall. A small placard beside the door read TAVERNA XINOS. They sat at a corner table in the gravel garden and ordered *taramo* and beet greens and *papoutsakia*, sautéed eggplant stuffed with ground lamb, cinnamon, tomatoes, and béchamel baked golden brown.

Heads together, they talked quietly about the script that Dominika would play back to Moscow. They agreed that she would report to the Center that she had seduced him, and he avoided her eyes for a second. She would report that he was starting to talk about his work, the clever little Sparrow winding up her target. They had two days to create the legend, stay away from her hotel room, watch for surveillance. There would be no contact whatsoever with the Station.

"You will never guess who is in Athens," said Nate, filling Dominika's glass with retsina from a battered aluminum pitcher. "Forsyth arrived two months ago. He's Chief here now."

Dominika smiled. "And *Bratok,* has he followed him?" she asked. She wondered if they knew of their secret affair.

"Gable? Yes. They're inseparable," said Nate. Conversation stalled. They looked at each other in silence. There was a heaviness in the air, a weight on their heads. Nate looked at Dominika and his vision dimmed around the edges.

"We have two days," Nate said. "It is important we go through the act. We need to fill the days."

"We must carry on the actual conversations, we must actually say the things I report to the Center. Everything must be, how do you say, *podlinnyj*?" said Dominika.

"Authentic," said Nate. "We have to appear authentic."

"It is important for me to live the details now, for when I report back," she said, remembering the interrogations in Lefortovo.

Then they had little more to say; they both were leaden with the lie, with the denial of their passion. His purple cloud never changed, as if he felt no conflict. Dominika closed her mind to him. Night fell. They were walking again, skirting the margins of the Plaka, along the narrow, dark side streets hard against the Acropolis walls. They went quietly up a narrow staircase with flowerpots on each step. At the top Dominika put her hand on his arm to stop. They stood in the shadow, looking down, listening in the night for the sounds of footsteps. It was still, and Dominika took her hand off Nate's wrist.

"Decision point," whispered Nate. "Do we split up, go to our hotels, meet early tomorrow?"

She didn't want to make it easy for him. "What if my room is monitored? You would be expected to take me to your hotel, and I would be expected to accept."

Nate fought the sensation of sliding headlong into frigid water. "In the interests of authenticity, of cover, that would be right. Authenticity."

They looked at each other for a minute. "Shall we go?" asked Nate.

"As you wish," she said.

Sergey Matorin stood naked in front of a full-length mirror in his room at the King George Hotel in Syntagma Square. He knew Dominika was staying at the Grande Bretagne next door, both venerable, jewel-box hotels of Old World elegance amid the discordance of the city. Matorin did not look at his body, crisscrossed with scars from combat in Afghanistan, or at the dimpled hole in his right shoulder where he had been wounded in the bazaar in Ghazni while leading a sweep with his Alpha Group. He concentrated instead on a regime of movements in slow motion: strikes, blocks, pivots, and traps, Apollyon performing tai chi, as the noise of the evening traffic roared outside his window. He bent at the waist, then straightened, his milky eye frozen in its socket, and took a deep breath.

He turned, picked up his small roller valise, and flipped it facedown on the bed. He twisted four set screws in the metal frame of the suitcase to unlock a tubular concealment cavity developed by the technical branch, and drew out his two-foot-long Khyber knife with its gently curved hilt. He returned to stand in front of the mirror and went through a combat drill of cuts, parries, and slashes. The knife whistled as he swung it in a backhand cutting blow.

Matorin's body glistened from his exertions. He sat down on a Louis XIV chair, his sweat staining the powder-blue brocade. He picked up a large ceramic ashtray embossed with the King George crest and turned it over. Matorin stropped the blade of his knife along the unglazed ceramic base, heel to tip, heel to tip. The metronome rasp of steel on ceramic filled the room, drowning out the sound of the street. In a while, satisfied with the killing edge, Matorin put down the knife and dug a small zippered pouch out of his suitcase with the word *insuline* printed on the leatherette side. He shook two thick epidermic auto-injector pens from the pouch, one yellow, the other red, field syringes designed to be injected into the thigh muscle or the buttocks. The yellow pen contained SP-117, a barbiturate compound designed by Line S. That would be for the questions. The red pen from Laboratory 12 contained one hundred milligrams of pancuronium, which would paralyze the diaphragm in ninety seconds. That would be for after. Two pens, the gold and red of Spetsnaz.

They took a taxi in silence to Nate's hotel, the St. George Lycabettus, nestled among the pines of Likavittos Hill. From the soaring balcony they could see the spotlighted Parthenon, and the flat sprawl of city lights winking all the way to the horizon, and the black strip of the sea, and the harbor lookout where Aegeus waited for a ship with white sails. Dominika peeked into the bathroom, switching the light on, then off. They kept the rest of the lights off; the ambient light from the hotel's façade was enough. Nate paced a little in the dark room, and Dominika, arms crossed, looked at him.

"If you are reconsidering our plan," she said, "I can report that my visit to your room lasted four minutes, and tell them your . . . ardor . . . was somewhat, how do you say, *umen'shilsya*?" asked Dominika.

"Abbreviated," said Nate. His color flared at the gibe.

"Yes," said Dominika, going to the other set of balcony doors and looking out. "The readers at Yasenevo would be delighted by the gossip that CIA officers' endurance is lacking. Your prowess would be well-known at our headquarters."

"I've always loved Russian humor," said Nate. "It's a shame there's so little of it. But in the interest of protecting our operational legend, I think you should stay overnight."

In the interest of our operational legend, thought Dominika. "Very well, I will sleep on this divan, and you will sleep in the bedroom, and you will keep the door closed."

Nate was matter-of-fact. "I'll bring you a blanket and a pillow," he said. "We have a long day tomorrow, doing nothing." Dominika did not slip out of her dress until Nate had gone into the bedroom and closed the door. Another moon, she thought sourly, it shone through the open balcony door. She got up to draw the gauzy curtains but stopped and lay back down, letting the moonlight wash over her, paint her silver.

She was tired of being used like a pump handle by all of them, the *vlasti,* the inheritors of the former Soviet Union, General Korchnoi, the Americans, Nate, telling her what was expedient, indicating what had to be done. How had Korchnoi done it for so long? How long could *she* last? She listened for Nate in the bedroom beyond the door. She needed something more from them all. She was weary of having her feelings denied to her.

Nearly 0300, and Nate dully registered the door to his room opening. A diffused orange glow from the streetlamps came through the sheer curtains. He turned his head slightly and saw Dominika's silhouette—that unmistakable catch in her graceful stride—move across the bedroom to the window. She reached out and drew the sheers open, first one side, then the other, until she stood backlighted against the sliding glass door, which she slid open. The night air wafted the curtains out and back, snaking on either side of her, around her, over her face, and across her body. She walked toward him, the curtains parting, and stood at the side of the bed. Nate propped himself up on one elbow.

"Are you all right? Is there anything wrong?" he asked. She did not reply and stood still, looking down at him. The case officer in him instantly wondered whether she had heard something, some noise at the door. Did they have to bug out of the hotel right now? He had checked the back stairwell earlier that evening. Still Dominika did not reply, and Nate sat up, reached out to take her hand softly in his.

"Domi, what is it? What's going on?"

Her voice was a whisper. "When we have made love, did you report it to your headquarters?"

"What are you talking about?" said Nate.

"In Helsinki and in Rome, when we were lovers, did you tell your superiors?"

"What we did was against the rules, unprofessional; it was my fault, we risked your security, the operation." She was silent, looking down at him. It was another second before she spoke.

"'The operation,'" Dominika said. "You mean we risked the continued collection of *razvedyvatel'nykh materialov*, the intelligence."

"Look," said Nate, "what we did was crazy, both professionally and personally. We nearly lost you. I thought about you all the time. I still do."

"Of course, you think about the case, about Dominika, *the national asset*."

"What are you talking about? What do you want me to say?" said Nate.

"I want to feel that sometimes we leave the operation behind, that there is just you and me." Her bosom heaved in her brassiere. He stood up and put his arms around her. His mind was a riptide of damage control battling the stirring of his passion for her. He smelled her hair, and felt her body. *You gonna slip a third time, Mr. Case Officer?* he thought.

"Dominika," he said, and the rushing in his ears started, the old danger signal.

"Will you break your rules again?" she asked. She saw his purple lust, it lit up the darkened room.

"Dominika . . ." he said, staring into her eyes. Her lashes caught some of the light from the window. He saw Forsyth's face floating in the air above his head, scary, unblinking. He wanted her, more than his power to resist, more urgently than it was possible to think.

"I want you to violate your rules . . . with me . . . not your agent, me," said Dominika. "I want you to violate *me*."

The lace of her brassiere rustled as she unclasped it. They fell onto the bed, and she was on her stomach, and she pulled Nate on top of her, heavy and hot, his lips at her neck, his fingers twined in hers. She held his hands tight. He fumbled, she teased him, and he trapped her hips with his legs and her breath came up sharp. She groaned, "*Trahni menya,*" and reached behind to touch him while he whispered in her ear.

"How many rules will you force me to break?"

She looked back at him, wordlessly, to see if he was mocking her.

"Shall I break five regulations, ten?" He kept his mouth close to her ear and began counting to ten slowly, matching the numbers with the cadence of his hips.

"*Odin . . . dva . . . tri . . .*" She was trembling but at a different hertz rate than before.

"*Chetyre . . . pyat . . . shest . . .*" She stretched her arms out, gathered fistfuls of bedsheet.

"*Syem . . . vosyem . . . dyevyat . . .*" Fingers like claws, she twisted the sheets around her wrists.

"*Dyesyat,* ten," Nate said, lifting himself off her back, hotly connected yet soaring above her glistening spine, and suddenly the gentle line of her back and buttocks arched, and she buried her face in the mattress, mouth gasping.

The bar of moonlight inched across the room and they watched it as they lay next to each other. Nate leaned over and held her chin in his hand, kissed her on the lips. She took his hand away gently. "If you say the wrong thing," she said, "I will put my thumbnail in your right eye and tip you over the balcony railing."

"I have no doubt you could do it," said Nate as he lay back against the pillow.

"Yes, Neyt," Dominika said, "and if I need anything more, your little Sparrow will lure you into bed again."

"Okay, okay, that's not what I meant. Can we get a few hours of sleep? Will you be still for a while?"

"*Konechno,* of course, good agents always follow instructions," said Dominika.

TAVERNA XINOS PAPOUTSAKIA (STUFFED EGGPLANT)

Brown ground lamb with diced onions and peeled diced tomatoes in olive oil. Season well, let cool, and add grated cheese, parsley, soaked day-old bread, and beaten egg. Halve eggplants lengthwise and sauté in oil until soft. Scoop out eggplants (reserve the flesh) and fill cavity with meat mixture. Top with béchamel sauce, drizzle with oil, and bake in dish (with chopped eggplant flesh and minimal water in the bottom) until tops are golden brown. Serve at room temperature.

37

Zyuganov gripped the receiver of the encrypted phone tightly. The instrument was as big as his head.

"Of course they will be looking for surveillance," Zyuganov said. "You'll never be able to follow them. Stay with your original plan. Do you have the materials prepared? Fifteen minutes will be all you need. One name, confirm it, then the killing stroke." Zyuganov swiveled in his chair.

"Look, I'm not telling you *not* to save her, but the name is more important than anything, than anyone. *Panimat?* Understand? I'm waiting for results, and keep your mouth closed. Out."

Their last day in Athens, the sun hot at nine a.m., both of them feeling tired and unplugged and drifty. They walked from the hotel down Pindarou, stopped for a fresh-squeezed orange juice in Kolonaki Square, sat elbow to elbow under a canopy as the waiter brought a pastry. They would stay on the move throughout the day, continue to rehearse how Dominika would report the contact to the Center. Dominika took a bite of the flaky roll and licked her fingers. She was feeling better and made an effort.

"Shall I tell them you forced me, or that I blindfolded you and locked you naked in an armoire?" She tore a piece of brioche and tried feeding him. He moved his head away.

"The Center would probably understand stuffing someone into an armoire," Nate said. He felt scratchy and irritable and guilty, no patience with morning-after love talk. Dominika's face fell when he said that. She put the brioche down on the plate.

"Well, that is *bezdushnyi,*" she said, turning to face him, heartless, soulless, but Nate's contrarian demons already had their hands in his guts, and he knew his feelings for her, but he knew his duty, and he knew what she wanted, and he knew what he could give, what the CIA would let him give, and that he had let his passion—oh, it was real passion, no doubt—take over again, *again,* goddamn it, on the day before she was supposed to return to Moscow and sit in front of the interrogators, and if she wasn't pitch-perfect, well, that would be his fault because he couldn't tell her no last night. Romantic, hopeless Russians. She wanted some sort of romance, but they were both intel officers, and there couldn't be any distractions. He looked at her—his last thought was that he probably loved her—but she saw the demons, read the purple bloom around his shoulders, and knew the connection of last night was gone.

She saw his guilty regret, and the washed-out color around him. Her own demons flew out of the cave like bats at sunset and she became Egorova, feeling the anger building, the *goryachnost,* the temper that General Korchnoi had warned her about. She stood up.

"I'm going back to my hotel for a shower and change of clothes," she said.

"Negative," said Nate, slipping into agent-handling mode. "It's the one place they can find you—and us. Benford definitely said—"

"Gospodin Benford might do without a wash and a change. I cannot. I will take ten minutes." Nate did some fast calculations. Stick with her? Cut her loose and meet her later? He had seen her face, knew the signs. She was furious at him; it would be best not to let her alone, she might disappear out of spite. Some report that would make back in Langley.

"Okay, ten minutes, no longer," said Nate, taking her arm. She smoothly took it away.

The Grande Bretagne Hotel stood in the sunlight of Syntagma Square, gilt railings and wrought-iron porte cochere glinting in the white light. Upstairs, Nate stood awkwardly in the huge sitting room, with elegant groupings of tables, chairs, and lamps, a thick Wilton underfoot. He looked into the bedroom as Dominika shrugged off her dress—he remembered the black lace bra and panties—and she bent to pull off her sandals, turning to face him, a defiant lingerie model against the backdrop of the massive silk headboard of the bed. Her seminakedness whipped at his senses, and she knew it, she could read him. She took a provocative step forward into the living room.

"Do I distract you?" she said, lifting her arms. She was seething.

"Dominika, stop it," said Nate.

"Please tell me," she said, pulling the cups of her bra tight. "Do I *disorient* you? Is the plan working?"

"Admirably. I cannot think that you could do your duty any better, Corporal Egorova," said Sergey Matorin, stepping out of the walk-in closet between the bedroom and the bathroom. He spoke Russian that sounded like a truck transmission filled with gravel. He was dressed in a dark sport coat, black shirt and slacks, and wore slip-on moccasins. He casually tossed a zippered pouch and a black cloth sheath onto the bed and began shrugging out of his sport coat, never taking his eyes off Nate. Black.

Silence, then electric shock and no hesitation, not a second, as the scraps of black lace launched at Black, her arms around his neck, a knee driving into his crotch. Nate noticed ballet muscles in her legs and her buttocks bunching as Black grunted and pushed her chin back and punched her in the throat, a killing blow, and she fell back on the rug, in her lacey undergarments, gasping.

Nate needed more time to get there in slow motion, thinking, *Someone's going to have to die, dead, as in killed,* because Black had heard them talking and they were a cell phone call away from meltdown, and he put his shoulder down and smelled ammonia and drove the thin body back against a little Hepplewhite in the corner, which made a crack when it splintered. They both pushed off the floor and three stones hit the side of Nate's face, bang, bang, bang, *oh, fuck,* Spetsnaz open-hand technique, and he locked the ropy arm and kicked behind the knee and Black fell and rolled and popped back up, cloven hooves high and smiling. Nate felt for a piece of furniture, and slung it at Black's feet, then stepped in to smell the ammonia again, and he started low and brought the heel of his hand up and through the chin, trying to remember other long-ago hand-to-hand techniques, as Black rolled again and reached the bed and pulled the whispered sheath off, and the blade was up and the point was making little circles, and it was time to back away, seriously, because this was no good and there were no weapons immediately at hand, nothing long enough and hard enough to deal with this bastard and the silver edge of the otherwise blue-mottled steel.

The windpipe strike had not killed her, as there were black lace panties and black lace cups holding the big blue-and-white vase, Ming, Limoges, Wedgwood, whatever, smashing it between Black's shoulder blades in a shower of shards, and he went down on one knee, but there was the whistle of the spinning slash and the blood started, a thin line on her thigh and diagonally across her belly, then she was red and slick, and she staggered back and fell with a bump, sitting up and looking at her legs, one wet, the other dry.

The brass lamp felt good to Nate and heavy enough to throw, but Black's backhanded parry was a blur, but at least it got him off her, and he closed with impressive speed, more like gliding, really, and Nate stepped inside the point of the blade, and he felt cool air on his arm and on his stomach where his shirt split open, then hot blood running down under his belt and down the front of his legs like pissing himself and the motherfucking sword was the real issue so he held the brocade chair like in the circus and the other sleeve of his shirt opened up and the hot blood pooled in his hand, and the point of the blade caught in the brocade of the chair, and he stepped in, not much more time on the clock, he reckoned, and tried to torque Black's knee with legs that were losing strength, bad sign, very bad, like his red footprints on the carpet, and the smell of copper in the air.

Dominika looked at them across the room, Matorin moving easily, swinging his Khyber knife, and Nate staggering sideways, sodden clothes red from the chest down. *My fault, coming back here,* idiotka, *he's going to fight until he dies,* she thought. *He's fighting for me,* and the rush of realization, *He does love me, he is buying me time,* and the *goryachnost,* the rage, picked her up off the floor, and she limped and weaved in an S to the bed and picked up the black pouch. She was looking for a weapon, any weapon.

Black was breathing easily through his nose, and Nate could feel something come loose as the blade ran across his biceps and he grabbed the blade and felt it slide across his palm and through his fingers, like a wet knife through a birthday cake. Black stood looking at him, and Nate concentrated on locking his weak knees so he wouldn't fall. This Spetsnaz guy no doubt was savoring the next cut, thought Nate, an upward rip to spill his long intestines on the Wilton, or the backhand strike at the side of his neck.

Then Liberté came over the ramparts like something out of Delacroix with one breast out of her bra and she drove the red and the yellow pens into his buttocks and his instinctive back fist knocked her down, head bouncing hard, but Black started melting and rasping, great heaving breaths on hands and knees with red and yellow tails pinned on the donkey, and he crawled toward the knife but was slowing down, crawling in slow motion and shaking his head from side to side, with a narcotized diaphragm and a skull full of barbiturates and the good eye rolling up into his head and the heels drumming on the pink-and-blue carpet and the death rattle and *Let's seriously consider sawing off his head, just to be safe,* but Nate's hand was under Dominika's left breast and he was glad of the fluttering heartbeat, her eyes opened, and he started to lay his head on the softness but remembered something important, he couldn't go to sleep just yet, he had a call to make.

Dominika had taken the phone from Nate's nerveless fingers and told *Bratok* where they were, and he listened good and brought a cleared embassy medic and a trauma kit, they were waiting on the street in the car. How Marty Gable got them both cleaned up and out of the hotel was a miracle, vintage Saigon and Phnom Penh. Bedsheets became bandages, Matorin's vinegary-smelling jacket was buttoned all the way up, Dominika's hair was slicked back. Gable motioned to her to yank the pens out of Matorin's ass, sheath the Khyber blade, check his pockets. He put Nate's arm around his neck and humped him out the service entrance, telling a limping Dominika to lock the door to the suite and throw the room key in a planter in the hallway.

They collapsed in Gable's backseat like Bonnie and Clyde, and the wide-eyed medic wrapped Israeli pressure bandages around Nate's chest, arms, and hand, another around Dominika's thigh, and taped the diagonal slice across her stomach. Nate's pulse was thready from loss of blood, so the medic started an IV, and Dominika cradled Nate's head in her lap, not talking, holding the plasma bag up as Gable slammed through traffic, cursing and pounding the steering wheel.

They banged up the hilly streets into Zografos, under the loom of Mount Ymittos, and Gable helped them up to a top-floor *retirée* in a quiet Greek apartment block where the Station kept a contingency safe house. They put Nate in the small bedroom, and the medic stayed with him until the embassy doctor arrived; they were both cleared, but Gable wanted them out as soon as they finished, twenty stitches in Dominika's leg, three times that for Nate. Gable held Dominika by the shoulders, looking at her over the tops of his glasses, but she shrugged him off and went into the other bedroom to sponge off the blood, insanely flashing to Ustinov, how long had it been? Her breaths started coming in gulps.

Gable thanked the doctor and medic—they wondered what the spooks were up to, but knew to keep quiet—and steered them out and gently closed the door. Dominika was in Nate's room listening to him breathe, and Gable shooed her out. She didn't want soup, didn't want bread, she closed the door to her bedroom, but in five minutes Gable heard her cross back into Nate's room, and he left her alone. Later that night Gable cracked open the bedroom door and heard her talking to him, he was still out from the sedative, color better, and DIVA sitting on the bed, talking Russian to him. Big ugly mess this was, but thank Christ they survived.

Forsyth snuck in the next day, after dark, wearing a paste-on goatee and wire-rimmed glasses—Greek cops knew his face, and there was a manhunt on for the young Russian woman at the Grande Bretagne Hotel who had disappeared, leaving a dead man in her room. Dominika's passport picture was all over the television and papers. There had been another man, a dark-haired Westerner, perhaps an American. Gable told Forsyth he looked like a Viennese sex therapist in that goatee, then briefed him on the scene at the hotel, nodded to the two bedrooms in back. Forsyth sat down and threw a stack of late-edition newspapers on the coffee table. The bloodfest at the Grande Bretagne was being covered in a media firestorm excessive even by Greek standards. Station translators had provided a list of headlines:

"KGB Slaughter Plot Sunders Athens Calm"—*Kathimerini* **(center right)**

"Cold War Massacre at Grande Bretagne Hotel"—*To Bhma* **(center)**

"Russian Beauty Sought in Sex Murder Tryst"—*Eleftherotiypia* **(center left)**

"US Disdain for Greek Patrimony, Antiques"—*Rizospastis* **(Communist)**

"Assassin Picks Low Season at Five-Star Abattoir"—*Tribuna Shqiptare* **(Albanian language)**

They made a little noise in the kitchen, waiting for Dominika to come out of her bedroom. A half hour later Forsyth got up and tapped softly on her door. Through the door she told him she wasn't feeling well, no, she didn't need the doctor, but she wanted to sleep. Forsyth came back out into the living room. "I'm not sure, something wrong, more than shock," he said to Gable.

Then a little stirring and Nate shuffled in, finally awake, holding the wall, orange Betadine showing around the edges of the bandages and tape. One side of his face was purple. He eased into an armchair, face wet from the exertion and pain.

"What're you guys doing here?" he rasped. "Some kind of emergency?"

"How you feeling?" said Gable, ignoring him. "Any dizziness? You have an appetite?" Nate shook his head, and Forsyth started talking softly.

"I've been on the green line with the Seventh Floor. I've been called in a half dozen times by the ambassador, who has himself been summoned by the Greek foreign minister twice. The entire Hellenic Police is looking for a Russian woman, trying to ID the dead guy, and the Russian Embassy claims to have no idea what's going on. The Greek Ministry of Foreign Affairs is just up the street from the GB Hotel, and the TV lights in Syntagma Square have been on for twenty-four hours."

"That's the best thing about a clandestine operation, the TV lights," said Gable, looking at Nate.

"Everyone at Headquarters is in a different stage of pissed, seriously pissed, and fucking outrageously pissed," said Forsyth. "There are recriminations flying back and forth: Why didn't we anticipate this kind of SVR action? Why didn't we yank you off the case? Why couldn't MARBLE warn us about the ambush? Most of it's bullshit.

"I received an email this morning from Chief Europe. Admiral Nelson suggested it was 'time to change the sails' in the DIVA case. Apparently C/ROD told Chief Europe he had his head up his ass. In front of the Director. That's all stuff we can handle.

"Then last night Benford called asking whether his guidance about *not going* to Dominika's room was unclear. He sends his regards. Explaining your performance to him, specifically, is something we—you—might not handle so easily. It will depend on Benford's inclination to flog you."

"I gave him my personal recommendation to do so," said Gable.

"Yet there is hope. Benford says this incident has created a narrow window of opportunity; he was very excited. He is arriving late tomorrow evening and until then he wants you to stay out of sight." Forsyth went to the sliding glass doors of the balcony and looked through a gap in the drawn curtains. "It's important that Dominika stay hidden so the Center keeps thinking the worst, that she's blown to the CIA, that their plot to ambush Nate is exposed. We've got a couple of days at the most."

Gable got up and walked down the little hallway and knocked at Dominika's room. He spoke softly through the door and then she told him to come in. They could hear his muffled baritone down the hall, and in ten minutes Gable walked back out and sat down. "Trouble," he whispered. "She's agitated. Not hysterical, just pissed. Splenetic. That temper, but this time it's serious. Doesn't know who to trust. Us, MARBLE, certainly not her own people." Nate struggled to get up out of the chair. "Sit the fuck down," said Gable. "Part of it is that she's frantic she almost got you killed, first thing she asked was how you are."

"She saved my life," said Nate. "That mechanic had me cold."

"You check out the room when you went up?" Nate avoided his look. "Didn't think so," said Gable.

"She's talking about not going back, about running away, defecting. She's shocky and betrayed and her leg's hurting her. Poor kid, just spent two days with droopy over here." Nate wasn't going to make things worse by telling them about the lovemaking.

Forsyth stood up. "Marty, stay with DIVA until

Benford arrives. Nate, we'll smuggle you into the Station tomorrow. I want you to start writing up what happened; Benford is going to want a full readout." Nate nodded.

"Right now let's give her space," said Forsyth. "We may have lost her as an agent. We probably won't find out until she does some thinking."

Forsyth left and Gable got up, rattled around the kitchen, came back out to the living room, said he was going to the corner to get a bottle of wine, some cheese and bread. "Stay off the balcony," he said, moving toward the door. He took a pistol out of his coat pocket, flipped it to Nate. "PPK/S," Gable said. "Ladies' gun. I brought it for you."

Dominika spent most of the first night on her bed, looking at the ceiling. Then she had gone into Nate's room to sit beside the bed, watching him sleep. She knew exactly what had happened. Uncle Vanya had tired of waiting for her to elicit the information about the American mole, had dispatched Matorin to solve the problem and protect his political flank. He apparently did not care that anyone in a room with Matorin was at mortal risk. Had he intended Matorin to eliminate her too? She was not sure, but for the moment she would assume the answer was yes. Another betrayal by Vanya and the *navoznaja kucha*, the dunghill of the Service.

She had told *Bratok* that she was not sure she wanted to continue spying. She was out of Russia, in the West, perhaps she would defect. Gable listened and softly told her to do what she thought was best. His aura was deep purple, he had no reason to be so serene, but she was glad.

Now it was the next night and late, the beacons on the microwave towers on the ridge of Ymittos the only pinpricks of light on the dark mass of the mountain until the orange streetlights of Zografos and Papagou. Forsyth and Benford sat in chairs while Dominika in a bathrobe lay on the couch so she could keep her leg elevated. She had heard Nate leaving the apartment earlier, but she didn't come out to see him. Nate was gone.

Benford arrived late, insisting on coming straight to the safe house. He asked to read the account of the attack, said that the Office of Medical Services wanted the SVR auto-injector pens in the next pouch. In the car he had listened to Forsyth and muttered that speed was of the essence.

"How are you feeling?" he asked her. "Can you walk?" She stood up and walked around the couch. She ran her fingers over the stitches, same side as her broken foot; this leg was getting a lot of wear.

"Forgive me," said Benford, "I need to know you can move around, because we have to go out on the street. You have to call Moscow." Dominika winced as she sat down. Benford put a hand on her shoulder. "Take your time. I want to talk to you first.

"Domi, I need to know whether you are willing to continue the relationship we started in Helsinki. We need to know whether you're willing to return to Moscow and work from there."

"And if I am not?" she asked. "What will become of me?" She knew these men, but her trust in them—in everyone—had faded. They were professionals, they needed results, they answered to an organization that was also the Opposition. Benford and Forsyth were bathed in blue, their words were tinged with it. Sensitive, artistic, devious, they would work her in layers, she knew. *Be careful.*

"What will become of you is that I will fly you to the United States and you will meet with the Director, who will award you a medal and a bank draft with which you may buy a house in a location of your choice—subject to security review—from the comfort of which you can read about current developments in Russia and the world. You will be free of a life of secrets, of intrigue, deception, and danger." Pulsing blue out of the top of his head.

Benford is so clever; I have met him once, yet he knows me, she thought. "And if I elect to continue working with you, what do you want me to do?"

"If you're in, I would ask that you make a phone call," said Benford, "to your uncle." Forsyth was silent and watchful in the other chair, steady blue, she could trust him—a little, anyway.

"And the nature of the phone call?" asked Dominika, knowing they were leading her through one hedgerow after another. "What do you want to accomplish?"

"Forsyth told me a little about the fight in the hotel room," said Benford. "And how you saved Nate's life. I want to thank you for that." He still had not answered her question.

"And the call to Moscow?" she asked.

"After all this drama, we need to pave the way for your return home. And to maximize the chances that you land a good job in the Center—assuming you agree to continue working." Benford pulsed blue at her.

"If I return, General Korchnoi will ensure that I have a good position. He and I will make a strong team."

"Of course, we're counting on that," said Benford. "But you must operate separately, stay in different orbits." Dominika nodded. "And the day will come when you will have to carry on in his place." Dominika nodded again.

"But to enable all this, you have to contact Yasenevo, an urgent call. You are worried, exhausted, you bribed someone, a veterinarian, a pharmacist, to sew up your leg. In your fatigue and anger you discard the basic rules about speaking openly over the phone. The Center's Spetsnaz assassin nearly killed you. Young Nash luckily prevailed. It's important they think Nash killed him. You are calling on the run, police on your trail, the Americans about to catch you. And you have to ask dear old Uncle Vanya to rescue you."

"I see," said Dominika. "*Gospodin* Benford, are you sure you don't have a little Russian in you?"

"I can't imagine that I do," said Benford.

"I would not be surprised," she said.

"There's something else you must do," said Benford. "During the call we must spread some disinformation, do you understand the word?"

"*Dezinformatsiya,* yes," said Dominika.

"Precisely. The operation against Nash has exploded in their faces, but you were able to coax a little out of him."

"What do you want me to say . . . in this *obman,* this deception?" said Dominika.

"You had an argument, still fighting the Cold War, still spying on each other. Nate blurted that a major Russian spy was just caught in the United States, an important person, managed actively by the Center."

"Is this true?" asked Dominika. *This must have been the crisis for Vanya,* she thought. *He is now probably in serious political difficulty.*

"Completely true and accurate," said Benford. "You must tell them Nate told you the Center tried misdirecting the mole hunt by indicating the spy had eye surgery. A false lead." Benford paused.

"Excuse me, but what is the purpose of this message?" asked Dominika. She thought it strange, but could not read Benford's face; his color was fading.

"Dominika, these details are important. We want to let the Center know that we saw through the deception. That's why mentioning the eye-surgery false trail is critical. And we want the Center to think you've done good work, we want them to rescue you. Is all that clear?"

"Yes, but I will tell them *I* killed their assassin," said Dominika. "*Me.* Because he was going to kill us both. Now Nash has fled and it is my uncle's *grubaya oshibka,* his blunder, not mine."

"Admirable," said Benford, "a subtle refinement." *MARBLE was right; she is something.*

"I've written down some details, where you're hiding," said Forsyth. "Then we can go out and make the call." They looked over his notes, then Dominika went into the bedroom to change, leaving Forsyth and Benford alone.

"Not telling her she's pulling the trigger on the general is going to upset her," said Forsyth.

"It's the only way," snapped Benford. "I don't like it, either. But she cannot hesitate or be aware of the canary trap."

"She'll figure it out. What if she's so pissed she quits?" said Forsyth.

"Then this converts to world-class debacle. I hope she'll see it our way," said Benford. "You have the Greek cops all set?"

"It's all arranged. She'll be arrested the morning after the call."

GIGANTES—GREEK BAKED BEANS

Sauté onions and garlic in olive oil. Add peeled chopped tomatoes, beef stock, and parsley, and boil until thick. Add cooked gigantes beans, mix well, and bake in medium-low oven until beans are soft and top is crispy, even lightly burned. Serve at room temperature.

38

Vanya Egorov was in his office working late. The sky had gone from pink to purple to black, but all Egorov noticed was the flat-screen monitor showing endless stories from Greek television, Eurovision, the BBC, Sky, the American CNN, about the incident in Athens.

The Athens *rezidentura* had confirmed that the dead man was Sergey Matorin. Vanya felt his bowels flip when the *rezident* informed him that the Greeks—inexplicably—had already cremated the body, making a forensic autopsy impossible. *Inexplicably, my ass,* thought Vanya. The CIA owned the Greeks, had for years.

Not important, not now. Vanya knew someone else had authorized the wet work in Athens, had dispatched the pie-eyed psychopath to Greece. Not the Director, not his counterparts at the FSB. Not even the dwarfish Zyuganov. Only one possible name. As if sentient, the VCh phone trilled, making Egorov jump in his seat. The familiar voice came through brutally, rasping and ragged, but evilly calm.

"The operation in Athens was a disgrace," said Putin. *Is he in his stocking feet?* thought Egorov. *Shirtless?*

"Yes, Mr. President," said Egorov dully. There was no point in stating that he had not authorized it. Putin knew.

"I expressly specified that there be no Special Tasks."

"Yes, Mr. President, I shall investigate—"

"Leave it," said the voice. "I looked for more successes from you. The loss of the senator is colossal.

The mole in your Service remains active. What are you doing to track this traitor down?" *If you had resisted your monstrous urges,* thought Egorov, *we might have him in the bottle.*

"As you know, Mr. President, I assigned a skillful officer to exploit the American handler. I was hoping for important information—"

"Yes, your niece. Where is she now?" *Here it comes, the worst.*

"She is unaccounted-for, in Greece." Silence at the other end.

"What is the probability that she is dead?" asked Putin. *Don't sound so hopeful,* thought Vanya.

"We are waiting for word," said Egorov. Another long silence. Dominika was a bigger threat to the president, more than the espionage flap in Washington, bigger than a mole in the Service.

"She needs to come home," said Putin. "See that she is safe." Which meant, *Ensure that she will never—ever—talk about the Ustinov* intriga, *the action, whatever it takes—whatever.* The line went dead.

Dominika was missing; if not dead, then presumably in hiding. How she could hide, alone, in the Greek capital, was a mystery. His little Sparrow must be resourceful, he thought. There was news footage of a cordon of gray-and-white Greek police vans around the Russian Embassy in Psychiko. The Greeks had considered the possibility that a Russian fugitive would seek refuge in the chancery.

News accounts included reports of another man, they didn't have Nash's name. Had Dominika gotten anything out of him? Had the CIA killed Dominika? Captured her? If she was alive, he had to get her back. *Spasenie,* salvation, would be possible.

The telephone on his desk purred—it was the outside line, and therefore nothing important. "What is it?" he snapped. His aide Dimitri was on the line.

"An outside call patched in from the duty officer, sir," he said.

"What is this nonsense?" Egorov raved.

"A call from overseas, sir," said Dimitri. "They traced it to Greece."

Egorov felt the skin on his head contract. "Put it through," he said.

Dominika's voice came in over the line. "Uncle? Uncle? Can you hear me?"

"Yes, hello, my child. Where are you?"

"I cannot talk long. It is very difficult here." She sounded tired, but not panicked.

"Can you tell me where you are? I will send someone to you."

"I'd welcome the help. I'm a little tired."

"I will send someone for you. Where can we meet you?"

"Uncle, I have to tell you that my friend, the young one, began talking. I made good progress. Like you hoped I would. But your man, that *d'javol*, almost killed us both."

"What happened?" asked Egorov.

"They fought. My young friend fled, I do not know where he is."

"The young American bested a Spetsnaz-trained fighter?" Egorov wanted to know.

"No, Uncle. *I killed him*. He would have killed me." There was silence on the other end of the line.

Hristos, *Christ*, Egorov thought, *what a demon*. How could she possibly have liquidated Matorin? His hand on the receiver was wet. "I see. What did your young friend tell you?"

"Yes. Something strange. He bragged that the Americans had just caught one of your spies, a woman; he said she was important. I told him I did not believe him." *You can believe it, all right*, thought Egorov.

"He told me you had tried to mislead the Americans, telling them the spy was sick, unable to work."

Egorov was about to scream into the receiver, to tell the little idiot to get on with it. He could feel his own pulse through the earpiece. "That's most interesting. Did he say anything more?"

"Just that the spy did not really have eye surgery, it was a false trail and the Americans saw through it. My friend seemed quite proud that they had caught the spy," said Dominika.

And now they will be less pleased when they lose their own spy, thought Egorov. *Korchnoi.*

"Nothing more?" *Korchnoi.*

"Nothing, Uncle. Our conversation might have continued if we had not been interrupted."

"Yes, of course. Now we must get off this line. Where are you? I will send someone for you. You must stay out of sight."

"I have been staying with a man I met, a stranger, in his apartment. He promised not to turn me in if I was nice to him. That's what you trained me to do, isn't it?"

Egorov missed the irony in her voice. "Can you stay there for another day? Are you calling from his phone?"

"I think I can stay. But I have to go out to call. I abandoned my phone in that hotel. The man has no phone, only a mobile, I would not like to use it to call you. There is a kiosk across the street. I'm calling from there, with a phone card." She gave him the name of the street and the building number in the working-class neighborhood of Patissia, north of Omonia Square.

"Be at the kiosk tomorrow exactly at noon," said Egorov. "A car will come for you. The driver will mention my name. We'll get you back home. In the meantime, stay off the street." He broke the connection.

If they could recover her, Egorov thought, he would be safe. He would cover her in medals if they bagged Korchnoi. First, a telegram to that *durak* in Athens to see if that jackass could manage to pick up an officer under hot pursuit, then order twenty-four-hour coverage on Korchnoi. No alarms, no alerts, no exfils by the Americans.

Even as he steeled his circus strongman's body for the wait, he began thinking about his old colleague who had betrayed him and helped the Americans find SWAN. "Get me Zyuganov," he called to Dimitri.

The Athens *rezident*'s cable arrived the next day in Yasenevo at close of business. It described the scene as two SVR officers entered the Patissia neighborhood to approach the kiosk and collect Dominika. They reported that no fewer than six Greek police cars and twenty police officers in white helmets and flak jackets were milling around the kiosk. It was chaos, the SVR men could not get close, but they saw two female police officers lift a handcuffed woman up the rear steps of a police van. They described the prisoner as "dark-haired and thin," nothing positive but likely Dominika. She was in their hands. Not two minutes after the arrival of the cable on his desk, the VCh phone on the credenza behind Egorov's desk began trilling with a sound unknown in nature.

It was past midnight, and the Moskva River bend visible from General Korchnoi's living room was a black ribbon between the high-rise lights of Strogino. The apartment blocks across the river were newer than the buildings on this side; construction cranes still towered above unfinished units. MARBLE made a favorite dinner of *pasta alla mollica,* tossed with anchovies, bread crumbs, and lemon. After washing up, he brought a glass of brandy into the living room, checked his watch, and went to the bookshelf that ran along the wall. He slid a small paring knife into the join of the top of the shelf, wiggling the blade to release two catches mortised into the wood. The top of the shelf opened on concealed hinges like a coffin lid, exposing a shallow compartment.

Korchnoi reached into the cavity and pulled out three gray metal boxes wrapped in a clean cloth. The first two were each the size of a cigarette pack, the third flatter and wider. Korchnoi connected the two small boxes end to end by fitting their tracked rails together. The flatter box—with a tiny Cyrillic keyboard—was in turn connected to the first two by a pinned plug. A stylus lay in a side clip holder. Using the stylus, Korchnoi depressed two recessed buttons to illuminate three tiny LEDs. The first was the battery/power indicator. Green, go. The second indicated whether the integral antenna in the top component could read the US Milstar Block II geosynchronous bird. Green, strong signal. The last LED indicated whether the transmission exchange, the *rukopozhatie,* the handshake, had been completed. Yellow light, standby.

Korchnoi used the stylus to depress keys to compose a routine message. He wrote plainly, eliminated spaces and punctuation, cryptic economies learned over the years while preparing secret-writing letters—he missed the tactile process of SW, rubbing the paper, preparing the inks, the featherweight pressure while printing the block letters.

He worked sitting in his armchair, the reading light over his shoulder, an old man on a Vermeer canvas, bent over his work. There was utter silence in the room. The message composed and signed "niko," the free-from-duress indicator, Korchnoi pushed the transmit button and watched the yellow light. His message soared heavenward in a super-high-frequency burst in the Ka band, washed over the satellite, tickling its sensors. The already-stored reply was activated and returned on an attenuated signal in the Q band in the space of three seconds. Moscow slept, the windows of the Lubyanka were dark, yet Korchnoi had reached upward to touch fingertips with the Main Enemy. The LED winked green. Handshake. Successful exchange.

Korchnoi unwrapped a cord from a recess in the keyboard unit and plugged it into the input jack in the back of the small color television he had received from a CIA officer in a midnight trunk-to-trunk exchange three years ago along the M10. The set had been modified by the CIA, and Korchnoi turned it on, selected a preset channel. Three keystrokes with the stylus and the snowy blank screen turned black, blipped once, then turned black again, displaying two words in light typeface. *Soobshchenie: nikto,* was the message: *Message: none,* it read. The period was missing, that was the real message, the signal flare: game begun.

Korchnoi turned off the television, coiled the cord back into its compartment, shut down power, and disassembled the commo equipment. He wrapped the components in the cloth and returned them to the concealment cavity, closing and locking the lid. He returned to his chair, his book on his lap, and took a sip of brandy. He reached up and turned the reading lamp off, and sat in the darkness of his apartment looking out at the city lights and the black river, certain in the knowledge that the SVR had seen and recorded everything he had done in the last thirty minutes.

From August to October 1962, the KGB mounted blanket surveillance on Colonel Oleg Penkovsky of the GRU, including in his apartment overlooking the

Moskva River. The colonel at the time was passing the West voluminous intelligence on Soviet ballistic missile capabilities. Officers of the FSB surveillance unit, who more than five decades later were watching General Vladimir Korchnoi, were too young to remember that Cold War case, but the measures they employed to gather evidence against their target were nearly identical to their predecessors'.

Across the river, from an apartment in a partially completed high-rise, three teams of watchers used colossal yoke-mounted naval binoculars to watch Korchnoi orient his covcom equipment to an azimuth of thirteen degrees to communicate with the satellite. From the apartment directly above, Korchnoi's watchers had down-drilled pinholes in the ceiling of three rooms fitted with fish-eye lenses and stick microphones, both slaved to digital recorders. They had watched Korchnoi access his bookshelf concealment device, assemble the components, and poke out his messages on the keyboard. They did not have the angle to read words off the screen of his television set, so they lowered a remote-head video camera on a fiberglass spar down the outside of the building to record words on the television through the living room window. Unlike with the Penkovsky case, they did not need three months. They had enough.

Midnight. Across town, another team was going through Korchnoi's office in the Americas Department on the second floor of Yasenevo. Apart from a thorough physical search of the office, desk, credenza, and containers, technicians minutely took swab samples from a number of surfaces: keyboard, desk drawer pulls, safe handles, file folders, teacup, and saucer. The next morning Zyuganov brought in the lab report and Egorov snapped it out of his hand: *Metka indicated in trace amounts, inside doorknob, right edge of desk blotter. Analysis: Compound 234, lot number 18. Host: Nash, N., Amerikanskij posol'stvo.* The American Embassy.

Korchnoi returned home from Yasenevo after work, the early twilight bright over the trees along the river. His legs were leaden and his chest felt constricted as he walked along the esplanade from the Metro stop. The building was quiet but for the murmur of television sets behind the doors, and smells of cooking food were heavy in the corridor. The instant MARBLE opened his apartment door, he knew he was caught. The key had always stuck; he normally had to jiggle it to turn the lock. Tonight the cylinder felt silky. They had sprayed graphite in the keyway to lubricate it.

There were five men in his apartment standing in a semicircle around the front door. Rough, lean faces, square-jawed and hard-eyed, wound up. They wore jeans, tracksuits, leather jackets, and they swarmed the old man the minute the door opened. He knew enough not to resist, but they grabbed his legs and arms and picked him up off the floor. They moved quickly, silently, a forearm around his throat, two others specifically holding his arms. *They always pick you up,* he thought, *but where am I going to run?* He said nothing as they forced a rubber wedge that smelled of drains between his back teeth (*Not to be biting down on cyanide capsule, please, comrade*) and they stripped him to his underwear, never letting go of his limbs (*Not to be using weapons or buttons or needles in clothing, please, comrade*). They forced an ill-fitting tracksuit on him and carried him bodily down the stairwell, passing at least ten other men in leather coats standing on the landings. He was wedged into the back of a dark-green van, their hands never letting go of his arms and legs. Pain ran through Korchnoi's body; he was losing feeling in his arms where the men were gripping him tightly. *It doesn't matter,* he thought, preparing himself for the next chapter. He knew what was coming.

The ride in the windowless van was long. They rocked violently as it made turns, jounced when it went over tracks, and tilted as they went around a traffic circle. Korchnoi knew where they were headed, he could track their route west through the city. When the van doors were flung open and he was dragged out, Korchnoi looked up. He thought he should take one last look at the sky, tonight inky black with an orange city glow, and breathe the air deeply, likely the last time he could do so. As they manhandled him to a small door, he also looked around quickly to confirm what he knew already. The crowded courtyard was littered and dirty, bleak walls of unfinished cinder block were topped by a jumbled lattice of barbed wire, the familiar ocher walls of the Y-shaped, five-story building were unmistakable. Lefortovo Prison.

Korchnoi knew what was inevitable: *vysshaya mere,* the highest punishment. He knew his final stop: *bratskaya mogila,* an unmarked grave. The only choice remaining to him was the manner in which he would go out. He already had decided not to make it easy for them, and that ironically meant he would talk, freely, but just not about what they wanted to hear.

To the mounting discomfort of his interrogators, he told them he had not been spying against Russia, rather, *he'd been spying for Russia,* first to defy the Soviet system, the system that strangled its people for fifty years, and now to confound the *podonki,* the current crop in the Kremlin. He told the steely faced men in the interrogation rooms that he had no regrets, that he'd do it again. His career as a spy overwhelmed them; he was a general officer. The damage assessment would take years. He could see it in their faces.

Contemplating his arrest and certain demise was made easier knowing that he had set in motion his legacy. He noted with satisfaction that Dominika was not mentioned during any of the questioning, nor was there any insinuation that she was under suspicion. She was safe.

Korchnoi answered their questions, and catalogued the intelligence he had provided for nearly a decade and a half to the Americans. Despite Korchnoi's total cooperation, Zyuganov told them to shift to "physical means," some of the old techniques from the original basement cells of the Lubyanka. It was Zyuganov's pleasure, perhaps a little payback because Korchnoi had betrayed them, the bendy cedar slivers under the nails, black and oozing red, the wooden dowels pressed between the toes, the oily knuckle pressed into the hollow behind the earlobe. In another room, the woman doctor, a urologist, looked at his face as she eased the wire up one more millimeter.

When the rough stuff suddenly stopped and they left him in his cell for an entire day, Korchnoi suspected Vanya had probably ordered a halt. The next day Korchnoi entered the interrogation room as he had been doing for the last days, to be confronted with a display of his CIA communications equipment laid out on a table. They waited for some time before Vanya Egorov walked in, motioning the guard to get out and close the door behind him. Vanya went around the table slowly, not looking at MARBLE, fingering the equipment and battery packs with a faint smile on his lips.

"I considered it might be you, briefly, some months ago," said Vanya, lighting a cigarette. He did not offer one to Korchnoi. "I told myself it was impossible, one of our best, the last person who could possibly engage in such disloyalty to Russia."

Korchnoi said nothing, held his hands in his lap. "All those years, all our work together, a life's career, everything undone so easily," said Egorov. "The trust I showed you, the love."

"This is about you, of course," said Korchnoi. "It always is about you, Vanya."

"*Zalupa,* dickhead," said Egorov, flicking his ash to the floor. "You have gravely damaged the Service. You have damaged your country, forsaken Russia." He was playing it up for the microphones, thought Korchnoi.

"*Zalupatsia* is more like it," said Korchnoi, Vanya playing the big man, taking airs. "What is it you want, Vanya? Why are you here?"

Vanya looked at Korchnoi for a second, then looked at the equipment on the table. "I came to tell you that it was my niece, your protégée, Dominika, who elicited the information that led to your arrest. She is a hero, and you are the *plodovyi cherv,* the cankerworm."

There it was, their succession *sekretnyi plan.* Korchnoi said a silent word of congratulations to Benford.

Vanya watched Korchnoi's face to gauge his reaction, and was satisfied to see the older man look down, as if in defeat. He gathered up his cigarettes and pounded on the cell door. Walking down the cement corridor past the steel doors, Vanya calculated. Loss of SWAN balanced out by the arrest of Korchnoi. Dominika. *Get her back.*

Myshinaya voznya. Mice games. Line T technical officers carefully moved the covcom equipment back to MARBLE's apartment building in Strogino, to originate the transmission from the usual coordinates. A knot of quiet men huddled on the roof looking out over the blue-black Moskva River and hit send and waited for the *rukopozhatie,* handshake, from the satellite over the Arctic Circle. The uppercase "NIKO" signature on the covcom transmission told Benford that MARBLE's message had been written by someone else, or by MARBLE under duress. Whatever the case, it meant that his arrest had finally come. Even though he and MARBLE had gone over and over the plan, Benford's instincts recoiled at the thought of his agent sacrificing himself, and he silently mourned the loss.

His Mercedes covered the twenty-five miles on the deserted Rublyovo-Uspenskoye Highway in fifteen minutes, but Vanya had to wait at the reception building for ten minutes before the duty vehicle arrived to take him through the black fir and pine forest to the neoclassical front entrance of Novo-Ogarevo. Vanya checked his watch. Nearly midnight, and he inwardly shuddered at the late-night summons to the secluded presidential dacha west of Moscow. *Just like you-know-who,* thought Vanya. Uncle Joe made men wait till three a.m. in an anteroom superheated by a roaring fireplace.

This was different than Stalin. Egorov was ushered down a curving flight of steps into a massive basement gymnasium that stretched the entire width of the building, brimming with machines and weight stacks glittering in the overhead lights. Egorov dryly noted that his Line KR chief, Alexei Zyuganov, was sitting in a chair next to an exercise station. *A witness,* thought Vanya, *bad sign.*

President Putin was shirtless, his hairless chest slick, the veins in his arms popping. His hands were through the grips of two nylon suspension straps, anchored to an overhead bar. The President of All

Russias leaned forward against the straps and, by extending his arms like Christ on the Cross, lowered himself face forward, nearly parallel to the mat, a foot off the floor. Shaking with exertion, he raised himself up by bringing his arms together, then lowered himself, then up again. That little *ulitka,* that escargot Zyuganov, never took his eyes off Putin. A matter of seconds before he would be licking the sweat off his benefactor's chest.

Putin continued raising and lowering himself, with hissing exhalations of breath, then stopped at maximum extension, raised his head, and looked at Egorov with eyes the color of an old glacier. Motionless. Levitating. Another second, and up again.

"I want her out of Greece, back in Russia," said Putin thinly. He mopped his face with a towel, threw it backhanded at Zyuganov, who caught it, flustered. Putin stared, his eyes bored into Egorov's, an unsettling habit, featuring himself as a clairvoyant, a savant. Some believed the president could read minds.

"I am working through several contacts," said Egorov. "The Greeks are furious."

Putin held up his hand. "The Greeks are incapable of such outrage, they're puffed-up little birds," said Putin. "We will show them Kuzka's mother." *In other words, he'll bury them,* thought Egorov, *right after he finishes with me.*

"The Americans are behind the Greeks; they control everything," said Putin, moving to a bench machine with stainless handles. "They will try to direct this to their advantage, to discredit Russia, *to embarrass me.*" There it was, the ultimate transgression. Egorov refrained from replying. Zyuganov squirmed in his seat. Putin lay back on the bench and began pressing the handles above his head. A weight stack behind his head rose and fell as he pumped.

"Egorova is a hero," Putin said, the clanking plates

echoing in the massive room. "I'm not interested in the details, or in the difference between tradecraft mistakes on the street and bureaucratic bungling in Yasenevo.

"I . . ." clank,

"want . . ." clank,

"her . . ." clank,

"back." Clank.

Vanya Egorov heard the clanking weight stack in his head, like Satan's bilge pump, all the way back to Moscow.

In the backseat of a separate, less luxurious car, also speeding back to Moscow, Zyuganov knew he had a narrow opportunity to cement his standing. He assessed that Egorov was hours away from being cashiered, purged, perhaps jailed. Putin would not reinstate him, regardless of the outcome with Egorova. There were too many failures, too many mistakes. If he, Zyuganov, could retrieve Egorova, promotion and rewards would cascade around his head. He could never have guessed that the CIA would be calling him to discuss that very thing.

PASTA ALLA MOLLICA (ANCHOVY SALSA)

Toast bread crumbs until the "color of a monk's tunic." In a separate pan, sauté anchovy fillets in oil until they dissolve into a paste; add sliced onions, garlic, and red pepper flakes and continue cooking until onions brown. Toss cooked, drained spaghetti into pan with anchovy-onion salsa, add parsley and lemon juice, and mix well. Sprinkle with bread crumbs and serve.

39

After her arrest, Dominika had been quietly turned over to Forsyth by the Greek police and had been moved to a new safe house in the beach town of Glyfada. On a windy, rainy afternoon Benford and Forsyth told her that there were "indications" almost certainly confirming the arrest of General Korchnoi by the FSB. She had set her face, emotionless. Another loss.

"We lived with the possibility it could happen," said Benford.

"But why now?" said Dominika. "We would have worked together. How did this happen?" Benford noticed that her concern was only for Korchnoi. She was not thinking about herself.

"We're not sure," said Benford. "After the loss of the US mole, Line KR has been looking for the leak. It could have been a mistake he made."

Dominika shook her head.

"After fourteen years? I do not think so. He was too good." Forsyth studiously did not look at Benford. Forsyth's blue mantle was paler today, perhaps he was tired. In contrast, Benford exuded an inky blue. *He is working, thinking, plotting,* she thought. Dominika knew something was not right.

Benford looked at his hands when he spoke. "You know, Dominika, Volodya had great admiration for you." Dominika watched him carefully, how he held his hands. He definitely was working.

"I believe he envisioned you as his replacement, to continue this work. We thought we had two years, perhaps three, to build this together. We could not have known. So now it falls to you, sooner than we want, but it falls to you, nonetheless." Dominika turned to Forsyth, who reached out to pat her hand, but she moved it slightly out of his reach. There was a lot of blue fog in this room, she thought.

"I am heartbroken over the arrest of the general. I will never forget him," said Dominika slowly. "But you are direct, *Gospodin* Benford. With him gone, you are telling me that it is *otvetstvennost,* how do you say it, *my responsibility,* to continue the struggle. That's it, isn't it? It remains only for me to decide whether I will continue working." She stopped and looked at them, reading their faces. "*Gospodin* Forsyth. What do you and *Bratok* think?"

"I would tell you exactly what Marty Gable told you," said Forsyth. "Follow your heart, do what you believe." Benford looked over at him, mouth pursing in annoyance. Forsyth could have been a little goddamned more persuasive.

"Your reasons to join us were complicated," said Forsyth, who knew what he was doing, to whom he was speaking. "Friendship with Nate, your despair over the disappearance of your friend, being undervalued and mistreated by your own Service. Having control of your life and career. Nothing about that has changed, right?"

"You should be a college professor," said Dominika, watching him waltz.

"We don't want to overwhelm you," said Forsyth.

"Yes, we do." Benford laughed. "Damn it, Domi, we need you." Inky blue like the tail fan of a peacock.

She looked at the bandage on her leg. "I am not sure I can agree," she said. "I must consider it."

"We know you will," said Forsyth. "If you do agree, the most important thing will be to get you back to Moscow quickly, securely. And that's why we three are the only ones who know where you are."

"Not even Nathaniel?" Dominika said.

"I'm afraid not," said Benford, his color unchanged. *At least he's telling the truth,* thought Dominika.

Awake early, Dominika stood barefoot in the spacious living room of the safe house. The triple doors were folded back, opening the whole room to the wide, marble-floored balcony over which stretched a blue canvas awning that lightly billowed and popped in the last puffs of the onshore sea breeze. Across the Glyfada coast road, the Aegean sparkled in the morning light of a sun still low on the horizon. Dominika felt the warmth building on the marble floor. She was wearing a belted cotton bathrobe and her hair was a tousled mess. A clean bandage was tight around her thigh. Gable had gone out for bread.

She jumped at the soft knock and stood to one side of the door and waved a folded newspaper across the peephole, waited, then looked out. Nate, standing in the hallway, looking down. Dominika turned the locks, opened the door. Leaning against a cane, Nate limped straight into the center of the room. She turned and went up to him, snaked her arms around his neck, and kissed him. She hadn't seen him since the first safe house, after she held the IV bag above his head in Gable's car. She had sat with him the first night, but then he was gone.

"Where have you been?" she said, pulling his hair. "I have been asking about you." She looked in shock at his purple face, which blended with his florid halo. "You saved my life, it was my stupid mistake, I made you come to my hotel room." She kissed him again. "How are you? Let me see your hand." She brought his hand up to her lips and kissed the back of it. "Why haven't you come to me?" He stepped back from her.

"Were you ever going to tell me about this safe house?" said Nate woodenly. "Were you going to let me know where you were?" His words came at her, each one a deep-purple disc in the air. It was as if she could feel them hitting her body. She moved out to the balcony.

"Yes, of course," said Dominika, "after a few days. Benford asked me to stay quiet for two or three days. To let things calm." She leaned against the railing. Nate followed and leaned against the door-jamb. His purple cloud pulsed as if someone were flicking a light switch on and off. Nate's hands were shaking and he put them in his pockets.

"How did you find me?" asked Dominika.

"Everything that's going on with this case—safe houses, signals, SIGINT—is being reported to Headquarters," said Nate. "I wrote some of the cables, but Benford and Forsyth apparently have written a few of their own, in restricted channels. I was able to read some of those, against regulations. I've read quite a lot, actually."

Dominika looked at him, watched his halo, read his face, felt his anger. This was what Benford had wanted.

"Do you know Vladimir Korchnoi has been arrested in Moscow?" Nate said brutally. "There's SIGINT, and collateral reporting, and the VCh line in Moscow is buzzing. Do you know he's in Lefortovo?" Dominika didn't answer.

"What did you say to your uncle when you called Moscow?" said Nate. His tone was flat, unemotional. Dominika's stomach felt heavy, weighted.

"Neyt, Benford doesn't want us to speak of this. He was quite clear."

"The cables said you called your uncle. You said that we had been together. The cables said that I had told you about the mole I handled in Moscow. Who told you to say that?" Nate stood sullenly, his hands by his sides, his color pulsing. "Do you know that your call probably got Korchnoi arrested? What did you say to Egorov?"

"What are you talking about?" Dominika said, confused, frightened. She felt the rage building, more so because it was Nate telling her these things. She needed to ask him once. "Do you believe I would *knowingly* do such a thing?" asked Dominika.

"So you didn't know? It's all in the cable traffic," said Nate.

"I don't care what is in the cables," she said, taking a step toward him. "Do you believe I would harm him, this man?" She remembered Benford's instructions to say nothing.

"When you didn't call me, when you went into hiding, I thought it was for security. But how could you have agreed to betray the general? Your call to Moscow was the trigger."

Dominika could only stare at him. "Did Benford tell you to do this?"

Nate ran his fingers through his hair. "You followed orders, you bought the plan. Whatever the goal, your placement as prime agent is assured. Congratulations." Purple and emotion, lava running downhill.

"What are you talking about?" said Dominika. "I did not sell anyone."

"Well, Korchnoi is in Lefortovo, thanks to your call. You're now number one. He's lost."

"You think I did this?" Dominika said. "You cannot speak to me this way." She wanted to scream, but instead spat the words out in a whisper. "After all we have gone through, after all that is between us." Dominika did not permit herself to cry.

"That's not going to help Korchnoi now," said Nate. He straightened and turned toward the apartment door. She could stop him with a word, a half dozen sentences of explanation, but she would not. The door closed on his luminous rage.

Forsyth had to restrain Dominika when Benford told her that her scripted phone conversation with Uncle Vanya had indeed directly resulted in the arrest of Korchnoi. "How dare you use me in this," spat Dominika as she pulled against Forsyth's arms. He steered her to an armchair and continued standing between her and Benford, while she gripped the arms of the chair. "You used me like a common *donoschik*, an informer." She made to get up again, but stopped when Forsyth put up his hand.

"You're all so smart, you could not think of anything better than this?"

Benford was pacing in the living room, trailing a dark-blue cape of deceit. The sea breeze blew through the balcony doors. "We made a decision, Dominika," said Benford. "I will tell you that Volodya conceived the plan, he insisted on it. For him it was the culmination of his career as an agent. He had you spotted and elected and prepared as his successor before you got out of Lefortovo. He would be satisfied now."

Dominika's hands gripped her chair. "You will let him die to continue the secrets? Is the stupid information more important to you than *this man*?" She got up and paced the room, her arms around her stomach, her hair in all directions.

"The stupid information is, in fact, the point of what we do. We all sacrifice to play the Game. No one is immune," said Benford.

Dominika looked at Benford and with great force swatted a lamp on the side table to the floor, shattering it on the marble. "I asked you if the information was more important than the man, than Vladimir Korchnoi," said Dominika, shouting. She was looking at Benford as if she were ready to sink her teeth into his neck. Forsyth was shocked at her fury. He moved a half step toward her in case she launched.

"To tell you the truth," said Benford, looking first

at Forsyth, then at Dominika, "no. But we have to move forward. It is now more important than ever for you to return. That is the task at hand right now."

"More important than ever? You make me responsible for killing this man. You have maneuvered me into this position. If I refuse, knowing what you made me do, the general's sacrifice will have been wasted." She pivoted and started pacing again. She looked at them through narrowed eyes. The hem of her dress shivered as her body trembled. "You are no better than they are."

"Compose yourself. There is no time for this," said Benford. "Volodya would tell you the same. You now have to prepare to return to Russia. We must take advantage of the situation. Cultivate your fame as the officer who identified the mole, who passed the critical information that resulted in his arrest. You must exploit the credit within your service." Benford's halo was as blue as an alpine lake. He was concentrating, nervous, anxious.

"*Khren,*" said Dominika, "bullshit. You did not tell me the truth. I never would have agreed to this."

No one spoke. They were in the living room, motionless, looking at one another. Forsyth watched Dominika's breathing slow, saw her hands unclench, her face relax. Was she going to go along? Benford broke the silence.

"We have to move quickly," he said. "Dominika, are you in agreement? Can you accept this?" Dominika straightened her shoulders.

"No, Benford, I will not accept this, I cannot." She looked over at Forsyth. "I am a trained intelligence officer in the SVR," she said. "I am familiar with the Game. I know about sacrifice, about doing *podlye shagi,* repulsive things, for operational advantage." She looked at them both. "But there are things more important than duty. Respect and trust. Between colleagues and partners. You require it from me; why should I not require it from you?"

"I want you to keep in mind that this situation is what Volodya *wanted*. I would not want to contemplate wasting his courage," said Benford, feeling the sand slipping between his fingers.

Dominika looked at the two men for a beat, then turned and went into her bedroom, closing the door softly. *Not good,* thought Forsyth. He turned to Benford.

"You think she's left us?" he said.

"Fifty-fifty," said Benford tiredly, leaning back on the sofa. "We don't have much more time. If she's going back, she's got to decide in the next day. MARBLE was convinced she'd agree. I don't want to think of the flap on our hands if we've let MARBLE get the chop for nothing, if she refuses to go back inside."

"But that's not all," said Forsyth, "is it?"

"You tell me," said Benford.

"You've got one final card in your hand. Something that will convince her to continue."

"I dislike the metaphor. This is not a game of chance."

"Sure it is, Simon," said Forsyth. "It's all about chance."

Benford sat on a couch under a potted linden tree in the atrium of the König von Ungarn Hotel in Vienna, in an angle of the Schulerstrasse behind St. Stephen's. Benford had returned after an amusing half hour at the Bristol Hotel with the SVR's Line KR chief, Alexei Zyuganov, who had appeared wearing an inexplicable felt snap-brim hat. He was accompanied by a dark-complected young man from the Russian Embassy. Over a glass of Polish vodka and a small plate of sweet-sour cucumbers, Zyuganov continued to profess ignorance of the bloodbath in Athens. He had refused to speak of Vladimir Korchnoi other than to repeat that he was guilty of treason. He insisted that Benford press the Greek government for the immediate release of Egorova to the Russian Embassy in Athens.

Benford with a straight face told Zyuganov that the Greeks were being obstreperous and were not only interrogating Egorova about the death of the former Spetsnaz officer in the Grande Bretagne Hotel, but also insisting that she participate in a press conference about *all her activities* in exchange for a lighter prison sentence. Zyuganov sat up straight and again insisted that Egorova be released, at which point Benford made his proposal. A half hour later a vibrating Alexei Zyuganov left the Bristol abruptly, without paying for his vodka. *That's all right,* thought Benford. *They're paying for it more than they could imagine.*

In his Kremlin office, the blue eyes blazed and the Cupid's-bow mouth turned up a fraction. The politician in him instantly saw the benefit in the Americans' proposal. The former KGB functionary in him appreciated the operational expediency. But the strongman bent on consolidating absolute power in his retooled Russian Empire would not accept second place, not even with these stakes. Zyuganov stood in the wood-paneled Kremlin office with head bowed as his president spoke softly into his ear, a paternal hand on the dwarf's little shoulder.

BRISTOL HOTEL CUCUMBER SALAD

Peel and seed halved cucumbers and slice thinly. Finely chop red onion and one chili pepper. Mix in bowl with white cider vinegar, salt, pepper, sugar, dill weed, and a drop of sesame oil. Serve chilled.

40

Benford, Forsyth, and Gable were in Athens Station. They sat at one end of a scarred conference table in the secure room—a thirty-foot Lucite trailer on Lucite legs inside a larger host room, under the harsh light of the fluorescent tubes arrayed on the top of the trailer. Their coffee mugs added fresh heat rings to the numerous old ones along the table. Nate was down the hall, in the infirmary, some stitches were coming out.

"It's going to be quite a scene if DIVA doesn't agree to return," said Gable. "The Russians will be so pissed they'll shoot MARBLE out of spite." Benford put a satchel on the table and unclipped the clasps on the flap. He turned to Gable.

"You will be pleased to hear that you have just been elected to convince DIVA not to defect, but to return inside, and in harness," said Benford. "Apart from our young superstar out there, she respects you the most. You are the only one she calls, what is it, bratwurst?"

"*Bratok*," said Gable. "It means 'brother.'"

"I see. Well, brother, she views me as having betrayed her, and by extension the entire CIA. For operational reasons we do not want to involve Nash too closely—besides, there is a fatal strain thanks to the ill-advised physical interaction between the two." He looked at Forsyth and then pointedly at Gable. "That is why I am entrusting this infinitely delicate part of the operation to you," said Benford. "*Bratok*, get DIVA to agree."

Benford opened the satchel and turned it upside

down. Papers and glossy black-and-white photographs spilled onto the table. Forsyth stacked them and looked at each one in turn, then passed it over to Gable. The glossies showed a rural river, smooth and slow, with a slash of foam over a weir and above it a two-lane highway bridge on concrete abutments, light poles with curving arms along the railing. Castles on either side of the river, one with a square tower, the other crenellated and squat. Rude little houses along the river and sooty apartment blocks in the distance against a gray sky. Articulated trucks with canvas tops were stacked up in a line on the bridge.

"The Narva River Bridge," said Benford, pointing at one of the photos. "On the right, Russia. On the left, the West, if that's what you want to call Estonia." He spun another photo around. "Control station. This crossing is quiet, mostly trucks, very slow. Petersburg is one hundred thirty klicks north." Benford tapped the photo. "This is where she'll cross."

"Why are we doing this?" asked Gable. "The Greeks could escort her to the airport and put her on a plane. She would be home in three hours." Benford studied one of the photographs, then finally answered.

"To use one of Forsyth's unfortunate gambling metaphors, we have broken even, more or less. On one hand, thanks to MARBLE, we have neutralized a mole in Washington. On the other hand, we have sustained the grievous loss of MARBLE. In exchange, DIVA has, we hope, immensely advanced her standing. I might add," he said, sipping his coffee, "that we were extremely lucky in that DIVA and Nash escaped mortal injury at the hands of that Spetsnaz assassin.

"For me, the one unsatisfactory aspect in all this is the ultimate price paid by a courageous old man. I tried to reason with him to continue as before, to avoid precipitate action, but he was adamant. He sensed his time was short." Benford looked at the faces around the table, then began shuffling through the photos again.

"I refuse to let it go at that," Benford said, lightly slapping the satchel on the table. "I want to address the one outstanding issue."

"The one issue?" asked Forsyth.

"MARBLE. I intend to get him back. He's earned his retirement," said Benford. It was quiet in the bubble. The rush of forced air coming through the Lucite vent was the only sound in the room.

Gable shook his head. "There's the small matter of his current status. Arrested Western spy," he said. "There's no work-release program in Lefortovo." Forsyth stayed quiet; he saw what was coming.

"I believe the Center will be glad to exchange MARBLE," said Benford.

"Exchange?" said Gable. "Who do you propose—"

"DIVA. They want her back badly enough to let MARBLE walk. It never would have happened with Stalin, or Andropov, but this is the new Russia. Putin is concerned about his image at home and abroad. DIVA knows a secret—several secrets—that would cause him a lot of trouble domestically."

"The Russians will never agree," said Gable. "They will never let MARBLE loose. They'll be thinking about future traitors, loss of face, looking weak."

"Actually, they already have agreed. Putin will have ordered the Center to make the deal."

"Let me get this straight," said Gable. "You made a deal with the Russians for a spy swap without knowing for certain whether DIVA will agree to return?"

"That is precisely why I am counting on you," said Benford. "Besides, it is inconceivable that DIVA will continue to demur when she is told that a decision on her part *not* to return will effectively annul the release of MARBLE by the Russians."

"Bitchin' trump card," said Gable. Benford looked up in annoyance. "That's no way to motivate this woman to return to Moscow as our clandestine asset. I mean, if she resents us, resents our manipulation, she might simply pull the plug out of spite. It'll be the last we hear from her."

"I expect you to vitiate the negative aspects of our manipulation of her. Motivate her anew. Sit with her and prepare her for internal handling. Emphasize that she alone holds the key to MARBLE's freedom," said Benford.

"Vitiate the negatives, got it. All right. I'll go out to Glyfada in an hour," said Gable.

"We have a deadline," said Benford. "I told the Russians we're in a hurry. We have days, hours left."

"Narva," said Gable. "Estonia. Jesus wept."

The two Georgians stood at attention in Zyuganov's office, looking at a spot on the wall above the dwarf's head. They were midgrade *chistilshchiki,* mechanics from SVR Department V, the Wet Works, the inheritors of General Pavel Sudaplatov's Administration for Special Tasks, which had eliminated the Soviets' enemies at home and abroad for four decades. Zyuganov read from a just-received report from a Greek police informant. The thugs left.

Zyuganov then called for Lyudmila Tsukanova. She entered the office slowly, chubby, hesitant, looking at her polished brown shoes over an ample if doughy bosom cinched tight by a uniform jacket a size too small. Her brown hair was cut unevenly and quite short. Her round Slav face was at first glance rosy with good health, but closer inspection revealed that the thirty-year-old woman suffered from rosacea. The red blotch on her chin looked painful.

Ill at ease, Lyudmila sat and listened to Zyuganov speak steadily for more than half an hour. Uncomfortable as she appeared, Lyudmila's black eyes, shark's eyes, doll's eyes, never left his face. When he was finished, she nodded and walked out of the office.

Beneath the surface, Gable later remarked, Benford had a large case of flop sweat as he laid out the Chinese-puzzle operational schedule in a narrative flood that suggested the drive belt of his tongue had slipped the flywheel of his mind.

"Forsyth, you must remain at Station to deflect the inevitable obstreperous cable traffic from the First Lord of the Admiralty, Chief Europe, and the other savants in Headquarters.

"I will fly ahead to Estonia to take the local young COS in hand and to liaise with the police—KaPo, they're called, once Russian-trained but now NATO and very earnest and intense. I expect the Center to be active, ticks all over Estonia, to see what they can pick up, even try a snatch to get DIVA back.

"You, Gable, have the most critical task. Hide her, keep her safe. Convince DIVA to return. You have one or two days in which to do this, then deliver her, at the end of the second day, to the bridge in Narva at 1700 local.

"Until that time, under *absolutely no circumstances* is anyone to use a phone, cell or landline. Moscow Rules, is that clear? Russian SIGINT is every bit as good in tracking mobile phones, and the Center still controls assets in their former satellite.

"I suggest, Gable, that you fly from Greece to Latvia, then make the trip from Riga in the early morning; it's three hundred sixty kilometers from Latvia on the E67, and the Narva Bridge will be closed by KaPo when the daily traffic subsides and before the night truck traffic begins.

"Gable, you must devote any available time to

coach DIVA on the exchange on the bridge. They'll be looking at her very closely.

"I want MARBLE out of Estonia within two hours of the exchange, out of their reach. The air attaché promised me a C-37 in Tallinn, but Forsyth, please remind him to have the aircraft there; I do not want to have to fly economy on an Estonian Air flight to Trondheim to get him clear."

Later, as he walked Benford to the departure gate at Venizelos, Forsyth took him by the arm. "Quite an operation you've put together here, Simon," he said. "You will have Russians, Estonians, SVR, and CIA at the bridge, all fingering their weapons nervously. God willing, MARBLE will be standing in the night fog, waiting to be exchanged."

Benford stopped and turned toward Forsyth. "Tom, Gable and DIVA *must* stay black. No cell phones, no contact, nothing that would give the Center even the remotest opportunity to attempt a hostile action."

"Gable's already disappeared," said Forsyth. "As of yesterday afternoon, even I don't know where he is."

Benford nodded. "We have no choice; we've got to move ahead as if she's already agreed. I want MARBLE there, physically, before they decide to execute him. This is our one chance." Benford stared out the window at the tarmac. "Gable will convince her. He has to."

In the Station in Tallinn, Estonia, the young Chief of Station put down his coffee cup and sat up when he read Benford's cable, relayed by Headquarters. He stuck his head around the corner and called his wife into the office; it was just the two of them, a tandem couple. Together they reread the cable several times. She stood behind him, her chin on his shoulder, making a list of things to do quickly, hotels, cars, radios, binoculars.

Per Benford's instructions, the young COS called

his liaison contact in KaPo, the Kaitsepolitsei, to ask for an urgent meeting. Escort in town? Follow car to Narva? Overwatch at the bridge? Kick our former Russian tenants in the bloody balls? Delighted, KaPo said. Everything will be arranged.

Benford arrived in Tallinn from Venizelos via Tempelhof on Lufthansa. With a brief stop at the Hotel Schlössle in the Old Town, Benford dragged the eager young COS on a pounding casing-and-timing run to Narva and back. A nondescript Lada followed them sporadically on the E20, but disappeared on the outskirts of Narva. The Russians knew where the action was going to be. On the way back to Tallinn, Benford stopped at a highway café grill, to see how the Lada would react. Surveillance proceeded two hundred meters and waited on the side of the highway. Benford made himself stretch out a lunch of boiled sausages, pickles, herring, Baltic *rosolje* salad, black bread, dark loamy beers. He hoped the goons in the car were hungry.

Benford's hotel room had been entered, but they had been very good. None of the traditional telltales Benford had left for them had been disturbed. The stray hairs, the talcum, the aligned corners of the notepad on the desk. But they weren't as good as Benford. COS Tallinn watched, fascinated, as Benford used a rice-grain-sized Stanhope lens concealed on the bezel of his wristwatch to examine the back cover of the decoy cell phone left in a side pocket of his suitcase. Benford looked up, nodded. The microscribe marks on the cover were misaligned. They had pried the back off and probably downloaded the useless memory.

Other preparations were under way. In Saint Petersburg, the director of the SVR office for the Leningrad Oblast was called by Yasenevo on the director's VCh phone. He was informed only that there would be an exchange. He was told to organize and deploy a team to handle a prisoner for release, and then to escort a "person of importance" from the Narva Bridge to Ivangorod, and then to Saint Petersburg in the shortest time possible.

The director was authorized to call the Saint Petersburg FSB and the oblast Border Guards Service to provide support during the exchange. A Colonel Zyuganov in Moscow ordered and stipulated that there should be no trouble whatsoever during the exchange and that it should be accomplished with the greatest secrecy.

The Saint Petersburg director acknowledged the directions, and subsequently asked for and received approval to transport the important person from Ivangorod to Saint Petersburg by Border Guard helicopter. A Yak-40 executive jet, part of the presidential squadron, would fly the repatriated individual—whoever the devil he was, thought the Leningrad chief—the rest of the way to Moscow.

The exchange for MARBLE was scheduled the next day at 1400 Zulu. Perhaps because they were all keyed up, perhaps because Forsyth worried about Gable, perhaps because he knew Nate had been frozen out of the operation and was headed to Washington, he took Nate out for a beer.

They were sitting under pale plane trees at the Skalakia Taverna in Ambelokipi down the hill from the embassy. Nate had been mooning around the Station, waiting for his flight, and Forsyth felt sorry for the kid; he'd been through a lot, been scratched up pretty good. Forsyth knew what else was nagging at him, apart from Nate's usual fretting about his hall file and career.

So Forsyth walked him down Mesogeion and up the steep flight of stairs to the polished wood entrance of the taverna, and they sat outside listening to the city quiet down for the midday break. Nate asked

Forsyth if DIVA was back in Russia now, after she had blown MARBLE up, then tossed back his beer and signaled for another.

Forsyth looked at him pretty sharpish, and Nate told him he had read the Restricted Handling file in the office when Maggie wasn't looking and knew the whole story, about Benford's plan, about Dominika burning MARBLE. Didn't we try to protect our assets? How could she? Russians. MARBLE wouldn't have done it; he was a guy apart.

Forsyth leaned into it, gave it to him between the eyes, told him he had his head up his ass. Forsyth said that he was considering kicking it farther up his ass for sneaking the RH traffic. Dominika hadn't known about the plan to burn MARBLE, Forsyth said; she was following orders, doing what Benford had told her to do, she had no knowledge of the canary trap, of the fatal words she was told to repeat. She was directed not to tell Nate any of it. She had discipline, she was the professional. She had broken down when they told her about MARBLE.

Nate was silent for ten minutes. He told Forsyth he was going to the safe house to see her. "Don't bother," said Forsyth. "We closed it up yesterday. She's with Gable, and even I don't know where Gable is." He told Nate about Benford's spy swap, about the two-lane highway bridge in Estonia. "We're playing this by Moscow Rules—well, Narva Rules, anyway—because we have only one shot at this."

Nate's jaw was set. "Tom, I have to see her. You have to help me."

"I couldn't if I wanted to," said Forsyth. "There's one point on the surface of the globe where it's *possible* that she will show up tomorrow, and that's fifty-fifty." Nate understood that Forsyth was telling him because he would let him go.

For Nate, the next twenty-four hours were a journey of self-loathing and guilt. He started the physical journey after getting up from the table and walking away from Forsyth, who let him go and knew what he was going to try to do, because if he didn't try, it would be even worse than it was now. He had a day to get there. The Athens traffic didn't move and the white Aegean light shone through the windows of the taxi and the sweat ran down his back onto the plastic seats and he threw the euros down and went into the terminal and bought a bag and a toothbrush and a T-shirt and a ticket on the next flight to Germany, to Munich, and the cattle in line didn't move and he almost started yelling but limped through security and didn't even register the lift as they took off and he wondered why the plane was flying so slowly over the Alps and the articulated bus in Munich circled the whole airport twice before coming to a halt at the sliding doors and he told himself not to hurry up the stairs, cameras were everywhere, and his stitches were acting up, itching. The endless concourse in Munich with a knackwurst and a beer, which he threw up five minutes later, and the two VoPos, cops with MP5s, asking him for his passport and boarding pass, almost told them he was too much in a hurry, and the epaulets in the booth looking at him for an extra beat, and he wanted to reach through and grab his papers but willed his hand to stay at his side, wet and trembling. The waiting lounge was full of lumpy Balts with string-tied suitcases and he wanted to shoulder his way through them and get to the gate but they clumped in front of him and the announcement of a two-hour delay sent his sour stomach sinking and he checked his watch for the hundredth time as he sat in the cracked plastic chair, hearing the Balts chatter, and smelled them eat bread and sausage and he made it to the bathroom in time and vomited on an empty stomach, an agony, and he lifted his shirt to check that he hadn't popped any stitches and his skin was pink and hot to the touch but nothing was leaking. Back out at the gate, he fell asleep in a sweat, seeing her face and hearing her voice. Someone kicked his feet going by and he woke to get in line, semiconscious and numb with a buzz in his head and packed tight and they made him wait on the tarmac until they resolved the technical difficulty, twenty minutes, forty minutes, an hour and the Balts wouldn't stop talking and Nate's head buzzed and his ears would not clear when they took off and the flight attendant asked him if he was all right. Two hours later, and they weren't descending because of the fog and they were going to divert to Helsinki, he couldn't bear that, and he closed his eyes and put his head on the seatback and the fog lifted in time and the customs table was stainless steel in the dinky-modern Tallinn airport and the anonymous, throwaway mobile phone purchased at the airport didn't work and the rental car had a steering wheel that was loose on the column but he didn't have time to swap cars and the little engine rattled and he was going too fast and fucked up on the roundabout outside Tallinn and went south on the E67 until a sign told him he was headed for goddamn Riga and he got turned around and on the E20 with the double-carriage rigs buffeting the wobbly little car and the radar cop pulled him over and took his time before tearing off the ticket and saluting him and the towns rolled past, alien names in an alien moonscape of flat hills and windbreak trees beside muddy farms and it was Rakvere, then Kohtla-Järve, then pissant Vaivara and the city limits of Narva, dingy Narva, and it was afternoon and the clouds were thick across the sky and he found the castle and the bridge, Russia across the water, but something made him get out of there, *Don't heat up the site,* the last scrap of operational discipline. He drove around town hoping for a glimpse of her but there was no chance and he fought the guilt and the shame and dredged up the last scrap of operational discipline, and he sat in a parking lot downtown, the car rocking as the trams went by, and Nate's hands trembled and he sat behind the fogged-up windshield, the minute hand on the dash was ticking backward, and he splashed cold water on his face and armpits and stomach—the stitches still itched—in the gas station and looked at his face, one side black-and-blue, like the Phantom of the Opera, some lover he had been, and he shrugged on the Greek flag T-shirt and ate a Narva sandwich with lettuce going brown on the edges and the lard oozing onto the waxed paper and Forsyth had told him sundown so he started the car and he couldn't feel his legs and feet on the clutch and he drove back toward the bridge, but the striped sawhorse was already up and the jeep was parked sideways on the center line and he told the soldier he was part of the clambake down the road, but the blue eyes beneath the forage cap and the buzz cut didn't understand "clambake" and was staring again at Nate's passport when he popped the clutch and went around the sawhorse and heard the police whistle but didn't think they would shoot and up ahead he saw a van and a jeep and Benford standing there and his vision blurred, *Don't know if it's the wobbly steering wheel or me,* and he let out the clutch and coasted down toward him, quietly, the last scrap of operational discipline left to him.

ESTONIAN BEET SALAD—ROSOLJE

Chop in half-inch dice boiled beets, boiled potatoes, pickles, peeled apples, hard-boiled eggs, cooked beef or pork, and salt herring (soaked overnight and cleaned), and mix with sour cream, mustard, sugar, pepper, and vinegar until incorporated. Chill and serve.

41

Gable dragged Dominika from the safe house—she came along grudgingly—and they went to ground. They talked for a full day in a room Gable had booked in alias at the Astir Palace twenty klicks out of Athens in Vouliagmeni overlooking the bay. They had registered as a married couple, easier that way. Gable never recognized the off-duty cop, moonlighting behind the hotel desk, but the cop knew the big American and picked up the phone.

Gable didn't even give it fifty-fifty. Dominika told *Bratok* that she no longer respected or trusted him; they had all used her. He listened with his purple halo in the Aegean light coming through the windows while she told him that ever since ballet school her choices had been taken away, she had been shoved this way and that, the things most dear to her had been stolen. It was why she had decided to work with them. Nate and *Bratok* and Forsyth had been like family; they knew what she needed. And everyone was so smart, so professional.

But the result turned out the same. They had colluded against her. Even the general had broken faith. Her Russian mind saw conspiracy, her Russian soul felt betrayal. She would not work with them. She told him she had decided that she would not stay in Russia either. She realized the futility of defying the system. The *vlasti* would always win. All that remained was to decide where she would go. If the Americans would permit her to resettle in the United States, she would go there; if they refused to accept her defection, she would consider settling in a third country. If the CIA blocked her, she would return to Russia as a civilian. But she was quitting. She was out.

Gable let her talk and brewed tea for her and put lemon in the Perrier and listened. When she became tired they sat on the balcony with their feet on the railing and looked at the turquoise water and he told her stories about his early assignments as a young officer and made her laugh. He kept her laughing over a lunch of fried calamari with parsley, lemon, and oil, and as the afternoon shadows lengthened they walked around the gardens. Gable told her that he was not going to try to persuade her to do anything. Dominika smiled and said, "Which is the first step in persuading me to do exactly what you want." Gable laughed and took her back to their room and let her take a nap in the bedroom while he sat awake on the balcony. That evening Dominika put on a summer dress and sandals and they took a rattletrap bus along the coast to a small fish restaurant in Lagonissi and Dominika ordered baked sardines in grape leaves, and shrimp *yiouvetsi* baked with tomatoes, ouzo, and feta, and grilled swordfish in *latholemono* sauce, and Gable ordered two wines, a bottle of ice-cold Asprolithi and an aluminum beaker of pungent retsina.

They stopped at another taverna for coffee and Gable ordered two glasses of Mavrodaphne, sweet and arterial-black from southern Greece, which once turned Homer's sea wine-dark. The Christmas lights on the canopy of the taverna glowed and small waves chuckled on the beach beyond, invisible in the night. Looking at Gable's big beefy face and brush-cut hair, Dominika waited, leaning back against the ropes, waiting for him to begin throwing punches. "You're going to talk to me now, aren't you, *Bratok*?" said Dominika. Gable ignored her and said he wanted her to think about the whole thing seriously, he wanted her to reconsider on her own terms. He would explain how he saw that, what that would mean for her. She agreed to listen, she expected his tricks, but his steady purple bloom told her he would probably tell her the truth. Probably.

Gable said he thought her original reasons for joining the SVR were just and right and fine. She could serve her country, she could excel at a demanding job. Turned out she was good at it. But the promise of it all turned to ashes because of the beastliness of the system. There was nothing left. "Am I right so far?" he asked.

Dominika sat back and nodded. His purple was steady and strong.

"Okay," said Gable, "now ops or luck or fate comes along and you meet Nate Nash, and he's unlike anyone you ever met before—and that goes for the other handsome senior officers in the CIA—and you stick your big toe in the water to see how it feels, maybe to get back at the bastards. It isn't about money or ideology, it's your self-worth." Gable signaled a waiter for two more glasses of wine.

"Then something screwy happens. You realize that you thrive on this life, on the risk and the trickiness and the ice and the deception and the secret in your head every day. You thrive on it, you develop a real taste for it." The wine came, and Gable sipped. "How am I doing?" he said. Dominika crossed her arms.

"So suddenly you're betrayed again, this time by the people you thought were the good guys, but that would be the wrong way to think about it." Dominika blinked at Gable sideways. "The general, and Benford, and all of us wanted you to assume the general's place as our top gun in Moscow. Maybe we should have asked you, but it didn't happen. So now we're in the last act, and Benford is trying to get you back inside Moscow, and sweetheart, it's up to you. No one can force you; you have to decide on your own." Dominika looked out at the black water, then back at Gable.

"What are you going to do without all this?" he asked. "What are you going to do without your fix?"

Dominika closed her eyes and shook her head. "You think I cannot live without this?" she said.

"Forget about the CIA. Think about the general; he'd tell you the same thing. Go back and get to work. Don't think about the CIA for the first six months, a year. Don't give those bastards at the Center an inch. Run them over. You have a head start now; begin building your career. Go back and finish with your uncle. Tell the Center what he did, make sure he gets what he deserves. You'll be on the winning side, and it'll make you seem unpredictable and dangerous. First you caught Korchnoi, now you demolish your own uncle. They'll be scared of you.

"Choose, demand, force them to give you an important job, something with a lot of access, somewhere in the Americas Department, Line KR, whatever. Run your shop like you mean it. Recruit foreigners, cause trouble, catch spies, make allies, throw your enemies off balance. Be bitchy around the conference table."

Dominika tried not to smile. "Bitchy, this means *zlobnyj,* I think," she said.

"Once a year, twice, you come out on an operation of your choosing and I'll be there. You tell us what you want to tell us. You call the shots on internal communications. If you need to see us in Moscow, I'll personally make sure you're safe. You want commo gear, we'll give you some. You need help, you got it. You want us to go away, we're gone."

"And would Nathaniel be involved in the future?" she asked.

"People think it would be ill-advised to bring the

two of you together, given the operational history. But I'm here to tell you that if you want him handling outside meetings, we can arrange that."

"You're being very accommodating," said Dominika.

"This work, Dominika. It's in your blood, you can't leave it alone, it's in your nose and under your nails and growing out of the tips of your hair. Admit it."

"I would never have come to dinner with you if I knew you were a *janychar*," she said. "Did the CIA take you from your crib and train you from youth?"

"Admit it," said Gable. The air was filled with purple.

"And now you're being *nekulturny*," she said.

"You know I'm right. Admit it." She was enveloped in it.

"*Mozhet byt'*," Dominika said. "Perhaps."

"Dominika," he said. His purple cloud had descended from above his head and was swirling between them.

Dominika's face was calm and clear. "Perhaps."

"Think about what I said. I want you to agree, you know that, but whatever you decide, you have to make up your mind by tomorrow."

"I see," said Dominika. "I detect another surprise from you. Why must I decide by tomorrow, dear *Bratok*?"

"Because we need you, Benford needs you, in Estonia tomorrow."

She looked at him coolly, her hands flat on the table. "Tell me why, please." And Gable told her about the swap in Estonia, watching her eyes narrow.

"Don't get mad again," said Gable. "I didn't tell you before because I wanted to talk to you without it hanging over our heads."

"And you are not making this up?" said Dominika.

"You're going to be walking past him on the freaking bridge," said Gable. "It would be difficult to fake it."

"I assume the CIA could build a bridge."

"Be serious," said Gable.

"All right, I will be serious," said Dominika. "By telling me this you are again making me the general's executioner. You are not giving me a choice at all."

"What did I tell you before?" said Gable. "It *is* your choice. You can decide right now, right here, not to continue. We already owe you a modest resettlement. You have a bank account. I will call Benford and then personally fly with you to the United States. Tomorrow."

"And the general?" she said.

Gable shrugged. "He was the best Russian asset we ever had. He lasted fourteen years. He engineered his own demise because he was at the end of his run; he thought he found in you a replacement for his work, he wanted continuity. But it was his decision. Assets live and die. You are bound by the situation to the extent you let yourself be."

"You do not believe this," said Dominika. "Nate has said you told him that the most important thing—ever—is the safety and well-being of your assets. Your conscience would not let you abandon him."

"Perhaps you're right," said Gable. "To rescue the general from the Lefortovo cellars would be a good start as we resume our work." Dominika stared at him and took a sip of wine. Gable raised an eyebrow and looked her in the eyes. She knew he was telling the truth.

"You all are such bastards."

"Flight to Latvia's at ten o'clock."

"I wish you a pleasant flight," she said.

They took the last bus back to the Astir Palace. They sat beside each other but did not talk for the fifteen-minute ride. They walked wordlessly through the lobby with the scent of bougainvillea and the sea and went out to the sweeping patio and ordered mineral waters and watched the lights of the ferry to Rhodes move across the horizon.

Gable didn't think he had reeled her in, she was too indignant, too angry. He could tell when someone was wavering and when someone had made up her mind. Dominika had what it takes, but she couldn't be bullied. Benford's face would fall when Gable showed up without her. The worst part would be seeing the guards across the bridge leading MARBLE away. No swap. Carry out the sentence.

But he had made his pitch, she knew he was her friend, she knew it was up to her. They took the elevator to their floor. The curving corridor of the hotel was quiet, it did not seem as if anyone else was on the floor. A magnetic servo whine from the elevator shafts was the only sound in the air.

Dominika unlocked the door and stepped inside. Neither of them heard the footsteps; the two men had taken off their shoes and were padding toward them from either end of the corridor in a silent rush. Dominika saw them as she turned, and tried to pull Gable into the room, but the men shouldered their way inside, flinging the door shut. Lamps on each bedside table gave the only light in the room.

One of the men in a low growl said, "*Ne boisya my s toboi pomoch'tebe,*" don't be afraid, we're here to rescue you, and Dominika registered that he used the familiar "you." The four of them stood stock-still for an instant, the silence before the explosion. She could see the butt of a pistol in one man's belt.

Both men were huge, giants from Georgia, judging from their faces. Dominika pushed past Gable and into the arms of one of the men, sobbing as if relieved to be rescued. The other monster launched himself at Gable, who stepped back a quarter turn and drove the man past him into the end table and lamp, demolishing both, but the man was up, too fast, too agile for his size, and they locked arms and wrapped legs and went down to the floor, each looking for openings, eyes, throat, genitals, joints.

Dominika put one arm around the neck of her man, which slowed him from doubling up on Gable. He smelled of wet dog and garlic, and she gagged and turned to look at the heaving mass that was Gable and the Russian. She realized with sudden clarity that she would not allow *Bratok* to be hurt. She pawed the front of her man's shirtfront and down to his belt and felt the checkered grip of the small pistol and did not bother to draw it clear, but reached in and thumbed the safety off and pulled the trigger as fast as she could, three times, four times, and the muffled shots were drowned out by the man's scream and he was on his back writhing, his shirtfront and trousers a mass of blood.

Holding the pistol at her side, Dominika walked over to the other Russian, who had Gable pinned to the floor with a forearm against his throat. *The second time a CIA man is fighting for me,* Dominika thought, and she reached for the man's hair and pulled his head back, relieving the pressure on *Bratok*'s neck. The Georgian's head swung around, eyes wide, to see who had pulled his hair, and Dominika put the barrel of the gun under his chin, turned her face to avoid the blood spray, and, careful to point the muzzle away from Gable, pulled the trigger twice. The Georgian spat blood, toppled sideways, and did not move. The first man continued writhing on the now-wet rug. Gable got up and reached to take the pistol from her, but Dominika turned away and would not let him. Amazed, Gable watched her walk over to the first man, bend down, and, shielding her face with her free hand, put the muzzle of the pistol against his forehead and pull the trigger twice. The man's head bounced once on the floor.

Dominika threw the empty pistol, its slide locked back, into the corner of the room. Gable had a bruise under his left eye and fingernail scratch marks on his right cheek and neck. They both knew there could have been no other way with these two mechanics. He studied Dominika intently in the nearly dark room, her chest rising and falling, a little blood on her arm.

"I will be a little bitchy from now on," she said. "*Zlobnyj*."

SHRIMP YIOUVETSI

Sauté onion, red pepper flakes, and garlic, add chopped tomato, oregano, and ouzo, and reduce to thick sauce. Add shrimp, stir in chopped parsley, and cook briefly; transfer to baking dish, top with feta cheese, and bake in medium-high oven until bubbling.

42

The next evening at 1700 hours a bank of fog settled low over the Narva River in an otherwise clear night sky. Thick and ragged as a plug of surgical cotton torn from the box, the fog occasionally licked up over the roadway of the bridge. The lamps along the bridgeway came on and caught the fog, blowing right to left, making it seem as if the bridge itself were moving on casters along the riverbank. Well above the fog bank, the tower of Hermann Castle on the west bank faced the deserted battlements of the Ivangorod Fortress on the east bank.

On the Russian side of the bridge, two light trucks were positioned lengthwise across the roadway. Six border guards in camouflage utility uniforms were slouching around the trucks. Behind them was a small armored personnel carrier, a Tigre, with a light machine gun mounted on a ring turret in the roof. There was no one on the gun, which was locked on its pintles, pointed at the sky. Behind these vehicles, parked along the side of the road that led past the convenience store and administration building, were five cars from Saint Petersburg SVR—two Mercedes and three BMWs. The drivers stood together in the dark talking. The rest of the SVR men had entered the checkpoint tollbooth and were waiting out of sight, following orders to stay discreet. On the sloping riverbank below the bridge two border guards stood completely enveloped in the fog, dripping wet.

On the Estonian side of the bridge Benford sat fifty meters from the bridge inside a van parked in the center of the road. He could look straight down the roadway of the bridge at the parked Russian vehicles. Next to Benford's van a small KaPo jeep was pulled over on the shoulder. Four black-suited troopers sat in the jeep smoking. KaPo had intended to put two spotters in the bastion of the Hermann Castle tower, but the ministry did not have the budget for nightscopes. The lights on the bridge would have to be enough.

There was a sound of squeaking brake pads and the crunch of tires on the gravel shoulder, a car coasting to a stop. Benford saw Nate get out of a little green compact, his hair down over his forehead, a ridiculous blue and white—no, it was the Greek flag—on his T-shirt. Benford got out of the van and walked back to the car.

"What are you doing here, Nash?" said Benford in a low, even voice. "And what is that ridiculous shirt you're wearing? Do you know what is supposed to happen in a half hour? Have the kindness to get into the van and stay out of sight. You need a shower." Benford steered Nate into the van and slid the door closed. The KaPo troopers in the jeep looked over and wondered what was going on. Benford walked over to them and accepted an offered cigarette. The troopers were respectfully quiet.

Benford could see more activity at the other end of the bridge. The light trucks parked lengthwise across the bridge were separated slightly and the Tigre APC had moved between them. A soldier had unlimbered the gun on the roof. From behind Benford came the sound of another vehicle, and Gable pulled up in a nondescript black sedan. He appeared to be alone in the car. Gable got out and walked toward Benford.

"Tell me what you have done," said Benford. "Tell me you have her."

"The Russians tried for her last night in Athens. A rescue team, they called themselves. I have no idea how they tracked us, someone the Russians have at the hotel, the cops, I don't know. She killed both of them, executed them." The KaPo troopers had climbed out of their jeep and were standing behind it, looking at the Russian side of the bridge through binoculars.

"*She* killed them? Where is she right now?" asked Benford. "Do we have someone to swap for MARBLE?"

"She told me no. For six hours it was no. Nothing I could say to change her mind. The next morning I was going to turn her over to Forsyth to fly her to the States, and she was waiting for me by the car. Waxing the two Center goons may have done the trick, I don't know. She's seriously furious." Benford looked as though he was going to pass out. "She's in the backseat, lying down; she got back there as we entered Narva. I wanted to change the profile." Benford blew out a stream of smoke. It had been nearly seventy-two hours of not knowing.

"She agreed?" Benford asked.

"Yes and no. Told me to go to hell, that she was doing it to spring MARBLE, for no other reason. Said she's going back to think about working with us. In the meantime, she intends to raise hell in the Center. We might have an agent, we might not. She'll let us know."

"What does that mean?" said Benford.

Gable ignored the question. "Another thing. Nash is an issue. She asked about him." Benford started laughing. "What?" said Gable.

"Nash is in the van. I don't know how he did it, but he got here from Athens and showed up. That's his car behind the van."

"State of mind?" asked Gable.

"Agitated, intense, exhausted. What are you thinking?"

"What I'm thinking is that we let them talk for a few minutes—might be good for both of them. Leave her with a memory to take back with her, settle him down. I can pull the car up and get her into the back of the van so no one sees."

"Okay, we're waiting anyway. But wait till I talk to Nash for a second." Benford slid the van door open, climbed in, and sat beside Nate on the middle bench seat. Nash had found a jacket in the back and had run his fingers through his hair. He looked tired, but presentable. Benford slid the door partly closed and leaned back in the seat.

"DIVA and Gable have arrived. She is in the car. Last night the Russians tried to rescue her and she killed two men. She has agreed to return to Russia only because of the swap, to free MARBLE. As for working inside, she has not made any commitment and we do not know the extent to which she is now, or in the future will be, our agent.

"We have a few minutes, and Gable believes it would be salutary for DIVA to speak with you. I need you to become her recruiting officer once again. I need you to be inspirational. I need you to speak to her of duty and mission and long-term espionage. There is only one way to play this that will not result in her arrest at the other end of that bridge—as a case officer preparing his agent. Otherwise it will break her composure. Can you do this?"

Nate nodded. Benford exited the van and Nate heard engine noise and the click of a door and the back of the van opened up and Dominika quickly stepped inside and the door slammed shut. She squeezed past the rear seat and sat down beside him. She was dressed in a simple navy dress with a light coat of the same color. Gable had insisted on sensible black laced shoes and beige hose. She had pinned her hair up and wore no makeup, a matron just out of

CIA captivity. The blue eyes were the same, and she looked at Nate, searching his face. He was bathed in a pale purple glow; it told her he was in pain.

For the first time in his young career, Nate did not automatically think about the ramifications of breaking the rules, of ignoring Benford, of blowing a hole in his rep. He leaned forward, grabbed Dominika by the shoulders, and pressed his lips on hers. She stiffened, then relaxed and finally put her hands on his chest and gently pushed him back.

"We don't have time—not remotely enough time—to tell you I'm sorry about what I said to you," said Nate. "There's no time to tell you what you mean to me, as a woman, as a lover, as a partner. And there's no time to tell you how much I will miss you.

"I'm supposed to talk to you about continuing our clandestine relationship, about how you should keep operating for the CIA in Moscow. I don't care about that right now. I know you're going back just to save the general; I would do the same, so whatever happens, you've delivered him. But I want you to stay safe; none of this is worth it. You're the only thing that's important, at least to me."

Nate looked self-consciously away, through the van windshield at the fog-shredded roadway, a time tunnel receding into Russia. Dominika turned to look at the same thing, making up her mind.

"You needn't worry about me, Neyt," said Dominika flatly. "I am going back to my country, among my own people. I will be fine. How convenient it has been for you to apologize and tell me you will worry about me five minutes before I cross the border. Please do me a favor," said Dominika, "don't give me a second thought." Dushka, *let me go,* she thought.

She got out of her seat, slid to the back door, and tapped on the glass. Nate watched her go. He stared at the fog, hands clasped behind his head.

Gable saw her eyes and knew she was holding on by a thread. Goddamn Nash. She needed stiffening, and fast. He steered her to the car, screened by the van.

"Get in," said Gable, "I want to talk to you." She slid across the backseat and Gable climbed in beside her, slammed the door. He played it rough, pretending not to notice her eyes.

"There will be about a dozen binoculars on you the minute you step outside this vehicle into the clear," Gable said. "Guards'll be worrying about security, but there will be others looking at you. Counterintelligence guys, the CI monkeys *looking specifically at you.* Do you understand?" Dominika avoided looking at him and nodded.

"When you cross, walk at a steady pace. Not too fast, but not hesitant either. It's important that you don't look at Korchnoi when you pass him on the bridge. He's a traitor, and you were the one who put him in prison," said Gable.

"They might call for you both to stop at the midway point on the roadway. It's marked with a line of asphalt, a little bump in the road. It's normal; the guards aren't happy unless they're shouting into bullhorns. They probably will be transmitting video images of you back to the Center to confirm your identity." Dominika was better. Gable could see she had started thinking about the walk ahead and not Nash.

"Steady pace right up to the trucks. It'll be a Leningrad knuckle-dragger in a bad suit who steps up to say . . . What will he say?"

"*Dobro pozhalovat,*" said Dominika, staring out the window. Welcome home.

"Yeah, well, do me a favor and kick him between the legs. Your behavior from then on is critical. Remember," said Gable, "you're coming home, freed from CIA custody. You're relieved and, well, *safe.*

Not exactly talkative, that would be inappropriate. You've accounted for three KIAs, your own frigging people tried to *kill you,* and you're pissed. You'll be surrounded by all those Leningrad thugs in the car or on the train, or however they get you up to Saint Petersburg."

"I am familiar with the species," said Dominika. "There will be no trouble from them. I have just come back from an operation *for the Center*. The only people I will talk to are in Moscow."

"Exactly. And once you're there, show them your Greek stitches and yell about the Spetsnaz maniac, and about Korchnoi and what took them so long to come get you. You're back, baby, you're back."

"Yes," said Dominika, "I am back."

"And we'll see you in six months," said Gable.

"Do not count on it," said Dominika.

"You remember the universal call-out number?"

"I threw it away," Dominika said.

"After you memorized it," said Gable.

"Tell Forsyth good-bye for me," she said, ignoring him.

Lyudmila Mykhailivna Pavlichenko was the storied Red Army sniper, the deadliest female sniper in history, with 309 confirmed kills during the Crimean campaign in World War II. This evening, on the ruined south tower of the Ivangorod Fortress on the Russian riverbank, her namesake Lyudmila Tsukanova, the primary sniper of SVR Special Group B, eased onto her stomach and settled herself. She was dressed in a baggy black coverall, a hood pulled over her head tight around her cherry-splotched face. Her felt-soled boots were splayed out flat behind her. She snugged the VSS Vintorez rifle, the "thread cutter," against her riotous, chapped cheek and sighted through the NSPU-3 nightscope three hundred meters diagonally across the water at the western end of the Narva Bridge—this would be a night shot comfortably within her ability. She was looking for a profile—a dark-haired woman who walked with a slight limp.

The medium Mi-14 "Haze" helicopter with the black Mickey Mouse nose was a civilian transport version painted red and white. It settled slowly into the empty parking lot of the Ivangorod Railroad Station. The mustard walls of the station's baroque façade flashed pink in the range lights of the helicopter. As the helicopter bounced on its gear, the engine note dropped from a scream to a whine to a purr. The massive rotors stopped spinning and drooped, hot in the chilly night air. No doors opened on the helicopter until two of the SVR cars that had been waiting down the road pulled up tight alongside. The side passenger door opened and two men in suits banged the metal stairs down and walked a frail white-haired figure to the lead car.

The two cars drove slowly up the road to the blocking trucks at the bridge, and the three men got out, one on each side supporting the smaller man. They squeezed past the trucks and stood silently, unmoving, while looking down the roadway at the dim figures at the other end. The border guards around the trucks unslung their rifles and the spotlights on the trucks came on, flooding the Russian side of the bridge in light. The railings and light pole stanchions cast slanted shadows across the roadway. There were half a dozen cherry pinpricks of light behind the window of the customs tollbooth. The Leningrad boys were smoking, watching, not talking.

They got out of the van and came around to stand in front, facing the Russians. The Russian spots came on and Benford signaled the KaPo jeep to turn on its headlights and single spotlight. The Russian side was now obscured by a glaring wall of light past which the fog continued to billow.

"We'll walk you to the start of the bridge," Gable said, holding Dominika's arm steady. Benford stepped close and stood on the other side of her, holding her other arm above the elbow. Nate had exited the van and stood to one side. Gable and Benford walked forward.

"Wait," said Dominika, and she leaned toward Nate and slapped him hard across the cheek.

"Atta girl," said Gable. The KaPo troopers in the jeep nudged one another.

Dominika and Nate looked at each other for a beat, no one else in the entire fog-shrouded world, then Dominika whispered, "*Poka,* be seeing you." She straightened and pulled Gable and Benford forward. "Come on," she said.

"Be cool, baby," Gable said out of the corner of his mouth. He and Benford steered Dominika by each arm, like custodians in a prison. Her hands were fists as she resisted their pressure. They walked up to the beginning of the bridge roadway and stood there, watching the fog spill over the span. At the far end of the bridge there were flashes of cars pulling up, impossible to make out details, and there was a flurry of movement, then three men silhouetted at the other end, a short one in the middle. A spotlight winked off, then on again, and Benford signaled the troopers to send the same signal. The KaPo lights glinted off a dozen binoculars looking at them. "Stop when you get to the center," Gable said.

Dominika contemptuously tore both her arms free of their grasp, told them, "*Yob tvoyu mat',*" straightened her coat, and stepped forward. With that slight hitch, she began walking into the fog, head up, ballet calves flexing, shoulders back. The short figure at the far end of the bridge also began walking.

"What did she say?" asked Benford.

"Sounded fairly obscene," said Gable.

Dominika's silhouette grew less distinct as she passed progressively through the faint circles of light on the roadway. She and the solitary figure walking the other way were nearly abreast of each other.

"She's at midspan with MARBLE now," said Gable softly. A bullhorn barked something and the two figures stopped. The two silhouettes were standing side by side in midspan, in the light of one of the lamps, fog swirling between them, soaking them. Dominika looked straight ahead, imperious, disdaining. She never turned her head, but she could feel his majestic purple presence, it was the last time she'd feel him. MARBLE looked over at Dominika, his white hair caught in the lamplight, and he shrugged off his overcoat and held it to her, an offering from one exchanged spy to another. Dominika took the coat and dropped it on the fog-wet pavement. Just as MARBLE had hoped she would do. The light glinted off a dozen binoculars.

MARBLE looked straight ahead, noting the city glow of Narva, the loom of the castle keep, the wink of a star in the western sky, the headlights and silhouettes of the men at the far end of the bridge. When lights on both ends of the bridge flashed again, he began walking. He heard Dominika's footsteps fading behind him. His body felt light, the pains were familiar, but the hollowness in his chest was gone. His head was clear and he concentrated on not walking too fast, he would show them to the last how a professional finishes. As he came nearer, the silhouettes turned into faces, familiar faces. It was more important to see his friends than it was to actually be free. Benford. Nathaniel. A spy swap. He almost laughed.

The 9x39mm round from Lyudmila's suppressed rifle passed through the left side of MARBLE's neck, severing his carotid artery before exiting his right pectoral muscle below the armpit. Tsukanova, intending a head shot, had held a touch low, and the cold night air had affected the subsonic SP-5 round. She was up and walking her egress route along the south fortress wall before MARBLE's legs buckled. The Russians on their side of the bridge did not know anything had happened.

Benford caught him, but MARBLE's dead weight slipped through his arms and the old man collapsed to the wet asphalt. Nate sat on the roadway and cradled MARBLE's head against his thigh, but the old spy was still, they had flipped a switch on him and he was gone, eyes closed, face strangely composed. Benford looked at his hands, red with Korchnoi's blood.

The KaPo troopers unslung their Galils and brought them up, but Gable screamed, "Stop!" and waved them to stand down. Across the bridge, Dominika turned briefly—she had heard Gable's bellow—but she was swallowed up in the searchlights' glare. She registered the dark knot of figures around the black lump on the ground, and she knew, instinctively, what had happened.

She screamed, *No!* once in her head, then willed herself to close down, to compose her face, relax her shoulders. She was hustled into a waiting vehicle, a heated Mercedes, luxuriously warm, which immediately sped off down the highway. The car rocked around the curves, and she contained her horror, replaying images of Korchnoi. She choked down her venomous rage as a yellow-draped Leningrad colonel filled the inside of the car with cigarette smoke.

Benford looked down at MARBLE, paralyzed, unable to move, unable to think. Nate's head was bowed, and his hands shook as he continued cradling MARBLE's head in his lap. This was violence too cruel; they were speechless, insensate with the finality, the irretrievability of MARBLE's lost life. They were shaken by the despot's towering treachery, by the enormity of the ruthless act.

All except Gable. He quickly stepped back out into the roadway and raised his binoculars. A jumble of silhouettes on the Russian side was moving around; the taillights of a luxury sedan receded into the night. Gable could not tell whether Dominika had seen what had happened, but he hoped she had, *Please God she knows what happened.*

The fog swirled around them, wetting their hair, touching MARBLE's placid face. The old man's sodden overcoat lay forgotten at the middle of the bridge.

ACKNOWLEDGMENTS

In counting the number of people who in one way or another materially assisted me in writing this book, I was surprised to see how many there were. I owe them all my thanks.

I must begin with my literary agent, the incomparable Sloan Harris of International Creative Management, who, in the early days of writing, acted as a sustaining guide and mentor, and later, as an unyielding advocate of the manuscript. I am certain that in another life Sloan was a farsighted Venetian doge or a conquering Byzantine sultan. Without him the book would not have been born.

Many thanks to the rest of the ICM team, including Kristyn Keene, Shira Schindel, and Heather Karpas, all of whom embody patience as a virtue.

I owe another debt of gratitude to my editor at Scribner, the legendary Colin Harrison, who simultaneously edited the manuscript with the acuity of a mapmaker while teaching me how to write good. His dedication to the science and art of writing is boundless, and he improved the final product beyond measure. Without him the book would not have been completed.

Thanks too to all the people at Scribner and Simon & Schuster, including Carolyn Reidy, Susan Moldow, Nan Graham, Roz Lippel, Brian Belfiglio, Katie Monaghan, Tal Goretsky, Jason Heuer, Benjamin

Holmes, Emily Remes, and Dave Cole for their support, encouragement, and the warm welcome into the S&S family. Special thanks go to Kelsey Smith for all her hard work. All these people are collectively responsible for creating the book, though I hasten to add that any error of fact or language or science is mine.

I must acknowledge a number of friends who helped me begin the effort, some of whom cannot be named. They know who they are: the discerning Dick K. of Beverly Hills; the eclectic Mike G. at USC; and superattorney Fred Richman, also of Beverly Hills.

Of course the book would not have come to pass without a career in the CIA, a life I shared with hundreds of colleagues beginning with my career trainee class, and including lifelong friends made in Langley and in all the foreign postings over thirty-three years. A number of them are still relatively young. I salute all of them.

As a young CIA officer I benefitted from the (at times) not-so-gentle guidance and patronage of a number of senior officers such as Clair George, Paul Redmond, Burton Gerber, Terry Ward, and Mike Burns, operators of towering talent and unshakable patriotism. In those days they were referred to as "barons" in the Directorate of Operations. And I sat at the knee of the laconic Jay Harris, a nuclear-physicist-turned-case-officer; together we reinvented internal operations in Castro's Cuba.

My brother and sister-in-law William and Sharon Matthews made critically important suggestions, and my daughters, Alexandra and Sophia, more than once reminded the author that eight-track tape decks are no longer sold at Woolworth's.

Finally I thank my wife, Suzanne, herself a thirty-four-year veteran of the CIA, for sharing an endlessly varied life with me, for the late nights, and the surveillance nights, and the evacuation nights, and for raising two sublime daughters, and for her patience while I wrote.

Turn the page for a preview of
the next thrilling novel by

JASON MATTHEWS,

continuing the adventures of
Dominika, the Red Sparrow, and
Nathaniel, her CIA lover . . .

CHAPTER ONE

Captain Dominika Egorova of the Russian Foreign Intelligence Service, the SVR, pulled down the hem of her little black dress as she weaved through the crowds of pedestrians in the red neon, pranging chaos of Boulevard de Clichy in the Pigalle. Her black heels clicked on the Parisian sidewalk as she held her chin up, keeping the gray head of the rabbit in sight ahead of her—solo trailing surveillance on a moving foot target, one of the more difficult evolutions in offensive streetcraft. Dominika covered him loosely, alternatively paralleling on the dividing island in the center of the boulevard and drafting behind the early-evening pedestrians to screen her profile.

The man stopped to buy a charred kebab skewer—typically pork in this Christian quarter—from a vendor who fanned the charcoal of a small brazier with a folded piece of cardboard, sending an occasional spark into the passing crowd and enveloping the street corner in clouds of smoke fragrant with coriander and chili. Dominika eased back behind a street pole; it was unlikely that the rabbit was using the snack stop as a way to check his six—for the last three days he had shown himself to be oblivious on the street—but she wanted to avoid him noticing her too soon. Plenty of other street creatures already had watched her passing through the crowd—dancer's legs, regal bust, arc light blue eyes—cutting her scent, sniffing for strength or frailty.

In two practiced glances, Dominika checked the zoo of faces but did not get that tingle on the back of her neck that meant the start of trouble. The rabbit, a Persian, finished tearing the strips of meat with his teeth and tossed the short skewer into the gutter. Apparently this Shia Muslim had no compunctions about eating pork—or slathering his face between the legs of hookers, for that matter. He started moving again, Dominika keeping pace.

An unshaven and swarthy young man left his friends leaning against the steam-weeping window of a noodle shop, slid in beside Dominika, and put an arm around her shoulder. "*Je bande pour toi*," he said in the crooked French of the Maghreb. He had a hard-on for her. Jesus. She had no time for this, and felt the smoldering surge in her stomach running into her arms. No. Become ice. She shook his arm off, pushed his face away, and kept walking. "*Va voir ailleurs si j'y suis*"—go somewhere else, see if I'm there—she said over her shoulder. The young man stopped short, made an obscene gesture, and spat on the sidewalk.

Dominika reacquired the Persian's gray head just as the man entered La Diva, passing through the scrolling lights framing the dance hall's entrance. She drifted toward the door, noted the heavy velvet curtain, and gave him a beat to get inside, this diminutive man who held the nuclear secrets of the Islamic Republic of Iran in his head. He was her prey, a human intelligence target. Dominika ran the edge of her will rasping across the whetstone of her mind. It was to be a hostile recruitment attempt, an ambush, coercive, a cold pitch, and she thought she had an even chance to flip him in the next half hour.

In her early thirties, Dominika tonight wore her brown hair down around her shoulders, a bang covering one eye, like an Apaché dancer from the 1920s. Her electric blue eyes were concealed behind square-framed tortoiseshell eyeglasses with tinted lenses, a Parisian Lois Lane out for the night. But the typing pool effect was spoiled by the low-cut black sheath dress and Louboutin pumps. She was a former ballerina, her legs shapely and knotted in the calves, though she walked with a slight limp from a right foot shattered by a ballet academy rival when she was twenty.

Paris. She hadn't breathed the air of the West since she had returned to Moscow after being exchanged in the spy swap on the bridge in Estonia. The images of the exchange were fading, the sound of her long-ago steps on the silver-wet bridge roadway increasingly muffled, draped in the fog of that night. Returned home, she had inhaled the Russian air deeply; it was her country, *Rodina*, the Motherland, but the clean bite of pine forest and loamy black earth was tainted by a hint of liquid corruption, like a dead animal beneath the floorboards. Of course she had been greeted back home enthusiastically, with the knobby kudos and good wishes from lumpy officials. She had reported for work at SVR headquarters in Yasenevo—the Center—immediately, but coming back once again to see her colleagues in the Service, the milling herd of the *siloviki*, the anointed inner circle, had collapsed her spirit. *What did you expect?* she thought.

Things were different with her now. She was learning (most of the time) to control her rage against this rotten service, this rotten system, feeding instead on an animal instinct to wait, to listen, to appear a wholly quiescent creature of the mephitic atmosphere of her service. To that end, she had demurred when several idiotic headquarters positions were offered to her—she would wait for a job with the kind of access the CIA really wanted. She feigned interest in the process and otherwise took the time to attend a short course in operational psychology and another in counterintelligence: It might be useful in the future to know how mole hunters in her service would be looking for her, how the footsteps in the stairwell would sound when they came for her.

She also tempered the rage by looking into their souls, for Dominika was born a synesthete, with a brain wired to see the colored auras around people and thereby read passion, treachery, fear, or deception. When she was five years old, Dominika's synesthesia had shocked and worried her professor father and musician mother. They made their little girl promise never to reveal this soaring precocity to anyone, even as she grew accustomed to it. At twenty, Dominika was lifted on maroon waves of music at ballet academy. At twenty-five she calibrated a man's lust by his scarlet halo. Now past thirty, being able to divine men's and women's spirits just possibly would save her life.

On her return to the Center from the West, there had been two clearance sessions with an oily little man from counterespionage and a saturnine female stenographer, and they asked about the *ubiytsa*, the Spetsnaz assassin who had almost killed her in Athens; and then about being in CIA custody; and what the CIA men had been like, and what they asked, and what she told them. Dominika stared down the stenographer, who was swaddled in a yellow haze, and replied that she told them nothing. The bear sniffed at her shoes, and nodded, apparently satisfied. *But they weren't*, she thought, *they never are.*

Her exploits, and near escapes, and contact with the Americans cast suspicion on her—as it was with anyone returning from active service in the West—and she knew the *yashcherits*, the liver-eyed lizards of the FSB, the internal service, were observing her, waiting for a ripple, watching for an email or postcard from abroad, or an inexplicable open-code telephone call from a Moscow suburb, or an observed contact with a foreigner. But there were no ripples. Dominika was normal in her patterns; there was nothing for them to see.

So they placed a handsome physical trainer to bump her during the "mandatory" self-defense course run in an old mansion in Domodedovo, on Varashavskoye Ulitsa off the MKAD ring road. The moldy, spavined house with creaky staircases and a green-streaked copper roof was nestled in a shaggy, unkempt botanical garden hidden behind a wall with a crooked sign reading VILAR INSTITUTE OF OFFICINAL PLANTS. A few bored class participants—a florid Customs Service woman and two overage border guards—sat and smoked on benches along the walls of the glassed-in winter garden that served as the practice area.

Daniil, the trainer, was a tall, blond Great Russian, about thirty-five and imperially slim, with sturdy wrists and pianist's hands. His features were delicate: jawline, cheek, and brow were finely formed, and the impossible lashes above his sleepy blue eyes could stir the potted palm fronds in the winter garden from across the room. Dominika knew there was no such thing as a mandatory self-defense class in SVR, and that Daniil most likely was a ringer dispatched to casually ask questions and eventually elicit from an unwary Dominika that she had colluded with a foreign intelligence service, or passed state secrets, or seduced multiple debauched partners in swaying upper berths of sooty midnight trains. It didn't matter what transgressions they harvested. The counterintelligence hounds couldn't define treason, but they'd know it when they saw it.

She certainly was not expecting to be taught anything along the lines of close-quarter fighting techniques. On the first day, with dappled sunlight coming through the grimy glass ceiling of the winter garden, Dominika was intrigued to see a pale blue aura of artful thought-and-soul swirling around Daniil's head, and out the tips of his fingers. She was additionally surprised when Daniil began instructing her in *Systema Rukopashnogo Boya*, the Russian hand-to-hand combat system: medieval, brutal, rooted in tenth-century Cossack tradition and with mystical connections to the Orthodox Church. It was normally taught only to military personnel.

She had seen the Spetsnaz assassin use the same moves in a blood-splattered Athens hotel room, not recognizing them for what they were, but horrified at their buttery efficiency. Daniil spared her nothing in training, and she found she enjoyed physically working her body again, remembering the long-ago discipline of her cherished ballet career, the career They had taken away from her. *Systema* put a premium on flexibility, ballistic speed, a knowledge of vulnerable points on the human body. As Daniil demonstrated joint locks and submission holds, his face close to Dominika's, he saw something in those fifty-fathom eyes you wouldn't want to stir up unnecessarily.

After two weeks, Dominika was mastering strikes and throws that would have taken other students months to learn. She had initially covered her mouth and laughed at the bent-leg monkey walk used to close with an opponent in combat and the swirling shoulder shrug that precedes a devastating hand strike. Now she was knocking Daniil down on the mat as often as he dumped her. In the dusty afternoon light of the room, Dominika watched Daniil's back flex as he demonstrated a new technique and she idly wondered about him. The way he moved, he could have been a ballet dancer, or a gymnast. How had he gotten into the killing martial arts? Was he Spetsnaz, from a *Vympel* group? She had noticed, with the eye of a Sparrow—a trained seductress of the state—that his ring finger was significantly longer than his index finger. The likelihood existed therefore, according to the warty matrons at Sparrow School, of above-average-size courting tackle.

Calm yourself. She told herself she was fighting the building stress of being back in Russia, the start of an impossibly risky existence. She missed the man she loved, a secret she would have to guard to her core because there was the small detail that he was an American case officer of the CIA. She waited for the overdue start of Daniil's sly elicitation, plausible after the earned familiarity of fourteen days of physical training. She would have to be exceedingly careful—no games, no baiting, no sarcasm. Everything she told Daniil would go back to the FSB, and then the Center, and be compiled with all the other pieces of the "welcome home" investigation, and ultimately determine whether she would retain her status as an *operupolnomochenny*, an operations officer. But my, those eyelashes.

Dominika held her head erect, elegant on a long neck, as she pushed through the musky velvet curtain into the La Diva club. The bouncer at the inner door—she hadn't seen him before—looked with professional approval at her little black dress, then glanced briefly into a tiny black satin clutch barely large enough to hold lipstick and a wafer-thin smart phone. He pulled the heavy curtain aside and motioned her to enter. *No weapons*, he thought. *Mademoiselle Doudounes, Miss Big Chest, is clean.*

Captain Egorova was in fact more than able to dispense lethal force. The lipstick tube in her purse was an *eqlektricheskiy pistolet*, a single-shot electric gun, a recent update from SVR technical—Line T—laboratories, a new version of a venerable Cold War weapon. The disposable lipstick gun fired a murderously explosive 9mm Makarov cartridge accurately out to two meters—the bullet had a compressed metal dust core which expanded massively on contact. The only sound at discharge was a single, loud click.

Dominika scanned the black-light interior of the club, a large semicircular room filled with chipped tables in the center and tired, leatherette booths along the walls. A low stage with old-timey footlights stood dark and empty. Parvis Jamshidi sat alone in a center booth—his usual place, she had learned while covering him in the club for three consecutive nights—pensively looking up at the ceiling. Dominika did a second quick scan of the room: no obvious countersurveillance or security coverage. She weaved between the tables toward Jamshidi's booth, ignoring the snapped fingers of a fat man at a table, signaling her to come over, either to order another *petit jaune*, or to suggest they go together for thirty minutes to the Chat Noir Design Hotel down the block.

The familiar feel of *beshentsvo*, the elemental rage that sustained her, rose in her throat, tightened across her chest, and switched on the glow-plugs in her stomach. Dominika eased into the booth and put the little clutch down in front of her. Jamshidi continued looking up at the ceiling, as if in prayer. He was short and slight, white-haired, with a forked goatee. His El Greco hands were folded on the table, long-fingered and languid. He wore the requisite pearl-gray suit with a white collarless shirt buttoned at the neck. A little man, a physicist, an expert in centrifugal separation, the lead scientist in Iran's uranium enrichment program. Dominika said nothing, waited for him.

Jamshidi felt her presence and his eyes lowered, appraising Dominika's figure, the slim arms, the plain, square-cut nails. She met his gaze until he stopped looking at the blue-veined cleft between her breasts.

"How much for one hour?" he said casually. He had a reedy voice and spoke in French. In the club's musk-cat air his words came out milky yellow and weak, all deceit and greed. Dominika noted with interest that the ultraviolet light in the club did not affect her ability to read his fetid colors. She continued to look at him mildly.

"Did you hear me?" Jamshidi said, raising his voice. "Do you understand French, or are you a *putain* from the Ukraine?" He looked up again at the ceiling, as if in dismissal. Dominika followed his gaze. A Plexiglas catwalk hung suspended from the rafters and a naked woman in heels was dancing directly above Jamshidi's head. Dominika looked back at his preposterous goatee.

"What makes you think I'm a working girl?" said Dominika in unaccented French.

Jamshidi looked back down, and met her eyes, and laughed. It was at this point that he should have heard the rustling in the long grass, the instant before the grip of fang and claw.